LINE BRAWL

By
Bianca Sommerland
Copyright 2015, Bianca Sommerland

ALL RIGHTS RESERVED
Cover art by Bianca Sommerland

Copyright © 2016, Bianca Sommerland

ALL RIGHTS RESERVED

Photo credit to:
Jenn LeBlanc/Illustrated Romance

License Notes

This e-book is licensed for your personal enjoyment only. This e-book may not be resold or given away to other people. If you would like to share this book with another person, please purchase an additional copy for each recipient. If you're reading this book and did not purchase it, or it was not purchased for your use only, then please return it to the vendor and purchase your own copy. Thank you for respecting the hard work of this author.

This book is a work of fiction and any resemblance to persons, living or dead, or actual events is purely coincidental. The characters are products of the author's imagination and used fictitiously.

Licensed material is being used for illustrative purposes only and any person depicted in the licensed material is a model.

Author's Note

For some reason, this book has been very different than any of the other Cobra books. Maybe because the anticipation for myself, and for the readers, to finally get Pischlar's book out there, made it even more important to really tell his story perfectly. But the best stories are imperfect. Which is what makes them stick with you, long after you've returned the book to the shelf. There can be no formula. The only expectation is the unexpected.

Like most authors, when I write, I have my doubts. I wonder if I have the talent, the skills, the *strength* to do the story justice. Whether anyone who reads this story agrees depends on their tastes, but there were two things I knew without a doubt.

I wasn't along for the ride with an ordinary hero.

And there will never be another quite like him.

Even the most messed up, complicated people deserve love. No one is immune to pain. And sometimes, everything you're convinced is the absolute truth will be questioned. If you want simple, this is probably not the book for you.

If you want 'Easy'?

This is him in all his glory. And I hope you enjoy getting to know him as much as I did. <g>

This isn't the end for him.

But it is one hell of a beginning.

Acknowledgements

This has been an amazing journey and as always, I have many people to thank. Let's start with the fans of the Dartmouth Cobras. You're all AMAZING. Your passion means so much to me. This team has become as real to you as they are to me, and every loss, every win, is something we've experienced together. And I hope we can continue to enjoy every one for at least a few more books. ;)

To Stacey, you amaze me with your patience and how much you believe in me, no matter how rough things get. You believing in me makes it easier for me to believe in myself. I can thank you in every book, tell you every day how much I appreciate you, and it still won't be enough.

Jennifer, for your friendship, for how much faith you've shown in my ability to get past the parts of the book I was afraid to write, because they ripped open old scars, thank you. You've dealt with so much of my crazy and I think you've earned sainthood for that! Lol!

My sweet, loving daughters, some days have been hard, but I hope, when you one day pick up these books, you read all the acknowledgements dedicated to you and remember the same precious moments I do. Sleepless nights and deadlines, then a day where we'd all shut away the rest of the world to just be us. I live for those days. You're both growing so fast, but I am so proud of the strong young women you are becoming. Just slow down a little. I'm still getting used to you being too big to pick up and hold for hours.

There are many that helped me with language, and medical stuff, and I have to say, you guys are awesome! Christine, you spent days going over different scenarios with me and I am so grateful for your willingness to share your knowledge. Any mistakes I made are my own, but close to real life as possible thanks to you.

To Jenn Leblanc and Robert Simmons, thank you for giving me a perfect image for the cover. I needed something unique for Pischlar's book, and I couldn't ask for better. You're both awesome to work with!

And last, but definitely not least, Milly. Damn, I have been thinking over what I would say to you for days, and I'm not sure I have words for all you've done for me. You are my sun, the one who made the darkest days seem bright, and your friendship is priceless. I have never known someone so selfless and giving and I'm so happy to have you in my life. You get me in a way no one ever has or ever will. The day can't come soon enough when I can see you again!

Dedication

To a season best forgotten, but a team that never will be.

A few words from Pisch…

Call me Easy. And let me give it to you straight.

You don't want a man like me.

What you want is a man who will say all the right things. Who will sweep you off your feet and make your heart race as you fall in love. He'll give you the happily ever after every woman secretly dreams of.

The man you really want has probably dreamt of that too.

My dreams are simpler.

In this moment, all I need is the taste of your lips, the feel of your flesh. Right now, I can make you feel things you've never dared to imagine. That you *couldn't* imagine, because the things you've experienced fit into a neat little box.

Even the kinky stuff.

So before you begin, let me tell you the rules.

I am not interested in long term. I don't tolerate jealousy. If you fall for me, you will get hurt, so be damn sure you keep your heart out of the game.

And it is a game. A game where no one has to lose. The prize is an experience you'll never forget. A beautiful memory.

But you can't keep me.

Dartmouth Cobra Roster

Centers

No	Name	Age	Ht	Wt	Shot	Birth Place
27	Scott Demyan	29	6'3"	198	L	Anaheim, California, USA
45	Keaton Manning	32	5'11"	187	R	Ulster, Ireland
18	Ctirad Jelinek	28	6'0"	204	L	Rakovnik, Czech Republic
3	Erik Hjalmar	25	6'3"	219	R	Stockolm, Sweden
4	Heath Ladd	19	6'1"	198	R	Bourke, Australia

Left Wings

No	Name	Age	Ht	Wt	Shot	Birth Place
16	Luke Carter	24	5'11"	190	L	Warroad, Minnesota, USA
53	Shawn Pischlar	30	6'0"	200	L	Villach, Austria
71	Dexter Tousignant	25	6'2"	208	L	Matane, Quebec, Canada
5	Ian White	26	6'1"	212	L	Winnipeg, Manitoba, Canada
42	Braxton Richards	19	5'11	196	L	Edmonton, Alberta, Canada

Right Wings

No	Name	Age	Ht	Wt	Shot	Birth Place
22	Tyler Vanek	23	5'8"	174	R	Greenville, North Carolina, USA
72	Dante Palladino	36	6'2"	215	L	Fassano, Italy
21	Bobby Williams	35	5'10"	190	R	Sheffield, England
46	Vadim Zetsev	28	6'0"	203	R	Yaroslavl, Russia
66	Zachary Pearce	33	6'0"	210	L	Ottawa, Ontario, Canada

Defense

No	Name	Age	Ht	Wt	Shot	Birth Place
6	Dominik Mason	33	6'4"	235	R	Chicago, Illinois, USA
17	Einar Olsson	29	6'0"	200	L	Örnsköldsvik, Sweden
74	Beau Mischlue	27	6'2"	223	L	Gaspe, Quebec, Canada
26	Peter Kral	29	6'1"	200	L	Hannover, Germany
2	Mirek Brends	35	6'1"	214	L	Malmö, Sweden
11	Sebastian Ramos	30	6'5"	227	R	Arlanza, Burgos, Spain
40	Max Perron	32	6'2"	228	L	Alamo, Texas, USA

Goalies

No	Name	Age	Ht	Wt	Shot	Birth Place
20	Landon Bower	27	6'3"	215		Gaspe, Quebec, Canada
29	Dave Hunt	21	6'2"	217		Hamilton, Ontario, Canada

Chapter One

Early May

Why had he ever thought it would just be an easy, no regrets, fuck?
Because everyone's right. You are *stupid.*

Ian White stepped up to the door of his best friend's apartment, a place he'd once spent more time at than his own, and for the first time, couldn't bring himself to just walk in. He had the damn key, on the *Deadpool* keychain Pisch had given him, but he left it in his pocket.

Things were different.

I fucked up.

But this was freakin' Shawn "Easy" Pischlar. Sex didn't mean a thing to him, no matter who it was with. But some lines couldn't be crossed, and Ian had trampled all over them like the big, dumb meathead he was. Fine, Pisch *had* fucked other friends, but he didn't see them all the time. He had his rules and made sure everyone understood them before he worked them out of their clothes and did what he was so fucking good at.

He was a damn good Dom because he was observant though, and he'd caught White's slip when he'd said his name while they were...

'*Don't fall in love with me or anything, Bruiser. I'll break your heart.*'

Love. Screw that. Falling in love with Pisch was the fastest way to get him to fucking disappear. And no way was Ian gonna risk that. Not for sex.

Not for anything.

They'd had fun. Shared a hot chick. That was over and now things could go back to normal.

Then why are you still standing in the fucking hall?

He jabbed his hand into his pocket to grab the key.

The door opened, revealing Pisch with a smirk on his lips as he leaned against the doorframe. "Finally grew your balls back, Bruiser?"

Ian scowled, staring at the center of Pischlar's bare, tattooed chest, because he couldn't deal with that damn arrogance aimed at him. Not now. "I just came to get my comic book. I wasn't sure if you were still sleeping."

"It's past noon."

"Yeah, but you were out late last night at the club." Probably fucking some cute little twink that some Domme—or Dom—had decided they wanted to share. Someone who wouldn't get all fucking confused and imagine the man would want more.

Maybe Vanek again. He ground his teeth as he pictured the Dartmouth Cobra's golden boy, Tyler Vanek, all small and wiry and in love with his Master and Mistress. Perfect for Pisch to play with.

You jealous?

He blinked at the weird little voice in his head he was sure had never been there before. He so needed to hack the source up into little pieces and bury it.

"Don't think so hard, you'll stress yourself out." Pisch gave him a playful slap on the arm. "Come in. And don't lie to me about why you're here. You gave me that comic book as a peace offering."

Yeah, I did. And he didn't really want it back, but he couldn't think of a better excuse, so screw it; he'd pretend he was desperate to get his hands on the damn thing. "I know, but I still haven't read that one yet... Can I borrow it?"

"Sure." Pisch's brow creased slightly as he held the door open wide, waiting for Ian to pass. "Sorry for being an asshole. I thought you came to get laid."

The laugh escaped Ian before what Pisch had said fully registered. He blinked, stopping with one foot over the threshold. He glared at Pisch. "Are you fucking serious?"

A careless expression smoothing all the lines on his face, Pisch lifted a shoulder. "Not that I'd mind, but I had to mess with you a bit. Keep things light."

"'Course you did." Ian made his way across the hall, heading to the kitchen to grab one of the beers from the case he'd bought last week. He twisted the cap, taking a few gulps since his mouth was suddenly fucking dry, and he couldn't face Pisch yet.

This was why fucking Pisch had been the most phenomenally stupid thing he'd ever done in his life. He'd be shoved into the potential repeat fuck category. So long as he didn't get too comfortable.

He *liked* how comfortable things had been before.

"Hey, I thought we were good. What's eating at you, White?" Pischlar's voice came from much too close. He touched the small of Ian's back.

And Ian almost broke another tooth on the lip of the beer bottle. He took a deep breath and managed not to jerk away. Or move closer.

This man should be illegal without a damn prescription. One with a warning: Might cause fatal addiction.

His gaze went to Pisch's bare feet first. Which was safe enough. He had a tattoo on one foot, barbed wire that looked pretty real, with 17 spikes and the words, 'Keep moving, even when it hurts' in long, elegant script.

Deep. Pisch's tattoo were all full of meaning—most of which Ian didn't get—and people who paid attention to them might see him as a sensitive man. But he wasn't. Pisch was damn tough. Ian was tough himself, but he wasn't sure he could deal with the pain of a needle jabbing into his damn foot.

"There a reason you're not looking at me, man?" Pisch put his hand on Ian's shoulder, turning him fully.

Giving Ian no choice but to meet his eyes. Eyes that were an odd green shade, like fog over the lush green prairies where he'd grown up near Winnipeg, Manitoba. Eyes that never missed a thing but hid so much.

Ian shrugged and glanced down at Pisch's chest again. The man was freakin' tight. Not bulging with muscles so much as carved with sharp definition; there was not a damn ounce of fat on him. Covered in wicked ink, multiple piercings in his ears and nipples, all badass and I-don't-give-a-fuck attitude seeping from his very pores.

Ian had never lusted after a man in his life, but Pisch…Pisch wasn't just any man.

He's my best friend.

Forcing what he hoped was a smile to his lips, he brought his eyes back to Pisch's face. "Just making sure you're whole, buddy."

Pisch smirked, like he wasn't buying what Ian was trying to sell, then made a dismissive motion with his hand. "All good. So I'm guessing you don't wanna talk about the fact we had sex?"

The beer, that had been going down nice and smooth with that last gulp, tried to drown him. Ian sputtered, coughing as the liquid hit his windpipe, handing Pisch his beer so he could cover his mouth while he hacked up a lung.

Gently rubbing his back, Pisch leaned close to whisper in his ear. "This would go so much easier if you admitted you wanted me."

Fucking hell. Ian growled and latched onto Pisch's forearms, shoving him against the counter by the fridge. The shock in Pisch's eyes gave him some shallow satisfaction as he moved his lips close to the other man's.

"You think anything about this is easy, *Easy?*" His whole body trembled, and he struggled not to drop his gaze as Pischlar's eyes hardened. He'd tried to remind himself he was straight, so this thing between him and Pisch couldn't happen. The confused emotions were new, and the playoffs were the wrong time to be exploring all this messed up shit.

But the man he cared about—the man he *loved*—more than anyone in the damn world beside his grandmother, was gonna turn into a stranger if they didn't clear the fucking air.

So he considered everything he hadn't let himself really think about and blurted out every single one. "When Sahara was with us, we were playing. It was a game, and we both knew the rules. I don't know the rules anymore, Shawn. I—"

"Don't call me that." Pisch flattened his hands against Ian's chest and shoved. "And you might be a fucking caveman, but you manhandle me in my goddamn house again and it will be the last time you ever set foot past the door."

Well shit. Nodding slowly, Ian backed away a bit more, giving Pisch some space. He'd gone and fucked up again. He hadn't meant anything bad by grabbing the man, but maybe he should be more careful.

He dropped his gaze, staring at the barbwire again. "I'm sorry."

"It's all right. And I think I get where you're coming from." Pisch grabbed another two beers from the still open fridge and motioned for Ian to follow him to the kitchen table. He sat, waiting for Ian to join him, a relaxed smile sliding across his lips. "You're not into guys, but you like all the things I do to you. And I'd be a shitty friend if I didn't warn you, you might start thinking there's more between us because all the feeling good hits the right triggers."

Maybe he's right. But... "What's that do to us being friends?"

"Absolutely nothing unless you let it."

"Unless I—" No, Pisch was right. He was the one who'd gone all cold after they'd joined the mile-high-club and then almost died when the plane forgot how to fucking fly right. He'd figured out that much, which was why he'd given Pisch the comic book.

The best way he could think of to tell Pisch he was sorry without leaving any doubt that he meant it.

He shook his head, picking up his beer and taking a sip so he could consider his words carefully. "I love you, man."

"I know. And I love you too." The way Pisch said those three words was no different than him agreeing that Iron Man rocked. Or

ACDC playing over and over on a road trip was an awesome idea. No big impact on life, they were on the same page.

One full of words that wouldn't change a goddamn thing.

Taking a deep breath, Ian ran his tongue over his bottom lip. "So where do we go from here?"

"That depends. You sure you didn't come here to get laid?" Pisch arched a brow then sighed when Ian shook his head again. "A shame. But we can chill with a movie or something. Two days, no practice; I've got plenty of time to seduce you."

Ian rolled his eyes. "You hit a dry spell or something? Jesus, Pisch, go take a cold shower."

"Why should I? You're here, and you're being rather difficult, which is damn sexy. I like a bit of a challenge." Pisch gave him a half smile over the lip of his beer. "Wanna bet I can put on your favorite movie and get you too distracted to watch it before the opening credits are done?"

"No, I'm good." Actually, Ian had never been less turned on in his life. Whatever had been between him and Pisch the times they'd fooled around was gone. And he wasn't sure why. "Can I ask you something as a friend, and not a fuck buddy or whatever you've decided I am now?"

Pischlar winced, inhaling sharply. "Bruiser, I'm not trying to—"

"Just answer the damn question, Shawn."

Eyes narrowed, Pisch inclined his head.

"Do I get the talk?"

The edges of Pisch lips quirked up. "White, I will still train you if you want me to. I will suck your dick—hell, I'd be doing it now if you weren't giving off 'don't fucking touch me' signals."

Tightening his grip on his beer bottle, Ian held Pischlar's amused gaze. He didn't move as Pisch came closer, close enough that the heat of his lips slid over Ian's.

He brushed his cheek against Ian's, speaking softly in his ear. "But you can't keep me."

This game wasn't one Shawn wanted to play with White. Probably wasn't one he *should* play. But the second he'd met White's eyes and caught the man looking at him *that* way…

A few guys and girls had looked at him like that before. Like he was a man they could fall in love with. That they *were* falling in love with. And he'd escaped every time without anyone getting hurt.

Too badly, anyway.

White had the advantage because Shawn had started falling for him a long time ago, but his reaction after they'd fucked had set off alarm bells Shawn promised himself a long time ago he'd never ignore again.

They could have great sex. Figure out how to hold on to their friendship. But if they tread down that muddy path toward an actual relationship, White would destroy him.

White was a good man. He cared about people, probably more than he should, but he wasn't built to balance in the middle of the spectrum for long. He was only twenty-seven years old, and one day he'd want a wife and kids. All kinds of normal.

As his friend, Shawn would make sure White got everything he could ever want. Now, and in the future.

What if you're wrong? What if White doesn't want all you've planned out for him? What if he really wants you?

There was no doubt that White wanted him. At the moment. Shawn was pretty impressed the man managed to front like he had no interest in getting off, but White was very responsive. The right touch would shut down all his objections, and he'd be fucking putty in Shawn's hands.

If they weren't teammates, weren't as close as brothers—which was pretty twisted, considering how often he thought about sliding his lips over the man's dick again—he'd use every trick he'd honed on those who meant nothing to him.

Instead, he made some popcorn and joined White on the couch, laughing at White's scowl when he stole the remote. He put on one of White's top ten favorite comic book movies, *The Incredible Hulk*. The newer one. White loved every comic book movie ever made, even the ones that tanked at the box office, but this one always got his full attention. He seemed to relate to the unstable hero.

Yet another reason Shawn had to keep him at arm's length.

"Not so rough, Steve. That fucking hurts." Shawn's head hit the edge of his bathroom sink as his boyfriend slammed into him, his fingers digging into his hips. *"Slow down. Why the fucking rush?"*

"My girlfriend's waiting for me, scheisskopf." Steve rammed in one last time with a loud groan—one loud enough to be heard throughout the house, but thankfully, no one was home. He pulled away, the sudden loss of support dropping Shawn to his knees. *"I told you this would be quick. You're not gonna be a total fag and cry about it, are you?"*

"No." Shawn dragged himself to his feet as Steve headed to his bedroom to get his clothes. He stepped gingerly into the room, his whole body aching. And not in a good way. *"And you don't get to call me a fag like you aren't one, arschgesicht. I might be the only one who knows, but—"*

Steve closed the distance between them in three short strides, grabbing Shawn by the throat and holding him against the wall. *"But what? You know that if you tell anyone, I'll fucking kill you, right?"*

"You know I won't."

"Then don't talk shit." Steve loosened his grip, smiling abruptly. *"We good?"*

"Yeah, we're good." Shawn rubbed his throat even as Steve kissed him. The other boy was the biggest, hottest, and most popular, jock in their high school. He got why Steve was so paranoid, but he hated it when he got mean and violent.

Things would be different after they graduated though. Steve didn't want to play football anymore. He was doing it for his dad now, but he wanted to be a doctor. And once he graduated medical school, he wouldn't give a shit what anyone thought about the two of them together.

Shawn just had to be patient.

And Shawn had been very, very patient. Put up with more bruises than he could count. Not that Steve had been abusive, really, but the one time Shawn had slipped up about their relationship in front of the other players...

Well, that hadn't been the first or last beating Shawn had gotten, but it was the one he'd finally learned from. He didn't just get off on control, he *needed* it. When he shared with another Dom he trusted, he could relax his hold a little, but never with a sub who had a hair trigger that could snap without warning.

He trusted White, so he didn't mind training him, but even in that, he'd have to set some very clear limits. If he planned to push White close to the edge, he'd likely restrain him.

If he let White in any deeper, he wouldn't have that kind of control.

Are you afraid of him?

Shawn's lips tightened at the thought. No, he wasn't afraid of White. But the man had gotten physical with friends in the past. He'd gotten physical with Shawn in the kitchen. Something he would never do with a woman.

The man would make a good boyfriend, maybe even a good husband one day. To a woman he would treat gently, who he could protect with all those fierce instincts that were fucking sexy and terrifying all at once.

Yeah, you got issues, man.

True. Issues he was well aware of and had a handle on. Enough of one to avoid diving in deep enough to drown. He could wade into the wild current of passion with White. But he wasn't reckless enough to let himself be dragged in all the way.

That settled, he let himself relax and admired the broad physique of his best friend. White was still wearing far too many clothes, but even in a T-shirt, he was a damn fine sight. Big muscles, a strong jaw, and warm blue eyes that didn't hide a thing. They were crystal clear windows to his soul.

Windows revealing pure confusion when he glanced over and caught Shawn staring at him.

"Shawn?"

Fuck, he doesn't listen, does he? Shawn arched a brow, leaned forward, dropping one hand over White's crotch to squeeze him through his jeans. "What did I tell you about calling me that?"

White's lips parted. He began to pant as Shawn rubbed his swelling cock through his faded blue jeans. His eyes drifted shut. "Shit. I'm sorry, Pisch."

"You're forgiven." Shawn shifted closer to White, brushing his lips up the side of his throat as White tipped his head back. "You into the movie?"

Shaking his head, then nodding, White groaned. "I..." He hesitated. Then opened his eyes and latched on to Shawn's wrist. "Kiss me."

Shawn blinked. He always remembered the hard limits of his subs. Fine, White wasn't exactly his sub, but if he trained the man, he would fall into the same category. White didn't kiss his casual flings. Shawn had teased him about how 'Pretty Woman' that was, but he was curious how the man had avoided kissing the many puck bunnies he fooled around with.

Of course, if they had their lips around his dick, or his mouth on their cunt, they probably didn't notice he was avoiding anything too intimate.

Which meant that was what White wanted from Shawn. Something more intimate.

He was a simple man, so he might *think* he wanted that now, but with the right distraction, he'd forget all about it. Shawn pulled his wrist free and snagged the button of White's jeans. "Kiss you where?"

"Fuck this shit." White pushed off the sofa and headed for the door.

And Shawn almost let him go, but he couldn't. *He* was the one who'd fucked up this time. White was afraid to lose their friendship, and Shawn wasn't helping.

"Don't go, White." Shawn chewed at his bottom lip when White stopped, head bowed, shoulders stiff. "I'm sorry. I'll stop."

"I didn't want you to stop, I just..." White groaned, lifting his arms to lace his fingers behind his neck. "You know what, you're right. This needs to stop. I want what we had before back. Can we just watch the movie?"

"Absolutely." Shawn picked up the remote and skipped back to the scene he'd interrupted with his fondling. "Wanna grab a couple beers while you're up?"

White laughed. "Sure."

"And tell me if you change your mind about watching the movie?"

Letting out a heavy sigh, White returned with two beers and handed Shawn one. "I won't."

They managed to chill out without further issue. After the third movie—apparently they were now doing an X-men marathon—Shawn teased White about having a man-crush on Wolverine. He offered to relieve some 'pressure'.

But White's answer never changed. He'd effectively shoved Shawn back into the friend zone.

Which fucking sucked.

Chapter Two

The baby isn't mine anymore. Why can't everyone just leave me the fuck alone?

After what seemed like days of labor—screw the doctor saying how 'easy' it had been— Samantha Carter was fucking drained. Only Oriana Delgado, who was gonna be the kid's mother, had been in the room with her at the time. Which worked, because Oriana got to hold the baby before anyone else. And if there'd been any doubts that Sam was doing the right thing, seeing the other woman carefully cradling the fragile little bundle would have erased them.

But I've still got a lot to think about, right? She sighed as she thought over what had gone down after she'd been rushed to the hospital. Jami Richter, her brother's girlfriend, had wanted to stay with her. She hadn't argued when Sam asked for Oriana, but that didn't make Sam feel any less shitty. Oriana's men—Sloan and Max—had thankfully left when things started getting seriously icky, but in a daze, Sam had suggested they should see their son soon as he was out of her body.

They're his family.

Seeing them together, she'd been happy. When Jami came in, she started feeling guilty, because apparently the baby looked a bit like Luke, which Sam couldn't comment on, because she hadn't held him yet.

"No one let you hold him?" Jami shook her head, planting a forced smile on her lips. *"Do you want to?"*

No.

No, she didn't want to. But she couldn't explain why and Jami wouldn't understand anyway.

Thankfully, before she had to think up a good answer, Sloan's father came in. And Oriana's siblings, and other people, and...and that was the last thing Sam remembered because she fell asleep. A nurse woke her up at some point to go to the bathroom. More nastiness and then Sam got to settle in for a good night's rest.

When she woke up the nurse brought the baby. Cute little thing, but he scared the hell out of Sam. She'd hoped Oriana would stick around to take care of him, but the nurse said Oriana had gone with Max to get something to eat. She'd been with the baby all night.

"Time for breakfast." The nurse was all smiles as she brought the little bundle wrapped in blue to Sam. "Just like last night. Follow his lead."

His lead for what? Sam blinked at the nurse.

"I don't think she remembers much of last night." A deep voice came from the corner of the room. Sloan rose from the armchair and stretched. "I'll give you some privacy."

Screw privacy! Maybe it seemed like a lot of people had been in and out nonstop last night, driving her nuts, but she needed the kid's *parents* here!

What if they changed their mind? They couldn't get attached to the baby if they weren't around him. And if they didn't take him, what was she going to do?

I'm not ready to be a mother.

"Don't go!" Her eyes teared as both the nurse and the baby startled. Damn it, she was already fucking up. "I'm sorry, I just can't—"

"Shh. It's fine, Sam." Sloan approached the nurse, and she placed the baby in his arms. "I can stay if you'd like."

"Please." The panic building up in Sam's chest lessened as she watched how comfortably Sloan held his little boy. The man was *huge*, with eyes that looked completely black at first glance and a deep scar cutting down his face, which made him seem dangerous. In a purely, *fuck, he's hot* kinda way. The type of guy she'd totally go for if he wasn't involved.

Or even if he had been, to be honest. She'd never bothered asking any of her exes if they were single.

Throwing herself at *anyone* stopped being a priority after she got herself knocked up though. Her life had become a colossal mess, and she'd never been more alone. Every kick reminded her it wasn't only *her* life she was screwing up.

But now, with the way Sloan looked at the baby, the world seemed like less of a clusterfuck. The kid would have the perfect daddy.

Two of them actually.

But then he brought the baby to *her*. She bit her lip, staring up at Sloan.

"He needs to be fed, sweetie. We talked about him needing that first milk that comes in." Sloan sat on the edge of the bed. If he hadn't been holding the baby, his presence would have been comforting. Instead, she was trying not to freak about the whole feeding thing. And she wasn't sure how to tell him she didn't want to do it.

His brow furrowed when she inched back. She dropped her gaze to the sheets covering her legs. "Last night wasn't enough?"

When he shifted away, she looked up to see his dark eyes soften with understanding. Sloan stood, still holding the baby close. "Unless the doctor thinks you need to pump for your own health, last night *is* enough. Do you want anything? I can text Max to pick you up a snack or whatever."

"I'm good." She leaned back, breathing easier now that no one was gonna make her breastfeed.

The nurse didn't look too happy, but she just checked Sam's chart before crisply stating she would go prepare a bottle. Sam pretended to sleep until the woman came back and left. Then she snuck a peek at Sloan, who'd returned to the armchair, baby tucked in the crook of one big arm as he fed the kid like he'd been doing it forever.

"She's gone. You can get up now and take a shower if you want?" Sloan lifted the baby up to his shoulder, gently rubbing his back. "Unless you'd rather wait until we get home? The doctor said you'd be released today."

He had to be the most perfect man in the world. Sam sat up and grinned. "I just wanna get out of here." Hospitals were depressing, and she was so done. But maybe that sounded selfish? The baby was fine, right? She should probably have asked about him before going on about how eager she was to leave. She made a face. "Umm...he's doing good, isn't he? I mean, the doctor seem happy with how...." She groaned as she glanced down at the baby. "I suck. What's his name?"

"James Weston Callahan Perron." Sloan chuckled when she blinked at him. "Yes, it's a mouthful. But we talked it over and decided to use both Max and my fathers' names."

Not Oriana's father? Sam didn't want to dig, so she just smiled and nodded. "That's a good name."

Sloan's brow furrowed. "Did you have any names you'd considered?"

"No. I think I always knew..." Her throat tightened. Yeah, she wasn't ready to be a mom, but sometimes what she was doing hit her. Like, she should have *tried*. Maybe she wouldn't have been a great mom, but was she being totally pathetic just handing off her kid?

Rather than pushing her to continue, Sloan simply waited, his expression still calm and supportive.

She took a deep breath. "When I felt him move inside me, I think it was the first time that I ever had to really worry about anyone else. I tried to picture my life with him in it and...I couldn't. When I was living with Jami, I pictured her taking care of the baby. I thought about going back to school, making something of myself, but the second I considered doing it alone, with the kid, I panicked. I know I should have been more careful, and he's my responsibility, but I have nothing to offer. And he deserves so much better than I can give him."

"He'll never want for anything, Sam. But that's true no matter what you decide. I know you're uncomfortable with people constantly asking if you're sure, so all I'll ask is that you don't hesitate to talk to me, or Oriana, or Max about any concerns you have. *Including* your options."

"What if I don't want to stay with you?" Where the fuck had that come from? Of course she had to stay with them. She didn't have anywhere else to go!

Unless she went back to Luke's place…

Hell no.

She covered her face with her hands and groaned. "Don't listen to me. I'm just…I'm confused. Not about the baby. It's messed up, and I know it makes me sound like a bitch, but if I have to see him every day it's gonna be like…like I *should* think about being his mom."

"According to who?" Sloan held up one hand, his lips curving up slightly. "Never mind. You don't have to answer that. If you'd like your own place, I can help you get settled somewhere. I'll need a few days though, but before you worry that anyone will put pressure on you, consider this. Some birth mothers spend absolutely no time with their child after giving birth. They don't take the baby home. They sign the papers and do their best to continue their lives."

"Is it horrible that I like that idea?"

"Why would it be horrible? His biological father had no problem with it. You might feel differently tomorrow. Or next week. But you're the only one who gets to decide how much this changes your life." Sloan adjusted the blanket covering his son. "I'm not a therapist, Sam. Emotionally, I have no idea how this will affect you. But if you want to get your own place, go back to school…no one has the right to make you feel guilty."

She took a deep breath and nodded. "Okay. Good. That's what I want. I was just afraid it would be weird if I go back to your place and…like, I don't change diapers and wake up with him at night."

"You can be as involved with him as you're comfortable with. If that's not at all, then that's fine." Sloan's brow furrowed slightly. "Would you feel better if I took him out of the room for a bit?"

Her emotions were a mess, because she wanted to say "yes", but at the same time, Sloan being close kept her calm. She couldn't very well tell him to send the baby away with someone else and stick around. If she wanted him to stay, she'd have to deal with the baby.

You really are a bitch. 'Deal with the baby'? He's your kid!

Fuck, she was really starting to hate herself.

But she needed someone to talk to who wasn't just here for the baby. Someone who didn't think she was completely heartless. She couldn't even be that person for herself.

Sloan seemed like he could be, but it wasn't fair to ask that of him. He was doing all the things a new father should.

Which was more important than worrying about her and all her fucked up shit.

"Sam." Sloan stood and approached the bed. His voice was deep, with a resonance that went right through her. She couldn't help but meet his eyes. And staring into them made it a little easier to deal with the baby being so close. "Something is bothering you. What is it?"

"I—"

"Sam?" Luke stepped into the room, his shoulders hunched, his hands stuffed into the pockets of his dark blue suit jacket. He wore a black Cobra ball cap backwards, which looked weird with the suit. He must have just come from a meeting or something. He hadn't been here since she'd had the baby—that she knew of anyway.

Did she want him here now?

She wasn't sure.

He couldn't stand her. And she didn't blame him, because she'd screwed up gaining his trust over and over. She kinda respected him more for not letting her kid make him all forgiving.

Unless that had changed? Maybe he was here to convince her not to give his nephew to someone else?

She really hoped he wasn't. She loved her brother, and she had no right to ask him for *anything*. But she needed his support. And if he couldn't give it, he needed to leave her the hell alone.

Sloan kept his steady gaze on her then inclined his head as though she'd answered a question he didn't even need to ask. "I'm gonna take James to see the team. A few of the guys have been stopping by, but I didn't want you to feel overwhelmed. I think some time with your brother would be good for you."

Before he could leave, Luke cleared his throat. "Can I see him? I know I'm not his uncle anymore, but—"

"What gave you that idea?" Sloan chuckled when Luke stared at him. "You're family, Carter. Did you really think I wouldn't let you be part of his life?"

"I don't know." Luke frowned, glancing over at Sam. "I mean, I don't know how this works."

"In the least complicated way possible. Do you want to hold him?" Sloan didn't hold the baby out or anything. He gave Luke the same patient look he'd given Sam.

Which seemed to relax Luke as he gazed down at the little bundle in awe. "Umm…maybe later? When he's a bit more solid and I'm sitting down on a pile of bubble wrap?"

"You've held Amia before, Carter."

"Yeah, but she was bigger."

Sloan laughed. "She really wasn't, but that's okay. Let me know when you're ready."

And that was it. Sloan left the room with the baby and suddenly, her lungs remembered how to expand, and her chest didn't feel like someone was sitting on her. She pressed her eyes shut, absolutely positive that she was the most messed up person on the planet.

"Are you okay?" There was a loud scraping sound, and she opened her eyes to see Luke sit in the chair he'd dragged up to the side of the bed. "You look really pale."

"Probably puffy too, right? And my hair's all gross." Sam sighed when Luke hunched his shoulders again. "Sorry, I'm in a weird mood. I had this plan. I would give birth, look like myself again, and everything would be back to normal."

"Yeah..." Luke's brow creased. "Pretty sure that's not how this works. Jami told me the dad signed the papers and got them back to Callahan's lawyer the same fucking day."

Did he? Sam wasn't really surprised. The 'I'm pregnant' convo had ended in an argument about her having an abortion. She didn't have an issue with women who made that choice, but even though she'd never considered actually keeping the kid, the baby had been real to her from day one. Real enough that she'd pictured him growing up. Wondered if he'd ever ask about her. Hoped he'd have a better life than she had.

Of course, 'he'd' been just 'the baby' at the time, but his future had always been separate. One that wasn't connected to hers. But still a life she'd wanted to know would go on.

"I'm happy he didn't fight to be the dad. I don't know what I would have done if he decided he wanted to keep the kid."

"'The kid'?" Luke rubbed a hand over his lips. "You don't...I mean, you're sure about this?"

"Yes."

"Okay." Luke inhaled sharply. "I'm not saying you shouldn't be. Just...I didn't want you to give him up because of me."

Okay, and I'm fucked up? Sam shook her head. "Luke, listen to me. You didn't do anything wrong. I'm the one who can't be a mom. I didn't choose to give him up because of you, I just didn't give him to you because...because I need some distance and I can't have that if you ended up being his father. Our family is a mess."

"Ya think?" The edge of Luke's lips quirked up slightly. "I think, if Jami got pregnant, I'd be a good dad. I'd have time to figure things out, you know? But when she decided we'd keep your kid it was like...real sudden. Like, me and you weren't good, and I could tell you weren't ready. If he was with us, you'd be more involved. But you don't want that, do you?"

"I really don't." Her brother was the last person she'd ever considered telling all this, but he was here, and she needed to talk to someone. And talking to him was a lot easier than she thought it would be. "I want to know he'll be okay without me. That I can walk away and not be a terrible person."

"I don't think you're a terrible person." Luke reached out and took her hand. "You chose amazing people to be his parents."

Her bottom lip quivered. Why did he have to be so nice all of a sudden? This was easier when he was treating her like she deserved to be treated. "*You* would have been amazing."

"I *will* be. Didn't you hear? I'm an uncle again!" He grinned. "And I'm real good at that. Gives me tons of practice."

"Does this mean you don't hate me anymore?" Her eyes teared as her brother stood and pulled her into his arms. That was the biggest regret she'd had. Giving him her baby would have forced him to forgive her. But that wouldn't have been fair to anyone. Luke was right. If the baby had gone to him, she would have felt even more obliged to stick around.

But she couldn't. She needed to fix herself, figure out where her life was going. Without worrying about how her choices would affect anyone else.

"I never hated you." Luke kissed her forehead. "I didn't like you very much, but I'm over it. Just…damn it, Sam. I love Jami. And she cares about you so much. Don't make her regret it again. Please?"

"I won't." She'd keep the promise this time. No matter what. She wasn't living with her brother and Jami anymore, so it should be easy. Sloan would help her get her own place. She'd build a life that she could be proud of. Maybe, when the baby grew up, he wouldn't be ashamed of the person she'd become.

If he wanted to know her, he'd see that she'd made the right decision for the both of them.

Either way, the idea of not having someone else to worry about while she sorted out her life was less scary. That's all it came down to, really. She wasn't really a grown up yet. Why anyone trusted her to make decisions for herself was a mystery. Making them for a kid?

Nope. She couldn't even wrap her head around that.

"Do you need anything? Not for him. I know there's people taking care of him, but what about you?" Luke held her hand between both of his, looking at her like she was fragile and broken, and he wanted to do something to fix her. "My mom wanted me to ask if you if you needed to talk to her. She's worried about you."

"I miss her." Sam swiped away the tears spilling down her cheeks. Luke's mother had been there for her more than her own. And she'd screwed that up too. She didn't deserve the woman's concern, but she wanted to reach out to her. To tell her again and again how sorry she was for everything she'd done. "I'd love to talk to her."

Luke inclined his head. "Good. I'll let her know."

"You're really not mad at me?" Yeah, that question was *way* too vague. She wouldn't blame him for still being mad about her stealing from his girlfriend. Or his mom. Or for walking into his life and leaving such a fucked up mess in her wake. She'd given Jami every reason to believe the baby would be part of her family. "I mean—"

"I'm not mad at you, Sammy." Luke laid a soft kiss on the back of her hand. "So, you want anything?"

She shook her head. She was just tired. So freaking tired, she just wanted to sleep and not worry about anything. At all.

And Luke had just made her believe she could actually do that. Which was awesome. The greatest gift he could have given her.

She woke after what seemed like a long time, her eyes shooting open to see her brother still sitting by her side. And she laughed because the strangest thought had just occurred to her.

"James Weston Callahan Perron." She shrugged, dropping her gaze when Luke stared at her. "That's his name. Not sure anyone told you. Is it weird that I can't think of him as 'James'? He doesn't look like a James to me, but I didn't look at him for long."

Luke grinned. "He doesn't look like a James to me either. West is a cool name though. I've been thinking of him as 'little Westy' in my head."

"I like Westy." Not letting go of his hand, she let her eyes drift shut. "Can you stay with me for a bit? And…it's okay if they don't bring the baby back in here. Is that bad of me to say? He's beautiful.

Perfect. But he's not mine, and I'm so tired of not being able to say that. Of feeling bad for thinking it."

"Don't feel bad. I can't imagine making the choice you did and having to second-guess it again and again. I get it, Sam. And I can do that." He adjusted the blankets over her without releasing her hand. "I'll stay. And you rest. No one will make you look back anymore. Consider it done."

Done.

Her throat tightened, but at the same time, all the pressure on her lightened as she drifted off to sleep.

The word was so final, but she needed it. She needed someone to actually understand that she meant it. That she didn't want to have to rethink what she'd decided. Because, of all the choices she'd ever made, this was the only one she was absolutely sure of.

The one that was right.

For her.

And for *him*.

Chapter Three

Over the past few days, Shawn had come to terms with the fact that his plans for White weren't going to work. He considered getting past the stiff goodnight White had given him the last two nights, at the respectable hour of exactly 9 PM, progress.

They'd had practice this morning, and a trainer had noticed White was favoring one side. So the man had been forced to endure a few hours of medical exams, deep muscle massages, and an ice bath. He'd come back to Shawn's place, looking utterly miserable.

Shawn wanted to cheer White up, but even his favorite meal of steak and potatoes had only gotten a quiet thanks and a brief smile. It was the playoffs, so Shawn didn't expect White to complain much even if he was hurting bad, but he had to do *something*.

After they watched a few movies, Shawn caught White's head drooping to the side, then snapping up as though he was trying to stay awake. He stood and held out his hand.

"Come on, buddy. You can crash here tonight." He took a deep, deep breath as White's warm, calloused hand surrounded his. Touching the man messed him up. He'd avoided it while readjusting their limits; it made it easier to shove aside all the lingering lust.

White's hand holding his brought it all slamming back, like a solid punch to the gut. And another to his chest.

"Shouldn't stay. Like how things are." White's forehead creased, as though he knew he wasn't making any sense. "Not here to fuck."

"I know, Bruiser. Hell, you're punch drunk tired. I don't take advantage of my friends." He pulled White close and draped an arm over his wide shoulders. "You can sleep in the guest room."

Where he usually slept when he stayed over. No need to point that out. Of course he'd sleep there.

That's not where you want him.

Yeah, well, what he wanted was irrelevant.

He took White to the spare bedroom. It was plain, with a simple queen sized bed, dark blue bedding, and a dark wood bedroom set to match the bed. But a few of White's comics were strewn across the dresser and he had clothes in all the drawers—clothes he'd left here and Shawn had put away for him, nice, clean, and folded. The Transformer pillow White traveled with was propped up on the headboard, where he'd left it after their last trip.

He mustn't have been sleeping good without it. Shawn should have taken it to him, but he'd been trying to give White the space he needed.

White's lips spread in a lazy smile. "I love this bed. Thanks for letting me stay."

"No problem." Shawn tightened his grip on White's shoulder when he moved to drop face first onto the bed. "You're not sleeping in your clothes."

"You want me naked?"

"Yes, but that's beside the point." Shawn chuckled when White blinked at him, confused. "I want you comfortable. Doc asked how you've been sleeping. Have you been?"

"A bit. But not good. Not sure why." White lifted his arms as Shawn drew his shirt up, letting him take it off. "I shouldn't let you do this. It's weird now."

Shawn went still, guilt wrapping around his throat like a thick, coarse rope. He hadn't meant for things to get 'weird', whether or not he managed to get White beyond his sudden obsession with making hot sex into something meaningful. He'd been taking care of

White in a way that had become so natural, he hadn't even thought twice about making sure he was comfortable.

But with his teasing and sly advances, White probably thought he had only one goal in mind.

"It's not weird, White. We're us. We watch out for one another. We talk about stupid shit and I make you dinner and you bring me coffee or tea. I wash your clothes, you tape my stick, and on the ice I always know where to find you." He inhaled as he undid White's jeans and pushed them down. Focused on what he was saying, rather than the surge of lust that hit him when he glanced down at the bulge in White's boxers. At least the man wasn't fucking hard. He was testing his own control enough as it was, thank you very damn much.

"I always know where to find you too, Pisch." White huffed out a tired laugh when Shawn pushed him back to sit on the edge of the bed. He caught Shawn's elbow before he could bend down to take off his socks. "You don't gotta do that."

"I want to." Shawn swallowed hard. Hell, if he kept this up, he might as well just kiss White. Stripping him down and tucking him into bed was just as intimate.

Which it hadn't been before they'd stepped all over those fragile lines in the sand. He almost wished White would go back to insisting he wasn't into guys. Accepting a straight guy wasn't into you could be tough, but it happened. Shawn would have gotten over his feelings for White. Found someone else.

A few someones. Uncomplicated, no-hold-barred someones that wouldn't leave him acting like a desperate, horny asshole.

He'd played with a couple at the club briefly. Showing them how essential oils could be used safely on the sub they shared. The girl was a beautiful, responsive woman, much curvier than the wife, but there was an admiration between them that told him right away both were comfortable in their own bodies, and with one another's. The husband balanced his affection nicely, and Shawn hadn't been concerned that he was encouraging a poly relationship that would become toxic.

The wife had sucked his dick to thank him, while her husband gave their sub aftercare, and he'd gotten off, but he had to be honest. He'd have been just as satisfied using his own hand.

Their dynamics didn't leave much room for him. He'd been a teacher. A prop. If he thought back, the last fulfilling scene he'd done had been with Vanek and Zovko. He didn't count the ones with White and Sahara. Sahara was an Ice Girl for the team who'd needed temporary care while figuring out her relationship with the team captain, Dominik Mason. She'd been the opening for him to play with White.

Complicated wasn't satisfying. It was…complicated.

Pulling off White's socks, Shawn straightened, tugging the covers out from under him, guiding him back to lay on the bed before pulling the blankets over him.

"Thank you, Shaw—Pisch." White rested his head on his favorite pillow. "I owe you."

This time, Shawn didn't hesitate before saying exactly what White needed to hear. "Make sure I don't get crushed on the ice and we'll call it even."

The soft, even breaths told him White had already passed out. He had to force himself to leave the room and head to his own.

He wanted to stay. To climb into bed beside White and hold him. Pretend it wasn't complicated at all. That this was his best friend and the man he loved and they could figure out the rest tomorrow.

But they couldn't. *Wouldn't.* And he'd decided to keep that particular door shut tight.

For about an hour he laid in his bed, staring at the ceiling, still wide awake, going over all his excuses to stay put. He heard White cursing softly. Crying out.

And he was back in the guest room without wasting a second to decide whether or not it was a good idea.

Kicking off the blankets Shawn had carefully covered him with, White twisted and turned, like he was struggling to free himself from something in his dreams.

His nightmares.

"I'm here! Please don't go, you don't know what happens!" He lashed out at his pillow, grabbing for it and knocking it off the bed. "I still need you. You can't go!"

Shawn wasn't sure if White was dreaming about Tim Rowe, their coach who'd died in a car crash only a few months back, or his father, who'd died in the mines when White was a kid. Either way, he couldn't bear to see his man suffer.

He sat on the edge of the bed and took a firm hold of White's shoulder. "Ian, I'm here. Wake up, kid."

"Come back!" White let out a low, pain filled growl, like a wolf who'd been shot, desperately trying to crawl to safety. "They're wrong. You have to stay. We need you."

'We'. He's dreaming of Coach then. Shawn's throat tightened. The loss of their coach was still a deep wound for him as well. As it was for most of the team. But for White, it was more. Tim had taken the place of his father. For him, it wasn't a deep cut. It was a vital organ, completely removed. One he had to learn how to live without, no matter how much he needed it.

"Ian—"

"Shawn, don't get in! I can't lose you too!"

Damn it! Shawn swallowed, the raw pain in White's voice tearing into him. He hated the idea of White seeing all those he loved being taken away. He'd hoped to wake the man gently, but fuck that.

He set his hands on White's shoulders and shook him hard. "Ian, wake up! It's a nightmare. I'm right here. I'm here with you and we're both okay."

White sat up suddenly, wrapping his arms around Shawn and pulling him close. His whole body shook as he inhaled rapidly, like he'd been running for a long time. "Damn it! I'm sorry, I...I'll let you go in a minute."

"No rush." Shawn laughed softly, rubbing White's back. "You okay?"

"I don't know. Just stay here. Stay where I can see you. All the time. And if you have to go, stay somewhere safe."

"You wanna put me in a bubble, Bruiser?"

"Yes!" White pressed his forehead against Shawn's shoulder. "I know that's stupid, but let me pretend for a bit. I can't do this again. If I lost you…"

Shawn didn't need White to finish. One thing he'd never doubted was that White considered him one of the few important people he'd let in his own *personal* bubble. Not many of his friends understood how precious their spot was, but Shawn did. White had every reason to believe everything he loved could be taken away.

And maybe Shawn couldn't promise nothing would ever happen to him. But he would make sure White knew he was here now.

"If I lie down beside you, are you gonna freak?" Shawn asked, lifting the blanket.

White shook his head. "No. Stay. If you leave, I'll see it all happen again. If I feel you, I'll know it's not real."

Nodding, Shawn lowered to the bed, the weight on his chest lightening as White let him pull him close. All the reasons why this was a bad idea didn't fucking matter anymore. He'd figure out how to balance their friendship and…whatever else they had going on between them.

Would probably be easier once White got over seeing them as potential relationship material. Shawn had thought his feelings never being returned was tough, but that was nothing compared to seeing everything he'd thought he'd wanted within his grasp and not being able to take it.

He's yours if you want him, Pischlar.

It wouldn't last.

Maybe it will.

Shawn pressed his eyes shut tight, grinning as White let out a soft, grunt-snore. He rested his hand on White's shoulder, loving how damn easy this was. What did they say about better to have loved and lost than—

I already love him. And I always will if things stay exactly the way they are.

Love could be toxic. As easy as holding White was, it was just as easy to see White freaking out if their relationship became public. Lashing out as he had in the past. Turning on Shawn and everyone else who was close to him. Him being a caveman was awesome on the ice, and kinda cute when they hung out, but that unpredictable temper would have most Doms avoiding him.

He wasn't a sub. Wasn't even a switch.

Wasn't the right man to play in Shawn's world with him.

That could change, but Shawn didn't want to change White. Sticking with the status quo was the only way to keep him.

Funny, considering Shawn made it perfectly clear to everyone, including White, that *he* couldn't be kept.

Pressing a soft kiss on White's temple, Shawn relaxed onto his pillow and whispered. "I'm gonna keep you, Bruiser. The only way I know how."

Chapter Four

Second round of the playoffs. Against the freakin' *Leafs*!
Justina Davis's hands shook as she did up her skates. Every single time she came here, she had to pinch herself to make sure she wasn't dreaming. She'd loved the Dartmouth Cobras since day one, and she'd loved hockey her whole life. She'd never really tried to play, she hadn't been the sporty type as a kid—hell, she'd been a pudgy little thing and getting picked last in gym was bad enough—but her dad watched hockey every night during the season and she loved how passionate he was about the game.

His passion was addictive. He taught her to skate when she was ten, never having had much time before that, but he'd gotten a promotion at his job in the packaging company where he'd worked for years and suddenly had time to spend doing fun stuff with her and her little brother, Chris. Chris had the skills to play the game, but Justina sucked with stickhandling.

One day she saw a special about the Dallas Ice Girls and she'd decided she *had* to be one of them. Maybe not in Dallas, but she would find a team.

She'd learned to dance, found out she was pretty good at it actually, and then started figure skating. Her mother had been thrilled with how dedicated she was. Often complimented her on how fit she'd gotten. How skinny.

Her mom had been overweight since childhood and suffered depression because of it. Justina thought her mom was beautiful, but it had been drilled into her head that being fat would make her miserable. So her mom's praise was even more important. Mom was proud of her and knew she'd do great things.

Her mom would be very disappointed if she knew how often Justina compared herself to the other Ice Girls and wondered if...well, if maybe she wasn't as pretty and fit and wonderful as her mom seemed to think.

Just thinking that way made her feel guilty. So she tried not to.

Which was difficult when some of the other girls whispered about how big she was behind her back. She'd gotten better at ignoring them though. She had friends who reminded her she looked absolutely perfect on the ice.

One of those friends, the Ice Girl's team captain, Akira, stepped up to her and tipped her chin up with a finger. "Very nice. You've gotten really good at putting on all the makeup."

"Thanks!" Justina smiled, praise from Akira meaning more than she could say. The woman was *amazing*. With long, rich brown hair that looked black out of the light, her features delicate, small in structure, but everything about her was strong. Not much older than Justina, but she was an Olympic level figure skater. She hadn't made it that far, but she planned to open her own school one day. Justina hoped she could convince Akira to let her teach there too.

If she ever got up the nerve to ask. She considered Akira a friend, but it wasn't like they hung out or anything. Or talked on the phone, or...

Stop it. Akira's busy, and it's not like you've ever called her.

Very true. She'd always been afraid to bother Akira, but Akira was so nice, she probably wouldn't have minded.

"Everything all right, sweetie?" Akira crouched down in front of her. "If anyone's giving you a hard time—"

"No, it's nothing like that!" Justina ducked her head, her face heating. She loved how Akira had stood up for her in the past, but she also knew bullies just got sneaky after they got caught. Even *if* there was a problem, she wouldn't go whining to Akira. She'd deal with it herself.

Nothing they said was *that* bad, anyway. She'd heard worse.

She took a deep breath, knowing she had to say something before Akira started to worry. "I was just thinking...you gave me your number, but, like, is that just for emergencies? Would it be weird if I called to hang out some time?"

Akira grinned and shook her head. "Not at all! Actually, I've been meaning to ask you to come do something. Things have been crazy, but maybe we could go out this weekend? I have plans with Jami and Sahara, but you get along with them?"

Justina nodded, excited at the idea of spending time with girls her own age. When she wasn't here, she was usually at home or at her brother's hockey practices. Both her parents worked a lot, so she tried to help out by taking care of Chris, which didn't leave much time for fun.

And her mom was always on her case about having fun. So...

Someone cleared their throat. Sahara, one of the alternate captains, joined them. "Umm...I love the idea of us all hanging out, but we're going to the club this weekend, Akira."

"Oh." Akira frowned. "Damn it, I forgot about that."

Justina throat tightened. They had plans...should she just laugh it off and tell them they could get together some other time? That would save her pride. She hadn't been clubbing in awhile, but Sahara, Akira, and Jami—the General Manager's daughter and one of the backup Ice Girls—were best friends. They probably didn't want to drag her along on their girl's night out.

Sahara looked over at Justina thoughtfully, her sleek blonde hair slipping over one shoulder. "Jami *did* mention bringing her some time though."

Jami did? She wanted me with them?

"Sahara, that's a bad idea." Akira folded her arms over her chest, her forehead creasing slightly as she looked down at Justina. "Sweetie, don't get me wrong. I'd love to spend some time with you away from all this, but the club is...it's not the place for you."

"But I love dancing!" *Don't you sound needy and pathetic.*

Sahara ran her hand down Justina's high ponytail. "Honey, it's not that kinda club."

"Then what kind of club is it?" She looked from Sahara to Akira, not sure what to make of them both pressing their lips together, heads titled to one side like they were thinking hard. "Come on, it can't be that bad?"

Letting out a long sigh, Sahara sat on the bench beside Justina. "It's not...*bad*. You know how Akira and I call our boyfriends 'Master'? And the rumors of some of the players being a bit kinky?"

She didn't pay much attention to rumors, but she *had* heard some things. Things that sounded straight out of the movies. Or the romance novels some of the Ice Girls giggled over.

Her face was on fire now because she'd pretty much needed the obvious spelled out for her. "So it's...it's *that* kind of club?"

"Yes." Sahara's eyes took on a mischievous glint. "You want to check it out?"

"Sahara!" Akira groaned when a few of the other Ice Girls glanced over, then sat at Justina's other side and lowered her voice. "I don't think you'd be comfortable there, Justina. It's nothing like what you've probably read about. Or seen on TV."

I freakin' hope not! Justina tugged the edge of her bottom lip with her teeth. "The only thing I've really seen is on CSI. And I wasn't allowed to watch the whole episode. My mom yelled at my dad when she saw the robo-spanker."

Both Akira and Sahara burst out laughing. Sahara put her arm over Justina's shoulders. "That's *awesome*! We've so gotta see if the club can get one of those!"

"That's a great idea." Akira's tone was dry as she glanced over at Sahara. "Maybe Dominik will use you to demonstrate exactly how it works."

"Umm, how about no." Sahara's face turned crimson. "I still can't believe he made me get up in front of that class, naked, for that demo on sensation play."

"You loved it!"

"Yes, but it was still humiliating!"

Justina swallowed hard, starting to think Akira was right. She wouldn't be comfortable there. Being naked in front of anyone was not her idea of a good time.

The teasing between Akira and Sahara continued until one of the trainers came into the locker room to tell them it was time for the show. Justina trailed a little behind, taking a few seconds to herself at the edge of the ice too cool off and clear her mind. She wanted to ask more about the club, but not here.

The other girls might be totally cool talking about sex and kinkiness where anyone could hear, but just the idea of voicing her questions made it hard to breathe.

Once her skates hit the ice, she stopped thinking about the many things she didn't know, and let what she had no doubt of take over. The music moved her as she skated away from the semi-circle of girls, the spotlight on her as she spun faster and faster, skidding out to bow her head as the lyrics began.

Unbreakable, by Fireflight, was one of her very favorite songs and she'd pretty much begged the choreographer to let her take one of the solo parts. She never asked for anything, but she'd *needed* to do this. She knew she'd nail it.

She swayed her body to the rhythm, mirroring the other girls for a few beats before gliding in a wide circle around them, speeding up to take her leap.

A little sound, one she shouldn't have heard at all between the music and her focus, reached her just as her skates left the ice. Her balance shifted, and rather than lean into the momentum, she prepared for the fall. Her bare thigh hit the ice, and she braced herself with one hand, protecting her face.

The sound came again. A giggle. The concerned murmur of the crowd drowned it out. Justina's heart pounded as she pushed back up to her feet. The open Zamboni ramp tempted her to race off the ice and out of sight where she could let the tears of humiliation fall freely.

But the music hadn't stopped.

This was her song.

Finish it, Justina.

As she took long strides, cheers filled the arena. She inhaled. Exhaled. And released into another leap. This time, she soared.

And landed perfectly.

The applause was deafening. Especially considering the stands hadn't filled up yet. She flashed a little smile at the crowd before joining the group for their finale pre-game song. *Centuries*, by Fall Out Boy, blared through the arena. The moves to this song were simpler, upbeat, pulling the fans into the excitement. More so since the players hit the ice halfway through.

Which is when the crowd really went wild. Justina grinned, waving as she headed off with the other girls while the announcer began to introduce the players.

The second she had her skates off, Sahara grabbed her hand, laughing as she dragged Justina into the hall. "Finish changing later! I'm sneaking you into the Wives' Room to watch the game."

"No, you most definitely are not." Justina laughed and tugged free of Sahara. "I've watched *Hockey Wives*. They probably don't like *you* being in there."

"Ha!" Sahara looped her arm around the back of Justina's neck. "I'll have you know they love me. And they'll all want to gush over your performance."

"You mean me falling on my butt?"

"It's so cute that you call it that. Come on, let me corrupt you a little." Sahara batted her long, black eyelashes and stuck out her bottom lip. "Akira's gonna be busy for a bit, giving Carrie shit about giggling to mess you up. And Carrie will deny it, of course, but everyone knows she's just jealous because you're awesome!"

Sahara was sweet to say that, but Justina knew Carrie—and at least half of the Ice Girls—didn't think she belonged on the team. Thankfully, as much as it might hurt, she wouldn't let them ruin what she'd worked so hard for.

"Sahara, I appreciate this, really, but I'm not comfortable going to the Wives' Room."

"Because it's against the rules?"

Well...yes. Obviously.

Sahara sighed and stopped trying to prod Justina down the hall. "Fine, but, honey, you've got to learn to live a little. Do something unexpected. I never see you having any fun."

"I have fun on the ice." Justina fiddled with her skirt when Sahara arched a brow at her. Maybe the other girl was right. Maybe she *should* make an effort to be a little spontaneous. She admired Sahara. And Akira and Jami.

They wouldn't want her tagging along if she was completely boring.

She took a deep breath. "I'll go with you to the club this weekend."

Big blue eyes wide, Sahara stared at her. "Are you serious?"

"Yes." And crazy too, apparently. Was she really going to do this?

Squealing and jumping up and down, Sahara caught her hands. "This is *awesome*! You're going to enjoy it, Justina, I swear. You don't have to do anything you don't want to. I'll talk to my master and make sure I can spend most of the night with you. And Jami and Akira will be there, so you'll never be alone."

"That's good, because if you leave me alone I'll probably end up chained to a wall somewhere. Getting..." She shook her head and laughed. "Robo-spanked."

With a snort, Sahara shook her head, tugging Justina in the other direction down the hall. "Not gonna happen. If you see something you want to try, Dominik will supervise. Have you met him?"

"Only in passing."

"I'll introduce you. Fuck, I love that man. He's a DM—a dungeon monitor—at the club. He's got a lot of experience, so he'll probably want to talk to you. Make sure you're there of your own free will."

Was it weird that she was just as excited as she was terrified? This all sounded so different than anything she'd ever experienced. Even if it totally wasn't her thing, she could at least say she'd given it a chance.

But she did have one last thing she had to ask before committing. "Sahara, there aren't actual cages in this dungeon, are there?"

The stupid game was finally over. Sam groaned as she pushed out of the uncomfortable chair in the press box where Sloan had been nice enough to let her chill while he was behind the bench and Max was on the ice. She'd tried to make small talk with Oriana's sister, Silver, and her brother, Ford, but all either of them wanted to know about was the baby.

Who she hadn't seen much of over the past few days.

Giving them both brief answers, she'd snuck over to the other end of the room the second they were distracted by the play, and promptly fell asleep. Jami came at halftime—or whatever the break from the game was called—and they went and grabbed a snack.

Jami, at least, didn't ask about the kid. She spent as much time as she could with him. And Sam had a feeling Luke had explained things to her.

Like how Sam was determined to prove she was just as selfish as everyone thought she was.

No one fucking thinks that, Sam.

Right. More like no one wanted to say it to her face.

The worst thing was life was going pretty good. Her room had been temporarily moved to the basement to give her some space until she found a place. Sloan was helping her with that, but kept reminding her she didn't have to rush. Her body was still achy, but not horribly so. She'd gotten plenty of sleep—never seemed like enough, but still—and she'd even gone to visit Luke a couple of times.

He was nice. Jami and Sebastian were nice.

They'd probably have been just as nice if she had some terminal illness.

She was grateful that people were putting up with her after everything she'd done though, so she accepted the nice. The careful smiles. The gentle encouragement every time she talked about plans for the future. She still wanted to go back to school. She wasn't sure about working with animals anymore because when Luke had tried to be sweet and show her all the courses she'd have to take…

Hell, she wasn't that smart. No way would she pass all those courses.

"You taking the loss hard, or are you just bored?" Sloan gave her a crooked grin as she sat up. "Ready to go?"

"Yeah…" She frowned, looking past him. "Where's Max?"

"He went to have a beer with a few of the guys. Oriana and James are sleeping, and I'll be there to get up with him if she's tired. Max probably won't stay out late, but I want to make sure he'll be good on the road. He's playing distracted."

Sam nodded slowly. "He's a new dad. That's gotta be expected?"

"Maybe so, but the more confident he is that Oriana can manage if he's not there every second, the easier it will be for him to get his head back in the game. We need him in top form out there and…" Sloan chuckled as she stifled a yawn. "You really don't care, do you?"

"It's not that. I'm just sleepy all the time, and I'm tired of it."

"You're still recovering. We'll get you home and right into bed."

Damn, a man like him, talking about getting her in bed, would have made her all kinds of hot and bothered before she'd gotten knocked up. Hell, even *while* she was pregnant she'd gotten turned on by all the sexy men on this damn team.

Sebastian might be fucking her brother, but when she'd been staying with them, she'd spent a good amount of time watching the man walk away. He had a damn fine ass.

Now though, her brain was definitely noticing all the sexy, but her body was like… *meh*.

Recovery sucked. She was never having another kid.

Stuffing her hands into the sleeves of the sweater she'd borrowed from Sloan—because none of her clothes fit right, the excuse she was sticking with no matter what—Sam followed him out of the press box. He seemed to know all the halls to take to avoid staff and press and people in general, which was awesome.

He was awesome. Sure, she'd given him a baby, but he knew she wouldn't take his son away from him, so he didn't have to keep checking up on her. He definitely didn't have to pour her coffee in the morning, or add her favorite stuff to the grocery list—after making sure he knew what she liked—or any of the other little things he was constantly doing.

No man in her life had ever treated her this good. She almost wished she could continue living with him.

But just almost. The cute little domestic thing he had going on with Max and Oriana really wasn't her style.

They were back at his place within twenty minutes, slipping in quietly so they wouldn't wake Oriana or the baby. After taking off his shoes, he headed straight to the kitchen and put on the kettle. She carefully placed her own shoes beside his and padded after him, clasping her hands in front of her so she wasn't tempted to touch anything.

He had a beautiful house. The kind of house you'd find in a magazine with the perfect little family standing in front of it. Nice, sturdy wood furniture, soft, natural colors everywhere, everything gleaming and smelling slightly of lemon cleaner.

She hadn't been upstairs much, but she knew Sloan shared a *huge* bed with Max and Oriana. Their arrangement confused her a little, but she didn't judge. Oriana was pretty and sweet and ideal wife material.

And Max was...damn, just his voice got her squirming when he spoke to her in that deep, southern drawl. He was nicely built, not like those greasy, scary bulging weight lifters, but with just enough muscles in all the right places. His smile was panty-melting and when he wasn't all scruffy—playoff beards were so stupid!—he was easily one of the best looking guys on the team.

Not as hot as Sloan, but she'd always been into tall, dark, and dangerous. Sloan had the look, but he wasn't an asshole like all the guys she'd fooled around with in the past. She couldn't blame Max for wanting a piece of the man. Hell, if she was a boy, she'd *still* want him.

"Do you want a tea?" Sloan glanced over his shoulder at her, holding up a plain, black mug. "Or you ready for bed?"

Dude, you've really got to stop bringing up my bed. Her cheeks heated a little, and she inhaled quickly before she started blushing and acting all giddy. "I'm not really tired anymore. The game was so bad, I got bored, but I was too nice to say so."

He snorted as he fixed them both some tea. "Cheeky brat. Do you want to watch a movie?"

"I'd *love* to!" She wouldn't lie. Not to herself anyway. Any excuse to spend time with him made her very happy.

Sloan's brow furrowed as he turned to face her, holding out the tea he'd fixed exactly the way she liked. With four teaspoons of sugar and just a splash of milk. He spoke before she could thank him. "I figured spending time with your brother would be enough, but you should be hanging out with girls your own age. Why don't you do something with Jami tomorrow? Go to the mall with her and her friends."

I'm not allowed to go to the mall anymore. She tongued her bottom lip and shrugged. "Maybe. The mall really isn't my thing, but I'll see if they wanna chill."

"Good." He gestured toward the living room. "For now, what would you like to watch?"

"Umm..." She sat on the cushy, brown leather sofa next to him and placed her mug on the rustic coffee table. As he flicked on the TV and began to scroll through new releases, she thought of a movie she'd wanted to see for a while.

Probably not his thing though.

"And you will tell me what that thought was, sweetie." Sloan placed the remote on the table and leaned back, his arm rested on the sofa behind her head. "Picking a movie shouldn't be this stressful."

"Picking one *you'll* like is."

His lips curved slightly into the little smirk that always gave her the strangest urge to lick him. "I didn't ask you what I want to watch. You clearly have something in mind?"

Many things. Many bad, bad things.

Telling him about the movie was probably the smartest thing she could do. Then she could stare at the TV, instead of at him. "Yeah...*The Boy Next Door* looks good."

Without another word, he did a search for the movie and rented it.

For the first ten minutes of the movie, she sat stiff beside him, finishing off her tea and trying to get into the movie.

He sighed and pulled her back once she set down her mug. "Relax. Are you enjoying it so far?"

She bit back a smile as she rested her head on his shoulder, and he didn't protest or act at all uncomfortable. "Yes. This is nice."

"Good."

Having him so close, letting her touch him, was way more than 'nice'. She considered all that she'd learned about the kind of relationship he was in. She'd read enough books to figure out he was a Dom. Which meant he could do whatever—and *whoever*—he wanted. He made all the rules.

Not a game she'd ever played, but she was willing to give it a shot. The characters on screen were fucking and her body chose that moment to let her know it was still functioning in every way. She was still a little sore, but her nipples hardened and her core clenched, urging her on.

Rising up on her knees, she leaned over Sloan, clasping her fingers behind his neck as she pressed her lips to his.

Damn he tastes good. She let out a soft moan as his lips parted and the sweet flavor of the honey he took with his tea hit the tip of her tongue. His hands settled on her hips and she pressed against him, more than ready for him to take her to her room, or to the floor, or wherever he wanted her.

"*Jeezus H. Christ!*" An angry, barely coherent voice broke through her wonderful, perfect haze of the moment. The low growl made all the hairs on the back of her neck stand on end. "Damn you to hell."

Sloan set her aside and strode across the room as Max turned around and headed right back out the front door. "Max, it's not—"

She winced as Sloan caught the door a second before it could slam into his face. He stepped around it then closed it softly behind him.

Shitshitshit! She really hadn't meant for that to happen. Well, for the kiss, yes, she'd totally meant that. But not for Max to walk in and freak out. Maybe she'd misjudged the rules a little bit. Maybe Sloan had to clear things with Max at least?

You're gonna end up on the streets if you keep this up, dumbass.

Slipping off the sofa, she headed down to her room. Figured things would go from great to fucking miserable again. She just couldn't do anything right.

No matter how hard she tried.

Max was pretty sure he'd never been so pissed. He sensed Sloan behind him as he walked along the front of their house, treading over the new grass that had been coming in as the ground finally thawed. He really wanted to turn around and crack the bastard right between the eyes.

What the hell was Sloan thinking?

What if Oriana had come down and seen him with Sam?

Spinning sharply, he rammed his hand into the center of Sloan's chest, shoving him against the brick wall. "We're a family, Sloan. A family with a child we swore we'd give a good, stable life. That little girl right there needs help. How could you—?"

"Fuck, Max, don't you think I know that?" Sloan dropped his head back and groaned. "She just…she caught me off guard. I was trying to figure out how to turn her down gently. If you'd come a moment later it would have been handled."

"Handled? You 'handle' subs at the club just fine. 'No' is actually quite effective. Did you try that?" Max fisted his hands in Sloan's shirt as the urge to lay him out grew. "If Oriana had seen you, you'd be fucking gone. You and the girl. My wife deserves better than—"

"Don't fucking do that, Max. Don't throw the fact that she's *your* wife in my face." Sloan pried Max's hand from his shirt, his eyes pure black in the night shade. "You're angry and I get that. But don't destroy everything we have because of one stupid mistake. One I had no control over."

"You're always in control, Sloan."

"I try. And I thought I could be there for her, but obviously she wants more than I can give." Sloan sighed and wrapped his hand around the back of Max's neck, touching their foreheads together, tightening his grip when Max tried to pull away. "She can't have me. All I have belongs to you and our woman."

Max pressed his eyes shut, struggling to suppress the still boiling rage. "I still want to fucking hit you."

Sloan chuckled, stepping back and holding his arms wide. "Then hit me. Do your worst, Max. Hurt me if it will help."

Rolling his eyes, Max shook his head. "No. Not my thing, and I'm not sure it would make either of us feel better."

"I disagree. I would feel much better." Sloan's smile faded at Max's level look. "You're right. I should have—fuck, I want her to be happy. To know she's going to have a good life and never second-guess leaving her baby with us. I keep thinking… What if she's scared and lonely and decides our son would be someone who won't ever leave her?"

Throat tightening, Max inclined his head. "She might could decide that, Sloan. She could change her mind a week from now, and there's nothing we could do."

Bowing his shoulders, Sloan dropped his gaze and nodded slowly. "Yeah. I guess she could."

"She talks to you more than anyone. Does it sound like she'll change her mind?"

"No. She still wants a clean break. I've been trying to help her find a place, but I don't like the idea of her being too far from everyone she knows. I looked for a small condo in Ramos' neighborhood." Sloan raked his fingers through his mussed up, black hair. "There's no way she could afford any of those places for any length of time. I could cover her for a few months, but—"

"She needs her independence." Max inhaled roughly. "We'll find her something, but she can't stay here anymore, Sloan."

"I know."

"And you have to make it clear that whatever she thinks is between the two of you…" Max ground his teeth, finding it hard to remember Sam was a troubled young woman and not one of the many females—or males—that would throw themselves at Sloan simply because he was one hell of a catch.

Subs have knelt in front of him, begging for his attention. How come that never bothered you?

Damn it, he didn't know. Maybe because at the club he knew what to expect. Same thing at games. Fans went nuts. Puck bunnies tried to cop a feel.

But this was their home. Which made what he'd walked in on even more of a shock.

Sloan's hand curved around the back of his neck again. Massaging the tense muscles gently. "Hey, listen to me. I will make it clear. In the morning, we will figure out where she can stay until we find her somewhere to live long term. You, Oriana, and our son are my priority. Please don't doubt that."

"I don't."

Lying awake, hours later, Max stared at the ceiling, what he'd walked in on playing over and over again in his head. He didn't doubt Sloan's commitment to their relationship, but one thing had become very clear.

Shit happened. Things out of their control. He'd seen some of the consequences while Oriana was in the hospital last month, but the three of them had been united as the world tried to pull them apart.

The challenges they faced would either make them stronger. Or it would destroy them.

He believed what they had was worth fighting for. He really did.

His words had told Sloan otherwise.

"If Oriana had seen you, you'd be fucking gone."

Spoken out of anger, but what if Sloan considered them as a crack in their once solid foundation? What if he questioned his place in their family?

Curving onto his side, he rested his arm over Oriana and his hand on Sloan's shoulder, careful not to disturb them. And he was finally able to sleep as he held on to the one thing no one could ever touch.

He'd never let either of them go.

Chapter Five

Whatever was cooking smelled *awesome*. Ian's mouth watered as he stepped into Pisch's apartment, practically tasting the peppercorn steak with bourbon sauce the man was making for supper. Arms loaded up with all the stuff Pisch had put on the grocery list, he backed into the door to shut it, toeing off his ratty sneakers so he wouldn't scuff up the floors.

They had the perfect arrangement. Pisch cooked, and Ian cleaned and ran and got whatever was missing for the meal. This time it had been all the healthy crap Ian was supposed to be eating. He thought he did pretty good with his diet, eating plenty of protein, but when he'd started getting tired all the time, the team doc put him on vitamin supplements and told Ian he needed ten servings of fruits and veggies a day.

Which was kinda nuts if you asked him. But Pisch agreed with the Doc.

So Ian was stuck eating rabbit food.

"Did you remember the almond milk?"

Ian rolled his eyes. "If you wrote it down, I got it."

"Good. Get in here and pour yourself a glass." Pisch sounded like he was trying not to laugh. The asshole knew Ian hated that nasty excuse for milk, but a smart man didn't mess with the person feeding him steak.

He lugged all the bags into the kitchen, looking from the table, all set for the two of them, to the counter where Pisch was cutting bread. The prep stuff he'd used to make the meal covered every available surface.

"Ah...where do you want all this?" Ian liked the routine they usually had. He'd get the groceries *before* Pisch started supper. Then he'd put everything away and hang out in the kitchen while Pisch cooked.

"Damn, I didn't plan this out very well, did I?" Pisch came over, grabbing a couple of the bags. "Sorry, buddy. With the playoffs, and you not being around as often, I didn't realize I'd run out of so much. Thanks for going, by the way."

Shrugging, Ian watched Pisch put the place settings on one side of the table, then set down the bags beside the ones he left there. "No problem. Thanks for having me over. *Again*."

Thanking each other for what had once been an everyday thing felt weird. He was spending most of his time here again, but more like a guest than like he belonged. He wasn't sure what had changed, but he hated it.

"Don't get all uncomfortable, Bruiser." Pisch started putting away the groceries. He motioned Ian away when he tried to lend a hand. "I've got this. Here, help yourself."

The almond milk. Damn, the man was determined to make him suffer.

Fetching a couple glasses from the cupboard, Ian filled both. And left them on the counter. "You think we're looking good for the game tomorrow?"

"Practice wasn't bad." Pischlar's lips thinned. "Except Vanek showing up late and Perron being there physically, but his head somewhere else. The rest of the guys seem solid enough."

"Vanek was late?" Ian hadn't noticed. The trainer had been drilling him on faceoffs, determined to get his average up. He couldn't rely on throwing down the gloves every game to prove his worth anymore, so he had to improve in other areas. He'd been moved onto special teams this year and was good on the penalty kill. He had one of the highest hits per game on the team.

But if he could bring up his assists and win more faceoffs, Dean Richter, the team's General Manager, would have a reason to extend his contract.

"Don't worry about Vanek." Pisch served up the plates and took a seat at the table. He waited until Ian was halfway across the kitchen before looking pointedly over at the counter. He continued as Ian grabbed the glasses of nastiness. "You're focused on the ice. More than you've been in a long time. The coaches noticed."

"You think so?" Ian smiled, taking a gulp of the chalky drink and managing not to gag. That accomplished, he settled in to enjoy the meal. He groaned as he chewed a nice big bite of juicy steak. "God, Pisch. Will you marry me?"

Pisch knocked over the glass he'd been reaching for. "For fuck's sakes, White. Don't even joke about that."

The man has completely lost his sense of humor. Ian smirked as he licked the bourbon sauce off his lips. "Why not? The idea of marriage scare you that much?"

"Yes." Pisch righted his glass and used a few napkins to clean the spill. "You'd make a horrible husband."

"Gee thanks, pal."

"You know it's true." Pisch brought a piece of steak to his mouth, chewing thoughtfully, all serious again. "Besides, even if you were gay, and ready to settle down, you're not a sub. And I need a sub."

Ian frowned and set down his fork. They hadn't talked much about why they'd friend-zoned one another, but he'd wondered if Pisch not wanting to be 'kept' was the only issue.

The lifestyle Pisch lived being a problem hadn't even occurred to him.

"You offered to train me."

"Yes. As a Dom."

"You sure I'm a Dom?" Once, Ian would have laughed at the idea of being anything else. He would have told anyone that asked that he was a tough guy, so of course he was a Dom. But he'd seen strong men kneel at the club. And he didn't think any less of them.

He wasn't sure where he fit in the dynamics, but he wanted to find out.

Especially if it meant one obstacle would be out of their way.

Using the last napkin on the table to wipe his lips, Pischlar studied him curiously. "You'd consider exploring the scene as a sub?"

"Maybe…I mean, Doms experience both, right? So I'd figure it out."

"Not all Doms do, but it does have certain advantages." Pisch inhaled slowly. "I've never seen any submissive behavior from you. The only people you answer to are the coaches and trainers."

Ian picked up his glass, giving Pisch a pointed look as he took a few long gulps. *Gah, so very, very horrible.* He used the back of his hand to dry his lips. "And you."

Well played, White. Shawn drained his glass, considering all White had said. Every day it was getting harder to convince himself they couldn't have a strong, lasting relationship. Which fucking terrified him.

He had plenty of reasons to avoid getting serious with White. Reasons that proved weak as the man doubled his efforts to show off how damn perfectly he could fit into Shawn's life. The dirtiest trick was making whatever was between them about more than sex.

Sex Shawn could handle. Even sex with White. Yeah, he'd probably have his little slip ups where his heart thought it had a say in what he did with his body, but he had absolutely no problem with him and White becoming fuck friends.

He understood White not wanting to risk their friendship. He didn't either, but they could easily have both.

Not sure he's good with that, Pischlar.

White was just confused. Hell, he had to be if he was talking about being a sub.

What if he is *a sub? Or can be for you?*

Yeah…very tempting. But when White figured out that nope, he wasn't even the least bit kinky, they'd be right back where they'd started. Or worse, left with nothing.

White's lips quirked as he continued to stare at Shawn. "Nothing to say?"

He's way too cocky for a sub. This will never work.

Shawn lifted his brow, finishing off his meal and taking his plate to the sink without bothering to answer. White wanted a taste of what it was like to be a sub? Very well.

It wouldn't play out the way White expected, but Shawn was game. "Clean up and join me in the living room. Then we'll talk."

Kicking back in the living room, his bare feet up on the coffee table, Shawn mentally laid out his strategy. Emotional investment aside, he did want White. He wasn't a fan of not getting who he wanted when he wanted them. Thankfully, he rarely set his sights on men or women in a relationship, but having a whole community of sexually open individuals to play with meant even some of them were available for one hot, wild night of passion.

He enjoyed his freedom, so that would be the first thing he made clear to White.

The 'you can't keep me' chat wasn't enough?

No. Not for White. One of the many things he loved about the man was that he was as straightforward as a person could be. He said exactly what was on his mind. Reacted to the words spoken, not what he thought someone was trying to say. If something was open to interpretation, or needed more digging, White usually didn't get it.

Which made some people thinking the man was stupid, but he really wasn't. He just didn't understand why people didn't say what they meant. Both a virtue and a flaw. Most people weren't that honest with one another. Or themselves.

He flicked on the TV, finding a comic book movie out of habit, leaving it as familiar background noise as he rested his eyes and waited for White to finish in the kitchen.

The sofa bounced as White plunked down beside him. "Done. Let's talk."

"Did you finish all your milk, or did you pour it out?"

White made a rough sound of irritation. "Yes, I drank my nut juice, *Daddy*. And now I'm having a couple beers to wash the taste out of my mouth. I brought you one if you want it."

Shaking with laughter, Shawn bent over, covering his face with one hand. "Damn it, White, how am I supposed to be serious when you say shit like that?"

"Are we being serious?"

Lowering his hand, Shawn studied White's face as the other man stared down at his unopened beer. "Do you want to be?"

Forehead creasing, White uncapped his beer. "I'm not sure what you mean."

Shawn nodded, not at all surprised. Other people might have pretended to understand, or assumed what suited them, but not White. He'd make Shawn be perfectly clear.

Which Shawn had every intention of being. "Are you looking for some kind of commitment from me, Bruiser? You want to come out to the team, your family, and the whole world?"

The question had White paling a little more with every word. He downed his beer in a few quick gulps. "Is there an option B?"

Should I be relieved or disappointed? Strangely enough, he was neither. White hadn't told him to go fuck himself. Or that he was straight and didn't need to come out at all. Ever.

Asking for an 'Option B' was close, but not a complete rejection.

"I'll train you. In public, it's no different than how most Doms at the club teach their same sex trainees. I'll show you what's expected of a submissive. Of a Dom. You'll learn the protocols, how certain tools feel when used on your flesh." He paused, enjoying the way White shivered at the last. This was going to be fun. "In private, we decide together what we want to do. We touch, we taste, and we fuck. And it's no one's business what happens behind closed doors."

Crimson spread slowly up White's neck and over his cheeks. He cleared his throat. "Ah...that makes sense. But you asked about commitment?"

"I did. And I'm glad you brought that up. You've heard the speech, White. I don't like feeling tied down, and I won't do that to you either." This part was a little harder. He didn't want restrictions, but he hated seeing White with anyone else. He couldn't have it both ways. If he wanted his freedom, his last shield against all the many things that could go wrong, he had to give White the same. "This will be...have you ever heard of an open relationship?"

White's shoulders dropped. "Yes, I'm not a complete moron, Pisch."

"From this point on, you will stop assuming I'm explaining myself because I think you're stupid." Shawn let his tone drop, with a rough edge that submissives tended to pay attention to. A deep, primal satisfaction filled him when White tugged his bottom lip between his teeth and nodded. Whether or not White was a sub, he did have a very basic need to please.

Inhaling noisily, White rolled his beer bottle between his hands. "Sorry, I just...so you want to be able to fuck whoever you want. And I can't get jealous."

"Will you be?"

"I don't know." White took another swig of beer. "Is that okay? I'll get over it. I won't hit anyone you're fucking. Especially not if it's a chick. I don't hit chicks."

I know. Shawn forced himself to smile, keeping his expression relaxed. "If you are upset, feel free to discuss it with me. I promise to do the same, but honestly, I don't see why it should be a problem. You might meet the perfect girl and decide you don't want to play with me anymore. And I'll still be your best friend. The point to all this is not losing what we have."

"That sounds good." White got up and headed to the kitchen. "You want another beer?"

Shawn chuckled as he grabbed his beer from the table. "I haven't started this one. But I will warn you, White. If you have more than three, I won't touch you tonight."

Silence. Then a steady banging. Likely White knocking his forehead against the fridge.

Smirking, he took a sip of beer. Still nice and crisp. Refreshing. He let White continue for a few second before speaking up. "It might be a bad idea to give yourself a concussion during the playoffs."

"You're killing me, man. A concussion is the *least* of our problems." White ambled over to stand in front of the couch, facing Shawn. "Is that it? We did all the negotiating thing and now..."

"No. We haven't even started negotiating, Bruiser. We were just leading up to that." Shawn noticed White had a beer in each hand. Since he'd only finished one so far, he was following the rules. *Good boy.* "I know you like blow jobs. Are you against giving them?"

A little evil, but he'd intentionally waited until White was drinking again before asking. He shifted sideways as White spit out half the beer he'd practically inhaled.

"I... Uh... you..." White pressed his lips together, then jerked on the sleeve of his black T-shirt to wipe his mouth. "I've never... I could..." He groaned. "You've done it to me. I'm sure I suck, but I can try."

"Sucking would be a good start, babe." Shawn used the endearment to test White's reaction. He grinned when White made a face. "I apologize. Would you prefer I call you something else?"

"Yes. Anything else. Babe is a pig." White blushed. "But I guess I shouldn't tell you what to call me?"

"Unless it's a hard limit, whatever you say will be taken into consideration. And likely used during punishment if I find it effective." Shawn's phone buzzed on the coffee table and he reached over to grab it, not looking right away because he was enjoying the conversation. "So I can look forward to blowjobs. That's definitely a plus."

White looked awfully cute, blushing while still trying to look all tough. "Do you want one now?"

Fuck yes! Shawn's dick throbbed as his blood pulsed strong and steady downward, but he shook his head. Toying with White might be fun, but as a Dom, Shawn knew better than to rush into anything a sub was clearly uncertain of.

"No. And don't expect me to say that often, but let's ease into you getting on your knees for me." Shawn kept his eyes on White, pretty sure he couldn't get any more red, but noting that he didn't react to the mention of being on his knees. "Are you a virgin?"

White blinked. "You know I'm not."

"No, I don't. I can assume, but I'd prefer not to. Has a man, or woman, ever fucked you? And to be clear, I mean anal." He was perfectly aware that he was pushing White to the limits, but if he was going to consider him a sub, he had to. He could deal with White never wanting to bottom, but to be honest, it would be disappointing. The man had a nice, round ass. To feel it, even once, Shawn would give almost anything. Both his heart and soul were fair game.

"Oh." White slumped onto the sofa, still holding his beer as he lowered his head to his forearms. "Then yes. I'm a virgin."

"Thank you for being honest. I know that wasn't easy." Shawn put his hand on White's shoulder. This was enough for now. White hadn't bolted. Or lashed out. They were making progress and he wouldn't ruin it by pushing any further. "I just gotta see who texted me. Then we can discuss what comes first."

White's throat worked as he swallowed hard. Then he nodded. "Okay."

Shawn squeezed White's shoulder. Tapped into the message on his phone, eager to put whatever it was aside so he could continue his night uninterrupted.

His plans changed the second he read the message. He had to read it twice. Make sure he wasn't seeing things.

"*Fuck!*" He checked himself before slamming his phone on the table. Breaking the thing would be stupid. And smashing it on the table wouldn't be as satisfying as throwing it across the room. But now that he'd had time to consider, neither seemed wise. "I have to go. Stay here."

"Is that an order?" White caught his wrist before he could move out of reach. Then released him quickly. "Sorry. I didn't mean to—"

"It's fine." Shawn didn't have the time to coddle White. And he was used to the man grabbing him, so no big deal. They'd work on it. "You don't want to come, Bruiser. This isn't your scene."

"What isn't?" White fisted his hands at his sides. "Please tell me what's going on. You're freaking me out."

"White, you don't want to know."

"Shawn, tell me what the fuck—"

"I told you not to call me that."

"And *you* told me our friendship was solid. You haven't fucked me yet, *Easy*. Don't cut me out."

Fuck me! Shawn groaned as he rushed across the hall and yanked on his shoes. White had every right to demand that he share in the same way that he would have before the rules had been laid out, but he wasn't sure he would have brought White along even then.

But how deep could he let White into his life if he hid things like this from him?

"Fine. You can come." He jerked the front door open, too pissed off to play nice. "But don't say I didn't fucking warn you."

Chapter Six

Ian didn't drive anymore. For some messed up reason, he couldn't force himself to get behind the wheel of a car. Pisch either drove him around, or he caught a lift from one of his teammates. Or called a cab.

Which meant he had no idea where they were going when he took shotgun in the new Mazda Pisch had upgraded to last month. The thing was red and sleek, even though Ian could picture a soccer mom sitting in the driver's seat. Decent, but Pisch should be driving a big truck. Or at least a muscle car.

Or a tank. He pictured Pisch behind the wheel of a big hunk of metal that roared when he revved the engine. Wearing army greens.

And fuck, he got hard at the image. Usually, his fantasies involved chicks with big boobs, not wearing much of anything. But Pisch fully clothed did things to him. Things he'd never felt before he'd crashed through the very obvious, clear cut, boundaries.

No point in looking back though.

About twenty minutes later, they pulled up in front of a club on the edge of the city, rolling past the parking lot, into what looked like the lot where the employees and management probably parked their cars. He shot Pisch a questioning look, but the man was already getting out of the car. Ian followed quickly as Pisch cut across the pavement, taking the steps up to the back door two at a time.

Jaw tense, Ian took in their surroundings. It wasn't even midnight, but the area was quiet, pitch black except for the small lights around the top of the plain, gray cement walls. The back door was heavy metal, knocking on it would be pointless, but Pisch immediately pressed a small buzzer Ian hadn't even noticed.

He's been here before.

Considering there was some kind of trouble, Ian couldn't help worry about the fact that Pisch had never mentioned this place. Ian wasn't a complete idiot, he knew Pisch hung out at gay clubs, but this one seemed different. Shady.

The door cracked open, and the silence was broken by the deep pulse of R&B music. The door swung wide, revealing a short, balding, middle-aged man who smiled broadly as he motioned Pisch and Ian inside. "Thanks for getting here so fast, Easy. I'm keeping him as safe as I can, but there's only so much I can do."

"I appreciate it, Skins." Pisch gave the man a quick hug, glancing over at the door at the end of a short, gray hall. "He still on stage?"

"Yeah. I'm not sure if he's drunk or just that fucking comfortable strutting his stuff. I'll be honest, man." Skins laughed and shook his head. "If you hadn't put your boys off limits, I might have made a play for him myself. He's one fine piece of ass."

Pisch has 'boys'? Ian shouldn't be surprised. He knew his best friend got around. And for the longest time, he'd just told the man he didn't want details. Which had probably been smart. His imagination was giving him more than enough to work with. Picturing Pisch with a 'fine piece of ass' sent a sharp pain straight into Ian's chest. One that lingered as though he'd been stabbed with a wooden spear that left splinters behind even as the source of the wound was removed by cold logic. They'd agreed to keep things 'open'.

No reason to get all worked up about Pisch still having other toys to play with.

Maybe not, but you sure you want to be one of them?

Folding his arms over his chest, Ian reminded himself he'd asked to come. He was here as Pischlar's friend. In case he needed backup.

I really hope he needs backup.

A fight he could deal with. These stupid emotions? Not so much.

Pisch's lips curved into a tight smile. "If he's as popular as you implied in your text, you might have a few unhappy patrons when I drag him out of here."

Skins nodded slowly. "I'm aware. Any way I can convince you to let him stay?"

Laughing, Pisch started across the hall. "I'll let you know when I see the damage. If one person has their fucking phone out taking pictures, I'm done playing nice."

Sidling past Ian, who was trying to stick close to Pisch, Skins made a low, irritated sound. "You know I don't allow that, Easy."

"Yes, but I also know you don't allow pretty, barely legal boys up on stage." Pisch's knuckles turned white as he grabbed the doorknob. "If you were smart, you would have stopped him."

"I'm a businessman, Easy." Skins put his hand on Pisch's forearm, jerking it away with his eyes wide when Pisch glared at him and Ian stepped forward. "He got up there with our regulars, and the crowd loved it. He's got skills."

"He does. Skills that belong on the ice, not on a stage cruddy with sweat and cum." Pisch turned the doorknob and paused. Hesitated as he met Ian's eyes. "Are you sure you want to do this?"

Is he serious? From the little Pisch had said, Ian had figured out it had to be one of their players out there. He wasn't sure which one, but they were a team. If one of their guys was in trouble, he didn't care that Pisch considered them one of his 'boys'.

Ian would help. And, with any luck, get a chance to lay out anyone who'd messed with the kid.

Had to be one of the younger guys. He wasn't looking forward to the fallout if it was someone like Carter or Vanek. They had solid relationships. What if one stupid mistake screwed up everything for them?

Hopefully he and Pisch had gotten there fast enough to prevent real damage.

He trailed after Pisch, his jaw clenched, hardly seeing the crowd pressing close to the stage. His mouth went dry as he caught who was up there. Not alone, there were five guys bumping and grinding as one song ended and another began.

But now he knew why Pisch had dropped everything to come. This was fucked up. The kid should not be here.

He probably wouldn't be if he wasn't so confused.

And Ian couldn't help but feel partly responsible for that.

The buzz of too many beers, mixed with a few shots, had Ian stumbling a bit as he walked across the hotel room. He tugged at his tie, wanting to get it off. Fuck, it was hot. He wanted to head to his own room. Strip and pass out on his bed.

But he had to keep an eye on the rookie.

With a soft sigh, Richards dropped onto the bed, one arm covering his eyes. "I think that last shot was a mistake."

"Yeah." Ian sat on the edge of the bed. "You okay?"

"I guess." Richards sighed again. "I just...fuck, I can't do this anymore. I keep hanging out with Hunt, and I love the man, but he doesn't get me."

Ian's head was really heavy. He dropped onto the bed beside Richards. "What do you mean?"

"I'm gay. Like, totally, completely, into guys." Richards turned his head, biting his bottom lip as he looked at Ian. "Go if you want. I know I shouldn't have said that."

"Why? I don't care who you fuck." Ian pressed his eyes shut. "I'm straight. Or I think I am. I don't know. It's fucking confusing."

"Is it? I don't think I've ever been confused." Richards rose up on his elbow. "Like, I've tried stuff with girls, but just because I thought I should. But when me and Hunt fool around with chicks, they don't get me hard. And that's where it's fucked up. We shared a chick once and...well, I was thinking about him the whole time. And I know he'd hate me if he knew."

Ian wasn't sure why Richards was telling him all this. But he wanted to help, so he slit his eyes opened and stared at the baby face above him. Damn, the kid was young. Ian couldn't remember being that young. And he wasn't exactly old.

"I don't think he'd hate you, but...maybe you're just into him? Like, maybe that happens? You're into someone and everyone else just...isn't them." His brain wasn't working right. So much had been going on lately, he was just damn tired. He should be having this conversation with Pisch. He loved Pisch. Not in a sex way…or, he didn't think so. He was absolutely, almost one hundred percent sure he was straight.

And then he wasn't and he could totally get why Richards was confused. Sometimes, you loved someone, and it didn't make sense. And it blurred all the things you thought you knew.

"But you don't have to be into someone for them to get you off?" Richards's tone changed. He moved closer. "I don't want to play with girls. I'm tired of pretending I do."

"Then stop." Simple enough, right? Ian watched Richards' tongue flick over his bottom lip and his cock hardened. He'd only ever reacted that way to one other man giving him that look, but he'd buried all those crazy urges deep. Because some relationships meant more than getting off. More than sex.

"I want to stop. But…I've jerked off thinking of Hunt. And that was good, but nothing compared to fucking the one man I really want." Richards slid his hand over Ian's chest, jerking away when Ian sat up. "I'm sorry. I don't mean I want you—"

"Okay, that's good. Because you're not fucking me, kid." Ian rubbed a hand over his face, his blood pounding into his dick, so fucking turned on he couldn't think straight. He wasn't even seeing Richards anymore. He was seeing Pisch. And that was so very wrong.

If Pisch was here, he would give the man anything he wanted. Thankfully, he wasn't. Ian wouldn't ruin their friendship because he was horny.

He should head back to his own room. Because he was horny. Like, so fucking hard it hurt.

"I don't want to fuck you, White." Richards hand slid down over Ian's rock hard cock. "But I want to suck your dick. I want to know I can do that without it meaning anything."

"Fuck." Ian's hips rose as Richards continued to stroke him through his pants. "I wanna let you."

"Why?"

"Because it not meaning anything sounds good. And that feels good. Maybe that's all that matters. Maybe I'll stop thinking so much if I just take what I can get."

Richards' hot mouth on his dick had felt good for a few seconds. But then he thought of Pisch, and shallow pleasure had his dick going soft. He stopped

Richards and called for room service, recalling that a hot chick he'd seen earlier was working the night shift. The rest of the night was a blur. He thought Pisch was there for real at one point, but he wasn't sure. He saw the man so often when he closed his eyes, nothing seemed real.

And Richards kinda enjoyed the girl—and her friend.

Neither of them talked much the next morning.

But Richards thanked him. Told him he was right. Sometimes, all that mattered was taking what you could get.

On that stage, Richards could get anything. Anyone.

Every man in the crowd wanted him.

And Ian wasn't completely immune. His legs seemed to have turned to stone as he reached the edge of the stage. The other dancers retreated, leaving Richards in the spotlight. The rookie was wearing a mask, like the one the Lone Ranger wore. Not covering enough to really hide his identity, not to anyone who knew him. Like teammates. Or fans.

Or anyone into hockey.

The song that came on was familiar. Ian recognized it from the movie, Miami Vice. He was pretty sure it was older though, and this version was a cover. *In the Air Tonight*...hell, his blood had left his brain. He couldn't remember the name of the guy who'd sung the original.

Then again, his own name might take him a minute to recall if someone asked right now.

Richards moved like his body belonged on a stage, bared to a crowd, tempting them to taste and touch everything he had to offer. In nothing but a pair of tight black boxers, he moved like a dancer trained to sell sex. Grinding down, dropping back, and bracing himself on one hand, he thrust his hips forward.

He glanced over the crowd without slowing, and Ian caught Richards' lips thin a little before he threw himself into a spin on his knees. Richards ran his hand down the center of his bare chest, flicking his tongue out over his bottom lip before bringing his fingers to his lips to suck one.

The boy was fucking hot. Ian wouldn't bother denying it. But if it got out to the media that he'd been stripping at a gay club—hell, stripping *anywhere* public—his career would be trashed. Little kids looked up to them; they were athletes and were supposed to set a good example. Not that they couldn't make mistakes, but the wrong mistake could get you traded. Or sent down to the minors.

Or worse, completely blacklisted by the league.

Ian didn't think Richards being exposed would lead to anything that extreme, but best not to take any chances. He looked over to Pisch, prepared to go drag the kid off the stage the second the man gave the signal.

Instead, Pisch was watching the crowd. Ian followed his gaze and spotted one of the cops he'd seen around the station when he'd been arrested for 'assault'. Decent guy. He'd been a bit of a jerk when Richards had asked him about his stolen bike, but he'd probably been busy.

The cop finished his beer, rubbed a hand over his face, and strode out the front door.

Pisch sighed and folded his arms over his chest. "Not the reaction the kid wanted. Hopefully, he'll drop the act now."

Huh? Ian shook his head, not sure what he was missing. "Shouldn't we—"

Holding one hand up, Pisch flashed him a stiff smile. "Not yet."

Arms folded over his chest, Ian continued to watch Richards. The rookie hooked his thumbs to the waistband of his boxers, easing them down over his ass. He didn't stop there. His hips rotated in time to the music as he got down on his hands and knees. Offering himself to the crowd.

A big, bald man in a leather vest vaulted onto the stage, coming up behind Richards.

Letting out a low growl, Ian took the steps up to the stage, two at a time, and jerked the man away from the rookie. The man was a fair match for him. He didn't think twice before cracking the asshole in the jaw.

Bouncers rushed the stage. Richards had disappeared. Ian faced the man as he straightened, more than ready to spend a couple minutes teaching the fucker why even trying to mess with the kid had been a bad idea.

Hands latched on to his arms. The man took the opportunity to snap his fist into Ian's nose.

Ian wrenched free. The bouncer that had grabbed him looped a thick arm around his neck.

Suddenly, Pisch was there, blocking a second punch from the dirty bastard the other bouncers still hadn't restrained. Pisch caught a fist in the eye and went down to one knee.

Red flashed across Ian's vision, and he drove his elbow back into the bouncer's stomach. Once free, he tackled the man who'd hit Pisch, wrapping his hands around the man's throat. He could fucking kill him. End him right fucking now.

"Bruiser, let him go." A soft, deep voice broke through the deafening pulse of rage. "Ian, that's enough."

Inhaling slowly, Ian pushed away from the man. Heat spilled over his lips. He blinked as he turned to Pisch. "I think the fucker broke my nose."

"You've had worse." Pisch grinned, resting his arm over Ian's shoulders and leading him off the stage. "You okay?"

"Yeah..." Ian squinted at Pisch as they hit the dark hallway. Richards was there. In one piece. He dismissed the kid as he tried to focus on Pisch's face while both his eyes watered. "Are you?"

"I'm good." Pisch squeezed his shoulder, then turned to Richards. "Kid, I don't know what you were hoping to accomplish, but that was fucking stupid. You over trying to get him to notice you?"

Richards rubbed his hands over his boxers. Which were thankfully covering him fully. "He *did* notice me. I was hoping he'd be the one coming to get me. Didn't mean for anyone to call you."

"You're lucky they did." Pisch sighed. "How drunk are you?"

Flashing a toothy smile, Richards straightened. "I'm sober, man. Didn't want him to think I was..." His smile faded. "That really was stupid. I met him here, you know? We had a good time, but he didn't call the next day. I kinda wanted to prove I'm worth his time."

Sympathy filled Pisch's eyes. "I get you, buddy. But sometimes a good time is just that."

Ian inhaled roughly. He felt bad for the kid. The asshole had used him.

Hitting a cop is bad, right? Might want to wait until I'm off probation.

After that, he and the cop would have a chat.

Groaning, Richards walked beside Pisch to one of the doors along the hall, stepping in and letting them pass. He started getting dressed. "I feel like such a loser. It was just sex."

Folding his arms over his chest, Ian leaned against the wall by the door. "Did you know that when you went home with him?"

Pisch arched a brow at him, then tossed him a towel from the collection on a nearby shelf. "I doubt the man seduced the kid with promises of a long lasting relationship."

Hey, fuck you, Easy. Ian ignored his best friend as he pressed the towel to his bloody nose. Richards was a sweet kid. He wouldn't have fucked around with someone knowing they were gonna use him.

Richards blushed. "I was kinda shy my first time here. Still hiding who I am, you know? He bought me a drink and asked me if I'd just come out. Said I had that look." He rubbed his arms, looking even younger now that he wasn't half naked. "I admitted I wasn't really 'out'. That I didn't have much experience. He was so easy to talk to. He kissed me and after that…fuck, I was willing to do anything. We went to his place, and he was…it's not like he kicked me out in the morning, you know? He dropped me off at home and told me to take care."

"Did he give you his phone number?" Pisch's tone was level. Like he understood a lot more about what had gone down than Ian did.

The rookie shook his head. "No. But I saw him with Laura once. I really wanted to talk to him, so I got her number from Vanek. And she passed him the phone, and he was all playing like I was calling about a stolen bike. I went along with it, figuring he just couldn't talk. But when I went to the station…"

"He made it obvious the 'bike' was gone. And you should stop looking for it." Pisch shook his head. "Kid, I'm sorry if you thought there was more, but he was in for that night. It's over."

So...there's no bike? Ian was lost. He kinda got that the cop had fooled around with the kid and hadn't wanted another round. Why not just say so? Why be so damn vague Richards felt like getting up on stage might get his attention? That was messed up.

People don't really do shit like that, do they?

The man was a cop. Maybe he was just working hard. But he could have at least tried to find Richards bike. Then taken the opportunity to be straight with him.

"So he used your bike as a way to tell you he's not into you?" Ian frowned when both Pisch and Richards stared at him. "Sorry, but the guy sounds like an asshole. Did you get a new bike?"

Richards snorted as Pisch muttered something while staring at the ceiling. "I don't have a bike, White. Never did."

Okay, that was just sad. Ian had thought Richards had a good childhood. He'd never had a bike?

This one must have been special.

"Bruiser, Richards wasn't neglected. I'm sure he had a bike as a little boy." Pisch put his hand on Ian's shoulder, waiting for Richards nod. "He means there was no bike involved in this situation."

"But..." *Oh.* Ian groaned. "Sorry. Maybe it's just me, but this is a whole lot of drama when the guy could have just said 'Hey, man, I just wanted to fuck you. No hard feelings?'"

"That would be nice, but unfortunately most people don't think the way you do, White." Pisch's eyes held the gentle, warm look that helped relax Ian. Made it not matter that he'd missed what was obvious to everyone else. Pisch cocked his head at Richards. "You seem all right, kid. I don't think this will hit the press. And you're good to drive yourself home. I came here thinking you needed rescuing, but I was wrong."

Richards ducked his head. "So not true. If White hadn't grabbed that guy, it would have been bad. I might not have stopped him."

What the actual fuck? Ian's jaw ticked. The man probably hadn't gone far. He could still go kill him. Unless that would be a bad idea? Maybe Richards was into being fucked on stage?

Pisch rubbed his shoulder and laughed. "Richards, did you want that guy to fuck you? Because being vague now is a bad idea."

Yes. Very bad. Ian hoped Richards was joking. Even though it wasn't funny.

"No, I would have felt like shit tomorrow. Tonight though?" Richards stared at the floor. "I didn't care. The man I want doesn't want me."

"Come back to my place, Richards." Pisch led the way out, stopping by his car and unlocking the door so Ian could get in. "We'll make you forget him. Even if only for a little bit."

Sitting on the edge of the passenger seat, Ian watched Richards hesitate on his way to a car parked at the end of the regular parking area. The car was new. A freakin' Zenvo ST1. Which was worth more than most rookies made.

Either the kid had a crazy contract, or he was being stupid with his money. Either way, the boy needed a mentor. And Ian couldn't be that for him.

Maybe Pisch could though. As edgy as he was, Pisch still managed to be a media sweetheart. He did tons of charity stuff. Got Ian involved in stuff he hadn't even considered. Ian trusted his agent to tell him what he should do, but the man wasn't helpful when it came to being generous. He'd stopped Ian from giving to a few charities that turned out to be real greedy and not doing much good, but he didn't offer alternatives. Pisch was on the ball with the good ones. He and Zovko, a player who'd been a huge buy for the team, but lost his sight after cracking his skull on the ice, took the lead with charities.

Ramos was another guy who was good with donations, but he didn't go public with anything. Ian had gone to the food bank he supported a few times, hauling around boxes when the man told him that's what they needed. He'd wanted to give some money too, but he'd dumped all his savings into brain research when his grandmother started getting worse.

He wouldn't tell any of the guys, except maybe Pisch, but he was broke. A doctor in the States had told him he could help his grandmother. Between funding the research and paying his grandmother's full time care, Ian could barely afford his own apartment.

Ian had gotten a notice last month about his phone being on the verge of being cut off. Some guys hired someone to handle all the bills for them, but Ian wasn't making that kinda money.

So, yeah...he drooled over Richards' car a little when the rookie pulled out and waited for them to pass. He might not drive, but he still appreciated a nice ride. His grandmother loved classic muscle. She'd taught Ian how to drive, and when he'd gotten signed, she'd talked about buying a real classic. Told him his dad would have been all over working on it with him when he had the time. Would have taught him how to take apart an engine.

She didn't remember those conversations anymore. But he did. And maybe if he proved himself in the playoffs, this summer he could visit and tell her all about his new car. Which he'd somehow manage to drive.

And she'd be well enough to get out and enjoy the ride. She'd remembered his name last time he called. She was getting better.

"Talk to me, Bruiser." Pisch pulled up in front of his apartment complex and parked, turning sideways, his focus on Ian. "You hurting?"

Hurting? He dropped the towel he'd been pressing to his nose every time he felt it leaking. It was better. Tomorrow, before the game, Doc might ask him about it. Tonight? He was sore, but in one piece.

"I'm good. Just looking at Richards' car. Grandma would love it." He smiled, even though he was a little sad. "My dad would have too."

"You should get yourself a nice ride." Pisch got out of the car, waiting for Ian on the sidewalk. "I know you don't like driving, but one day you might...I don't know, see it differently? If you do well during the playoffs, your agent could push for a sweet contract."

"He could, but there's some new research that doctor was telling me about—"

"I'm sure there is." Pisch sighed and shook his head. "I think the man's milking you, Bruiser. But I get why you're doing this."

"Thanks." Ian bumped shoulders with Pisch as they joined Richards on the walkway leading to the apartment entrance. "So you guys wanna try out the new Assassin's Creed? Got some sick graphics."

Richards bit his bottom lip as Pisch pressed the button to call the elevator. When Pisch ignored the confused look the rookie was giving him, Richards turned to Ian and cleared his throat. "I don't think I'm here to play games, man."

Pisch chuckled as he stepped onto the elevator. Arms folded over his chest, he gave Richards a lazy smile. "I wouldn't say that, kid. I'm just rigging the game so everyone wins. You'll learn to play my way."

Ian's pulse picked up a notch. He swallowed hard as he watched Richards' cheeks redden and his eyes glaze with lust. The way the rookie tongued his bottom lip sent heat surging down. The elevator suddenly felt way too small to contain the hot wave of arousal coiling around them.

Which was pretty fucked up. Richards did absolutely nothing for Ian. Yeah, the kid was attractive. Moved his body in a way that had Ian's thoughts taking a nosedive into the gutter, but he'd had his mouth on Ian's dick and the lack of chemistry had been pretty damn obvious. And embarrassing.

With that in mind, Ian's blood cooled. He stepped off the elevator first, wondering if he should tell Pisch to have fun and take off.

Richards needed whatever Pisch wanted to give him. Needed a chance to put the asshole he was crushing on out of his head. He wouldn't ask Pisch for more than tonight.

That wasn't enough for Ian. He couldn't pretend to be okay with watching them together. Not yet.

Will you ever be okay with it? Richards ain't the first, and he won't be the last.

Shoving his hands into his pockets, Ian inhaled a slow, even breath. He didn't know the answer to that question, but he wasn't in a hurry to find out. He let out a rough laugh, shrugging when Pisch stopped at his side.

"You two have fun. I'm gonna head home and—"

"*Ian.*" Pisch moved closer to him, backing him into the wall. His tone gained a depth that reached straight into Ian's core, like his voice alone lit a long fuse, one Ian couldn't snuff out. All he could do was watch it burn until ignition, blasting down the crumbling remains of Ian's resistance. All that by simply saying his name. And he didn't stop there. "You're breaking the rules. Either we all play, or no one does."

Pressing his eyes shut, Ian rested his head back against the wall, praying for some relief from the intensity of fear and desire and need. For a break from all Pisch represented. All he couldn't hold on to.

He exhaled after a long silence, mentally accepting Pisch's offer. He'd been dealt a strong hand. He could stay in the game a little longer at least. Figure out what he had to gain if he didn't fold.

"What are the rules, Pisch?"

A smooth gentle warmth pressed against his lips. His head spun as he realized it was Pischlar's lips touching his. Too lightly to really be called at kiss, but close enough to give him the dizzying sensation of zipping around the loop of a roller coaster.

"The rules, Ian?" Pisch released a soft laugh. "Haven't you noticed? I'm making them up as I go along."

Chapter Seven

There was a strange sense of calm that came over Shawn when he settled into his element. Inside his own home, with two men he knew very well, any doubts he'd had disappeared.

White was a wild card, but one Shawn knew exactly how to play. Not the careless way he might with someone who wasn't invested in the game, but...

You might want to stop considering this a game, Pisch. He asked for the rules for a reason.

Very true, but it didn't have to be all or nothing. Not tonight.

Tonight, White would get a taste of what Shawn meant by them being open. See all the benefits to not putting a hard, cold label on whatever was between them. They could enjoy what they shared, for as long as it lasted.

No one had to get hurt.

You sure you won't be when he finds his perfect girl?

Of course not. Shawn was in complete control. The same way he played on the ice. Reading every move like a chess player, always one step ahead.

He slipped into the kitchen, taking White's last three beers out of the fridge and carrying them to the table. When he set them down, he sensed White watching him.

"You've only had two. You're permitted to have another."

Ian's lips quirked at the edges as he took one of the beers. "I'm permitted, am I? Your accent just got real thick, buddy."

Had it? Shawn frowned, annoyed for some reason that he had a tell that he hadn't known about. He'd lived in the states since his early twenties and had spoken English quite well even when he'd lived in Austria. His accent had faded to the point his mother noticed when he called.

He cleared his throat and took a swig of beer. "Would you like a beer, Richards?"

Richards glanced between them and then nodded, taking the last beer without a word.

"So…" White rested his hip on the edge of the table. "Just to be clear, are we just having fun, or do we gotta call you Master?"

Apparently the man had shoved aside his reservations and was in the mood to test his limits. Which pleased Shawn. He didn't want to spend the entire night trying to convince White to enjoy himself.

"I'm not training Richards, so no, he doesn't have to call me 'Master'." Shawn smiled at White over the rim of his bottle as the man reddened. "I have a gag you may use if you're uncomfortable with protocols."

The color faded from White's cheeks so quickly, Shawn wasn't sure if the man would hit the floor. But he recovered just as fast and shook his head. "Naw, man. I'm good. Master, Sir, whatever. Can I put gags on my hard limits contract thing?"

Shawn had to fight not to laugh. Damn, White was adorable when he was flustered. Still big and tough, but cute. "Since you're not usually chatty, I'm not sure it needs to go on your list of hard limits."

"I think it does."

All right, this was the first time he'd ever felt the need to debate a hard limit. Not that he considered gagging White a priority—hell, he needed to force the man to speak up half the time—but if a gag was a hard limit, anything that truly tested White's boundaries would be near impossible to attempt.

So he took a few gulps of beer, watching White swallow his own down, his throat working hard, knuckles pale. The issue wasn't the gag. "Are you afraid I'll go too far if you can't speak?"

"No! Fuck, I trust you, Pisch. You know that, right?" White set down his beer and scowled. He looked like he wanted to close the distance between them. Shifted forward, then groaned and rubbed a hand over his eyes. "Tell me what to do. I guess a gag wouldn't be so bad. Honestly, I don't know my limits. I've seen stuff at the club, but...but it was always a big 'Hell no!' because I couldn't picture any of *them*, any of those Doms, doing that stuff to me."

The 'I would let you' was unspoken. But it was there.

A heavy sense of power threatened Shawn's steady balance, but he regained it with a slow nod and a smile. "Fair enough. Then let's set the limits for tonight. You can join in the conversation any time, Richards."

Richards choked on his beer. Poor kid had probably felt completely ignored. And quite comfortable being so. He sucked in a breath. "Umm...I don't like pain. And I don't top. And I want my limits to include White warning me if I piss him off, because if he punches me, I'm done for the season."

White winced. "Damn it, kid. I'm not gonna hit you."

"You sure? Because I wanna suck your man's dick. Prove I ain't all that bad."

"You—damn it, am I ever gonna live down that night?" White grabbed his beer and tipped it back against his lips. "I'm sure you're awesome at giving blowjobs. I just don't like them from guys, okay?" His face went crimson when Shawn arched a brow at him. "That ain't fair, Easy. Consider yourself the exception." He lifted his beer to his mouth again. "And by the way, rookie. He ain't 'my' man."

Glad that's cleared up. Shawn grinned, not minding the discussion turning to his dick at all. The blood was pumping into his cock, nice and steady. It was about time they moved this party along.

"I have condoms in my night table, Bruiser. Be a good boy and go fetch them." He was careful not to react when White spilled half his beer over the front of his black Ultron T-shirt. "There are a few options for flavor. Pick your favorite."

Jaw ticking, White set his beer on the edge of the table. The very edge.

Richards caught it before it hit the floor.

Nice save.

Shawn was absolutely positive White would tell him to go fuck himself. Instead, he got to enjoy the sexy view of the man's round ass as he strode out of the room. Fuck, he needed to talk White into wearing tighter jeans, but even those baggy, threadbare, faded blue jeans couldn't hide the biteable curves.

Richards hopped up to sit on the edge of the table, letting out a rough exhale. "Dude, this is freaking me out. I never would have made a play for White if I'd been sober. He's like, *uber-straight*. What the hell are you doing?"

Snorting, Shawn rested his hand on the table by Richards' hip. "You sucked his dick and you're still convinced he's 'uber-straight'?"

The rookie's forehead creased. "Yeah…either that, or I'm really that bad."

"I promise to be a fair judge of your performance." Shawn rubbed the rookie's rumpled, pale brown hair when the kid blushed. "Don't worry about White. Are *you* okay? I got the impression you didn't get the reaction you wanted from the cop?"

Wrinkling his nose, Richards shook his head. "No. He saw me, I made sure of it. But he just watched for a bit. Then walked out. You saw him."

"I did. I was hoping he'd intervene before I was forced to."

"But he didn't."

"No. He didn't." Not that Shawn could really blame the man. Richards was a nineteen-year-old boy, only just beginning to accept his own sexuality. From what he'd expressed so far, he wasn't the least bit attracted to women, but he'd slept with them to maintain his image. Even if the cop was ready for a serious relationship, the rookie had nothing to offer.

He still needed to grow up. Run a little wild.

Too young for a commitment, but old enough for Shawn to enjoy without regrets.

"Richards, I will be very clear with you. Tonight will be all about pleasure. I may push your limits. I will make sure you're able to play tomorrow. I consider you a teammate and a friend, but don't expect more from me." Shawn had lost count of how many times he'd had this conversation. The fact that the 'teammate' addition wasn't new was interesting. He really should stop messing around in his own backyard.

The rookie's lips spread into a nice, relaxed smile. "Is this the speech? I've heard people talk about it."

"Have you?" Shawn snorted. "Apparently my lovers have big mouths. But it does save time with you knowing what to expect."

"Good. Because I'm totally in. You don't gotta worry about me getting all clingy, I'm not..." Richards ducked his head, frowning down at his beer. "Damn it, I'm not *usually* the type to get all crazy. Hamilton was a one-time thing. I've learned, and I won't do that again. If you don't call me tomorrow, it won't be a thing, okay?"

"Considering you'll likely be in my bed in the morning, and I'll see you at the game, calling you would be a bit excessive." Shawn slid his hand over Richards' shoulder, resting it on the back of the rookie's neck as he heard White returning. "I don't want you to feel used. If you're uncomfortable, at any point, let me know. I want this to be for you. A way to forget all you can't have."

Richards leaned against Shawn's hand, his eyes drifting shut. "I want that too."

"Good." Shawn glanced over at White, who was holding enough condoms in his hand to go down on the entire US Navy. "What about it, White? Are you cool with helping our boy forget this night ever happened?"

The condom wrappers made a harsh, scraping sound in White's fist as his throat worked hard. He stared at Richards. Then inclined his head. "Yeah. I'll help him forget that asshole. I still want to destroy the bastard though."

"Except, this isn't a video game, Bruiser." Shawn's whole body relaxed as White came close enough for him to reach out and touch the man's shoulder. "We can't destroy people."

White nodded slowly. "But it *is* a game."

"It is." Shawn slid his hand over White's solid chest. Trailed it down to the man's erection, which strained against the zipper of his jeans. "Are you having fun yet?"

Shuddering, White shook his head. "Not yet."

"Then I guess it's time for us to hit the next level." Shawn stroked White, loving how easy this was. White didn't pull away. Didn't say a word. "Are you ready?"

Huffing out a breath, White laughed. "No. But I'm getting there."

Shawn grinned. "Good boy. Ask nicely, and I'll make this so much easier."

White groaned and braced his hand on the edge of the table. "Damn it, Easy. Tell me what you want, and it's yours."

The words dug in deep, taking hold. Refusing to let go.

And Shawn's answer wasn't part of the game.

It was the truth.

"Everything." He stared at White's lips, wishing he could taste them. Not in a gentle, teasing way, but in a way that would take all White had to give.

Instead, he pressed his lips to White's throat.

"I'll take everything."

The soft brush of Pischlar's lips along the length of Ian's neck had his knees buckling. If this kept up, he was gonna have to get them checked. Of course, the doc would laugh at him if he was totally honest about *when* his knees gave him trouble.

No part of his body really worked right around Pisch lately. Well, *one* part was fully fucking functional, working overtime, actually, but his cock didn't get an opinion. It had betrayed him in the past.

Nothing like getting hard for a hot chick who assumed all pro-athletes were crazy rich. Of course, his brain being slow to catch on to the obvious didn't help. He'd even had one chick asking him details about his contract, and it hadn't clicked until he'd refused to take her to an expensive restaurant on their third date.

Sexy and shallow as hell. He probably should regret the cash he'd dropped on the first couple dates a bit more, but the woman could do things with her hands and mouth and body that were probably illegal in most states. Worth every penny.

At least he hadn't gotten attached, but it was too late to avoid that with Pisch. A pleading noise escaped him before he could stop it as Pisch raked his teeth lightly over his flesh and continued to massage his cock. He sucked in a breath as he felt a tug at his belt. Not Pischlar doing it, he had one hand in Ian's hair and the other sliding down to his balls.

"Shit." His whole body jerked as a hand curved around his dick. The hand was soft. Gentle.

Not Pisch.

He pressed his eyes shut tight, doing his best just to feel. Not to think. That's what Pisch wanted, but fuck, it was hard.

And *he* wasn't gonna be hard for much longer.

He tried to enjoy the stimulation, but he saw the rookie, so messed up, looking for a good time that Ian couldn't give him.

Him...

Grinding his teeth, Ian fought the urge to pull away. It was messed up, but for some reason, when he'd fooled around with Pisch and Sahara, he'd managed to convince himself whatever happened was cool. He'd lost himself to the lust and pleasure.

With Pisch alone? Well, he'd only gone there once.

And he'd fucked up. Flipped out and almost destroyed their friendship.

He wouldn't do that again. If this was what Pisch wanted, he'd do it.

But his body decided it was done cooperating.

Pisch's hands left him for a second. Then Pisch touched his cheek. "Stop, Richards."

The air came easier to his lungs when Richards' hand released his cock. He didn't open his eyes though. His cheeks were blazing, and he didn't want to look at either of the guys. He didn't want to be the shy prom date, completely naked, all in until there was a pair of balls in his hand.

And just to think, a few minutes ago, he'd brought condoms and hadn't even hesitated at the idea of having Pisch's balls in *his* hand.

"Look at me, Bruiser." Pisch pressed his thumb under Ian's chin, tipping it up. Not speaking again until Ian looked at him. "Tell me what's not working for you."

Richards ain't a girl. That answer would be easy, but it wasn't the whole truth. He tried to find the words to explain why he couldn't let go of all the fucked up thoughts in his head. "This is...different. Me and Richards fooled around while I was drunk. Maybe if I had a few more—" He wasn't surprised when Pisch shook his head. "Shit. Okay, but, no offense, I'm not into the kid. All I keep thinking is he needs more than I can give. And I need to give something. But he's a guy, and I guess that's still a thing. Not with you, but don't ask me why. I don't know."

Liar.

Okay, he kinda knew. He loved Pisch. The man hit every fucking one of his 'hell yes!' triggers. Even with Sahara, Ian probably wouldn't have touched her without Pisch calling all the shots.

His brow furrowed.

"Tell me what you're thinking, Bruiser."

Ian took a deep breath. "Well, I mean, Sahara is hot. And doing girls has never been an issue, but without you there, I would have been thinking about how tough she's had it. Maybe wanted to hug her instead of let her suck my dick. But you took over. I didn't *have* to wonder if I was doing the right thing. I trusted you to know."

Pisch's eyes darkened as his lips slid into a slow, dangerous smile. Dangerous to Ian anyway because it meant Pisch had figured him out. "Good. That was perfect, my man. I know what you need. Thank you for being so honest with me."

Moving away from Ian, Pisch undid his belt. Slid it free of the loops and folded it in his hand.

He best not be thinking of hitting me with that. Ian frowned. His lips parted.

Pisch pointed at a chair. "Sit, Bruiser."

He'd used the same tone he might with a dog. And Ian obeyed before even questioning if it bothered him. The hard wooden chair dug into the back of his thighs as he sat forward.

"Lean back and relax, Bruiser. This isn't a fight." Pisch smoothed his hand over Ian's hair. "You want this. Even if you only want it for me, you do want it."

All the tension in Ian's body evaporated as he leaned back. Put that way, yeah, he wanted it. He rested against the back of the chair.

"Very good. Hands behind you...no, Ian. On the other side of the chair." Pisch's light tone made the embarrassment irrelevant as Ian put his hands in a place that made sense. Clasped around the back of the chair. His chest swelled at Pisch's low hum of approval. "Fuck, you're hot like this."

Sweat broke out over Ian's flesh as Pisch bound his wrists. With the belt. Which was obviously why he'd taken it off.

No beatings. That's good, right?

He tugged at his wrists when Pisch was done. His chest rose and fell with his deep, rough inhales. He'd never been tied up like this before. And he wasn't sure he liked it.

"Relax, Bruiser." Pisch's low, soothing tone put Ian into a calm zone that made breathing less of a struggle. The way he rubbed Ian's shoulder eased him completely. Then he leaned close, whispering in Ian's ear. "I want to see his mouth on you. To have your mouth on me. I won't let you regret this, Ian."

Ian's eyes drifted almost completely shut. Fuck, that sounded good. His whole body was secured. His mind was...kinda fuzzy. In a good way. Like he could go along with anything and not have to pick every move he made apart. Because he wasn't making a single one. Someone else was calling the shots for him.

"You seem quite comfortable with your body, Richards. It's about time you remove some of those layers." Pisch tugged at the collar of Richards' shirt when the rookie shifted closer. He hauled Richards forward, so the young man was standing with one legs between Ian's, leaning over him as Pisch spoke against his lips. "And in case that wasn't clear enough, I want you naked before you touch my man."

Ian's dick had no issues with that order, but his head was kinda torn about the way Pisch sucked Richards' bottom lip. Kisses were an issue for *him*, but they weren't for Pisch. He kissed the guys, and girls, he fucked. After laying out his rules.

But he wouldn't kiss Ian. He'd come close, but Ian wasn't sure if he could count their lips touching for a few seconds as any kind of commitment. Everything Pisch said made it clear he'd only give so much.

But he'd told Richards Ian was *his man*.

Which made him different, right? He could deal with them being open if he wasn't just another warm body.

Richards shed his clothes with the erotic grace of a stripper, but Ian didn't watch him as he had when the rookie had been on stage. There'd been distance then, he'd been able to admire the young man without wondering if fooling around with him would be weird. Kinda like his issues with driving didn't change how much he enjoyed watching stock car racing. He wasn't the one behind the wheel.

And he wasn't driving this show either, but damn, shotgun at 200mph was just as dangerous.

Standing by his side, arms folded over his chest, Pisch watched Richards kneel between Ian's thighs. Ian kept his eyes on Pisch as the rookie covered his cock with a condom. He wanted that hazy feeling back. It had made going through with all this fucked up shit seem not so bad.

Heat surrounded his dick. Rough, dry pressure. He winced as Richards sucked and the pressure increased. If not for the condom, he'd be begging for damn mercy. Actually, he was getting there anyway.

"Richards, what in the world are you doing?" Pisch fisted his hand in Richards' hair, tugging him away from Ian.

Because he was all kinds of awesome. Ian's dick softened, deflating in relief. And probably self-preservation.

Richards gapped up at Pisch. "I wanted it to be good for him this time. Last time he looked bored."

"And this time he's in pain. Please tell me you didn't do that to your nice police officer. He might not have played you at all. He may be very afraid."

The rookie's cheeks reddened. "Things moved kinda fast. I didn't have a chance to mess up. He fucked my mouth for a bit and told me what he liked."

"That's actually very helpful, Richards. Thank you." Pisch ran his thumb over Richards' bottom lip. "Seducing a 'straight' man takes patience and experience. You have neither. But I can help you with that."

Grinning, Richards licked Pisch's thumb. "I'd like that."

Pisch laughed. "I'm sure you would. Now, for starters, slow down. This isn't a race to see how fast you can make him come—which you never would have the way you were going. True, Bruiser?"

Ian scowled. This whole lesson thing wasn't much of a turn on. If they were gonna have a chat, he wanted his dick in his jeans. Far away from Richards mouth. "Can you untie me, man? He can practice on you."

Yeah, don't really want that either.

"Let's be nice, White. You won't regret giving him another chance. I promise."

Don't promise that. I already regret it.

To make things even more *awesome*, Pisch left the room.

Ian prepared for awkwardness, but Pisch returned too fast for either he or Richards to exchange a word.

He handed Richards a bottle of lube. "Try this. It's got a nice citrus flavor that will make your mouth water. Your lips should slip over his dick nice and smooth. Start slow and work your way up to taking more of him in your mouth." Pisch met Ian's eyes, his lips slanted as he grabbed Ian's half full bottle of beer off the table. "I'll keep him relaxed, but remember, he has no control. I've taken it all."

Sucking in a harsh breath, Ian stared at Pisch as the bottle was tipped to his lips. He gulped down the still cool, malty liquid. And groaned as Richards' slick hand slid over his dick. The boy was definitely better with his hands. He got Ian hard again with a few steady strokes. Then his tongue circled the head of Ian's cock.

Oh fuck, that...that's much better.

"Very good, Richards." Pisch framed Ian's jaw with one hand, challenge in his eyes. "Were you paying attention? You have less experience than he does, and if you hurt me, it will not go well for you."

"I won't." The response came so automatically, Ian didn't have a chance to consider what Pisch was actually talking about. After a few seconds—while Pisch unzipped his own jeans and rolled a condom over his hard, long, uncut dick—Ian was able to put two and two together. His brain was having a harder time than usual keeping up as Richards took him in deep. Without gagging. Hell, maybe he'd been wrong about the rookie. A few tips from Pisch and he was a goddamn pro.

His dick throbbing as he reached the edge of release, he rasped in a breath and swallowed. "Ah...might be safer to wait until he's done."

"Might be, but I trust you." Pisch leaned down and drew Richards away. "Give him a moment. Then continue. I'm impressed, you're doing even better than I'd hoped."

Licking his lips, Richards smiled. "Dude, I wasn't gonna let him ruin my reputation."

Yep, because I'm gonna go right to the locker room and let all the guys know you give great blowjobs.

Speaking of the locker room, would things be weird now? They'd been fine before, because people did all kinds of crazy shit while they were drunk. He'd gone to Vanek's room once to see if the kid had some pain meds the day after a bad fight on the ice—Vanek had left the latch open so the door wouldn't lock—and found him and his two buddies, Carter and Demyan, sunbathing on the balcony. Naked.

He didn't ask. He got the meds and got the fuck out. He really didn't want to know.

This time, he wasn't drunk.

Being drunk would be good.

"Another sip, my man?" Pisch held up the beer, letting Ian take a few more gulps when he nodded. "You ready?"

Was he? Fuck, he didn't know. But he was willing to try for Pisch.

Only, how the hell was he gonna do anything tied to the chair? "Uh, you untying me now?"

"No." Pisch poured some lube into his palm and slicked up his dick. "Let me lead you, Ian. Just relax."

One hand curved around his neck, Pisch drew him down, his fist gripping his own dick as he ran the tip gently over Ian's lips. The solid heat was strange, but Ian pressed his tongue against the sheathed head of Pisch's cock. The lube tasted like starburst candy. Not bad.

He opened his mouth a bit more as Pisch pressed forward. The flavor filled his mouth and his licked and sucked, hoping he was doing this right. It was hard to focus with Richards working his cock, hard and fast. If his attention hadn't been divided, he'd have come already. Instead, he concentrated on the smooth length slowly dipping deeper into his mouth. He didn't have time to wonder if he *should* do this. He *was*.

The thick length went in, an inch at a time, but the condom seemed to numb his mouth a little. He didn't taste flesh. The lube was almost overpowering at first, like he'd stuffed his mouth full of hot candy, but after a bit, there was only lingering sweetness and his own saliva.

More pressure and he tipped his head back, his dick swelling painfully as Pisch stroked his hair and murmured his approval. He tried to move against Pisch's slow thrusts, but Pisch took hold of his hair, keeping him still.

The haze was back and Ian let the muscles in his jaw relax. His body didn't seem like his own anymore. Everything that happened to him, Pisch controlled. The brief glimpse of Richards' head, moving up and down, was a blur. The sensations, the taste, the heat...

It was all Pisch.

"Take him, Richards. Slowly."

The words meant nothing, but suddenly there was a weight on his thighs. A vise grip on his cock. He moaned as Pisch pushed in until he couldn't breathe. Then eased back so he could.

"Give me a color, White. Are you still with us?" Pisch cupped his cheek, letting his dick slip from Ian's lips.

A color? Ian wasn't sure he knew what colors were anymore. There was black and white. What was good, and what was bad. And he wasn't seeing any bad.

"White." He grunted as the grip on his dick stroked down harder. "Shit, this is good. So good."

"Does the rookie have a tight ass, Bruiser? He's taking you so deep. The way he moves...damn, he was made for this."

Blinking, Ian made out Richards' back. His ass as he rode Ian's cock. It didn't matter who he was. He was all heat, and the heat was everywhere. And it was perfect.

But it wasn't Pisch.

So perfect was the wrong word.

He needed Pisch.

"Easy, I need to give you...I need..." Fuck, everything felt so good, he wasn't sure what his brain was trying to get past his lips. Or why he couldn't move. Or why Pisch was so far away.

"Shh, I've got you, my man." Pisch's dick filled his mouth again. And the hiss of pleasure Pisch let out soothed the riot in Ian's head. His praise relieved the tension that had wormed its way into his chest. "Just like that. Fuck, Ian, your mouth is heaven. So fucking good."

All the tension Ian had released gathered in the base of his spine. And burst out from his balls as he thrust up and turned his head away from Pisch to let out a low curse.

"Fuck!" Richards shouted, repeating Ian's word. "Oh fuck, yes!" He leaned back against Ian, resting all his weight on Ian's lap.

And all the feel goods in Ian had him wanting to hold the rookie. To tell him that had been…good. Awesome really.

Does he regret it? Will he? Will you?

Too complicated for Ian's brain at the moment. He twisted his wrists, almost falling forward with Richards when Pisch undid the belt.

His arms were heavy as he wrapped them around Richards. He kissed Richards' shoulder. "I take it back. You're the best cock sucker in the world. I'm glad I got to fuck you."

Pisch's lips parted. He made a strangled sound and then shook his head.

Richards burst out laughing, tipping his head back to give Ian a light kiss. "I love you, man. Not in a weird way. I won't try to 'keep you'." He gave Pisch a sly look. "Fucking tempting though. If you're this good tied up, how good would you be free?"

Ian shuddered as Richards' body clenched around him. The pressure on his oversensitive cock gave him a harsh dose of reality. What if Richards wanted more? Everything he had belonged to Pisch. He was still coming to terms with the fact that he'd have to find someone else if he needed a relationship that would last.

Someone who could deal with Pisch being a constant in his life. Someone Pisch wouldn't believe he was moving on with.

Richards couldn't be that someone. As fucking hot as fucking him had been, Ian still preferred girls. And Pisch.

Why couldn't he have both?

Be kinda hard if the kid gets attached.

Yeah, but he couldn't very well tell Richards that right after fucking him.

"Are you good with not keeping me? We're still friends, right?" Was that the right thing to say? He was still holding Richards. Things weren't weird. Yet.

Richards pressed his lips to the center of his forehead. "Totally cool, man. You good with me moving?"

Moving? Damn, Richards was still holding him snug in his body. And he hadn't even noticed. He nodded, his throat suddenly dry. None of this *should* be okay. This wasn't him.

But clearly it was.

This is fine. It happened. Just don't be an ass to the kid, he's more fragile than Pisch.

Pisch. Was Pisch okay with this?

Had he even gotten off?

His head was heavy and didn't seem to want to move much. So he reached out.

And felt Pisch's strong hand take his.

Richards' squirmed uncomfortably. "Bruiser?"

"Yeah…yeah, I'm good." Ian helped Richards stand with his free hand. "Uh…you're not rushing out, are you?"

The rookie's youthful face creased. "Not unless you want me to? I'm still living with Coach Shero and, like…him and his wife are really sweet, but it would be weird to go back there after…"

"Stay, Richards." Pisch tugged Ian to his feet. "You're both staying. I've got a big bed."

That was the truth. Ian hadn't paid much attention before, but as he ambled sleepily into his best friend's room, he realized there would be plenty of room for the three of them. He dropped onto the bed after kicking off his jeans and let his eyes drift shut.

Realizing he wished the bed was smaller.

Wondering if he'd ever accept having to share it with anyone other than Pisch.

I am so gonna need a nap before the game.

Shawn slipped out of bed, careful not to wake White, who was snoring softly. The man had one bare leg half off the side of the bed and his pillow in a stranglehold against his chest. Shawn had gone to the spare room to fetch the one his man—*that* White—usually used when he crashed here unexpectedly. A few weeks ago, Shawn had found a vintage Ninja Turtle pillowcase and bought it for him in a rare sentimental moment. He hadn't actually given it to White, but White found it in the linen closet while grabbing a towel and claimed it.

He'd never asked why Shawn had it. Maybe he didn't know it had been intended for him. Doubtful, but at least things hadn't gotten awkward.

This morning might be awkward, but he had at least an hour before White would stumble out of bed. Obviously, Richards was already up, but the rookie had a laid back attitude about pretty much everything. He might come off as shy, but away from the team he'd shown a different side. Given both Shawn and White a glimpse of a young man owning his sexuality. Comfortable going after he wanted.

Hopefully, that attitude would spare him losing his heart to any more men who were only looking for a good time.

Like you?

Shawn sighed and shook his head. He needed coffee before he'd start considering the consequences of last night. Richards was less experienced than the men he usually fucked around with. And White ..

Yes, coffee is a very good idea.

In the kitchen, completely naked, Richards stood at the counter, pouring two cups of coffee. He gave Shawn a naughty grin as he glanced over his shoulder. "I figured you'd be up first. Want some?"

The double meaning was intentional. Shawn folded his arms over his bare chest; happy he'd taken the time to change into black silk pajama pants before crawling in bed. Meeting the rookie in the kitchen naked would have put him at a disadvantage. Not that his pants did much to hide his swelling erection, but the cheeky—*very* fucking cheeky, damn the kid had a nice tight ass—young man was still somewhat vulnerable. No matter how sure of himself he came off as.

"You 'figured' I'd be up first and assumed I'm appreciate you being naked in my kitchen?" Shawn arched a brow when Richards' lips parted. "Last night was a one time thing, Richards. I was very clear."

Brow furrowing, Richards held out one of the coffees. He didn't speak until Shawn went to the fridge to add a splash of cream.

"You said I couldn't expect more from you. Like, a commitment." Richards took a sip of coffee and made a face. The he jutted his chin up. "I don't want that. I just want to fucking make you come. You didn't when White was sucking your dick. I would have finished you off, but you looked all worried about him."

Nodding slowly, Shawn took a sip of his own coffee. Which taste like dishwater.

Richards clearly didn't drink coffee regularly. He'd made it for Shawn. Badly, but the effort was appreciated.

Not so much that Shawn would drink the weak shit, but he'd be patient with the boy.

"White had never been with another man." *Besides me, but that's none of Richards' business.* "I probably shouldn't have pushed him so far, but he did well. Fun was had by all. The end." Shawn set his mug on the counter, giving Richards a pointed look when the rookie stood there, staring at him. Finally, Richards moved so Shawn could get to the coffee maker. "Don't drink that. I'll show you how to make a proper pot of coffee." He noticed a jar of instant coffee by the machine and spit out a laugh. "You didn't seriously make instant coffee in the coffee maker?"

Red spread across Richards' cheeks. "What's the difference?"

Shaking his head, Shawn cleaned the filter, washed every piece of the coffee maker, then prepared a proper pot with his favorite French roast. "The difference is the result. When you rush things, you end up with the cheapest, weakest, possibility. When you take your time..." Shawn turned to Richards, brushing his fingers over the rookie's cheek. Down to his lips. Moving closer as he let his tone deepen. "You have something worth so much more. Even if it's just for the taste."

The way Richards trembled, his breaths coming out in sharp little bursts, ruined Shawn's intention to teach the young man a lesson. He couldn't ignore how fucking sexy, and available, and *willing* Richards was. The toned, naked body in front of him was tempting as hell, and he had no reason to deny himself.

He pinned Richards against the fridge, reaching down to cup his soft, smoothly shaven balls. "You know what? I've changed my mind. Go to my room and get a condom and the lube from my bedside table. If you wake White, you'll pay."

With a shudder, Richards nodded, rushing off the second Shawn released him. He was so quiet, Shawn didn't even notice him returning as he enjoyed the first sip of perfectly brewed coffee.

With the rich flavor still on his tongue, he crooked his finger at Richards, pulling his wiry body close as he claimed his lips. He kept the kiss light, seductive enough to have Richards squirming against him, but leaving no doubt that this was all about sex.

And the low moan Richards let out as Shawn pushed him against the counter made it clear the rookie understood. He didn't need sweet words or promises. He'd been honest when he'd said he wouldn't ask for more than a good time.

From Shawn anyway, but that was all that mattered now.

Wasting no time after quickly slipping on the condom and slicking Richards' tight hole with lube, Shawn sank into the snug heat, groaning as he found no resistance. The tight grip on his cock reminded him that he hadn't found release last night. His body was a little too eager to claim it, but he held back, determined to make their last time together good for them both.

Hands gripping Richards' hips, he ground in, sucking lightly on Richards' shoulder as he fucked him. He hit the same spot over and over when he heard Richards whimper and slammed in deep and fast as the rookie came hard.

His own release came as a steady, satisfying rush. Much like finishing off his first cup of coffee. Not life changing, but very satisfying.

The satisfaction was cut short as he heard his front door slam.

Chapter Eight

Second home game of the second round of the playoffs and Justina was a nervous wreck. Not for herself, she'd done fine during the pre-game show, but after letting Akira convince her to watch the game from the press box, she wasn't sure she could take much more of her beloved team being absolutely decimated by the Leafs.

The *Leafs* of all teams. She'd kinda been happy for the fans of the team when they'd made the playoffs, which they hadn't done since 2004. The loyal fans deserved something good after all this time, but not at the expense of the Cobras.

Only, from the way Dean Richter cursed every bad play, the Cobras clearly weren't doing what they should be to win. There was something off. Key players were making stupid passes. And their small mistakes became bigger ones when the rest of the team struggled to figure out what the hell they were doing.

Luke Carter, one of the top six, lost control of the puck, leading to a giveaway that almost ended up in the back of the Cobra's net.

And Richter slammed his fist on the ledge of the window cutting the press box off from the crowd. "His contract is done this summer. That's it. I'm looking into what we can get for him."

Justina bit her bottom lip, her throat tightening. She loved Carter. He was an awesome player, and she didn't want him going anywhere.

Silver Delgado, Richter's fiancé—*girlfriend?*—let out a soft laugh. "After approaching Ramos's agent about a contract extension that could get interesting. But Jami has dual citizenship, right? I'm sure she'll let us visit when she's done hating you."

"I won't keep a player because my daughter is *involved* with him."

"And you shouldn't. But you *should* keep him because he's one of the highest scoring players on our team. And also because you love your job and Keane will fire you if you made a trade like that."

Richter huffed, but he didn't mention trading Carter again.

Letting out a soft sigh of relief, Justina glanced over at Akira when she laughed.

Akira shook her head. "You're adorable when you watch the game. And I'm sorry you heard that." She lowered her voice even more, though she'd already been careful to make sure the GM couldn't hear her. "I keep forgetting you haven't been exposed to some of the drama around here. Ford comes home in a bad mood every time a stupid trade even becomes a rumor. Last week it was another one about Perron getting a *huge* offer. And he has a no-trade clause. But Ford is worried about his sister and her new baby, so he got pissed, and no one would tell him anything."

That had to be frustrating. But the team was a family business, wasn't it? Justina had never met Keane, but she'd heard of him. She assumed he worked with the Delgado family. Which meant Ford had a say, right?

"How's the baby? Or…is it okay to ask? I don't wanna be nosey, just you and Jami are friends, and I heard Jami planned to adopt the baby, but she seems to be doing okay…" Damn, she sounded like she should never be out in public, didn't she? 'How's the baby' would have been enough. The rest was stupidly intrusive.

Nudging her shoulder, Akira laughed. "We're *friends*, Justina. You're allowed to ask stuff. Stop looking like you feel guilty about opening your mouth."

"I don't have many friends."

Loser. Why would you say that?

Akira frowned. "I know. But you have us. Me, Jami, and Sahara. And I am gonna get you out of that damn shell if I have to pry you out." She grinned. "The baby is doing good. He's such a cutie! Makes me want one, but don't you *dare* tell Ford. Cort's still kinda freaked out at the idea of kids, but Ford has this look in his eyes... I swear, my period is ten times worse since Westy was born. My baby maker is punishing me. Part of me sees Ford holding his nephew and is like 'I want that for us!'. But I have plans. And I know I'd regret it if I didn't put everything I have into making my dreams a reality. I want my child to come into a world where I can show him or her that I'm the person I want to be."

Akira is my freakin' hero. Justina smiled and nodded. "That makes sense. Both my parents have jobs they hate. They love me and Chris, but... well, they always tell us to do what we want with our lives first. They were so happy when I made the team. My mom said I need to listen to my trainers and make sure I don't get..."

Her throat tightened. She hated using the word 'fat'. She'd seen how depressed her mother got when people whispered behind her back when she squeezed into a chair. Justina knew she was lucky to be in good shape, but whenever she gained a few pounds, she heard her mother crying, like she had when she tried on clothes while shopping. When someone told her they didn't make clothes for women like *her*.

Akira and Sahara had stood up for Justina when the Ice Girls' old manager had come down on her about being bigger than the rest of the girls, but her mom... her mom had told her to listen to the criticism and take their advice. Go on a diet. Exercise.

'Don't let yourself go, baby. You can't come back from that.'

She exercised all the time. Ate all the right food. When she looked in the mirror, part of her was proud of her body. She was fit. Her body was strong enough to do all she asked of it.

But if she bent over and her stomach bulged a little, her mother's voice came to her. Telling her one wrong move and she would be miserable.

"Justina, I'm sure your mother is a wonderful woman, but you need to be happy with the person *you* see in the mirror." Akira put one arm around her and gave her a tight squeeze. "Enough of that though, unless you need to talk." She nodded when Justina shook her head. "Okay, so our boys are not doing well tonight. And Cort is gonna be thrilled that his team is sweeping their series, so things will be tense at home. I kinda wish he and Ford would kiss and make up, but they'd rather bash each other's teams and be complete jerks. If we're lucky this weekend, Cort will be practicing the single tail on the man we both love. You wanna watch with me?"

Really? She loved Akira, but she couldn't believe how open the woman was about her sex life. She wanted her boyfriends to kiss? Not a bad thing, but shouldn't she be loving all the attention?

Justina had never watched guys kiss. Or anyone kiss, really. Yeah, she watched movies, and more than kissing happened, but her parents were usually there, so she'd find something else to look at. Like the wall.

Get over it. You'll be seeing a lot more than that at the club.

"You just went pale. What's wrong?" Akira put a hand on her shoulder, her brow drawn with concern. "White's taken worse hits. I didn't even realize you were watching the game—"

"I wasn't." Justina bit her bottom lip as she watched Ian White, one of the team's fourth line enforcers, who didn't see much ice time, struggle to rise from the ice, shaking his head and waving Scott Demyan, the team's best sniper, away. She watched the replay of White being slammed into from behind as he dug the puck out of a crowd. He'd been hit right in the numbers. Cracked his head into the boards.

Should have been a penalty. When one wasn't called, the crowd went nuts.

She ground her teeth. "Those refs hate us! That hit will be reviewed by the league! How the hell did they miss it?"

"I know, right?" Akira watched with her as White skated to the bench. Then disappeared into the locker room. "He's tough, but I don't think his head can take much more."

"He's only been in ten fights this season. Yeah, it was a bad hit, but he was skating fine." Justina had read a lot of random things about hockey then started researching everything she wasn't sure of. Like head injuries. She'd watched enough clips of players that ended up with a concussion that she was willing to bet White was fine.

But she could be wrong.

She hoped she wasn't.

"OMG!" Akira pointed at the ice. "Pischlar *never* fights, but he dropped the gloves the second the puck dropped."

Shawn Pischlar was one of the few guys she had never seen without his helmet on, but as he dodged a punch from the Leaf's heavy hitter, his helmet went flying. The jumbotron gave a nice close-up before the refs jumped in.

Her pulse quickened, and she leaned closer to the glass to get a better look. The man was…hell, she wasn't sure exactly what he was, but it was somewhere between all her favorite candies and double fudge chocolate ice cream, drizzled with chocolate syrup. So tempting, so forbidden. From his devilish smile, sexy as sin even with blood slick on his bottom lip, to his magnetic gaze, with eyes that were the most beautiful shade she'd ever seen. Rich green with a hint of silver gray.

A bit closer and she conked her head on the glass.

Letting out a heavy sigh, Akira pulled her back and lightly rubbed her forehead. "Sweetie, please tell me you're not drooling over Shawn 'Easy' Pischlar."

I'm drooling? Justina's cheeks heated as she quickly wiped the heel of her palm over her lips. "The 'Easy' is because he's a smooth puck handler, right?"

"No."

"Oh." Justina glanced back down at the ice as Pischlar headed to the penalty box. Not that she'd *really* thought she'd have a chance with a man like him, but now she knew she should forget even wishing she could. He was the kind of man her mother had warned her to avoid at all costs.

He'd ruin her, break her heart, and she would be miserable.

"Honey, don't look so upset! I mean, he's hot. I guess. Not my type, but I don't blame you for enjoying the view. Just thought I'd give you a heads up. He'd be so bad for you."

Nodding slowly, Justina considered all the other things she'd gotten a heads up about. Because they were 'bad for her.' All the things she'd never gotten to touch, or taste, or experience.

"My mom says all the sweets I fucking crave are bad for me too." Justina chewed on her bottom lip when Akira's eyes widened. Her new friend had never heard her swear. She took a deep breath and kept going. "I want to go with you and the girls to get ice cream before we head to the club. And…and when we get there, I want to meet him."

Chapter Nine

Living here fucking sucked.
Sam finished scrubbing the counter, looking around the kitchen and hoping it was up to Chicklet's standards.
Max must *really* hate her to have convinced Sloan to send her here, of all places. Chicklet was such a bitch. She had absolutely no sense of humor, and she was always watching everything Sam did. Sam hadn't gotten a moment alone with either Raif or Tyler since she'd moved in a few days ago. Almost like the woman didn't trust her or something.

Had Sloan or Max told Chicklet that she'd kissed Sloan? It hadn't been a big deal, but still, kinda private.

Letting out a heavy sigh, she went to the sink to wash the breakfast dishes. She so needed to get a job and find her own place. At least Laura was nice. She'd made breakfast and stayed with Sam in the kitchen while the other three ate in the dining room. They'd chatted a bit about random stuff. Like where Sam was planning to go to school and where she could find a job even with her horrible track record.

Too bad Laura had had to go to work. Now Sam was stuck with the scary Amazon woman and two men who were acting like losing a damn game was the end of the world.

Slow steps warned her that someone had joined her in the kitchen. She turned around and her chest tightened as she watched

Raif feel his way along the kitchen island. He had a mug in his hand. He probably wanted a refill. Had Chicklet told him to suck it up and serve himself?

She really is a horrible person. The man is blind*!*

"Let me get that, Raif." She moved to take the cup from him.

He jerked away and cracked the mug against the edge of the counter. "I can...*Jeba te led*!"

Blood dripped onto the dark gray tiled floor. Sam grabbed a towel and rushed to his side. "Please let me help you. I hate being useless."

Lifting his uncut hand to his forehead, Raif nodded and let her take what was left of the mug then compressed the nasty cut between his thumb and his finger with the towel. "I apologize for my language, child. I understand feeling useless."

"But you're *not* useless. You're just adjusting. You've got a big hotel thing going on in Vegas. Even without playing hockey, you're...*amazing*. There's so much you can do." She wished he wasn't wearing sunglasses. Not that it would matter if she could meet his eyes, he wouldn't see it. But...but she would have a better idea of his expression. If her words were helping at all. "I know nothing I can say will make this better, but when I look at you, I see a fucking sexy man with everything going for him."

His lips quirked up slightly. "You certainly aren't bad for a man's ego, *slatkica*. And I appreciate your words."

She grinned up at him, feeling damn good for having made him smile. Even just a little. She rose up on her tiptoes to give him a quick kiss.

"Are you fucking serious right now?" The sharp tone had her jerking back. Then forward, because fuck Tyler being all stupid jealous.

Raif was bleeding, but at least *he* liked her.

She scowled at Tyler as he stepped up beside Raif. "Are you? He's hurt, and you're an asshole for fucking making him get his own coffee."

"He wanted to do it himself!" Tyler's normally cute face—not so cute with all the golden scruff he'd let grow in, but still not bad—

darkened to a harsh crimson shade. "That doesn't explain you kissing him! Are you that desperate for attention?"

Pulling away from her slowly, Raif fisted his hand around the towel and turned to face Tyler. "Desperate? Well, I'm flattered. A pretty girl giving me any attention must be desperate."

"That's not what I meant!"

"Then what did you mean?"

Oh boy, I better get out of here before...

Yeah. Too late.

She tried to hide behind Raif as Chicklet stepped into the room, leaning on the doorframe with her arms crossed over her tiny breasts.

Chicklet didn't look at all bothered by the way the men were yelling. "And the Carter siblings claim another victim. Tyler, you kissed her brother. I can't see Raif making out with her in the kitchen, but even if he did, fair play and all."

"So you're cool with her going after a married man, then coming here and hitting on Raif?" Tyler gave Sam a cold look, like she was a snake that had just slithered into his home that he couldn't convince anyone else to get rid of. "Because I'm not."

"Sloan is a big boy. He is capable of—and *did*—tell Sam that what she did was inappropriate. Raif will do the same if it bothers him." Chicklet smirked when Sam glared at her. "I'm sorry, sweetheart. Do you not like people speaking as though you're not in the room?"

"I don't give a shit. If you want to make a big deal over a little kiss, you can do it without me." Sam hugged herself, hating that just a look from Chicklet made her feel like she'd done something wrong. She *hadn't!*

Not this time, anyway. Kissing Sloan might not have been her brightest move ever.

"Did you listen to a word Sloan said when he brought you here? You're like a child, which is why he put up with you being clingy."

"That's not what he said!" Sam stomped her foot. Then realized her action were proving the evil Amazon's point. "He told me he wanted me to know I wasn't alone, but I misunderstood his attention for something more. Could have happened to anyone."

"I'm sure," Chicklet said dryly, shaking her head. She turned to Raif. "Do you want to fuck the girl?"

Raif pulled off his glasses and rubbed his eyelids with his thumb and forefinger. "No."

"Good. Just so there's no further misunderstandings. Why don't you take your coffee to your room, princess? My men and I need to have a few words." Dismissing Sam, Chicklet latched on to Tyler's jaw and whispered against his lips. "My naughty, possessive angel. Do you know how much trouble you're in?"

Ew. Sam rolled her eyes and slipped out into the hall. She heard Tyler let out a strained moan. Then Raif's deep laughter.

Knowing that Tyler had fooled around with her brother—*and I'm the slut?*—explained why he was so cold toward her. Luke probably hadn't had a chance to explain that they were cool now. But Chicklet's attitude didn't make any sense. She was Sloan's friend, but Sloan hadn't been pissed. He hadn't told her much, other than it would be better for them all if she stayed here until they found her an apartment, but she wasn't stupid. Max had demanded Sloan get rid of her.

Where Oriana stood on the issue was a little harder to read. She'd asked Sam to call if she needed anything. Hugged her and asked Chicklet to take care of her. She'd been nice, but no one could be *that* nice.

Could they?

Maybe Oriana was just being careful so Sam wouldn't take the kid back. Not like that would ever happen. Even if she had any urges to be a mom, where would she keep a kid? She was having a hard time finding a place willing to keep *her*.

Finishing off her coffee, she half watched some reality show on TV about a bunch of rich chicks crying over dresses. She'd almost nodded off when the door opened.

Chicklet gave her a sad look before coming over to sit on the edge of the bed. "Sam, I think we need to talk. I have a feeling we got off on the wrong foot."

"Why? I don't care if you hate me." Sam sat up and wrapped her arms around her bent knees. She pressed her eyes shut when Chicklet simply sat there, like she was waiting for something. "Look, I get it. I have nowhere else to go, and I'm grateful that you're letting me stay. But...I don't know, I guess I'm not good living with people. I was on my own a lot growing up. And I was good fending for myself."

"When did you start stealing?"

Sam blinked. What did that have to do with anything? "Huh?"

"At some point, you decided there were things you didn't have, that you wanted. So you learned to take them. Maybe it felt wrong at first, or maybe it gave you a rush. Either way, you don't worry about the consequences until it's too late." Chicklet put her hand on Sam's shoulder, a small, tired smile on her lips. "I think that's part of why you went after Sloan. You convinced yourself it was 'no big deal'."

"He's in a relationship with two other people. He's a Dom. He can do whatever he wants."

Chicklet's eyes widened. Then she laughed. "Oh, sweetie, please don't try to understand power dynamics like that. Those three are in a committed relationship. Doms *never* just do what they want, but we're not getting into that now. I don't like the way Tyler flipped out, but he's very protective of Raif, and *they* are in a committed relationship. I am in a more open one with Laura, Tyler, and Raif, but we communicate before doing anything with anyone else. Does that make sense?"

Yeah. Clear as mud. Sam shrugged. "I'm not trying to get with Raif. I was trying to make him feel better."

"It sounded like Tyler caught you kissing him."

"A quick peck on the lips. It was nothing."

"To you, maybe not. But would you do that to a married man who was in a traditional relationship?" When Sam shook her head, Chicklet inclined hers. "No, because the boundaries are clear. I don't know what kind of kinky books you've been reading, but they are fiction. The reality is much more complicated."

"Yeah, I kinda get that now." Sam grazed her bottom lip with her teeth and studied Chicklet's patient expression. Maybe the woman wasn't so bad after all. She hadn't come in here yelling, which Sam had expected. Sam liked Chicklet not being pissed at her. "Do you think I could get a job at your bar? I need to be doing something. I'm bored, and I feel stuck, and I really need to put my life together."

"Yes you do... But it's not my bar. It's Ford's." Chicklet's lips thinned. "I'll talk to him, but I can't promise anything. Your habit of taking things that don't belong to you isn't a secret."

I'm fucked. Sam nodded, shoulders hunched.

Chicklet tugged her hair lightly and laughed. "Chin up, kiddo. Ford has a shady past. If I promise to keep an eye on you, he might give you a chance."

"Really? You'd do that for me?" Yep, Chicklet was awesome. People didn't usually give Sam a second chance. Or even a first one.

The older woman's eyes narrowed. She tipped Sam's chin up with a finger. "I will, but don't fuck with me, Sam. You steal from Ford under my watch, and I'll have you arrested. You're rude to a single customer, slack off, or show anything other than respect to me and anyone else you're working with and I will fire you myself. I won't leave you homeless, but if you push me too far, I'll ship you off to my father's place. You won't be able to get in any trouble—or have any fun—out there. Got it?"

Sam's mouth went dry. Whoever had raised Chicklet must be a serious hard-ass. Being arrested sounded less scary than being shipped off. She nodded, determined not to screw up this time.

But...there was one problem. "Does that mean I can have fun *here*?"

Snorting, Chicklet sat back, bracing herself on her hands behind her, looking much younger all relaxed. "Absolutely. So long as the man—or woman—is willing, go wild. Check relationship status though."

"Yeah, yeah. And stay away from Sloan."

"If you want me to continue being pleasant that would be a good idea. I love Oriana. Thankfully, she sees you as a confused little girl and wasn't upset over what happened. If she was..." Chicklet's lips slid into a slow, devious smile. "I would make your life miserable."

"Isn't that what you've been doing?"

Chicklet laughed. "Oh my sweet, summer child. No, what I was doing was forcing you to be a contributing member of the household."

Which was fair. Sucked when she had to do dishes and the guys ate a bazillion meals a day, but she wasn't paying rent or anything. However, that didn't explain why Chicklet had been bitchy.

Saying that would be crazy though, so Sam worded her question carefully. "You didn't seem to like me very much when I first got here."

"I didn't. You're a little punk." Chicklet hopped up, reaching over to ruffle her hair. "But you're cute, in a clueless kinda way. And you were honestly trying to comfort Raif. Which puts you in my good books. Next time, either a quick hug or a blowjob. No one will get confused."

As Chicklet sauntered out of the room, Sam stared after her, lips parted. Then shook her head and giggled. The woman was outrageous. Completely nuts.

She might make a good friend now that they understood one another.

Unless Sam got on her bad side.

Then she'd make a very, *very* bad enemy.

Chapter Ten

A block from a destination Ian hadn't even realized he'd set out for, he turned around and headed back the way he'd come. The team was heading to Toronto tomorrow. He could figure out where things stood with Pisch then. When he didn't have a choice but to be near him for hours on end.

Sounds like fun.

The worst thing was he'd *lied* to Pisch. Right to his face. More than once.

He'd told him he was fine with an open relationship.

He'd agreed to the 'no keeping' terms.

He'd even told Pisch he was 'over' seeing him fucking Richards.

Lying was a coward's way out, but the truth was, Ian wasn't sure how he felt about any of the shit that had gone down. In the moment, the sensations, the sex, had been fucking amazing. The mess the next morning? Not so great.

Inhaling the damp, ocean air as he jogged along the small business district around the edges of Dartmouth, he let himself go back to the moment he'd woken up in Pisch's bed. He'd been...happy. Like that was where he belonged.

The pillow, covered in the cool Ninja Turtles pillowcase Pisch had obviously gotten for him, was tight against his chest. Pisch had brought it to him. Which was sweet, and not many people did sweet things for Ian.

The sex stuff was over, so Richards would take off and Ian and Pisch could hang out. Spend time together like they always did, only with a new...hell, he didn't know what to call it. A stronger bond? The beginning of something that could last a long time if he didn't try to change Pisch into the ideal boyfriend.

He'd actually thought that too. Of Pisch being his boyfriend. And he'd chuckled, because Pisch would cut and run so fucking fast if that label ever crossed Ian's lips.

Should have freaked Ian out a bit too, but nah. He couldn't suck the guy's dick, love him more than he'd ever loved anyone, and then cling to being straight. Or even gay for Pisch, because he'd *fucked* Richards.

Maybe he was fluid. Which was cool. He could deal with that.

Feeling good at having settled all the tangled shit in his head, he'd climbed out of bed, went to the spare bedroom to get dressed, and headed for the kitchen.

Then straight out the door without looking back. His chest had hurt just as bad then as it did now, while he pushed his body harder, lengthening his strides and breaking into a full out run.

He wasn't even sure if seeing Pisch fucking Richards was what really got to him. It was the pure bliss. The way Pisch let go as he slammed into the rookie's tight little ass.

The same one Ian had fucked the night before.

Only...Ian had been *with* Pisch then. All he'd felt, all he'd experienced, had included Pisch.

When he'd saw Pisch with Richards, part of him was crushed because he realized he wasn't needed.

He'd been warned. The terms of their relationship had been spelled out for him, very clearly, but he still hadn't gotten it until reality was staring him in the face.

And the reality was that he was more alone now than ever.

Lungs burning, he slowed near an intersection, walking for a bit along a street lined with restaurants and grungy little bars. His throat was dry, and to be honest, he wanted a damn drink. Maybe drinking the night before a game wasn't smart, but he knew his limits.

No matter how pissed he was, he wouldn't pass them. The game was his life.

All he had that he could control.

Somewhat.

We're two loses away from elimination. How you gonna control that, dumb ass?

He turned into the next bar, grabbed a stool, and rested his elbows on the bar top, inhaling roughly. "Jack on the rocks, please."

"White?" Ford dropped the rag he'd been using to clean behind the bar. He grabbed a bottle of Jack Daniels and scooped some ice into a glass as he stared at Ian. "You all right, man?"

Ian shrugged, pulling his sweat soaked tank from where it was sticking to his chest. "Yeah. Just need something to take the edge off."

"You wanna talk about it?" Ford set the drink in front of Ian. Because he was a damn good man.

"Not really." Ian took a sip of whiskey, focusing on the burn. Then wondering if he could consider Ford a friend. Maybe talking to someone would help. That was part of a bartender's job, right? He'd leave Ford a big tip. "Can I ask you something?"

Ford folded his arms on the bar top and grinned. "Go for it, Bruiser. I'm all ears."

"If you saw Cort fucking another guy, would it bother you?"

The man's jaw nearly hit the bar. Ford straightened, blinking at Ian like he'd just slugged him between the eyes. "Huh?"

"You're close, right? And you're with the same girl, so I'm sure—"

"I'm not fucking Cort. The asshole would probably fuck one of his beloved Redwings, but do you see me caring? Nope." Ford's tone sharped as he grabbed the rag and started scrubbing the bar like the soft cloth would sand out the watermarks. "He's like a brother to me. Most of the time. And Akira loves him. So I guess that would be a better question for her."

Maybe Ian shouldn't have asked. Ford didn't look uncomfortable. He looked mad.

Had Cort fucked one of the Detroit players? That would explain a lot.

And if Ford was a friend, maybe Ian should find the guy and give him a message.

"Are you in an open relationship?" Might as well clear that up first, since apparently it was a thing.

With a rough laugh, Ford shook his head. "No. Why would you ask that? You got a thing for my man?"

'*My man*'. That's what Pisch had called Ian. He hadn't meant it, but Ford clearly did and Ian didn't want him getting the wrong idea. "Fuck no. Just tell me the name of the player and I'll deal with him, pal. Fucking with another man's...man? That shit ain't cool."

Taking a deep breath, Ford shook his head again. Then laughed. "For that, your drink's on the house. You're a great guy, White. But no worries. Cort isn't my...we're not like that. He's not fucking anyone else."

"Just you and Akira."

"Yeah...wait. *No.*" Ford groaned. "Dude, did you and Pisch finally hook up? Is that why you're stuck on me and Cort?"

"I'm just trying to help." Ian took another gulp of whiskey. Damn, he was slow. He'd thought he and Ford had something in common. He'd been very wrong. "And me and Pisch—"

Ford snarled abruptly, cutting him off. "You're supposed to be working the floor, Sam! You gonna fuck her on the damn pool table, Cort?"

The big man, who worked security for the team, drew away from where he'd bent over the pool table, showing a cute little blonde how to adjust her aim. Harmless enough, but Cort apparently didn't appreciate Ford's comment.

He strode through the quickly parting patrons and slammed his fist on the bar. "You got an issue with me, Ford? Fine. But don't take it out on that little girl. She's been working all night. She gets to take a break."

"Well, if that's the kind of 'break' you're taking with her—" Ford slammed a glass into the sink, smashing it. "Take it into the fucking alley."

"Jesus, what's your fucking problem?"

"We have a girlfriend. Or did you forget Akira already?"

Cort swung his fist at Ford's face.

Ian latched onto the man's arm before he could connect. "You don't wanna do that, man."

Letting out an irritated growl, Cort twisted away from him. He pulled up straight, glaring at Ian. Then tipped his head back and sighed. "You're right. I don't." He wet his lips with his tongue, resting both hands on the edge of the bar and facing Ford. "Akira's been here, playing pool with the guys. A few of them have given her tips, and it wasn't a big deal because we know they respect her and aren't gonna try anything. I thought you knew me better, Ford. Sam's having a rough time. I was being nice."

"I saw that." Ford carefully picked up the glass shards from the sink and tossed them in the trash. "You done?"

Grinding his teeth, Cort inclined his head. "Yeah, I'm done."

With that, Cort went around the bar, grabbed his jacket, and left.

And one thing became clear to Ian. Jealousy could be damn ugly. He totally got why Ford wouldn't like seeing Cort touch another girl—he was probably worried about how Akira would feel. Except...Cort had made a good point about them letting her play pool with other guys.

It didn't mean anything. And it *shouldn't*.

There seemed to be more going on than Ford protecting Akira, but Ian couldn't dwell on that. He'd reacted the same way over Pisch fucking Richards. Angry and jealous and unwilling to discuss anything.

He wasn't sure he'd ever be cool with seeing Pisch with other people, but he'd gone into this knowing exactly the kind of man Pisch was. And he still loved him.

So if he couldn't deal, he needed to tell the man. And if he could...well, he needed to tell him that to. One way or another, he had to decide.

"You think I was a complete asshole, don't you?" Ford refilled Ian's glass and poured himself a drink, continuing when Ian couldn't come up with a good answer. "You're right. I should go talk to him. Probably before he punches a brick wall and hurts a poor, innocent building."

Ian snorted. He could picture Cort doing just that.

"Mind watching the bar for me for a bit? Chicklet stepped out for a late supper with Laura, but she shouldn't be long."

"Sure thing, man." Ian smirked over the rim of his glass. "Not implying anything, but blowjobs are as good as duct tape for fixing stuff."

After giving him the finger, Ford headed out.

Moving his drink across the bar, Ian went to stand on the other side. He served a few drinks, double checking the prices on the menu, and poured himself another glass of whiskey.

The cute little barmaid came over, her blue eyes wide. "Am I in trouble?"

"Nah, I don't think that really had anything to do with you." Ian smiled at her, finding it almost impossible to tear himself away from those cornflower blue eyes. He'd always thought using a flower to describe eyes was stupid, but they were his grandmother's favorite flower and the girl's eyes were a perfect match.

She bit her plump bottom lip and ducked her head. "Oh good. I seem to be messing up everything lately."

"I hear you, I feel the same." He chuckled, his gaze drifting to the stark red streaks in her blonde hair. She was adorable, looked young, but the red gave him the impression she had a wild side. He glanced down at the swell of her breasts, pressing against the buttons of her tight white shirt. His dick approved, but he didn't wait to be reminded that her eyes weren't down there. He cleared his throat, grateful for the bar, which hid his swelling dick. "You want a drink?"

"Yes please!" She bounced in place, which made it even harder not to stare at her tits.

But he managed.

Kinda.

"Oh, and here's the order." She passed him a paper with barely legible scribbles. "My name's Sam. Nice to meet you."

He held out his hand. "I'm Wh—Ian. My name's Ian."

"Do you play?"

Play? She really needed to clarify. Did she mean hockey? BDSM? Backgammon? "Umm...I play different things."

She giggled and put her hand on the back of his. "Pool?"

"Yes. Pool. I definitely play pool." Damn it, this girl was exactly what he needed. Once he got his head on straight again. She was sexy, sweet, and he wanted to get to know her. Even if just while shooting a few rounds on the tables. "When do you get off?"

"When the bar closes. But Chicklet said I can play a couple games when things are slow. The customers like watching me bend over the table." She winked at him. "And then they tip better."

"Are you looking for tips from me?" He cursed himself after the words left his mouth. He tried not to let chicks know he was an idiot before they'd gone on their first date. "I mean—"

"No, I get it. You're making sure I'm not flirting with you for a few bucks." She nibbled at her bottom lip, her eyes sparkling. "And I promise, I'm not. I just think you're sexy."

He liked how straightforward she was. He didn't have to guess her game plan.

And a plus, she didn't seem to recognize him. So she wasn't a puck bunny.

Not that he minded the bunnies. They'd given him some awesome memories. They were usually upfront about what they wanted. It was the girls with an agenda he had to watch out for, but this girl didn't seem like one of those. He was wearing faded jeans and a black tank top. No way she thought he had money.

"Can I ask you a question?" He filled out the order she'd brought him, only one last thing he needed to know before he played *any* kind of game with her. "Have you ever played pool before?"

She arched a brow. Then smiled. "No. But I won't lie. I do like how *helpful* guys can be showing me how to hold the stick."

"There's a few guys in here that would be helpful."

"True, but I'm bored of them. I have a feeling you wouldn't bore me."

He grinned, glancing over at the door as Chicklet came into the bar. He was free to enjoy the rest of his night.

Skirting around the bar, he stepped up to the girl's side, steadying her tray when she almost turned right into him.

He leaned in close to whisper in her ear. "Honey, the last thing I am is boring. Get back to work. I'll be waiting."

This job *rocked!*

Sam couldn't believe how lucky she was. Her tips were adding up to a good half a month's rent after just one night. She'd gotten a couple of free shots, and everyone here liked her.

Granted, they probably liked her ass and tits more than anything, but she would take their smiles and sweet words, no matter how dirty their thoughts might be. No one treated her like a fuck up. No one looked at her like they needed to nail down their valuables.

And absolutely not a single person brought up the baby.

Because here, she wasn't a girl who'd gotten knocked up and had given away the kid without a second thought. She knew how rare it was for a girl to get her figure back so quickly, but she would take it. She'd always been skinny, so her figure wasn't back to that. Actually, she had more curves, but her stomach didn't look that different unless she looked really close.

The men here weren't looking for flaws. They were simply looking.

Enjoying what they saw.

The attention gave her a nice buzz. She hadn't even considered shorting a single one of them on change, never mind stealing from them.

She might be getting better. Look at her go!

To top it off with whipped cream and extra cherries, she'd caught the attention of the hottest guy here. She shuddered when he whispered in her ear. Had to force herself to go deliver all the drinks. To smile and flirt with the patrons so she'd keep getting those tips.

When she looked back at the bar, she saw Chicklet talking to Ian. Chicklet caught her eye and gave her a thumbs up.

Damn, that felt good. Chicklet's approval was like first place in a race. Like a winning scratch ticket. Like...the best thing ever.

She wasn't sure if Chicklet was cheering her on for doing a good job here, or thought Ian was a good catch, but either way, she was happy with Sam.

It took about an hour, and last call, before she was able to join Ian at the pool tables. He was playing with a few random guys, laughing as he cleared the table and took their cash.

She took the opportunity to admire his hard body, her gaze trailing down from his broad shoulders, to muscular arms that she wanted to feel around her. To touch. Hell, maybe even lick and bite.

When he'd been bent over the table, she'd enjoyed the view of his nice round ass. She imagined it being firm, with just enough give to dig her fingers into. The thought had her feeling flushed, but by the time he noticed her, she had herself under control.

Barely, but enough to avoid jumping him, right here, right now.

"Hey, cutie." Ian motioned to the table. "You ready?"

Taking a deep breath, she inclined her head, watching him rack the balls. "Yes. I kinda want to take you home, but we can play first."

He positioned the stick to hit the white ball. Nodding like he hadn't heard her.

Then the end of the stick snapped into the table. The white ball rolled a little to the left. And he stared at her. "Damn, girl. If you want to distract me, it's working."

Grinning at him, she rested her hip on the edge of the pool table. "Is it? That's good." She waited for him to set up the white ball again. Then decided turnaround was fair play. She leaned close, whispering in his ear. "But I meant exactly what I said. I want to take you home and do dirty things to you."

He dropped the stick on the table and took her hand, pulling her against him. His lips hovered close to hers, but he didn't kiss her. He let out a ragged exhale and laughed. "Do you think Chicklet would let me steal you away early?"

"She would." Chicklet stepped up behind Ian, gathering his collar length, light brown hair in one hand tugging until he met her eyes. "Get out of here. Take her to your place and treat her right. You'll answer to me if you hurt her."

"Yes, ma'am." Ian's tone was totally serious. He obviously respected Chicklet.

And they knew one another well. Did he come here often?

Chicklet release him and pointed a long, black painted nail at Sam. "Remember what I told you."

Sam made a face, but she knew Chicklet was right. Between Sloan, Raif—which she hadn't really done anything wrong with—and Cort, men in relationships were becoming more trouble than they were worth. What seemed like harmless fun to her got other people pissed off.

She didn't want to deal with any more drama.

After grabbing her long black sweater from behind the bar, she gave Ian her arm and walked with him out to the street, letting him lead her as she considered how she would ask that very important question Chicklet had told her to.

Might as well be as blunt as she'd been with everything else. "Do you have a girlfriend?"

Ian snorted. "No. I wouldn't be taking you home with me if I did."

"That's all I needed to know." She hugged his arm as they strolled down one block. Then another. This was getting to be a long walk.

"Umm...how far do you live? Did you leave your car at home so you could drink?"

"Uh...no. Actually, I stopped in after a jog."

"How long was the jog?"

"About three miles."

Damn... I'm definitely getting my exercise for the day. "So should we make small talk to pass the time? What do you do for a living?"

His jaw tensed. He shook his head. "Would it be weird if I didn't want to talk about my job yet?"

Was he a criminal? From what Chicklet had implied, Ford had been into illegal stuff. And Cort...Cort reminded her of some of the bikers that hung out at the parties she used to go to. She liked them both, and she wasn't in any position to judge. But Ian seemed like a nice guy.

Maybe he worked some crappy job and didn't want to think about it.

"Not weird at all. You know what I do. Not much conversation there!" She wasn't sure what else would be a good topic. When she fooled around with a guy, there wasn't usually much time to talk before. Or much need to after. She looked around at the dimly lit streets, loving that all the snow had melted and everything was green. "It's nice out. Not too chilly."

He chuckled and freed his arm to put it around her shoulders. "I agree. Good night for an extremely long walk."

"Yeah..."

"Tell me what you're into. What do you do when you're not flirting with drunk guys?" He shook his head and groaned. "Sorry, that was a stupid thing to say."

He really was a sweetheart. Most guys would have said worse and not thought twice. She smiled at him. "Not stupid. Honest. Makes me feel like you really want to know."

"I do."

"Well... I was thinking of going to school to work with animals, but I'm not smart enough to pass all the courses. So I need to figure out what I can do." She wrinkled her nose. "The only thing I was ever good at is doodling in class when I was supposed to be learning. Not like I'm a great artist or anything. I like drawing stuff like you'd see in comic books."

"Really?" His face lit up, like she'd just told him she owned her own personal gold mine. "Do you like comic books?"

"I *love* them! I used to borrow them from my guy friends all the time. I still have a few I never gave back..." She cringed, realizing she'd almost let it slip that she was a thief. Most of the books she'd 'borrowed' without letting the guys know. She *had* returned some, in exactly the condition she'd taken them, but she had over a hundred in a box in her room. None of which she'd paid for.

Ian's bright smile never faded. "Do you like the movies? I know some suck, compared to the books, but I love them all."

"So do I!" She giggled, relief flooding her. They had something in common that could fill the rest of the trip to his place. And he didn't think any worse of her. "I started watching the old Batman episodes, and they're so corny, but I think they're fun. I can watch them for hours. And I don't care what anyone says, all the Xmen movies *rock*!"

"I *almost* agree with you. First Class was *lame* though."

"It wasn't that bad."

"Meh...I agreed with everything Cinema Sins said about it." His lips quirked at the edges. "You gotta admit, Mystique not getting all the love was fucked up."

"True. Mystique is fucking sexy." She would so do that woman. With or without the full body paint. "She's definitely in my spank bank."

"That you have a spank bank and admit it is damn hot."

"It's not weird that a chick is in there?"

"Fuck no! I have chicks in mine."

"Duh. Do you have any guys?" The way he pressed his lips together made her wonder if she'd gone too far. Most guys didn't like even the idea of doing shit with other guys. Accepting her brother wasn't straight had made her way too comfortable. "Sorry, I was just teasing."

His shoulders lifted. He laughed and shook his head. "Hugh Jackman is hot as Wolverine. I'd do him."

Heat pooled in her core and she couldn't keep walking. She pulled up short, dragging him down to her so she could lick his bottom lip. "You just had to say that. How much farther?"

He groaned as she rubbed against him. "About ten blocks."

"Too far." She grabbed his hand and led him into the closest alley. It was late. They hadn't seen a car pass in forever. If she didn't feel him inside her soon, she'd combust. "I want you. Please?"

He pressed her against the brick wall, his lips parted against hers. "Baby, I'm not fucking you in the alley."

"But I want you to!" She gasped as he slid his hand between her thighs. "I don't want to talk any more. I don't want to think. I just want to feel."

Lowering his lips to her throat, he nodded. "I'm so hard for you, sweetie. But I don't want you to feel used."

"I won't." She tipped her head back as his fingers nudged her panties aside and dipped into her. She'd stopped bleeding a lot faster than the doctor had expected. She was normal again. She could have this. Have *him*. "I will beg."

"You don't have to." He slid his fingers in deeper, reaching back and tugging out his wallet. He flipped it open and used his teeth to take out a condom.

That he'd clearly done this before got her even more worked up. She didn't have to worry that she was playing with some poor nice guy who always did flowers and the right amount of dates before making sweet love to a girl. Ian was ready. Willing. Unattached.

She could just take whatever he had to give.

He managed to get the condom on without slowing the steady thrust of his fingers. Her pussy ached when he drew away, but he lifted her up and the thickness of him pressed against her.

The fullness was amazing as the head of him stretched her. Her body wasn't ruined. Maybe she wasn't as tight as she'd been, but he didn't seem to notice as he sank in deeper and deeper, so careful, but his restraint was torture.

Until the stretching became painful.

She pressed her eyes shut at the sting of tears. It wasn't the stretching at all. She was still tender, and his thrust sent a hot wave of pain stabbing into her.

"Aww, sweetie. Why didn't you say something?" Ian drew out almost all the way. Holding her close and whispering to her as he moved in shallow thrusts. "If I'd known, I would have been more careful. Tell me if you want me to stop."

Stop? The very idea was horrifying. She wasn't sure what he'd wanted her to tell him, but the gentle way he moved eased the pain and stirred the pleasure. She clung to his shoulders, whimpering as the sensations boiled at a steady pulse, rising until she could feel the edge of release, lingering so close.

"Don't stop. Fuck, that feels good." She dug her heels into his back. "Just like that is perfect. I'm so close!"

He pressed his lips to her throat. Drew his dick out until only the thick head teased her. "How close?"

"Ah!" She pressed her head to his shoulder as every muscle within rippled with white hot waves of pleasure. Her nails dug into the back of his neck as she choked back a scream of ecstasy. He sank in all the way and shuddered, one arm around her waist, hand under her ass, the other pressed into the wall as he came.

Her body clung to him, and she prayed he wouldn't move, because she'd never been this sensitive. If he tried to pull away it would either hurt, or she'd come again.

He didn't seem to be in a rush to let her go. He simply held her, kissing her neck and whispering sweet nonsense.

After what seemed like forever, she unwrapped her legs from around his waist. His dick slipped from her body and her face heated when she saw the blood.

"Hey, it's all good. We can take a shower at my place." He tossed the condom in a nearby bin, covered himself, then smiled at her. "I don't know why you were cool with me being your first, but you won't be sorry. I promise."

There had to be a special place in hell for a girl that let a guy believe she was sweet and innocent when she wasn't. But Sam knew she was damned already. Maybe she could earn forgiveness if she was the type to believe in all that stuff.

She didn't though. And either way, she wanted this. Wanted to feel special and cherished and taken care of.

Her first time had been rough and cold. The guy had given her cab money while she was still feeling sore and vulnerable. He'd gotten her name wrong a few times while he'd fucked her. And she didn't remember his.

There was no way to get another first time, but this was close enough.

And she'd take it.

If he didn't tell her to take a hike in the morning, she'd tell him the truth.

Until then, she'd let him believe whatever made him continue looking at her like she was precious. She couldn't remember the last time a man had looked at her like that.

She wasn't sure any man ever had.

"Just hold me, Ian?" She closed her eyes as he straightened her clothes and pulled her into his arms. "Hold me tonight, and I won't regret a thing."

Chapter Eleven

A soft buzzing woke Ian, but he figured it was Pisch's phone and ignored it. No one really called him. Not this early, anyway.

Unless it was his grandmother's nurse?

He squinted at the clock, his throat tightening. It was 7:25 AM. A call this early couldn't mean anything good. He brushed away the long, soft strands of hair sticking to his arm, and his stomach flipped when he realized two things.

He wasn't at Pisch's place.

And there was a girl in his bed.

Sam. Her name is Sam. She wasn't one of his random hook ups. She'd been a virgin, and he'd fucked her in a damn alley.

Which made him a horrible person. Forgetting she was here, at his place, in bed with him, was even worse. What the hell was wrong with him?

Too much whiskey?

No, he wouldn't blame the alcohol. He hadn't been drunk, he just hadn't been thinking.

His phone buzzed again, and he slipped out of the bed, grabbing his jeans and taking his phone out as he quietly left the room. Thankfully, the call wasn't from his grandmother's nurse.

It was from Pisch.

He quickly called Pisch back. "Hey, everything all right?"

"Yeah, everything's fine, I just wanted to make sure you don't miss the bus. We're leaving in two hours." Pisch cleared his throat. "Figured we could grab a coffee before heading out."

Shit. He'd completely forgotten to set his alarm. Or mentally prepare himself for the flight. His stuff was all packed, so he didn't have to rush, but hanging out with Pisch would give him a chance to get his head where it needed to be. And they could make sure they were cool.

But he couldn't just kick Sam out and take off.

He sighed and shook his head. "Umm...maybe? I've got a couple things to take care of, but I'll let you know if I can make it."

"Please do." Pisch went quiet. Then spoke softly. "White, I understand if you're not ready to discuss what happened yet, but I'll be here when you are."

Ian swallowed, holding the phone away from his mouth so Pisch wouldn't hear him. He hated how things had gone down. Hated even more that he had to carefully consider what he should say to Pisch.

But he liked that Pisch wasn't being pushy. That he was giving Ian the space he needed. While not giving him too much. He pressed his lips together, leaning against the fridge and nodding.

"Thanks, man. I needed to hear that."

"Good. Because I have no problem repeating myself." Pisch let out a soft, tired laugh. "I'll see you in a bit."

Hanging up, Ian put on a pot of coffee, waiting until it was full before heading back to his room to wake up Sam. She looked so cute, curled up on his bed, her hair strewn across her face and his pillow. He half wanted to climb back in bed with her, snuggle for a bit, and wake her up with a nice, long kiss.

Only, he hadn't really kissed her yet, had he? Their lips had touched a few times, but everything had gotten hot and heavy really fast. Too fast.

He wasn't even sure if it had meant anything to her. She'd come on strong, which had made him think she had experience, but he'd been so very wrong. Which left him feeling like the worst kind of scum.

To top it off, he had to tell her about the flight in a few hours, and how he'd be gone for a few days. He could call her, but would that be enough? She'd probably think he was blowing her off now that he'd gotten in her pants.

Or under her skirt since she hadn't been wearing pants.

"You know, I can almost feel you thinking very hard." She smiled, not opening her eyes as she turned sleepily toward him. "If you tell me your girlfriend called, and you need to get me out of here before she gets back, I'm going to punch you."

His eyes widened and his lips parted. He plunked down on the edge of the bed, staring at her. "Fuck, why would you think that?"

Her eyes slit open, and she shrugged. "I don't know. You get a call then come back in here all quiet. I'm just assuming the worst."

"I *don't* have a girlfriend." But if he was going to call her, and see if there was anything besides one brief quickie between them, he should probably be honest. "There *is* someone in my life, but we're not in a committed relationship. I'm not a cheater."

She pushed up to a sitting position, cocking her head slightly as she rubbed her eyes with one hand. "Really? So she's cool with you taking other chicks home?"

"Yeah..." *Honesty, Ian. Spit it out.* He tugged at his bottom lip with his teeth. "*He's* fine with it. Or I think he is. He should be; he fucks other people."

"Oh!" She giggled and leaned toward him. "Wow, you're bisexual? That's so fucking cool! Is it horrible that I'd love to watch you with your man? I think two guys together are hot."

"You *do*?" He wasn't sure what to make of her reaction. Didn't most chicks want a stable relationship? Unless they weren't looking for a relationship at all, but a virgin would probably be considering one, right? "I mean, me and you... Where do you want this to go?"

Her smile faded. "I don't know. I'm kinda happy you haven't told me to leave yet."

"Leave? Why would I do that? I may be an asshole for what happened last night, but if I didn't have a game tonight, I'd stay and—"

"A game?" She groaned and shock her head. "Wait, this can't be a coincidence. The Cobras have a game tonight. You're on the team, aren't you?"

That seemed to bother her much more than him being...bisexual. Or in a relationship with a man, open or not.

"Yeah...sorry I didn't mention it?" His brow furrowed as she muttered to herself and rolled to the other side of the bed to grab her clothes. "Wait, do you have a problem with hockey players?"

"Not really, but I wish Chicklet had given me a head's up. Going back to her place is going to be awkward. She's gonna ask what happened, and she knows I'm not into the game, but I was considering dating a player?" She let out a bitter laugh. "This is gonna suck."

"You don't have to go."

"What?"

What? The voice in his head sounded just as shocked as she did, but it was the perfect solution. Apparently, she lived with Chicklet. And didn't want to answer a whole bunch of questions.

He couldn't do much for her before he had to go, but he could do this. "Stay here. There's some food in the fridge, I got a big TV and tons of movies you'll like. You'll still have to let Chicklet know where you're atat, but you won't feel stuck telling her anymore than you want to. And I won't feel like I completely abandoned you."

"So this is partially for selfish reasons?"

She didn't say it like that was a bad thing. And she was smiling.

So he smiled back and nodded. "Exactly. You'd be doing me a favor."

"Well, in that case, sure! I'd love to stay. I'll take care of your place, tidy up a bit, and make sure the food in your fridge doesn't go bad." She practically skipped across the room, leaning against him and wrapping her arms around his waist. "You're crazy, you know that? I'm a complete stranger."

"Not a *complete* stranger." He kissed her forehead, the weight of regret easing from his chest. "I'm glad you're taking this so well. Grab some coffee while I get you the spare key. I don't have much time, but I'll give you the WiFi password, and show you where everything is."

"Free WiFi! I've died and gone to heaven!"

He snorted as he grabbed the key from the junk drawer in the hall table. Only one other person had the key to his place, but he couldn't remember Pisch ever using it. They usually hung out at his place.

Probably because Pisch's place was bigger. Ian looked around at his comfy little apartment. The kitchen wasn't huge, but it had all the important stuff. He needed a new fridge at some point; the one that had come with the apartment was old when he moved in. And that was like, five or six years ago.

Damn, had he really been here that long?

All his stuff was worn, but in a familiar way. He hadn't planned to stay here forever, but he didn't hate the place.

He preferred Pischlar's, but he wouldn't think too much about that now. Sam would be comfortable here.

"Aww shit." He groaned as he considered anything else she might need. Staying at Pisch's so much meant he'd neglected a couple things here. "I washed some towels a few days ago, but I forgot to put them in the drier. They're probably smelly now."

Turning to him, with a mug of coffee held out, Sam laughed. "No biggie. I'll just air dry."

He managed not to pour the hot coffee down the front of his bare chest. Damn it, between her and Pisch, his sanity couldn't take much more. And his dick...well, the poor guy needed a break. All kinds of sex and it was still constantly hard.

Beautiful naked chick, strutting around his apartment while he was in another damn province. Fate was determined to punish him for something.

Sam took a sip of her coffee, her eyes sparkling with amusement. "You're too easy. Don't worry, I'll wash the towels again. And save walking around, water dripping all over my naked body, for when you get back."

He cupped the hot mug in both hands, burning his lips, but gulping down a mouthful anyway. The pain centered him and he smiled at her. "You're a cruel woman."

"I can be."

"Do you need anything else? I gotta get dressed, but I'll call you tonight and see how you're doing." There was more. Had to be. He frowned. "Should I leave you my credit card in case—"

"*Dude*! There's sweet, and then there's... Ian, you are not leaving me your credit card. I'll be fine." She leaned up to kiss his cheek. "Go get ready."

Another gulp of coffee and he went to get changed into his suit. He stuffed the tie in his pocket, grabbed his rucksack, and met Sam back in the kitchen. He still felt like he needed to do something. Something to let her know last night had been special.

Sliding his hand around the back of her neck, he pulled her close. "This is crazy, right? I told you I'm with someone. We haven't gotten to discuss anything, and now I'm leaving."

"But I'll be here when you get back." She set down her mug and wrapped her arms around his waist. "He's not here. No one else is. But you want me to be."

"Yes." He brought his lips to hers, brushing them gently with his own, tasting her as her lips parted. His bag hit the floor as the sweet taste of her coffee flavored mouth flooded his senses with heat and longing, and he couldn't get enough.

Her tongue teased his, and he let out a soft moan as he pulled her up against him. She fit so perfectly in his arms, and he hadn't gotten a chance to touch and taste every fucking beautiful inch of her. Another hour wouldn't be enough time.

But having her here, waiting for him, guaranteed he'd get that chance.

She raked her fingers into his hair, sighing as she drew away. "I can't ask you to stay, can I?"

"Please don't, I might consider it." He kissed her again, softly this time, knowing it was time to say goodbye. "I'll call you tonight?"

"You might need my number." She gave him that cute little cheeky grin, slipping her hand into his pocket to grab his phone. "I'm gonna watch *First Class* while you're playing."

He snorted and shook his head. "So much for asking if you'd be cheering me on."

"Oh, I'll be cheering you on, babe." She winked at him and gave him a playful shove toward the door. "When you get home."

Chapter Twelve

Apparently, having time to kill came in handy. Since they needed one of their best players to voluntarily leave his house and get on the damn bus. Sooner, rather than later.

Thankfully, two thirds of the trouble triplets had been planning for the inevitable. Shawn was along for his 'Dom' influence. When Luke Carter, first line left winger extraordinaire and mouthpiece of the team, suggested Shawn would be perfect for the job, Shawn had laughed and asked "Why not Mason or Callahan?"

Carter had stared at him. *"The kid needs a nudge in the right direction. He don't need tough love. Come on, Easy. Please?"*

That impish smile, with just the right amount of respect, and a dash of temptation, had Shawn wondering what he should ask for in return for this 'favor'. Ramos didn't share his subs anymore, unfortunately, but that could change.

If Shawn wasn't knee deep in a mess of his own making, he might have negotiated a little more. Instead, he decided to be a good friend and help, no strings attached.

As he pulled up in front of Vanek's house, something cold touched the back of his neck, and he jumped, driving right onto the sidewalk. He put the car in reverse, scowling as Carter laughed and Demyan struggled to get the situation in the backseat under control.

"You are aware that if we're late, you'll both be dealing with Callahan." So would Shawn, but his defense of temporary insanity might earn him some pity. The trouble triplets were hard to resist.

Carter leaned over the seat and planted a big wet kiss on his cheek. "Aww, don't be like that, Pisch. We won't be late. Just head on in, and make sure Chicklet don't wanna kill us."

Ah... That explains a lot. He chuckled as he got out of the car. If Chicklet hadn't been informed of the crazy plan, they needed someone to protect them from *her*. No wonder they weren't worried about the assistant coach.

The front door opened before he could even knock. Chicklet folded her arms over her chest, her eyes narrowing. "Are they insane?"

"Possibly?" Shawn watched both men being dragged across the walkway, grinning. "Which one would you like me to hold down for you first?"

Chicklet snorted. "Depends on whether this works. I imagine Carter used his charm to pull this off?"

"I'm here, aren't I?"

"Yes." Chicklet arched a brow. "Looking for brownie points? I notice you let your own boy run wild. I'd had such high hopes for you two, but he's gotten wound up in his own trouble, which takes it off my hands, so I'm not complaining."

Is she talking about White? She didn't sound worried, which made it easier for him not to, but he didn't like being in the dark when it came to his own man.

He's not yours. You made sure of that.

That remained to be seen. He wasn't sure what he could do to mend things between them, but he was willing to negotiate. Maybe fucking other people in front of White was the deal breaker. He hated the idea of not being able to share the experience of someone new with the man, but if it hurt him, he would manage. Not like it would happen often. He still hadn't gotten to experience everything he wanted to do to White yet.

He would though. And they'd both enjoy every damn minute, with no more regrets.

Unless he's moved on already?

Shawn stepped aside as Carter and Demyan finally made their way into the house. He crossed the threshold, standing by Chicklet's side as she closed the door. "Care to tell me who 'my boy' is running wild with?"

Chicklet laughed and shook her head. "Oh no, you're not dragging me into this. If he wants you to know, he'll tell you. If he doesn't, you've got bigger problems."

"You think so?" Shawn tried to sound doubtful, but Chicklet's smirk told him he'd failed miserably.

"The fact that you're finally, at least subconsciously, accepting that he's yours is a good sign, but if you're pretending nothing has changed? Yeah, you're gonna have a mess to clean up." She sighed as she met his eyes. "I suspect you already do."

"Nothing I can't handle." He returned his focus to the mess he was dealing at now. Vanek had come into the hall with Zovko, hovering close to the other man like he wanted to take his hand and lead him, but hesitated because Zovko seemed determined to manage on his own.

Letting out a low whine, the dog Demyan and Carter had adopted for Vanek and his family tugged free, sniffing the carpet, eyeing Vanek and Zovko as she inched closer to them.

Vanek's eyes went wide. He looked close to tears as he glanced over at his two best friends. "How did you manage to get her so fast? I thought it was gonna take at least another week for the paperwork?"

"I've been going in every morning for the past week." Carter closed the distance between him and Vanek, pulling the younger man into his arms as tears wet Vanek's cheeks. "I get it, man."

"I know you're trying to, but I can't leave. I just...I *can't.*"

Silent this whole time, Zovko took a knee, holding out his hand as the dog nudged him. "A dog?"

Shawn folded his arms over his chest, tempted to go hug Vanek himself when the young man's face fell, as though he took those two words as a rejection of his gift. There was no telling how Zovko would react to why Vanek wanted the new pet for him, but they were about to find out.

Vanek cleared his throat and wiped his eyes as he pulled away from Carter. "Yeah...umm, she has special training. She's a service dog whose owner passed away almost a year ago. She's been in the shelter ever since. No one wanted her because she's so big. And she doesn't listen so good anymore, so they weren't even sure she would *be* a good service dog. But I thought you... Well, you could teach her to be good again."

"Do you mean she will be with us temporarily? Until she's seen fit to serve someone in need?" Zovko's words and his tone were at odds. Almost as though he didn't believe *he* needed a dog specially trained for people with disabilities, but he really did want to keep her. He buried his hands in her thick fur, smiling as she gave him a hesitant lick on the cheek. "I don't like the idea of her having to be displaced too often. She should have some stability."

Biting his bottom lip, his lips quirking up slightly, Vanek crouched down beside Zovko. "She really should."

Zovko put his arm out, resting it over Vanek's shoulders as he continued to pet the dog. "What is her name?"

"Thora."

"Thora. I like that." Zovko leaned forward, touching his forehead to the big dog's. "Welcome home, Thora."

Tension eased from Shawn's shoulders, and he grinned at Chicklet as she flashed him a relieved smile. This wasn't a done deal, but hopefully, Zovko accepting Thora would make it easier for Vanek to leave his man for a few days.

Inhaling roughly, Zovko lifted his head, turning toward Vanek. "Describe her to me."

Fresh tears spilled down Vanek's cheeks. He squared his shoulders. "She's beautiful. They told me she's a bit of a mutt, but mostly Caucasian Shepard. She's got thick fur...okay, well you can feel that. It's almost black around her head, but there's pale brown around her eyes and on her muzzle. The rest of her fur, down her body, is brown and black...her legs are a light brown. She looks kinda like a small bear."

Chuckling, Zovko pulled Vanek close, kissing his lips softly. "She sounds like a magnificent animal. And so far, very well behaved."

Shawn smirked, glancing over at Carter and Demyan, who were both shaking their heads as though they didn't want Shawn to tell Zovko how much trouble they'd had with her.

The man needed some warning though. He shifted closer to Zovko, scuffing his shoes on the carpet so the man wouldn't be surprised by his approach. "She's a bit stubborn and needs to know who's in control. I doubt you'll have any trouble, considering you manage with this one."

Tipping his head up, Zovko's lips slanted in a crooked grin. "This is true. But someone else will have to 'manage' him on the road. Is that way the children brought you along?"

"Hey!" Demyan grunted when Carter elbowed him in the stomach. "Dude, I ain't a damn kid. I *have* a kid. You and Vanek are gonna need to find another third. You're ruining my reputation."

"*Dude.*" Carter poked Demyan in the center of the chest. "You earned that reputation before I was even born."

"Before I was five? How the hell do you figure?"

"You're only five years older than me? Damn, sorry man. The way you've been acting lately, I thought it was a lot more."

Demyan gave Carter the finger.

Carter leaned into him, taking the tip of Demyan's finger into his mouth.

Chicklet shook her head, stepped forward, and tugged Carter back by the collar of his shirt. "None of that in my house. If you two wanna play, fine. I suggest permission slips from both of your Masters or it could get ugly."

Scowling, Demyan stepped away from her and Carter. "First of all, Zach isn't my Master. Two, me and this kid? Never gonna happen."

"Thanks for ruining all my slash fantasies." Chicklet sighed. "My vibe was getting some good use on you two."

Both men's jaws nearly hit the floor. Vanek and Zovko both frowned, likely wondering why she'd need to picture any other men when she had them.

Shawn let out a soft laugh, sidling up to Chicklet's side, curving his arm around her waist, and brushing his lips against her ear. "You know, I think it's been *way* too long since we had a nice, intimate party. I don't think it would be difficult to give you some more visuals to add to your spank bank."

Chicklet reached back, sliding her hand right between his legs to grab his balls through his jeans. She chuckled as he went perfectly still. "Very tempting, Easy. I have some very nice visuals of you and my men, but I thought you didn't do sequels."

Toying with Chicklet was very, *very* dangerous. The woman wouldn't try to keep him, but she'd likely leave a few marks to remember her by. His dick hardened despite the painful pressure on his nuts. He couldn't play with her without surrendering much more control than he was accustomed to, but for the experience alone, he'd consider it.

He caught her earlobe between his teeth, wincing as she tightened her grip. Then he whispered to her. "You would be worth making a few exceptions to my rules."

"Mmm." She released him, patting his dick lightly as she glanced over her shoulder at him. "I might take you up on that. Win some games and you may deserve a party. Is it my boy you want to play with again, or are you looking for a piece of me?"

The woman wasn't difficult to read. She knew his answer already, but part of the game was laying all his cards on the table and leaving no doubt of his intentions. So he smiled at her as he hooked his thumbs to the loops on his black slacks.

"Both."

"Umm, do I get a say in any of this?" Vanek stared at them, his cheeks red. Fuck, the young man was damn sexy, all shy and uncertain. Shawn rarely looked back and wished he could have another taste of a man or woman he'd already enjoyed, but there was something about Vanek.

Something uncomplicated and erotic. Simple.

Zovko stood, one hand on his new dog's head, his jaw hard, his sightless eyes narrowed. "I certainly do have a say. Focus must be on the game, Pischlar. I agree with Chicklet. If you win, a celebration will be deserved, but what do you have to offer in exchange for our boy?"

Exchange? Shawn frowned. Fuck him, this conversation wasn't much fun anymore. He had himself, obviously. Wasn't that enough?

His jaw hardened. "I'm not sure what you're getting at, Zovko. If you don't want me to touch your boy, I won't. You know that."

Moving to Chicklet's side, taking her hand when she reached out to steady him, Zovko seemed to stare right through Shawn. Which was strange, because he couldn't see him. But his expression seemed as though he was seeing more than he would even if his vision wasn't gone.

"You take whatever you please, but you risk nothing. If he is willing, I will offer him to you. But you must offer one that belongs to you in return." The edge of Zovko's lips tipped up. "White."

Fuck! Shawn's stomach dropped. Not because he didn't like the idea of White joining in their twisted games. Yes, part of him snarled and tugged at the chains he'd put on any jealousy he let himself feel long ago. He ignored it. The issue wasn't whether he would mind seeing Zovko—and likely Chicklet—play with White.

He had no claim on the man. He wasn't even sure *how* he could stake one, not without shifting his entire live-free-with-no-strings-attached existence.

Yes, he'd considered it. But to play the game Zovko proposed, he and White would need some stability. A solid foundation. One they didn't have.

Yet.

White wasn't okay with the lifestyle Shawn led as it was. He couldn't even consider bringing him to a party like this. And wouldn't for a long time.

There had to be a way around Zovko's conditions.

"White isn't in the scene." He made the comment as lightly as he could, like the whole idea was amusing and mildly interesting. "Make me another offer and I'll consider it. There's no rush."

"Indeed. But we shall see." Zovko shrugged, as though their plans weren't important to him either. "The game is entertaining, but not all can play. No hard feelings if you can't anymore."

"*I* can. You know very well White can't."

"Really? I think he'd enjoy himself very much. Unless he's uncertain how it would change things between you?" Zovko arched a brow. The man might be blind, but he saw much more than Shawn was comfortable with. "I would not consider any entertainment my subs, or my sweet Mistress, don't enjoy indulging in. You're a good Dom, Pischlar. I don't imagine you would ignore the feelings of any under your care."

"I wouldn't." But White wasn't 'under his care'. Still wasn't really his at all. And he hated putting those facts to words for anyone else to judge. He might be able to pass his intentions off as casual to a sub. Or someone not in the lifestyle. But both Zovko and Chicklet were very observant.

In approaching their sub as a potential plaything, he'd just given them both the right to pick apart his own worth as a Dom. And judge the only relationship he had worth a damn.

"Good. Then when you're both in the right place, we will discuss this again." Zovko reached out, his brow furrowing when his hand found nothing. He'd misjudged how far he'd moved from Vanek, but the young man quickly stood and took his hand. And Zovko immediately relaxed. "Freedom can be pleasant, but when you have someone that will always be by your side? It means so much more. And when life is challenging, it is worth more than I can say."

The truth to Zovko's words hit Shawn like a solid cement brick landing on the center of his chest. Sure, his life was pretty good now, but if that changed? He'd managed to drive a wedge between himself and White. And *Ian*. How fucked up was it that he still used the last name of the man he loved? But he knew exactly *why* he did it. It kept distance between them. If he called Ian 'White' in his head, he was just a friend. Another player.

And yet, Ian was so much more. He was a man that owned a part of Shawn that hadn't been available to anyone else. And shouldn't be now, because he wasn't ready. If anyone asked, he could give a nice long list of all the reasons he and Ian wouldn't be a good match.

Ian was too rough. Which was a hard limit.

But Ian was willing to fix that for him. He'd already caught his mistakes and tried to correct them. He cared enough to be as gentle with Shawn as he was with anyone he considered special.

Ian needed commitment.

A much better argument, but Ian was testing the waters. He'd reacted badly to seeing Shawn with Richards, but Shawn knew very well he'd gone too far. He should have waited to see how Ian felt the next morning. Talked it out.

No matter what excuses he came up with, the truth was, Ian wasn't the problem.

Shawn was.

His silence had everyone's attention returning to the most important matter at hand. Demyan and Carter went to the car to grab the huge bag of dog food, the dog bed, and all the treats and toys they'd thought Thora might need.

And Chicklet and Zovko joined efforts in trying to convince Vanek to grab his stuff and get ready to leave. The two Doms working together was almost enough to make *Shawn* consider dropping to his knees. Which he might do for them one day—while being manipulative as fuck for their mutual pleasure.

But Vanek faced them, his jaw set, his arms folded. "I agree, having Thora will help, but it's gonna take time for her to learn to do all you need from her."

"And I'm incapable of working with Raif on her training?" Chicklet rested her hands on her hips, frowning at Vanek. "I'm insulted by your lack of faith in me."

"That's not what I'm saying!"

"Then what are you saying, *zlato moje?*" Zovko slid his hand around the back of Chicklet's neck, massaging gently as she glared at their sub. "Surely you're not envious of the time we will spend together?"

"That's the problem! You *won't* be spending that much time together. Chicklet has to work! You'll be alone all day and—"

"No, he won't." Chicklet leaned her head on Zovko's shoulder, stroking his chest when he scowled. "Don't get upset, Raif. You don't need a babysitter, but you still need someone around to help you adjust to living without your sight. Your independence will come. For now, I asked Ford for a few days off. Which means Tyler has absolutely no excuse not to go do his job."

Vanek groaned, obviously seeing he'd been out maneuvered. "It's just a fucking game."

Oh shit. Shawn winced as rage darkened Zovko features.

Zovko stepped forward, his tone dropping as he made a violent gesture, his hand cutting through the air. "Enough! I will never play that 'fucking game' again! Do you think you do anything for me by putting your life on hold? I am doing all I can to keep living mine, to prove I can still be a strong man, a good Dom. You're proving to me I am failing at both!"

Eyes wide, Vanek stepped up to Zovko, lifting a hand to touch his cheek. "You're not failing. I just want you to know I'm here."

"How many different ways must I say that I don't *need* you here?"

Ouch. Time for Shawn to step in before things got any worse. He put his hand on Vanek's shoulder as the young man retreated, looking lost. "Kid, your man knows you love him, but what he needs, what we *all* need, is for you to help us even up this series against the Leafs. Get your stuff and let's go win some games. For Zovko, for…for everyone who can't be with us. We've fought hard to get this far. We can't quit now."

"I know, but it's getting hard to believe the game means anything." Vanek's shoulder bowed as he stared at his socked feet. "If this is what you want me to do, I'll do it, Raif. Just don't hate me."

"*Kiragu*! I don't hate you, my boy. Come here." Zovko sighed as he gathered Vanek in his muscular arms. "You are stubborn and you are driving me insane. But I will always love you. I only want to see you..." Zovko inhaled sharply. "To *know* you are doing all I wish I could."

"If it's that important to you, I'll go."

"I need it to be just as important to you." Zovko released Vanek, turning at the sound of Vanek heading down the hall, probably to grab his stuff. He shook his head and rubbed his hand over his face. "This is difficult for him. I have no idea how to make it easier. Please watch over him, Pischlar."

"You know I will." Shawn squeezed Zovko's forearm.

Carter and Demyan came in, struggling to get through the door with the boxes loaded with dog stuff, Carter tripping over the dog bed that he had under one arm. The thing was basically just a huge black and beige pillow, but it was awkward to carry one handed.

Making two trips would have been smarter, but no one had ever accused the mouthpiece of being overly bright. Shawn rolled his eyes and took the dog bed.

Thora chose that moment to show Carter how much she appreciated all the treats he'd gotten her. Rushing toward him, she rose up on her hind legs, putting her big paws on his chest and knocking him right off his feet.

Into Demyan.

Both men hit the floor and Thora barked, sounding like she was laughing as the stepped over them. She licked both their faces while they struggled to get out from under the mess they'd made.

Chicklet burst out laughing. "You boys are adorable. Can we keep them, Raif?"

"I think their Masters might object." Zovko smirked at Demyan's grumbled protest. Then Zovko's expression became serious. "Thora. Come."

The dog immediately stopped licking Carter and trotted over to sit at Zovko's side.

He smiled and patted her head. "Good, girl."

Halfway across the room, carrying his sports bag, a small rucksack, and a suit bag, Vanek stopped with his gaze fixed on Zovko and the dog. He met Shawn's eyes, then inclined his head.

Seeing the dog respond so well to her new Master, to *his*, seemed to finally give him the assurance he needed that Zovko would manage without him. Shawn thought he understood why. Yes, Chicklet was here, but she would only give Zovko what the man asked for. She'd watch him like a hawk, but she respected him too much to force him to take any assistance he didn't want.

Thora would be by Zovko's side whether he'd admit he needed her, in the same way Vanek likely was. She would provide support, affection, and likely still remembered enough of her training to know if Zovko was in any danger and alert Chicklet—or Laura, when she was home.

And no matter what he said, that was probably the root of Vanek's fear: That Zovko would be hurt, and no one would know. He'd likely seen himself as the only one who could watch the man enough to keep him safe.

"She's got him, Vanek." Shawn met Vanek in the hall, grabbing the suit bag and the rucksack so Vanek's hand would be free while he said his goodbyes. "I promise, he's gonna be fine. Now promise him we'll make him proud on the ice."

"I will." Vanek swallowed and gave Shawn a shaky smile. "Thanks for coming, man. The guys are awesome, but I'm not sure they get it. They think Raif is tough and are like, what am I worried about?"

Shawn nodded. Putting himself in Vanek's place wasn't difficult. Ian had gotten in a lot of fights, and every single time, Shawn wondered if this would be the one that ended his career. That fucked up his head so bad that he might fall asleep and not wake up.

He'd sat by Ian's side in so many hotel rooms, watching the man for any signs of concussion, waking him up every two hours on recommendation from the doctors. His throat tightened every time it took a bit longer for Ian to open his eyes.

"I get it. It's hard to be there, but not overdo the 'I need to take care of you' instinct. Just remember that, as hard as this is for you, he's the one that's dealing with his whole life changing." Shawn didn't want to be cruel, but Vanek needed someone to be straight with him. "Seeing you give up everything you love puts more pressure on him. I know you don't mean to, but sometimes, the best thing you can do is show some things won't change."

Vanek bit his bottom lip and inclined his head. "Yeah...makes sense. I'll try harder."

"That's all you can do, kid."

Heading outside to put Vanek's stuff in the car, then wait there with Carter and Demyan so the young man could have a few moments alone with his lovers, Shawn took the time to think over the advice he'd given the kid. Maybe that would be the best thing he could do for Ian while they figured out how their relationship would work.

Show him all the ways nothing had changed.

They were still best friends. Ian was still one of the most important people in his life. Hot sex wasn't worth losing that, but even if they fucked like a pair of horny teenagers, they didn't have to lose what already worked for them.

Chicklet hinting that someone else had caught Ian's attention might make that a little more difficult, but in the end, what he had to do remained the same.

He loved Ian.

No matter what came next, he always would.

Now he just had to prove it.

Chapter Thirteen

The coach must absolutely hate Ian. There was no other reason for him to sit him next to the baby of the team on the flight. The kid was a mute. Like, seriously, Ian wondered if Ladd spoke English at all. Sure, he'd heard him speak short sentences in interviews, but maybe he'd just memorized the words the PR told him to say?

Naw, he's said stupid shit that got him in trouble. He can talk just fine when he wants to.

For some reason, he didn't seem to want to talk to Ian during the two-hour flight. Or close the window cover when Ian said he really didn't want to watch them crash.

He'd laughed a little at that. Like he thought Ian was joking.

But he didn't say shit.

Fucking obnoxious little fucker, aren't you? Ian shut his eyes as Ladd pressed his face against the window, not even putting on his damn seatbelt, even though the flight attendant had reminded them to. The kid was gonna get sucked out the window or something, then Ian would feel bad for thinking he was annoying.

Thankfully, the plane landed without killing them all. Ian grabbed his bag from the overhead compartment, standing in the aisle as the team slowly made their way off the plane. He spotted Pisch a few seats ahead of him and wondered if the man was pissed that he hadn't met him for coffee. Or talked to him before the flight. He'd planned to talk to him *during* the flight, but Callahan and Coach Shero had been all moody about some of the guys showing up late and had rushed them around, not giving anyone any time to chat.

They'd made the flight, and were back on schedule, so hopefully things would be cool now. They'd go to the hotel, chill for a bit, then head to the rink for the pregame warm-up.

Except, things were never that simple. There were always fans that managed to find out where the team was staying, and the media obviously got as up close and personal every chance they got. Which meant when their bus pulled up in front of the hotel, Cam—Dominik Mason's younger brother, who worked security for the Cobras—and Cort were the first ones off, clearing the way for the team.

Callahan stood at the front of the bus, looking out then glancing back with a stiff smile. "All right, guys, you know the routine. 'No comment' is all you have to say. If they want interviews, they'll wait until we get to the Air Canada Center in a few hours. Until then, get to your rooms and get rested up."

Ian nodded, like the rest of the guys did, and made his way off the bus. There were security gates set up and even a few cops standing with Cort and Cam, keeping the crowd contained. They had a bit more trouble as the guys started walking toward the side entrance of the hotel.

"Carter! Carter I love you!"

"Max Perron! Oh my God, you're my favorite player! Please, can you sign my jersey?"

"Where's Zovko? Vanek! Vanek! Didn't he come with you?"

A few feet ahead of him, Vanek stumbled. Both Demyan and Carter slowed to steady him and Ian quickened his pace, moving up behind Vanek to lend his support and help the kid get into the hotel a little faster.

Mason held back, herding the rookies who were overwhelmed by all the attention. He had to physically pull Ladd away from a few girls the dumb kid had stopped to give autographs to. With a wild crowd like this, you didn't stop. *Ever.*

The boy had probably learned his lesson though. Ian actually felt bad when he saw the kid's pale blue dress shirt was ripped, and he had scratches on his face. Fuck, he hadn't seen a crowd this nuts in a long time.

He stood outside the door of the hotel, looking over the players that still hadn't gotten in. He hadn't seen Pisch.

Then he spotted his man, standing by the barrier with some big dude who had a firm grip on his wrist. Neither security nor the cops seemed to notice. They were distracted by the teenage girls trying to get over the barriers as Ramos passed.

Bower came off the bus last, and the crowd got even worse. Ian squeezed past Kral and Brends, ignoring Kral when the man asked him where the fuck he was going.

Pisch was speaking to the guy that was so fucking huge he was either a pro wrestler or some kind of body builder. Ian wasn't exactly small himself, but looking at the massive muscles bulging in the guy's arms, completely bared by the wife beater he wore, Ian wondered if maybe he should be spending more time at the gym.

Either way, the guy didn't scare him. Pisch was trying to twist free.

The man wasn't letting him go.

Ian latched onto the guy's thumb with one hand and his throat with the other. "Back off, pal. Or I—"

A fucking boulder cracked into Ian's jaw. Or maybe it was just the guy's fist. He wasn't sure, but he stumbled back as his head rung and blood filled his mouth. Red flashed across his vision. A firm grip on his arms stopped him from tackling the man, which he fully intended on doing once he got loose.

"Bruiser, let's get the fuck out of here." Kral shouted in his ear.

There was a big black shirt, right in his face. Cort shoved him back. "I've got this, man. Get the fuck in the hotel."

So many words, but they did nothing to dampen Ian's rage. Where was Pisch? If that man still had Pisch, he was going to fucking kill him.

"Ian, come on." A soft voice in his ear, so calm and steady, so familiar. He swallowed as he met Pisch's eyes, and the man grabbed him by the back of the neck, touching their foreheads together. "I'm fine, okay? I need to take care of you now."

Me? Ian wasn't sure what Pisch was talking about, but he let him and Kral lead him inside.

One of the trainers gestured to them, leading them to a small room past the receptionist's desk.

Mason and Ladd were already in there. Another trainer was cleaning the deep scratches on Ladd's face while Mason paced.

"Why is it so difficult for you to follow simple instructions?" Mason's dark face had a red tinge, and he looked damn mad, but when Ladd hissed in pain, he sighed and sat beside the rookie. "You're lucky that crazy chick didn't take your fucking eye out. You good, kid?"

Ladd nodded. "Yeah. Bloody hell, I've never seen them this bad."

"It's the playoffs. You never know what to expect." Mason shook his head. "Your sister is gonna have my head. I promised I'd take care of you."

The rookie's lips quirked. "She's a scary little one, isn't she?"

"You're telling me!" Mason chuckled. Then looked over at Ian. "How you doing, Bruiser?"

The trainer was poking at Ian's lip, but with the adrenalin rushing through his veins, he didn't feel much of anything. He shrugged then looked at Pisch. "Who was that guy?"

Pisch shifted his gaze away, his jaw hardening. "An old…friend. From back home. He came all this way to see me. I guess he expected me to be a lot happier than I was."

"How's your wrist?"

That got the trainer's attention. He grabbed Ian's hand and had him hold some gauze against his mouth as he gently undid the button of Pisch's light gray dress shirt to expose his wrist.

There were already dark bruises forming in the shape of the man's fingers.

"I'm going to go kill that guy now." Ian spoke as calmly as possible as he stood.

Unfortunately, Callahan came into the room right that minute. He glared at Ian, pointing at the chair.

Ian sat.

Callahan glanced over at Ladd, seemed satisfied that the rookie was in good hands, then turned to Pisch. "The cops grabbed that guy and want to know if we want to press charges. I'm trying to avoid getting White too involved. He's still on probation."

Already shaking his head, Pisch pulled his chair closer to Ian. He looked pretty calm, but the hand he placed on Ian's knee was shaking. "No. It was a misunderstanding. Please tell them to let him go."

What the fuck? Ian couldn't look away from the bruises. A misunderstanding?

"Easy, you need to be honest with me." Callahan crouched down in front of Pisch as the trainer prodded at his wrist. "Is that guy gonna be a problem?"

"No." Pisch's lips thinned. "And that's all I have to say on the matter." He turned to the trainer. "I'm fine. White's the one who needs your attention."

The trainer put a couple of small butterfly bandages on Ian's lip and told him he was good to go. Callahan took off, probably to talk to the cops. By the time they left the room, the hotel lounge was quiet and their teammates had all disappeared into their rooms.

Pisch had gotten both their room keys from Coach Shero. He handed Ian one when they reached the team's floor. Hesitated after they got off the elevator, like he wanted to say something, then turned away.

No fucking way am I leaving things like this. Ian cleared his throat. "Sh—Pisch. Can you—"

"Call me Shawn if you want, Ian." Pisch turned to face him, his lips curving up slightly. "I've fucked things up between us with all my rules. I'm not sure getting into it before the game is a good idea though. You don't need the distractions."

"You fucking disappearing on me is gonna be more of a distraction than anything." Ian's jaw throbbed, and he wondered if he should go take one of the painkillers he always kept handy. They made him tired, which wasn't a bad thing, since he needed a nap before the game anyway, but he needed to clear things with Pisch first.

With *Shawn*. He smiled, even though it hurt. Something had changed if Pisch was letting him use his first name.

"What do you want from me, Ian?" Shawn moved toward him, his eyes on Ian's lip, his brow furrowed. "Damn him for hurting you. I'm sorry."

"Why are you sorry? He did it, not you." Ian double-checked his room number. The coach had gotten one of the guys to bring his bags up. He wanted to change out of this damn suit and crash in some fresh jogging pants for a bit. But not alone. "You wanna come chill in my room?"

Shawn smiled. "Yeah, I'd like that."

A weight seemed to evaporate from Ian's chest. He led the way to his room, his eyes watering as the pain in his lip increased. Nothing he couldn't handle, but he wasn't gonna try to be tough and manage without the meds. Shawn was right. He didn't need any distractions.

Of course, Shawn was the biggest distraction of all, but one he couldn't avoid. Didn't *want* to.

If Shawn was with him, he could handle pretty much anything. That had been true for as long as he could remember.

And it meant more than he could say that at least that hadn't changed.

After getting a bottle of water for Ian from the vending machine down the hall, Shawn watched Ian take a couple of painkillers and reclined on the bed when Ian insisted he'd sleep better with Shawn close.

Focusing on Ian made it easier not to think about what had gone down outside, but once the weight of Ian's head on his arm let him know the man had fallen asleep, all he could do was lay there and let the memories play back, dragging him right into the paralyzing fear and confusion he'd felt when he saw Steve standing at the other side of the barrier.

Shock apparently wasn't the reaction Steve had expected.

"Aren't you happy to see me?" Steve reached out like he wanted to hug Shawn, then lowered his arms when Shawn stopped a few feet away. "Say something."

"What are you doing here?" Shawn ignored the fans yelling at him, only hearing noise all around as his heart hammered in his chest. The last time he'd seen Steve, the man had beaten the shit out of him with his football buddies. He'd spit in Shawn's face before walking away, laughing.

Did he really believe Shawn would forget that?

"Look, I know things ended badly between us, but that was almost thirteen years ago. I was a stupid kid. You freaked me out, and I reacted badly." Steve smiled, as though his words alone could erase what he'd done. "That's in the past. I looked you up a few months ago. Found out your team had made the playoffs and wanted to come show my support. My wife and I have tickets to tonight's game. And to a couple in Dartmouth. She's been bugging me to travel for a while, and I figured this was perfect."

Shawn planted a stiff smile on his lips. "I hope you enjoy the games. Thank you for coming."

Before he could move away, Steve grabbed his wrist. "Not so fast, pal. I want to see you tonight."

Shawn wasn't surprised. Steve had fucked chicks because that was what was expected of him, but he didn't enjoy them. He was gay. And deep in the closet. Not all gay men ever came to terms with their own needs, and he'd accepted Steve never would a long time ago.

Playing the part of a good husband must have been a struggle for Steve. Shawn almost felt bad for him, but just almost. There was something in Steve's tone that put all his instincts of self-preservation on high alert.

But he didn't want to assume the worst. So he simply nodded. "Sure. You want me to meet your wife after the game? I can do that."

"You fucking know that's not what I want from you." Steve pulled him closer to the barrier, his fingers digging into Shawn's flesh. "I fucking warned you to

keep things private, but you had to go and tell me you loved me in front of the team. I had to...damn it, if I didn't fuck you up, they would have thought I was gay."

"Fine. It's in the past. I'm not sure what you expect from me now."

"Don't make me spell it out. I can't stop thinking about you."

"That's not my problem. Let me go, Steve."

"No. Tell me you'll see me. You've got a room here. I'll come to you. We can see if we're still as good together as we used to be." *Steve's eyes filled with lust. A look that used to get Shawn hard, but did nothing for him anymore.* "I'll fuck you so good—"

Suddenly, White was there, grabbing Steve's hand and latching onto the bigger man's throat as though he didn't notice the man was big enough to swat him away like a fly. "Back off, pal. Or I—"

Steve's fist slammed into White's jaw, and White fell back. Cort had looked over just at that moment and rushed over to restrain Steve. Kral helped Shawn get Ian into the hotel. Ian seemed completely blind with rage, but he'd responded to Shawn's soft words. Moved on his command.

Laying on the bed beside Ian, staring down at his swollen bottom lip and the bruises on his jaw, Shawn's chest tightened with a painful twinge of guilt. He couldn't even be angry about Ian being violent. He would have done the same if he'd seen someone hurting his best friend. Actually, he *had* during the last game. He wasn't a fighter, but when he'd seen Ian go down, he'd been bent on revenge.

But he couldn't let Ian get involved in the fucked up history between him and Steve.

Keeping him out of it seemed easy enough during the half an hour Ian was asleep. But the second Ian's eyes opened, Shawn could see the determination in those shadowed, blue eyes. Leaving the past in the past was going to be a challenge.

"Look, I get it." Ian sat up, rubbing the sleep from his eyes, the sheet still covering half of his wide, muscular bare chest. "Maybe it's none of my business, but you're my best friend. And we both just dealt with Sahara having an abusive ex. You get why I'm worried, right?"

Comparing the situations was almost funny. But Shawn wouldn't laugh. What Sahara had gone through was too serious to be made light of. He flattened his hand on the center of Ian's chest, pushing him down and leaning over him.

"It's nothing like that, Ian. Steve and I fooled around for a bit in high school. He was on the football team. I was obsessed with him, and I was afraid to lose him, so I did something stupid and paid for it." Even thinking back on that day was embarrassing, so he tried not to, but he didn't want Ian to worry, so he had to give him something. "He wasn't abusive when we were together. He just snapped when I tried to force him to accept his sexuality. That was wrong of *me*."

"Maybe, but it's pretty fucked up that the first thing he did after not seeing you for years was hurt you." Ian took Shawn's wrist gently, stroking it with his thumb. "And you didn't look happy to see him."

"I wasn't. He is a part of my past I'd rather not remember." He didn't want to talk about Steve anymore. Maybe now was a good time to ask Ian about the new person he had in his life. But carefully. He didn't want to bring up what Chicklet had said. So he kept his question vague. "What about you? I haven't seen you in a couple days. What's new?"

Ian's brow furrowed. "I met someone."

"Yeah?"

"Yeah... She's cool. I like her." Ian frowned. "I feel bad, leaving her like I did. But I think we're good."

A woman. No surprise there. Knowing Ian had a new woman in his life, after the confrontation with Steve, who was now a married man, became a tangled mess in his head. He wasn't sure how he should feel. Once, he would have just taken it as the natural order of things. Ian enjoyed women. A lot. He might be bisexual, but he was more attracted to women than men and could live out his life, perfectly happy, with the typical one woman, one man arrangement.

The time when Shawn could walk away without fighting to keep his place in Ian's life had passed.

He stroked his hand down Ian's side, resting his hand on his hip. "I suppose it's only fair that I have to share you. Do you think she'll have a problem with how greedy I plan to be?"

"You plan on being greedy?" Ian's body responded predictably, his cock swelling beneath Shawn's wrist, but it was his tone that pleased Shawn on a whole different level. He liked the idea of Shawn claiming more of his time.

Lips sliding into a sly smile, Shawn bent down, flicking his tongue over Ian's bottom lip, careful to avoid the cut. "Would you enjoy that, boy?"

Ian's eyes narrowed, and he shifted as though to sit up, growling when Shawn held him down. "Don't call me 'boy'. It's what you call Richards. And Vanek. And all those cute little subbies you fuck."

Well now, I believe we've hit a sensitive spot. Shawn worked his hand under Ian's head, taking a fistful of his hair to jerk his head back. "Do you still want me to train you, or will that be a problem for your new girlfriend?"

"She's not my..." Ian blinked then tried to shake his head, tensing when Shawn didn't loosen his grip. His breath came out in a shallow pant. "I don't know what she is, she's just staying at my place and we fucked and she was a virgin. I can't abandon her, but I still want you, Pisch."

Damn it, Bruiser. They were going to have to discuss this strange girl suddenly rooming with his man, but not at the moment. She wasn't here. And so far, it didn't seem like she had come between them.

Focusing on training would be a much more productive use of their time.

Shawn brushed his scruffy cheek against Ian's. "If 'Shawn' is difficult for you, Ian." His lips grazed Ian's throat as he spoke. "Feel free to call me 'Sir'."

"*Fuck!*" Ian pressed his eyes shut, squirming as though he was incredibly hot and wanted to shed the layers covering him. But he didn't try to get away from Shawn. "You're not playing fair."

Shawn smirked. "I never said I would."

"This isn't supposed to turn me on so much." This time, Ian moved his head, as though testing Shawn's hold on his hair.

Leaning more weight on him, Shawn tugged a bit harder. "Why? Because you're not a 'cute little subbie'?"

"Yeah."

"But you admitted you *could* be a sub. That you would explore the possibility pleases me, but if I'm to train you, we'll have to work on how you speak to me." Damn, the way Ian relaxed under him when he mentioned being pleased was a perfectly timed green light while driving on cruise control. He made a soft sound of approval. "You're comfortable with that."

"Yes, but I don't know about calling you 'Sir'. It would feel weird." Ian's brow furrowed as Shawn rose up, nodding for him to go on when he went silent. He sighed. "I know it's a thing. Like 'boy' and 'pet' are a thing. But they don't feel like *our* thing."

"Would you be comfortable with '*Bärchen*'?" Shawn hoped he was. He liked the idea of using a special pet name for Ian, but he didn't want it to be anything the man took negatively. "It means 'little bear'."

Cheeks going red, Ian tongued his bottom lip, huffing out a laugh. "I ain't exactly little."

"No, but compared to an actual bear?" In the leather scene, White wouldn't be considered a bear at all. He had a nice amount of chest hair, but not enough to claim the title. Bringing up the community Shawn used to play in quite often would either confuse the man, or bring on more uncomfortable jealousy.

Better to leave that conversation for another day.

Ian inclined his head, shifting so his dick wasn't pressing against Shawn's hand anymore. "I like bearkin."

Close enough. Shawn smiled. "Good. And when we're in high protocol, you can call me 'Mein Herr'. It's something like 'Sir' and it can be ours."

"So when we do a scene?"

"Yes."

"Are we doing one now?"

So fucking tempting. Using the excuse of a scene could get Shawn anything he wanted from the man, but he wasn't a wanna-be Dom using the lifestyle to get his own way. Yes, he played some twisted, kinky games, but Ian needed more from him.

"We've got to be on the ice in a couple hours, so we can't do anything too heavy. But I would like to clear the air." He slid his hand down to the tie on Ian's jogging pants. His lips slanted when Ian jerked and inhaled sharply. "You told me you were fine seeing me with Richards. Were you?"

Sinking into the mattress, Ian sighed and shook his head. "No. Not when it was just the two of you."

Good boy. Undoing Ian's pants, Shawn worked his hand into his boxers, curving his hand around the thick, hot, *hard* length. "Is there a reason that bothered you more?"

"Jesus, Easy. Do we really need to talk?" Ian lifted his hips, trying to move his dick in Shawn's loose grip. He went perfectly still when Shawn released him and cupped his balls. "Oh fuck… I got it! Don't squeeze."

"We do need to talk. I'll do what I must to encourage you."

"I'm encouraged. Very, *very* encouraged." Ian panted, his dark blue eyes glazed with lust. He bit hard into his bottom lip, leaving the plump flesh red when he finally spoke. "I hated that you didn't need me. Doing stuff together is cool. Hell, you wanna get all kinds of freaky with different people? I'm down with that. But if another guy is taking my place… I don't wanna know."

"So the issue isn't about us being open?" It mustn't be, considering Ian hadn't hesitated to take a woman home with him. Shawn studied Ian's face when his gaze shifted away. "Or is that still part of the problem?"

"I'm trying not to let it be. I've been thinking it over a lot, and the idea of you ditching me because I broke your damn 'You can't keep me' rules freaks me out more than knowing you're fucking other people." The tension left Ian's body as Shawn went back to lightly stroking his dick. "Damn, that feels good."

"I always appreciate, and will reward, you being honest with me, Bärchen." He wouldn't push his man to share much more, this had to have a happy ending if he wanted to teach Ian how...*enjoyable* communicating could be. But as much as he didn't want Ian thinking about the girl, Shawn would use this opportunity to learn a little more about her. "You said your girl was a virgin. And she's still at your place?"

"Mmm." Ian moaned as Shawn ran his hand up over the swollen head of his cock. "She didn't want to go back to Chicklet's place."

Chicklet's 'trouble'. Great.

"How long have you known her?"

"Met her last night. Fuck, don't stop." Ian's fist hit the mattress when Shawn did the exact opposite of what he'd asked, languidly passing his hand up and down, keeping Ian aroused, but not letting him find the release Shawn could tell was close by the tightness of the flesh against his palm.

"Do you feel responsible for her?"

"Yes! But I don't want to talk about her! I don't want to talk about Richards, or the other people we fuck. I'm with you!" Ian's jaw hardened and his hips bucked up with the quickening motion of Shawn's hand. "Please let me come!"

The rough pleading had Shawn's own dick throbbing painfully. He bent down, impulsively pressing his lips to Ian's. Feeling his rapid breaths, tasting the sweetness of whatever sugar cereal the man had eaten, his chest tightened as Ian rose into the kiss, his lips parted.

Shuddering, Ian came and the hot spill hit Shawn's wrist. More soaked into his pants and his dress shirt. He lifted a hand to Shawn's shoulder, as though to pull him close.

His hesitation told Shawn how badly he'd fucked up. He didn't want Ian to be afraid to touch him. To be careful, yes. But not so careful he second-guessed his every move.

Rather than make a big deal about it, Shawn pulled Ian into his arms, laughing as the bigger man tried to fit snug against his side. "Ready to finish your nap?"

"Yeah, but...I'm a mess." He made a face as he rested on the wet spot on the sheets where the cum had smeared from Shawn's wrist. "I've gotta strip the sheets. And leave housekeeping a *huge* tip."

"I love how thoughtful you are, *Bärchen*." Shawn pressed his lips into Ian's hair, smiling as he let his head settle on the pillow. "But let's rest for a bit. I can deal with you being a bit dirty."

Ian snorted as his head grew heavy on Ian's shoulder. He was so quiet, Shawn was certain he'd fallen asleep. Until he cleared his throat. "You kissed me."

"Yes." Shawn had known it would mean something to Ian, but he'd crossed so many lines already, holding back anymore simply didn't make sense. He couldn't ignore that it had been a limit though. "Does that bother you?"

"No. I kissed her...I wanted her to know she wasn't being used." Ian's voice faded, as though he was slowly drifting off to sleep. "If that's all it means...that's okay. I'll take it."

It means more. So much fucking more. The lure of sleep escaped Shawn as he stared at the ceiling. He wished he hadn't asked. He didn't want what he had with Ian to be compared to a relationship with a girl who'd somehow managed to dig her claws into his man after a damn one-night stand.

Jealous much? The cruel voice in his head was laughing at him. With good reason.

If this was even half what Ian had felt when he'd walked in on Shawn and Richards...

Suffer, asshole. Shawn ground his teeth, holding Ian a little tighter, careful not to wake him. Grateful that he hadn't fucked up so badly that he'd lost the opportunity to hold the man he loved. *You deserve it.*

But he hadn't lost Ian. He'd come close, but never again.

I hope the girl doesn't mind sharing.

She'd told Ian she didn't, but Shawn found that hard to believe. He'd reserve judgment until he met her. Until he had a chance to let her in on one simple fact.

He's mine.

Chapter Fourteen

The huge loading area on the bottom floor of the Center was the perfect place for some warm up before they headed onto the ice. Ian and seven other players were bumping a soccer ball between them as they stood in a wide circle. Ian kneed the ball toward Richards, laughing when the rookie dived forward to bounce the ball off his head.

Things weren't weird with the kid, which was cool. He'd wondered for a minute when he and Shawn had first gotten here, but Richards talked to Shawn like nothing had happened. He'd been a little wary of Ian at first, but when Ian brought up the new *Avengers* movie coming out that summer, he'd relaxed and that was the end of that.

Richards wasn't hung up on Shawn. They'd had their fun, and now life could go back to normal.

Well, normal with the team anyway. Things were anything but normal between Ian and Shawn, but not in a bad way. He'd hated digging up all the uncomfortable stuff when they talked, but Shawn had made it feel good. So…well, it had been worth it. They were both in a better place. Understood one another.

He still wasn't sure how things would work with him getting serious with Shawn, while seeing how things developed with Sam, but there was no pressure. He'd been honest with both of them. A few players on the team had relationships with more than one person, and while he'd never seen that kinda life for himself, well…why not? Shawn didn't like to feel tied down. And Ian was doing everything he could to make sure he didn't.

His phone, which he'd tucked into the waistband of his snug, black Under Armour shorts, buzzed and he held up his hand so the guys wouldn't bump the ball his way. He checked the message and his face flamed as he saw the picture Sam had sent him.

She was sitting in the middle of his bed, folding laundry.

Completely naked.

Holy fuck, that girl is hot.

Someone ran into Ian's side, shoving him playfully. "Whatever has you blushing like that's gotta be good. Is Easy sending you nude photos from the locker room?"

Ian's eyes narrowed as Carter grabbed his phone. "Dude, you gotta thing for Shawn too?"

"I fucking knew it! You're calling him 'Shawn' now? Or is it 'Master'?" Carter ducked behind Demyan, who was trying to check out Ian's phone too. Then Carter made a choking sound. "Holy shit! This is my fucking sister." He slammed Ian's phone into the center of Demyan's chest. "I need brain bleach. What the *fuck*, White?"

Sam is Carter's sister? Ian's mouth went dry. He snatched his phone back before Demyan was tempted to take another look. *Shit, this is bad. Really, really bad.*

All the guys were staring at him.

He was shocked that Carter hadn't tried to punch him yet. He tucked his phone away and held up his hands. "I swear, Carter. I didn't know. I met her at Ford's bar and… I'm sorry?"

"*You're* sorry? Why the hell would *you* be sorry?" Carter paced away, then back, raking his fingers through his hair. "My brain is broken. I'm done. Tell my mom I love her. Tell Jami and Seb that I…that I will try to come back to them if I ever regain consciousness." He stopped and grinned like a crazy man as he faced Ian. "I've got a better idea. Maybe if you hit me really hard, I'll get amnesia! That would be *perfect*!"

Hit him? The kid had lost his mind.

Demyan put his hands on Carter's shoulder. "Calm the fuck down, buddy."

"Nope. Can't do it." Carter twisted away from Demyan, pointing at his jaw as he approached Ian. "Right here. Don't hold back."

Should I? Ian didn't have any siblings, but he could imagine seeing them naked would be fucked up. Not *this* bad, but if it would keep Carter from being mad at him, he'd try to help him erase the memory.

Punching him before a game wouldn't be the *best* way to accomplish that though. He looked around at the other guys. Maybe Carter just needed another image to replace the one of his sister?

"Hey, Richards, you were cool stripping?" Ian grinned when Richards gave a hesitant nod. "Get naked so Carter can picture you instead of his sister."

"Dude!" Carter slapped his hand over his face. Then laughed and looked between his fingers at the rookie. "Actually, that's not a horrible idea."

"So not happening." Richards frowned, folding his arms over his chest. "I promised someone I wouldn't do that anymore."

A few feet away, Hunt had gotten very interested in his sneakers. Vanek was on his phone, smiling as he spoke softly. Not very helpful.

The last man, the youngest member of the team, Heath Ladd, looked around at them. Then shrugged.

"I'll take one for the team." Ladd pulled his snug white tank top over his head. Tossed it aside, smirking when Hunt stared at him, lips parted. "See something you like, goalie?"

Hunt snapped his mouth shut, gave Ladd the finger, then spun around as Ladd started to work his shorts down his hips.

He slammed right into Mason, whose eyes were blazing with rage.

"What the fuck is going on here?" Mason grabbed Ladd's shirt off the floor and tossed it to him, turning to Carter as though he knew the mouthpiece had to be responsible for the insanity. "If this is some twisted hazing ritual, I will fucking report you to team management. This boy is my responsibility. Whatever games you're playing, keep him out of it."

"I'm not…I didn't…I just…" Carter pressed his lips together, his face paling as his gaze fell on someone just past Mason.

Ramos.

Things had just gotten so much worse.

And it was all Ian's fault. He swallowed as Ramos folded his arms over his chest, his eyes narrowed.

Ian could just imagine how Carter felt. If Shawn had looked at him like that, he'd feel like dirt. He'd always liked when Shawn was happy with him, but now that they were exploring the lifestyle, it meant even more.

He cleared his throat. "Look, Carter wasn't doing anything—well, the asshole shouldn't have taken my phone." He gave Carter a pointed look. The man wasn't completely innocent. "But he saw his sister naked. And he don't hate me, which is cool. So I was trying to help him."

"At which point did Ladd getting naked come in?" Mason stood close to Ladd's side, like he needed to protect the kid.

Ian lifted his shoulders. "Well…Richards wouldn't take his clothes off. Ladd was being helpful?"

"For fuck's sakes." Mason groaned and shook his head. He put a hand on Ladd's shoulder. "They are a very bad influence. Keep your distance."

Ladd pulled his shirt back on. Then he glanced over his shoulder at Mason. "I appreciate all you've done, mate. I really do. But I haven't needed a father in a long time."

At that, the young rookie walked away from his mentor. Mason fisted his hands at his sides, mumbling something under his breath before following.

In the meanwhile, Carter was coming up with every possible excuse in the world to explain himself to Ramos. Repeating one in particular over and over. "Temporary brain damage. She was naked. *Naked!* And I feel dirty seeing that. Not a good dirty. My first suggestion was for White to knock me out, but he refused. He's a cruel man." Carter rubbed his eyes with his fingers. "Did I mention my sister was naked?"

"You did." Ramos's lips quirked, like he was trying very hard not to laugh. "May I ask why you took his phone?"

"Because I thought he was looking at something hot, and I'm stupid." Carter frowned at Ian. "You could have warned me."

"I didn't know she was your sister." Damn, now Ian felt bad again. "I...umm, I didn't use her or anything. She's staying at my place and we're seeing where this goes. I didn't realize how...innocent she was."

Carter's brow furrowed. "She's at your place? I thought she was at Chicklet's."

"She was, and if I was smarter, I would have made the connection. But I didn't. And she was probably saving herself for a better guy, but...I'll treat her good."

"Saving...?" Carter shook his head. "Dude, what are you talking about?"

"Ian thinks your sister was a virgin." Shawn joined them, his lips in a hard, thin line. "Don't *ever* question how smart you are, Bruiser. Some people are manipulative, and you're too straightforward to see it. That's on them. If I had figured out the girl you were with was Carter's sister, our conversation would have been *much* different."

Ian's cheeks heated. He knew Shawn hated it when he called himself stupid, but how could he not? Carter's sister had just had a baby. One she'd let Callahan and Perron and their woman, Oriana, adopt. He hadn't remembered her name. Or paid much attention when people talked about her. It was none of his business.

Well, it *hadn't* been.

He wrapped his arms around himself, thinking back on when he'd been with Sam. On what she'd actually said. She hadn't actually claimed to be a virgin. Hadn't denied it either. She'd just wanted to be held.

To not feel used.

"She never said she was..." Damn it, this was personal. He needed to talk to Sam. Not Carter. Not the team. Not even Pisch. "Look, I didn't mean for this to blow up. Carter, I mean it. I'll be good to her. I'm glad I got to know her without knowing who she

173

was, but now that I do…it doesn't change anything. You know where she is. She's safe."

Carter moved away from Ramos, his expression the most serious Ian had ever seen it. "White, I'm not worried about her. I'm worried about *you*. You're my friend, and I don't want you getting mixed up in her mess. She…she's got a lot of issues."

"So do I." Ian could feel Shawn staring at him, and it pissed him off for some reason. He didn't want Shawn, or Carter, or anyone to think he couldn't manage on his own. Yeah, he needed to talk to Sam. Clear things up. But that was between him and her. He hadn't had a say when Shawn fucked Richards in the kitchen. He'd questioned everything about their relationship. Their friendship.

With Sam, he'd been able to forget.

Maybe she'd needed the same from him. Some time to forget all the fucked up shit.

He had no idea what would happen next.

But he wanted to find out. He wouldn't turn his back on her because of what anyone else thought. Just like he wouldn't give up on Shawn because he was 'Easy'. Because commitment was his damn kryptonite.

When the other men headed to the locker room, Shawn stayed, his expression hard, like he wanted to say more, but wasn't sure he should.

Ian decided to make it easier on him. "I love you, but we're open, right? I don't get a say about who you play with. And I've accepted that."

"Ian—"

"No, let me finish. You're in control when I'm with you. That's what we've agreed on. What I need." He took a deep breath. He didn't like closing off a part of his life from Shawn, but he had to. He couldn't deal with Shawn doing his thing without having something of his own. "As a friend, if I can still talk to you, that would be great. But if you can't separate being my Dom, and the man I can talk to without judgment, without restrictions, then consider this a hard limit. She's in my life. You don't get a say."

Shawn dropped his gaze. His jaw tensed slightly then he nodded. "You can talk to me about anything. That will *never* change."

"Good." The vise Ian had felt clamped around his chest, tightening more and more as he tried to figure out how to make this work, just snapped, relieving all the pressure. He ran a hand through his hair, grateful Shawn was still here for him. That he still had his best friend. "I kinda wish Carter had punched me. How fucked up is it that the first naughty picture she sends me, her brother sees?"

"That is messed up." Shawn's lips curved slightly. "Can I see?"

His first instinct was to say 'yes', but Sam might get pissed if the pic she sent got passed around.

"I'll ask if she minds." He needed to reply anyway, so she didn't wonder if he'd gotten the picture.

He pulled out his phone.

Ian: I guess there are clean towels now? Lol

A long pause. Then her writing back.

Sam: That's all you've got to say? I'm insulted.

Ian: Sorry, was trying to keep things light. Your brother saw the picture.

Sam: Luke???

Ian: Yeah

Nothing for a very long time. Ian chewed the inside of his cheek, hoping she hadn't decided to pack up and leave.

Maybe he should let her know he wasn't mad?

Ian: I didn't mean for him to see... Sorry? It was HOT.

Another long pause. He felt Shawn close to him, not trying to see the texts, but somehow offering silent support, which was good.

Finally, Sam answered.

Sam: I had a baby. I get it if you hate me now. And if Luke told you I steal, I swear, I didn't take any of your stuff. I'll leave. I won't ever bother you again.

Carter hadn't said anything that bad about his sister. From what he *had* said, Ian wondered if her having had a kid was the only thing against her. Which was stupid. She was young. If she wasn't ready to raise a child, that was none of Ian's business.

It did explain why it had hurt her when they'd had sex. Callahan had mentioned his new kid not that long ago. Perron was all distracted about leaving his son. She must be going through a lot too, having given up a child.

No way would Ian let her believe he hated her.

> **Ian: I wish I had known. I would have been more careful. I don't hate you at all. Are you okay there alone? I still feel bad leaving.**

He could tell right away she was typing her reply.

> **Sam: How did I get so lucky? I love your place. I'm good. You having fun with your man? Is he the only one on the team you're fucking? Because I might get into hockey if I know who's getting it on.**

She was a very naughty girl. He wondered what she would have thought of Ladd all ready to strip.

For her brother.

Yeah...not as sexy.

> **Ian: He wants to see your picture.**
> **Sam: Show him.**

Scrolling back to the picture, Ian held out the phone for Shawn. He watched Shawn's face as the other man stared at the picture.

When Shawn handed back the phone, Ian had no idea what to make of his expression.

Or what Shawn asked him to text back to Sam before he walked away.

> **Ian: He said to tell you: Very nice. Challenge accepted. Not sure what he's talking about, but I gotta go. Game's about to start.**

A brief pause. Then a smiley face.

> **Sam: This is gonna be fun.**

Oh good, she's not pissed. Ian grinned, typing in his last text for the night.

> **Ian: Heading onto the ice. Thanks for doing the laundry. Do I get more pics?**
> **Sam: That and more. Give your man a kiss for me, sexy!**

Snorting, Ian headed over and pressed a light kiss on Shawn's cheek. "That's from her. I think you're going to like her. She's cute and funny and she doesn't blink at different stuff. Exactly the kind of girl that fits, right?"

"Right." Shawn's smile looked a bit tired. Maybe he hadn't gotten a good nap. Ian would have to make sure he'd get plenty of sleep tonight. But at least his smile never faded. "I look forward to meeting her, *Bärchen*. She seems to know exactly what she's getting into."

She really did, didn't she? A damn relief, right there. He walked to the locker room with Shawn, ready to play the fucking game. Out there on the ice, he always knew what was going on.

Out here? Well, he had Pisch. And now Sam.

They were both smart. And the whole 'open' thing made more sense to them than it did to him.

Which meant he had absolutely nothing to worry about.

Chapter Fifteen

Fucked. I'm fucked, game over.

Sam paced from Ian's kitchen, to his living room, then back, wondering if she could make it any cleaner. She'd never been a neat freak, and Ian didn't seem like one either, but she'd hoped coming home to a spotless house would make him happy.

Which was even more important after the texts they'd just exchanged.

That he hadn't told her to get the fuck out of his house, out of his life, freakin' shocked her. He'd actually been really nice. He was a nice guy.

Just nice? You're going to a lot of trouble for 'nice'.

Well, the fact that he was sexy, and fun, and the first guy she'd ever imagined spending more than a few hours fucking didn't hurt. Yeah, there had been other guys she'd *hoped* would want more, but deep down, she'd always known that she was just an easy lay.

With Ian, she *knew* she could be more.

But he was gonna be hard to hold on to. There was something in the tone of his messages, in the way he'd talked about the guy he was with, that told her she had some serious competition.

'Challenge accepted'.

Hell, the man hadn't even met her, and he already saw right through her. They both knew she wasn't good enough for Ian. And her attempts to snag Ian's interest were transparent as hell.

One night together and she was sending nude selfies.

Lame, much?

Worse, her *brother* had seen it. Which had made her want to curl up in a ball and disappear forever. At least she'd managed to play off light and happy, and Ian had been awesome.

There was a wet spot on the kitchen table. She grabbed a rag and scrubbed at it, well aware that her obsession with cleaning Ian's house wasn't gonna change a damn thing. He and his man might be in an open relationship, but if the guy saw her as a threat, he'd tighten the leash.

Speaking of leashes…

Taking out her phone, she went back to the website she'd come across earlier while checking out the team to see if she could find anything interesting. Hard as she tried, she couldn't get into hockey, but she would do her best to show some support. Be a good girlfriend to Ian.

He fucked you once. *You're not his girlfriend, dummy.*

Not yet, but she was staying in his damn apartment while he was gone. She had a foot—maybe even half her leg—in the door.

Anyway, the website was full of naked pictures of the guys, stories by chicks who claimed to have fucked them—some had, since they were in the pictures with different guys, naked with their tits and pussies fuzzed out, the player of the night fast asleep behind them—and blogs speculating about every aspect of the player's lives.

Most of the blogs were kinda boring. One, posted just a few days ago, listed all the reasons 'Our God Sloan' should name his new son 'Sloan Jr.'.

These chicks were obsessed, but a few of them seemed to know the men well. Beyond a brief hook up. One post had talked about going to an exclusive club where the players got kinky. The girl and her friend had taken a photo with Ian before heading in. A simple, metal sign in front of the club read 'Blades & Ice'.

Puck Goddess—the girl's blogging name—admitted she hadn't been there long, but she'd gotten an eye full. Guys from the team fucking their tied up girlfriends or wives. Whips being used. All kinds of props and toys and moaning and begging...

Sounded hot.

Sam had read some pretty kinky books, so she knew what BDSM was. If Ian had taken those girls, he must be into it, right?

No way was his man a sub. They probably shared chicks, taking turns being the man in charge.

Which meant, if she could become a good submissive, Ian would want her that much more. She was already cleaning for him. Dressing up in a cute little apron and nothing else wouldn't be too bad. She wouldn't mind being spanked when she was naughty, and being gagged and tied up, waiting on her knees for whatever erotic games he wanted to play...

She wrinkled her nose, not loving the idea of the kneeling part.

You've got standards? Now?

Swiping off the website, she dropped onto the simple gray armchair in the living room and sighed. Ian was probably used to experienced submissives. What did she really have to offer? She knew books weren't the real thing, but even the stuff that *did* seem real, she'd never done.

But maybe she knew someone that had? Someone who knew enough to give her some tips?

"My naughty, possessive angel. Do you know how much trouble you're in?"

Sam sat up and grinned. This was perfect! Chicklet had a submissive. Actually, she had *two*! She would be able to tell Sam exactly how to make Ian happy. She'd seemed pleased with Sam's choice of him, so she wouldn't mind, right?

Finding Chicklet's number on her phone, Sam pressed send. Her whole body shook with excitement as she waited for Chicklet to answer.

Only, she didn't

Damn it! Sam almost threw her phone, but checked herself. She couldn't afford to replace it. And she was supposed to be an adult. Adults didn't throw fits because nothing ever fucking went the way they planned.

She jumped as her phone rang.

"Hello?"

"Sweetie, why in the world are you calling *during* the game?" Chicklet sounded irritated.

Were the Cobras losing again? The team had some good guys, including her brother, but with the last two losses, Sam was starting to think they must suck.

"I'm sorry. I can call later."

"First period just ended, it's fine." Chicklet's tone softened. "Are you all right at White's by yourself? You know you're welcome here."

"I'm good, I just…I need your advice." Talking over the phone about this was weird. It was too personal. Sam loved the freedom of staying at Ian's place, but she was lonely already. "Would it be weird if I come over for a bit?"

"If you're not here in twenty minutes, and I have to come get you and miss part of the game, I will not be happy." Chicklet chuckled. "See you soon, honey."

The call ending got Sam moving. Chicklet was the *last* person she wanted mad at her. She seemed to kinda sorta like Sam now, and that was good. Damn essential at this point.

Within fifteen minutes, she was climbing out of a cab in front of Chicklet's house. The place didn't look that big from the outside, but she and her men and Laura had plenty of room. The house sat on the corner of the street, on the edge of downtown Dartmouth, close enough to the harbor for a good view, but not so close that the tourists got annoying.

Dartmouth was a cool place to live, but…part of her still felt like she was visiting. She could stay as long as she wanted, thanks to her mom being born in Ontario and her grandparents still living in Hamilton. She hadn't thought she had dual citizenship, but Sloan had looked into it and apparently she'd had it since she was a kid.

Which worked, since she had no idea where she'd end up. Here was as good a place as any for now.

It was a bit cold outside, but Sam hated wearing even a light coat after all the snow melted. Of course, that meant she was standing outside after ringing the doorbell, shivering in her practically transparent, loose black sweater, wearing nothing but a tank top underneath. Her leggings and her knee high Doc Martens kept her legs warm, but her tits were turning to ice under her lace bra.

She really had to start dressing better for living this close to the ocean. Was it ever gonna get warm?

The door opened, and Chicklet waved her in, shaking her head as she looked Sam over, closing the door behind her. "I can't even.. what are you wearing, girl?"

Not enough. She shrugged, hiking her chin up. "Clothes?"

"Uh huh. You brought a ripped shirt and leggings to change into after your shift at the bar? Do you need help getting new clothes?"

Sam's face blazed with humiliation. She knew her style was weird, but it suited her. Once, she would have gotten all mouthy, maybe called Chicklet old and made a smart-ass remark about *her* clothes, but that wouldn't make the woman want to help her.

Besides, Chicklet looked *damn* good, older woman or not. In her fitted jeans and a snug white Cobra's T-shirt, she was casual and well put together all at once. She seemed almost ageless, and her confidence made Sam feel like a frumpy kid.

"These are new, but...well maybe I should change up my style a bit." Sam blew a stray bit of blood red hair away from her lips. "I don't want to dress all cutesy...unless Ian's into that?"

"Ian? Oh, honey, you don't need to dress up any special way for White. He's not fussy." Chicklet grinned and put her hand on Sam's shoulder to lead her to the living room. Raif was sitting on the sofa with a massive dog sprawled beside him, his entire focus on the announcers. Well, their voices anyway. The TV was turned up very loud.

Eyes on the dog, Sam lifted her shoulders. The dog was watching her, its tail wagging, but it didn't move away from Raif.

Maybe it wouldn't attack her. She hoped not, because that dog could tear her into little pieces. She wasn't scared of dogs...exactly. Cats were just a lot easier to deal with. They didn't jump on people and lick them and bark and...

All right, fine. She just wasn't a dog person.

Chicklet looked from her to the dog, one brow lifted. "Thora won't hurt you. Do you want to pet her?"

"Do I have to?" Sam ducked her head when Chicklet rolled her eyes. Across the room, Raif stroked the dog's back, still mostly focused on the announcers, but he was frowning now. Damn it, she couldn't lose the only people willing to help her because the dog made her nervous. She chewed on her bottom lip. "Umm...she won't jump on me, will she? Because if she does, she'll break me."

Raif laughed. "No, *draga*, she won't jump on you. Come."

Oh good, he's not mad. She still didn't want to get too close to the dog, but she trusted Raif. He would control his new pet.

As she approached, Raif reached out, pulling her wrist gently until she knelt in front of the sofa, facing the dog. He lifted her hand to Thora's muzzle. The dog's fur was soft, and as Sam petted her, she didn't move at all. She panted a little, her tail still wagging.

"See? She only looks big and scary." Raif's brow furrowed. "She..."

He didn't actually know what she looked like. Chicklet or Tyler, or maybe Laura, had probably told him, but that wasn't the same.

Sam blinked fast, forcing a smile when Chicklet put a hand on her shoulder. Chicklet's expression wasn't hard to read.

Don't make this worse for him.

"She doesn't look scary at all. I'm just a wimp, but she's putting up with me anyway." She'd kept her tone level, but Raif still didn't look happy. She leaned closer to the dog, laughing as Thora licked her face. Kinda gross, but the dog was sweet and seemed to mean a lot to Raif. So she'd put up with the slobber. "I think I've been accepted."

"You have." Raif relaxed back into the sofa, smiling now. "The second period is starting in a moment. Sit with us—we can discuss your issues with White during the next intermission."

Nodding, Sam took the small spot left at the other side of the sofa, while Chicklet settled into the armchair. Both Chicklet and Raif were very focused on the game. Sam tried to follow what was going on, but other than the game being tied at one, she wasn't sure if the team was doing well.

She winced when Chicklet cursed and slammed her fist on the arm of the leather chair. "Perron needs to sit the next shift. Where the fuck is his head? I've never seen his passes this sloppy."

Digging her nails in her palms, Sam tried not to consider exactly what Max Perron's problem was. He'd been forced to leave his son and was playing distracted. Even with how little she knew about the game, she could see the hesitation in his every move. Heard the guys yelling for him to keep his head up.

What if his son proved to be too much of a distraction? Started affecting the way he played to the point that he had to choose between his place on the team, and the baby?

He'd choose the baby, right?

You didn't choose him.

Wrapping her arms around herself, she tucked her feet under her butt and paid a bit more attention to the game. The name on the back of one jersey had her sitting forward and holding her breath.

Her brother was good at this hockey thing, right? The way he moved with the puck, dodging big bodies, told her he had some serious skills. She rose to her feet as he neared the goal.

"Shoot! Shoot!" She groaned when he snapped the puck across the ice. "No!"

"Yes!" Chicklet jumped up, pumping her fists in the air. "That's our boy! Raif, Tyler just scooped up a damn fine pass and tucked the puck in right behind the goalie! Cobras are leading!"

A brilliant smile split across Raif's face. "I knew he could do it."

The excitement got to the dog, and she hopped off the sofa, running between Chicklet and Raif, letting out excited little whines. She rose up on her hind legs as the intermission started and Raif stood.

"Let's get you outside to get rid of some of that energy." Raif didn't move, but Thora ran into the hall. And returned with what looked like a harness. She nudged Raif's hand with it and he took to a knee, feeling the straps and slowly working them onto the dog.

Chicklet slipped past Sam and crouched beside Raif. "Let me—"

"I can do it."

"Okay. Just let me know if you need help." Chicklet straightened, never taking her eyes off Raif, her jaw tensing as he struggled to straighten the harness. The tension left her when he finally got it on right, and Thora led him outside. She rubbed a hand over her face and dropped back into her chair. "Men can be fucking impossible. I'm lucky, I have two good ones, but you've got a rough road ahead of you. Sit and tell me all your troubles, little girl. Not sure why you're having problems with White already. The man is as straightforward as they come."

"He is. And he *was*. Which is why I'm worried." Sam felt silly laying it all out there. She'd known Ian for one night, but she really saw them building something good together. Better than anything she'd ever had before. So she told Chicklet everything. From how they'd had sex in the alley, Ian thinking she was a virgin, and what had happened when he found out she wasn't.

By the time she was finished, she expected Chicklet to be looking at her with disgust.

Instead, the older woman regarded her with intense interest. "What do you want from him, Sam? Don't think about it, just answer."

"I want to be the kind of girl he needs. He's amazing and sweet, and I don't think I deserve the chance I'm getting with him. But I have it, and I want to see if we can keep this going." She took a deep breath. "He's into the same stuff you and Laura and Raif and Tyler are, right? Can you teach me how to be submissive for him?"

Chicklet shook her head.

And all Sam's crazy dreams turned to dust.

I should have known. Chicklet doesn't really wanna help. She likes Ian, and I was only good for a little bit. Not long term.

"I don't miss being so young that everything is the end of the world. Sam, look at me." Chicklet braced her hands on her knees, holding Sam's gaze as she leaned forward. "I don't think there's anything submissive about you. You could probably play at being one for a bit, for the right Dom, but you wouldn't get much out of it."

"But I want to try!"

"Because you think that's what he needs. Which is sweet, but all wrong. White isn't a Dom. If he and Pischlar are getting serious, he's likely exploring the scene as a submissive himself. He might *think* he'll eventually become a Dom, but I imagine he'll be very comfortable giving up control." Chicklet's brow furrowed. "Pisch cares about him. Maybe even loves him. But he doesn't want commitment. And I can see White needing it, eventually."

"I can give him that." Sam scowled when Chicklet's lips quirked up. "I *can*. Yes, I like flirting, but that's because I was single, so why not?"

"True. But if he needs to give up control, can you take it?"

Take him doing that with other people? She shrugged, not too worried. If he wanted to get his freak on with someone like...well, like Chicklet, or Raif, she'd be fine with that. Neither of them would try to push her out of his life.

Shawn Pischlar, the man who'd accepted her 'challenge', would.

"When he mentioned being in an open relationship, it didn't bother me. I don't need to be fooling around with all kinds of people, but it would be fun to go to some kinky parties and just like...go wild!" She could see Ian kissing other guys, and girls, completely free to take whatever pleasure he could find. While she did the same. "But Shawn doesn't like me."

"He doesn't know you. Don't worry about him for now. His relationship with White is between them. You can only work on yours." Chicklet cocked her head. "I think you missed what I was asking though. Do you think *you* could take charge? Does the idea of being in control turn you on?"

The question had her thinking back on when she'd dragged Ian into the alley. He would have waited. He'd wanted to take her somewhere better, but she'd been so worked up, she'd refused.

Her body hadn't been ready, but she had. And part of the appeal had been having a man willing to give her whatever she asked for.

"I *was* in control." Her whole body was hot, as hot as it had been in that alley. She would give anything to feel that way again. "I liked it."

"Interesting." Chicklet tapped her fingers on her chin. "You're a mess, so I would suggest you get yourself in a better place before you dive in too deep, but with some work, you might make a good Domme."

Eyes wide, Sam stared at Chicklet. "A Domme? Really?"

Chicklet laughed. "Yes. I can picture White as a sub. He'll have fun with Pisch, until Pisch gets bored. He's still learning, so your inexperience might not be an issue. So long as you're willing to learn."

"I am!"

"Good. And I'm willing to teach you. If your brother isn't going to the club this weekend, I say we start there." Chicklet's eyes shone with pleasure, as though the very idea pleased her. "Most of the Dommes I've met are boring. There are some great ones out there, but locally? Mostly just chicks that think it makes them better women if they're spitting in their man's face while he's on his knees. There are two at the club that I respect. I'll introduce you to them. They'll give you some good pointers and watch over you when I can't."

Am I really doing this? Sam tried to picture the Dommes she'd seen in porn, the ones she'd read about. They were surreal. Got off treating their men like dirt. Putting them 'in their place'.

Even that had been kinda hot, but not what she wanted. She didn't want Ian kissing her boots.

But kneeling for her? Waiting for her to tell him how he could please her?

Fuck yeah!

"I see you like the idea. Good. You'll have to prove you have more control over yourself, but if you're dedicated, if this is something you need, maybe you'll lose some of those self-destructive tendencies." Chicklet glanced over at Raif as he stepped into the room. "My man likely won't mind showing you how to handle your boy."

Raif's brow shot up. He stopped in the middle of taking off Thora's harness. "Her boy?"

"White. I know he's caught your interest, and I'll be training Samantha as a Domme."

Shaking his head, Raif tried to set the harness on the table. He scowled when it hit the floor. "White has a Master."

"He has a playmate. He deserves more, and she's willing to give it to him."

"Is she?" Raif didn't sound sure. "What if he and Pischlar become more serious? Is she willing to accept another Dom? To share?"

"I don't have a problem with Shawn. He doesn't like me, but maybe we can get past that." Sam doubted it, but everything they were talking about was unconventional. If Shawn saw her making the effort to give Ian what he needed, maybe he wouldn't feel so threatened. "I want to do this. Please tell me I'm not being stupid."

"Not stupid, *draga*. Naïve." Raif returned to his spot on the sofa with Thora, just as the third period was about to begin. "Power exchange is complicated. Open relationships are even more so. You are very young. I find it hard to believe you know what you want."

"I want Ian."

"You want him now. This is exciting and new." Raif reached over Thora, feeling along Sam's arm until he found her hand. He let out a soft sigh. "I am not saying I won't help you. But I will reserve judgment until I see what this is worth to you. What *he* is worth."

That she could understand. Raif was Ian's friend. His teammate...even though he couldn't play anymore.

And she really wasn't sure how much she had to offer. She didn't want to get obsessed with hockey, like some of the chicks dating players. She didn't want to go to all the games, and talk about the game all the time, and pretend she cared if the Cobras made the playoffs.

But she *would* listen to whatever Ian wanted to talk about. Support him as much as she could.

He was the first good guy who'd ever wanted her.

And she needed to keep him.

Whatever the cost. He was worth it.

Chapter Sixteen

Justina was in *way* over her head. She wasn't sure she should be here at all.

But the fact that Sahara had included her in the frantic 'Please help me!' text had her determined to figure out a way to be useful.

She just wasn't sure she had the experience to deal with a raging teen and a toddler on his worst behavior, taking cues from his big sister.

The apartment Sahara was 'kinda' sharing with Dominik Mason, her boyfriend, was a mess. There was food everywhere. And apparently the place hadn't looked like this when Mason left, so Sahara was freaking out.

She *needed* everything to be perfect when he came home. She'd told him she could manage his two new wards, the siblings of a rookie he'd be watching over on the road. A rookie the coach had decided he should mentor.

Heath Ladd, who had a sister who'd just hit her teens, and a brother who rarely spoke to anyone. Bran was adorable. Looked like a tiny version of his brother.

And loved his brother very much. Apparently, he'd done all right without his brother for almost a year. But now that they'd reconnected, the poor little boy couldn't accept that he wouldn't see his big brother for days.

He wouldn't eat. He threw anything Sahara put in from of him. And his big sister, Kimber, wasn't helping.

When Justina had shown up with Jami, Akira, and Ford, Sahara and Kimber had been in the middle of a screaming match. If Bran refused to eat, Kimber wouldn't either. And it was apparently Sahara's fault. She couldn't make the right food. She was trying too hard, but not enough. And, by the way, she wasn't their mother.

Within seconds of walking down the hall to the apartment, Justina just wanted to give Sahara a big hug. Kimber might be going through a rough time, but the things she'd said to Sahara?

She wasn't being fair.

Teenage girls weren't 'fair' though. But maybe an intervention would help. Kimber had gone quiet when they'd stepped into the apartment. Then she'd disappeared into her room.

The consensus was to give her a few minutes. Justina and Akira started cleaning while Jami made Sahara sit and talk with her at the dining room table.

Ford went to the living room to get Bran to calm down.

So far, it didn't seem like he was having much luck. Justina used a rag to scoop a pile of spaghetti off the kitchen table, listening to Bran sob as Ford held him, speaking softly.

"I know, buddy. You miss your brother." From where the table was set up, Justina could see Ford on the sofa with Bran. "Do you want to watch a bit of the game? Last time I checked, our boys are winning. Heath almost scored!"

Bran sniffled. Then started crying again.

"Yeah, that doesn't help right now. You're really tired. Wrap your arms around my neck. Let's walk for a bit." Ford held Bran close, walking down the hall, leaving the game on as background noise. "You had a nanny before, right? Did she help you sleep?"

Bran shook his head, his bottom lip quivering as he looked over at Justina and Akira cleaning the kitchen.

"I bad. Made a mess."

"Did you eat at all?" Ford frowned when Bran shook his head again. "Are you hungry?"

"No! I want Heath! I want Dominik! Tell them! Tell them!" Bran's voice pitched to an ear shattering level. "Come home! They come home!"

"They can't tonight, buddy. But they will soon."

The little boy screamed and shook as he began to sob.

Ford rubbed his back as he paced up and down the hall. "I know. It's hard when you have to let someone go. When you need them with you, but know you can't have them."

Akira set down her rag and looked over at Ford. She didn't say a word, but Justina could see how sad she was. Ford was missing someone too, and Akira wanted to help him.

But she couldn't. Any more than Ford could help Bran.

Justina bit her bottom lip. She'd seen her own little brother like this. They'd had babysitters, but mostly had just hung out, not doing anything special when either Justina or Chris had been upset.

Ford was trying. Akira had a good man.

But maybe Justina could give him some ideas. Stuff that had worked for her brother.

She approached Ford, holding her arms out. "Can I try?"

Bran held tight to Ford.

Ford gave her a helpless look. "Might not sound like it, but I think he likes me holding him."

He was right. Justina hugged herself. "Okay, well, when my little brother got like this, I used to walk and sing to him. Maybe try that?"

"That's a good idea." Ford continued to walk up and down the hall. "Would you like that, kid? I don't know any good songs, but people seem to like my singing. Want me to try one I know?"

The little boy sniffled and buried his face in Ford's neck.

And Ford began to sing softly. At first, Justina didn't recognize the song, though it sounded familiar. Ford had a really nice voice, and she couldn't move as she listened to him. When he reached the chorus, she knew the song.

Mirrors, by Justin Timberlake. But slower, with deeper notes, giving the song a whole different feel. Bran calmed, listening to Ford.

He relaxed in Ford's arms and started sucking his thumb. Then drifted off to sleep.

Warmth at her side had Justina glancing over. Akira rested her head on her shoulder.

"It's getting very difficult to convince myself not to give him a dozen babies." Akira let out a happy sigh. "Damn, I love that man."

Justina grinned and watched Ford carry Bran to his room. "You're a lucky girl."

"You'll find someone, sweetie. I still think you should spend some time with Heath Ladd. He seems like a nice young man."

"Are you still trying to convince me not to go to the club?"

"If you're going there with any intention of spending time with Pisch? Absolutely." Akira folded her arms over her small breasts, ignoring the heavy sigh Jami let out as she joined them. "If you're into older guys, there's always Hunt."

"Who is what, a year older than her? Besides, he's too moody." Jami put on some coffee, sitting up on the counter and studying Justina thoughtfully as she sat at the table. "There's always Cam."

Sahara came into the kitchen, shaking her head and nudging Jami off the counter. "Cam is currently dating three different girls. We are not letting Justina become the forth."

"You, of all people, know Pisch won't get serious with anyone." Akira frowned at Sahara. "Why aren't you on my side on this?"

"Because Pisch has done a lot for me. He's a good man." Sahara looked around the now clean kitchen and smiled. "I appreciate this so much, you guys. Thank you for coming to the rescue."

"You're changing the subject."

"Yes, I am. I think Justina's smart enough to make her own decisions. And I think you're too set on people aiming for perfect relationships, because you're in one now." Sahara pulled out the chair beside Akira. "You were with Dominik for a bit, and you knew it was just for training."

Biting her bottom lip, Justina looked from one girl to the other. She couldn't believe they could discuss all this so casually. Wasn't it weird to talk about guys they'd both been with?

Akira's cheeks reddened. "That's different. I was never in love with him."

"But I *was* in love with Ford." Jami began pouring the coffee, carrying the cups to the table, two at a time. "Of course, that was a bad time, but it was an experience. I think that's what Sahara's getting at. Whether Justina goes to the club and hits it off with Pisch, or Hunt, or whoever, it's an experience she wants to have."

"Ugh, fine! So long as he doesn't break your heart." Akira gave Justina a fiercely protective look. "Then I'll have to hurt him."

Steady footsteps sounded in the hall. Ford stood in the doorway, a slanted smile on his lips. "Who we hurting, Shorty? Should I get my sisters to set aside some bail money?"

Hopping up off her chair, Akira slid up to Ford and hugged him tight.

Sahara giggled, leaning close to Justina. "How much you want to bet she's pregnant within the next month?"

Jami's coffee mug hit the table hard. "Shit. I'm gonna be sick."

Because of all the sappiness? Justina stood, watching with concern as Jami dashed across the room and disappeared into the hall. She clearly *was* going to be—was being—sick.

Ford sighed and went to pour himself a cup of coffee. "Well, this should be interesting."

Both Akira and Sahara had gone after Jami, so Justina sipped her coffee, not sure what to say to Ford's comment. She didn't know him well, but after seeing him with Bran, she thought he was kinda awesome.

He was dating Akira and had been with Jami. She was curious about the history of the different people connected to the team. But asking a man she hardly knew for details on her new friends didn't seem right.

Actually, there was nothing she could say that wouldn't seem out of line. The girls would tell her what she needed to know.

Which meant all she could do was sit here, feeling out of place.

Taking Jami's abandoned seat, Ford smiled at her, looking totally relaxed. "It's nice to see you hanging out with my girl. I heard some of the trouble you had with the old manager. My sister speaks very highly of you."

"Which one?" Probably Silver. *Obviously* Silver. Justina shook her head. "Never mind. I'm sorry, I'm not very good at conversation."

"You're doing just fine, kid. Silver's very invested in the Ice Girls, and she sees you as the future of the squad. Do you think you'll be with us for a few years?" He chuckled when she stared at him, nodding silently. "Good. You'll likely be the captain eventually, but I'm hoping to have a few of the girls become part of the organization after they retire. If you're interested in a position, I could help you take the classes you'd need. We need media relations, chorographers, trainers… I'm thinking it would be good to set up a scholarship."

"I would *love* to be involved. I was hoping to help with Akira's school when she sets it up, but I could do both. I'd be interested in being a trainer. Working with the girls…" She couldn't believe Ford Delgado, the man who was in charge of the whole Cobra Ice Girls team, was considering her to work with them long term. "Just tell me what I need to do."

"Exactly what you've been doing. I'll have an application for you to fill out for the scholarship, but you have three letters of recommendation already. I just wanted to make sure you were interested." Ford looked up as Kimber slipped into the kitchen. "Hey, you."

Kimber wrung her hands, looking from Justina to Ford, her bright pink hair hiding most of her face. "Is Jami going to be okay?"

"I think so." Ford stood and went to the fridge, calling out over his shoulder. "Hungry?"

"A little." Kimber hovered close to Justina. Then burst into tears. "I'm sorry for being a miserable bitch! Couldn't be bothered just telling Sahara I miss my brother and Dominik. You can tell me to piss off if you want. I deserve it."

The girl had a very thick Australian accent. One that made her words hard to understand, but Justina could tell she was very upset. So she stood and pulled Kimber into a gentle hug.

"We all get it. You've been through a lot, and you had a bad day. Let Ford make you something to eat and sit with me. I'm new to all this too." Justina tugged a chair closer to hers then used her sleeve to dry Kimber's tears as they sat, facing one another. "Do you take care of your brother a lot? I used to take care of mine all the time, and then I'd get so mad when no one else understood why I was stressed. Kids are hard!"

"Right? They are!" Kimber sniffed, muttering thanks when Ford handed her a napkin. "I used to have to take care of him on my own. Sahara helps a lot now, but...well, I was worried because he wasn't eating. And she couldn't fix it. But that's not her fault."

"You're right. And you need to take it easy on her. But I'm sure she understands."

"I hope so."

"She does. Now come on, let's go watch the rest of the game. The boys were doing pretty good when I was watching at home. I bet your brother scored!" Justina put her arm over Kimber's shoulders as they headed for the living room. "I know it's not the same as being there, but if they win this game, they'll be playing here on Sunday. And we can see them up close!"

"They better win." Kimber sat at her side on the sofa, groaning when Justina put the game on and they both saw the score. The Cobras were tied at two. With five minutes left. "Bloody hell, this doesn't look good."

"Five minutes is plenty of time for them to close the deal."

Kimber shot her an amused look. "Guess they could give it a crack."

When Ladd hit the ice, Kimber sat forward. She grabbed Justina's hand when he took a hard check into the boards. Then covered her eyes when he spit a mouthful of blood onto the ice.

Ford stopped in the middle of the room, his jaw tense.

"Move!" Both Justina and Kimber yelled.

Shifting out of the way, Ford set the bowl of Spagetti-Os on the table for Kimber.

On screen, from out of nowhere, Pischlar nailed the player who'd blindsided Ladd. A legal check, but the other player didn't take it well. He rammed the butt of his stick into Pischlar's jaw.

Another Cobra, #5, abandoned the play, dropping his gloves and grabbing the big Leaf. The challenge was accepted, and both men started swinging. The fight ended when the Leaf player dropped to the ice, looking dazed after the last punch.

"Fuckin' A!" Kimber bounced in her seat. "That man, White? He's bloody fine. The things I would do to him…"

Justina snorted as Ford stared at Kimber like she'd just sprouted a tail and horns.

"Watch your language, Kimber." Sahara came to stand beside the sofa, frowning at Kimber. "Dominik warned you you'd lose your laptop for a week if he heard you speak like that again."

The young girl pouted. "He ain't even here, mate."

"Maybe not, but I am, and I'd appreciate if you wouldn't swear."

Paying no attention to either of them anymore, Ford moved up to the edge of the sofa, leaning forward. Justina caught the play that was exciting him.

Vanek was on a breakaway. He moved so fast, neither his own team, nor the Leafs, could keep up with him. He feinted to the left. The goalie came out to meet him. Vanek lifted the puck to the right, momentum sending him flying over the goalie's leg as he tried to avoid the netminder.

He slid right into the boards.

The goal light went off.

"Fuck yes!" Ford jumped up. He pointed at the TV. "Fucking finish this, you fucking sons of a bitches! Show my fucking man his team ain't got shit on us!"

On her feet beside Ford, Justina laughed as he turned to hug her, and Sahara stuttered, looking torn between cheering herself, or giving Ford hell for using *all* the swear words.

Kimber was giggling, squeezing in to be part of the hug.

"He's not interested in hockey," Jami said from the doorway, still a bit pale, but smiling as she nudged Akira with her elbow. "Not his thing at all."

Akira smirked. "I've noticed."

Plunking back down on the sofa with Kimber, Justina grinned. Coming here had turned out to be a great idea after all. She'd managed to be helpful and had fun hanging out with everyone. She actually felt like part of the group for once.

So she didn't hesitate to add her own lighthearted remark. "I take it 'his man' isn't a fan of the team?"

"*Our* man is a Detroit fan."

"Ah." Justina wrinkled her nose. "And you haven't dumped him yet?"

"Thank you, Justina." Ford said, distractedly.

Akira stuck out her tongue at Ford, then gave Justina a mock serious look. "Don't encourage him."

"Shh!" Ford didn't sit back down as the game neared the end. When the Cobras lost the lead with seconds left, he threw his arms into the air. "Are you fucking kidding me? Tell me they're fucking kidding me? They *had* this!"

Halfway through his rant, Justina covered Kimber's ears. Pointless, but it made the kid smile. And Sahara looked a bit less likely to walk over and punch Ford in the nose.

Folding her arms over her chest, Akira tapped her foot. Then cleared her throat. "Ford, the goal is under review."

"What?" Ford moved closer to the TV.

Justina stood, holding her breath.

Shero, the team's head coach, had used the Coach's challenge. The refs stood by the timekeeper's bench as the goal was called in. A replay began well before the goal, showing something none of them had noticed.

The Leafs had gone into the attacking zone ahead of the puck.

Offside.

It seemed to take forever, but the ref finally made the announcement.

"No goal."

They all cheered. The fans in the Air Canada Center were booing. The Leaf's coach looked pissed.

The game resumed, and the Cobras finished with a win. If they won game four, they'd tie the series.

"You can all come back here to watch the next game," Sahara said, hugging Akira then Ford, before they headed out. "Thank you so much for everything. I think Kimber enjoyed your company. I know I did."

"Any time, sweetie." Ford glanced over at Jami and Justina. "Do you ladies need a lift home?"

Jami nodded. "Yes, please. I need to take Bear for a walk before bed."

"You should bring him next time. Then you can spend the night." Sahara turned to Justina. "You're welcome to stay."

Before Justina even had a chance to consider anything, Kimber was grabbing her hand and jumping up and down excitedly.

"Please say you'll stay! We can stay up late watching movies. Bran tires Sahara out, and I know she wants to go to bed, but I can't bloody well sleep after that!" Kimber gave Justina the sweetest smile. "Please?"

Sahara did look tired. Maybe keeping Kimber busy would give her a chance to relax? Justina liked Kimber, and she wasn't sure she'd be able to sleep either. Going back to her parents to sit up all night, alone in her basement room, wasn't very appealing, considering the alternative.

She met Sahara's eyes. "Are you sure?"

"I wouldn't have asked otherwise, silly!" Sahara laughed. "I'll get you some pjs. Kimber, I don't mind you watching *one* movie, but go get changed and brush your teeth first."

Goodbyes finished, the house became quiet. Justina changed into the pjs Sahara lent her, simple pink pants with hearts and a pink tank top, and joined Kimber in the living room.

Sahara came to sit with them for a bit while they watched *Pirates of the Caribbean*, but stepped out quietly when Bran began to fuss.

Half asleep by her side, Kimber tipped her head up, a wistful smile on her lips. "Is it weird that things feel *too* good? Like, that scares me more. I don't know what to expect."

Poor kid. Justina gave Kimber a little squeeze and kissed her hair. "Not at all. You've had a rough go of it. But no one *ever* knows what to expect. The way I see it, if you have a good day, then it's yours to keep. No matter what happens after, that day is all yours."

"I haven't had many of those." Kimber's brow furrowed slightly. "Well, lately, I've had more I guess."

"You guess?"

"No, I know. But it's so much worse when you're not ready for the next bad thing." Kimber sighed. "I know that sounds stupid. I just like being prepared."

Justina shook her head. She understood exactly what the girl was going through. In high school, when kids had picked on her, she'd gone home miserable, then headed back, feeling sick because she expected more of the same. It was easy to say 'appreciate every moment', but when the good moments were rare, all you could do was keep fighting. Keep seeing everything as a fight you had to win.

"It doesn't sound stupid. And you have every right not to trust that this is gonna last." Put that way, Justina couldn't help but look at her own situation. She had friends now. Had so much going for her. But what if she lost it all? Would she manage as well as she had before on her own?

Sure you will. You learned to be enough, to not need anyone. You won't forget.

But Kimber needed to learn a bit of trust. She was too young to lose faith that anyone would take care of her. She had Sahara and Dominik. Her brother. And so many people who would always put her first.

She told Kimber as much.

"Should I trust them, Justina?"

"Have they earned your trust?"

"Yes."

Smiling, Justina rubbed the girl's shoulder. "Then you've answered your own question. Being prepared is good, but you have to give people a chance. No more or less than they deserve."

"That sounds perfect." Kimber snuggled up to her side with her eyes closed. "Are you giving them a chance too?"

Not even hesitating, Justina nodded. "Yes."

"Good. I like the idea of you sticking around." Kimber giggled. "You're one of my people."

Kimber fell asleep, but for the longest time, Justina couldn't. She found herself doing the same thing the teen had done. Wondering if this was too good to be true.

But then she took her own advice and let herself relax. Tomorrow might be uncertain, but for now, one thing was true.

She really did belong.

Chapter Seventeen

Tying up the series in game four should have put Shawn in a good mood. And it had, until the team headed back to the hotel and White decided he wasn't interested in going out with the team for celebratory drinks. Or back to Shawn's room for a different kind of celebration.

Within seconds of hitting the locker room, White had pulled out his phone and whatever he saw had him calling the new girl. He'd spent the night alone in his room, likely having phone sex or sending her dick pics, because apparently, that was his new thing.

Shawn wasn't sure whether he should be disgusted or concerned. What the hell was it with this chick? Did her pussy taste like bacon? Did she have some lust inducing super power?

Must I ask again? Are you jealous?

Fuck yes! If White was choosing an erotic phone call over a real life blowjob, Shawn must be losing his touch.

He'll always choose a woman over you.

Gritting his teeth, Shawn walked into Blades & Ice, pleased to see the busy Saturday night crowd. He'd killed some time today shopping for some new leather pants and found a pair with lacing up the sides that made his ass look fucking fantastic. The boots he'd splurged on made the outfit though. Knee high, combat style, and a man could never have enough sexy boots.

Not having White along to tell him otherwise had sucked though. He might say he hated shopping, but he'd always tagged along, grinning despite the grumbling, letting Shawn bully him into getting new shoes and a few suits.

You could have invited him. Would have been fun. You, him, and his new girlfriend.

Right. The three of them could probably have crammed in the dressing room together for a wild, risky, quickie. Shawn didn't mind sharing, right?

Fuck that.

He wouldn't have any trouble finding someone to play with tonight. And fuck if he would feel the least bit guilty about it. White had been so distracted the last time they spoke, Shawn wasn't even sure he'd see the man until the game tomorrow. Sam wanted to spend time with him. Sam missed him. Sam was so cute and sweet and White was sure his grandmother would love to meet her.

Fuck, I hate that bitch.

Sam. Not White's grandmother. He would meet the older woman this summer when he went with White for a visit. And since she'd done a great job raising the man, she was probably a lovely lady.

But Sam…something about her irked Shawn. He wasn't sure if it was all the stories he'd heard—and he'd heard a few over the past couple days—or just how completely enamored White was with her.

That her cutting between him and White, leading to him distancing himself and thinking of the man as 'White' instead of 'Ian' again, pissed him off even more. Of course, he knew he couldn't lay all the blame for that at her feet, but she deserved at least some.

You're acting like a sulky toddler, forced to share his toys. You're the one who wanted things open. Deal with it.

Open, yes. But he had a bad feeling a woman like Sam could easily slam that door in his face. He had no doubt White was bisexual, but he was more comfortable with women. He could probably live out his life, perfectly happy, with one.

A life Shawn had wanted for him.

Still did.

But *Sam* wouldn't be that woman. She was all the things White wasn't. A schemer. A liar. Someone who used others to get everything she wanted.

The last he'd learned from Vanek, who'd been all too willing to tell him *exactly* what he thought of Carter's little sister. Apparently, she'd come on to Zovko. After being kicked out of the home of the assistant coach—who was adopting her baby with Perron and his wife, Oriana—for kissing Callahan.

White didn't know any of this. And at this point, even if he found out, he probably wouldn't care. He tended to see the best in everyone. Until they proved him wrong.

Sometimes, more than once.

Which meant Sam would have plenty of chances. And the opportunity to do some real damage.

And there wasn't much Shawn could do to stop her.

A chair pulled up beside where he sat at the bar. He glanced over, forcing a smile when he saw Demyan. Unlike Shawn in all his black leather and silk, Demyan was dressed casually in blue jeans and a light blue sleeveless shirt. Still sexy as hell, his golden blond hair tussled in that constant just-been-fucked style he had.

He's taken, Easy. Very, very taken.

Smart of Pearce and Becky to nail the boy down. Unfortunate, because he'd be fun to play with for a few hours. Shawn would forget how damn alone he was, slamming balls deep into that tight ass.

Find yourself another piece of ass before you do something stupid, man.

Right. Any ass will do, he was 'Easy'.

Which wasn't as appealing as it used to be.

Demyan motioned Ford over, his expression very serious. "I think we need to get the man a drink. Or five. I've never seen him scowling this much."

Ford immediately came over with a bottle of rum.

For some reason, one look at the bottle stole all the color from Demyan's face. He sat back. Started to stand.

Shawn caught his wrist, recognizing a trigger. He wasn't sure what it was, but he met Ford's eyes. "How about some tequila?"

Eyes shadowed with concern, Ford stashed the bottle and grabbed the tequila, pouring three shots and laying out a small plate of lemon slices. "You okay, Scott?"

"Yeah. I'm good." Despite his words, Demyan was trembling. "Talk about something. *Anything*."

"Do you want me to get Pearce or Becky?" Ford leaned over the bar, hesitating, then putting his hand over Demyan's other wrist. "Or your boys?"

Chuckling, Demyan shook his head and pressed his eyes shut, his whole body trembling like he was chilled to the bone. "No. Pearce is being all helpful with 'training'. And we couldn't get a babysitter, so Becky stayed home. We were gonna stay too, but she insisted."

"So you're here to have fun, right?" Ford looked at Shawn as though certain Shawn would come up with a solution.

Unfortunately, Shawn didn't know enough about Demyan's past to be very helpful. He knew how he'd handle a sub hitting a trigger, but…

But nothing. Demyan might not be a sub, but a trigger was a trigger.

He moved his hand down to squeeze the other man's. "Have you spoken to a professional about this? Don't tell us more than you're comfortable with, but I need to know that to help you."

Demyan's lips thinned. "Yes. And I don't need help."

"Scott." Shawn brought his hand up to the other man's jaw, turning his head until they faced one another. "What did he suggest you do in this situation?"

Chewing at his bottom lip, Demyan rolled his shoulders. "She…she has these steps. She calls it a panic attack, but it's not that. Like, I'm not freaking out, I'm just…"

"What did she tell you to do?"

"Acknowledge, wait, do something. Repeat. And end." Demyan shook his head. "We tell the girls something like that in the self-defense courses. There's some therapy worked in. Damn it, I thought I was better."

"What was the trigger?" Shawn was pretty sure he knew, but the 'acknowledge' meant Demyan had to accept it himself.

And he did. He swallowed hard. "The rum."

"Got it. And I assume the 'wait' means giving yourself time before reacting. Which means now would be a good time to do something." Shawn forced a smile, even though he felt like a chunk of lead sat in the pit of his stomach. Demyan was a strong man. A good one. Whatever had happened to set him off at the mere suggestion of a drink had to be bad. "Do you want to dance?"

"With you?" Demyan looked down at their clasped hands. His palm was sweaty, and he was still shaking. He took a deep breath when Shawn inclined his head. "Sure. But don't give me the speech. I don't need it. I'm taken."

If the man could joke, he'd be fine. Shawn chuckled as he drew Demyan away from the bar and led him to the dance floor. "I'm aware."

He let go of Demyan's hand as they joined the crowd, simply moving to the heavy beat of the music. With most of his focus on Demyan, he couldn't help but notice the man's dark glare fixed on the play area. He glanced over his shoulder and lost the beat.

White had come to the club. With the girl. And they were setting up a scene.

Chicklet, of all people, was showing her how to use a flogger. While Pearce restrained White to a Saint Andrew's Cross.

A firm grip on his hips brought his attention back to Demyan. The music had changed to a song many Doms loved for the rhythm. He was pretty sure the song was by Cradle of Filth. Not a bad beat to whip someone to.

Or to dance.

But the man he was dancing with was in a bad place. Whatever Demyan felt about Pearce participating in a scene was amplified and he'd skipped over the 'wait' part of his therapy. Which was Shawn's fault.

The distraction might have helped a bit, but feeling Demyan fucking hard, pressing against him, tested his control. He didn't play with people in an exclusive relationship. And while Peace might help with training at times, or participate in the odd scene involving head games, he had limits.

Demyan never played without him and Becky.

Pulling him closer, Demyan whispered in his ear. "You're not as scary as everyone says. I'm giving you the perfect opportunity."

"Are you?" Shawn brought his hands to Demyan's hair, forcing him back just enough to speak close to his lips. Taking control and giving Demyan a taste of what he was asking for. "Then maybe you need the speech after all. Do you really want to play, Scott?"

"Zach is playing. I need him, and he's..." Demyan went still. Shook his head. "He doesn't know."

"No, He doesn't."

"I need him."

The revelation came too late. A hand settled on Shawn's shoulder, turning him roughly. Pearce's rage filled face was suddenly too close. Good intentions were irrelevant. Shawn braced himself for pain.

But it never came.

"You don't fucking get to be mad at him, Pearce. While you were having your fun, Easy was here for Demyan." Ford had somehow gotten there just in time to stop Pearce from throwing the punch. His voice cut over the throb of the music. "And so was I. You wanna hit me too?"

"What the fuck's going on Scott?" Pearce pulled away from Ford, looking confused. "We came here to chill for a bit. I'm helping a new Domme train."

"Nothing's wrong! I'm fine!" Demyan spun away from them all and went back to the bar. He downed one of the shots he'd abandoned before. Then another.

Pearce moved to follow, but Ford blocked him.

The younger man's eyes were hard. "I'm not sure what's going on, but if he's this messed up over being offered a drink, you have no business fucking leaving him to play with other people."

Perfectly still, Pearce met Ford's angry gaze. "What drink?"

"Rum."

"Fuck." Pearce shook his head. "I'm sorry." He looked over at Shawn. "I thought you were making a move. He seemed all right... This was my mistake."

'*All right*'? Shawn frowned. He considered Pearce a good Dom. Fine, Demyan wasn't a sub, but he still belonged to Pearce. Why in the world would the man leave him on his own, at the bar of all places, knowing about that particular trigger? It didn't seem like him.

"He needs you, Pearce." Shawn took a deep breath. He hated getting involved in other's drama, but he needed an idea of what had gone wrong. "You know that."

"I do." Pearce rubbed a hand over his face. "But she seemed to need me more. She's having a rough time. She's not sure her own brother even likes her. She just gave up a child. I thought I was in a position where I could help her explore who she is. To meet her needs and the needs of the man who wants to submit to her." He gave Shawn a weary smile. "I know he means something to you, but not enough for you to want to change. I'm not saying you should. But I've never seen him this happy."

The man might as well have taken a dagger and stabbed it right into Shawn's gut. Yes, Shawn had been there for Demyan. But only because he'd left his own man needing more than he could give. Their positions could be switched so easily if Sam hit a trigger with White. And Shawn could be the one being told he'd left White vulnerable. And alone.

At least Pearce and Chicklet were helping her learn. They knew White. They'd watch over him.

Somehow, in trying to retain his freedom, Shawn had given up his right to shelter White. Others had stepped up in his stead.

He had to find a way to fix that. But for now, Demyan was the one who needed a solid place to land.

And despite how fucked up things had been so far, he had one.

"He'd just come to terms with the fact that he should have told you he'd hit a trigger. Why he didn't is between you, but you should probably remind him that no matter what happens..." Shawn inhaled roughly, wishing he could say this to White. Wishing White could understand how important it was. The girl would never change it. "You're here for him."

Pearce nodded, glancing back at the scene Chicklet had continued smoothly, guiding the girl easily on her own. "I can't help you with this, Shawn. I wish I could, but I have no idea what either of you want."

"Don't worry about it. We'll figure things out." Shawn forced another smile. He was doing that a lot lately. "I wouldn't mind playing with your man, but I'd rather do it in a way that doesn't end with your fist in my face."

"He doesn't play like that." Pearce looked uncertain. His eyes narrowed as he watched Ford pour Demyan another shot. "At least, I didn't think he did."

Shawn shrugged. "He might be curious. He's watched both his best friends shared with others. Or at least heard details."

"Both involving you."

"True." This time, Shawn's smile was genuine. He didn't regret playing with either Vanek or Carter. An experience both he, and they, would remember. And their friendship hadn't been damaged. "I'm easy."

"You don't say?" Pearce chuckled, then shook his head. "I've heard rumors of a party. Will you be there?"

"Naturally." The party could be used to his advantage. But he had to find the right place. The right time. "Are you interested?"

"That depends on what you're getting out of it. I'm not stupid, Pisch. Your games are fucking twisted."

"Yes, but what's the point of a boring game? I'd love to see your boy play with his friends. And I'm not the only one. But there should be an exchange. You've played with others, but your subs have stood back, not getting involved." This was part of the lifestyle Shawn enjoyed. Reaching for the edge, pushing the limits a little. "Are you willing to let them play?"

"I might be. But I have to see how Scott's doing. I'd be with him already if he didn't seem so comfortable with Ford."

A smart move. Demyan *did* look comfortable. And across the room, Cort, who was working as a Dungeon monitor for the night, had taken notice. He was observing a fire play scene, but his attention was torn. Thankfully, he wasn't the only DM on staff. Mason stopped by his side, nudging him when he appeared too distracted.

"I don't see Ford being available to play with anyone."

Pearce followed his gaze and smirked. "Maybe not. But he should have the opportunity, no?"

Shawn knew he liked Pearce for a reason. Pearce's first time with Demyan had been at a party. Their relationship had been rocky for some time after, but they seemed to have a solid foundation with their woman. A play party might interest them.

"I've discussed organizing something with Chicklet and Raif. Maybe—"

"No." Pearce gave Shawn a sheepish smile. "There's too much history between me and Raif. Scott wouldn't be comfortable."

"You're becoming much more interesting, Mr. Pearce." Shawn took a moment to admire the other man. He was a few years older than Shawn—not obvious from looking at him. He was Shawn's height, but slightly bigger, with more muscle. He dressed conservatively, even at the club—he was wearing black shirt and pants now, though he'd ditched the tie and jacket before the training scene—but under the clean cut layers were tattoos. A body that moved with the sleek grace of a wolf on the prowl. Demyan was more Shawn's type, a little unpredictable and blatantly sexual, but he wished he'd paid more attention to Pearce when the man had been single.

Pearce shook his head, his lips curving slightly. "Don't look at me like that, man. I haven't decided whether I'd be willing to play with you at this party you're planning. We'll see where your head's at as well."

Brow lifted, Shawn laughed. "Where *my* head is at? I'm open for anything, Pearce."

"I can see that. How's that working for you, by the way?" Pearce looked back at the scene, where Chicklet was using the flogger on White. Her strikes were playful, light, and she stopped after a few to let Sam try. Pearce nodded as he turned back to Shawn. "Are you good with losing him?"

"I haven't."

"Right." Pearce shrugged as though unwilling to push the issue. He hesitated when the girl whispered something in White's ear and White burst out laughing. "One of the strangest set ups I've seen in a long time. Chicklet is keeping the training very light. Not her style, but I wouldn't have agreed to anything too intense. Sam is a hot mess. She might make a good Domme in a few years, but right now? Best to keep her in the kiddie pool."

"Which makes the idea of White playing with her pretty fucked up."

"You think?" Pearce quirked a single brow, his lips slanted. "From what I've seen, he's not ready for more."

"I disagree." Time to turn the tables. There was nothing he could do about the situation with White at the moment, short of heading over and creating all kinds of drama. Which wasn't *Shawn's* style.

Giggles from behind the bar created the perfect distraction. He grinned, tonguing his bottom lip as Ford's sweet girl, Akira, kissed one of her Ice Girls while Ford and Demyan watched.

Well now, what's going on here?

He approached the bar slowly with Pearce, nudging the man as he got an idea of the game being played. "You are aware that I won't let you hit Ford."

Pearce's lips thinned. "Fair enough. But I don't think it's me you need to worry about."

After a long, very *hot* kiss, Akira put her arm around the other girl's shoulders, letting her hide her red face against her neck as Akira shot Ford a challenging look. "Your turn."

Ford's face went crimson. "That ain't fair. He's done this before."

"So?"

"Shorty, this isn't *American Pie*."

"Chicken." Akira hopped up on a stool and shrugged. "That's fine. You lose."

Sitting up on the bar, Demyan tipped back yet another shot, his shoulders shaking with laughter. "Honey, you've got a mean streak. Leave the poor guy alone. Ford, you don't gotta—"

Ford's eyes narrowed as he jerked Demyan down by the collar of his shirt, almost pulling him right off the bar. His lips slid into a cold smile as he met Demyan's eyes. "I don't lose."

Ouch! Shawn winced as Ford slammed his lips down on Demyan's so hard, it was like he'd been challenged to an endurance test, rather than a kiss. But Demyan took over quickly, framing Ford's jaw with a hand as he whispered to him. He flicked his tongue over Ford's bottom lip, teasing him into a soft, sensual kiss that had Shawn's dick straining against his leathers.

Akira and the new girl cheered them on.

Which, naturally, gave Cort plenty of time to cut across the room, looking ready to rip Demyan limb from limb.

"Are you fucking stoned, Ford?" Cort was restrained just out of reach of the two men. Because Mason was on his fucking game.

And, quite frankly, not stupid enough to miss how quickly this situation could get out of control. Not that the girls, or Shawn and Pearce were stupid, but none of them could have stopped Cort.

Ford seemed to be in a strange mood. He curved his hand around the side of Demyan's neck, stopping the other man from pulling away. "You know I don't get stoned anymore. I'm just playing, Cort. Why? Jealous?"

Cort blinked. Then shook his head, pulling away from Mason, who'd loosened his grip when Cort had visibly calmed. "We ain't discussing this here."

"Cool." Ford bent closer to Demyan and then glanced over at Cort like he was surprised the man hadn't left yet. "Anything else?"

Rubbing a hand over his face, Cort looked from Ford to Akira—who was biting her bottom lip, guilt tightening her features—then stormed off, shoulders hunched, hands shoved in the pockets of his black jeans.

"Damn it!" Akira hesitated by her friend's side. Then met Shawn's eyes. "If you hurt her, I will kill you. Got it?"

"Me?" *How the fuck am I the bad guy here?* Shawn watched Akira rush after Cort, glanced over at Pearce, who'd motioned for Demyan to get off the bar, then focused on the sweet little thing, all on her own now.

Her big, blue eyes trapped him. Damn, she had shy and innocent written all over her. Typically red flags, but the curiosity in her level gaze had him wanting to push beyond his status quo. Hair a soft, tawny brown, in loose, long flowing waves. Taller than Akira, and just as fit, but the snug black dress showed off all her beautiful curves. The deep V neckline showed the pale swell of her breasts, which weren't enhanced by a pushup bra. Or any bra at all. Holy hell, just a glimpse of her nipples pressing against the tight material had his dick standing at attention.

You're staring, asshole.

He shifted his gaze, but her hesitant smile was no less fucking alluring. Almost as though that alone said she wanted to dive into his world, but hadn't a clue where to sample her first taste of the forbidden.

He could show her.

You shouldn't. It would be so very wrong. She needs safe. Gentle.

Easy.

I can give her easy.

He shouldn't, but something about her made him want to prove he could give her that taste without being all that she'd been cautioned to avoid.

He approached her, holding out his hand and waiting patiently as she tried to compose herself. The club was almost too much for her. Kissing Akira had probably smashed any intention she'd had to take things in slowly.

She was still blushing and ducking her head. And it was too freakin' cute.

You don't do cute.

Cute was risky. Cute was new. And untouched. And vulnerable.

But most of his rules had been broken already. Why not add another to the jumbled mess?

"I am everything they warned you about. Likely much worse. But I'm in a good mood." He winked at her. "So I'll play nice."

She put her hand in his and took a deep breath. "I hope so. Because I'm not sure I can play at all." She tugged her bottom lip between her teeth. "Akira just kissed me."

He grinned. Damn, adorable had never been this tempting. "Did you enjoy it?"

"It was...okay. Do you think it will be weird tomorrow?"

I'm going to hell. Save me a spot. He stroked the back of her hand with his thumb and she trembled. "No. Akira's probably forgotten it already. She was just having fun. Were you?"

The girl ducked her head, her cheeks flushed. "I liked watching Ford and Scott kiss. So it was worth it."

"That wasn't an answer, *Röschen.*" He touched her cheek, red as a rose, and decided that was the perfect pet name for her. If she'd allow it. But first he had to see if she even wanted to stay. "Had you discussed kissing her before you came here?"

"No!" The girl shook her head. "I came to meet you, actually."

"Oh?"

"Yeah..." She looked down at her hand, still in his. "I'm Justina."

"And I'm Shawn." He motioned for her to sit on the stool across from him. For some reason, keeping her off balance didn't appeal to him. Not yet, anyway. She wasn't ready. And he wasn't in a rush. "I've not seen much of the Ice Girls, but I think I've watched you perform."

"Cool! But...can we talk normal stuff here? I figured I either needed to be ready to do a scene or leave."

You should make her leave. With the wrong Dom, she would be in a lot of trouble.

But she wasn't with the wrong Dom.

She's with you. Even worse.

Not necessarily. As he'd mentioned, he was in a good mood. "Do you *want* to do a scene?"

The color faded from her cheeks. Not so fast that he felt the need to escort her out of the club—or get her medical attention—but enough for him to tread carefully.

"Let me re-word that. Don't assume you must do the scenes that you've seen. You're curious, yes?" He waited for her to nod. He wouldn't force her to speak. Yet. "You came with friends. And stuck close to the bar. Kissing Akira was different. But you tried it for fun."

"Yes." She took a deep breath. "Kissing isn't so bad."

Fuck me, why does it sound like kissing is something new? Back away slowly, Easy.

He ignored the paranoid voice in his head and studied her, enjoying the mix of innocence and wonder in her eyes. "Did I just witness your first kiss?"

"I'm almost twenty. Of course not." She hiked her chin up in a defensive way he took note of. Her inexperience was a sore spot. She'd probably accepted the kiss from Akira just to prove she could. But she didn't often explore her own desires just for the hell of it. Something her friend likely wouldn't have picked up on, but Shawn couldn't help notice.

He wouldn't play with an inexperienced sub—and damn, if this girl wasn't a sub, he'd retire from the game, on and off the ice—while they were trying to prove themselves to others. But she had no one to impress at the moment.

Aside from him.

"So you've kissed many men and women. That's quite remarkable for one your age. Though maybe it shouldn't be. Girls do all kinds of freaky stuff in college." The edge of his lips inched up. "Is this yet another thing you'd like to explore? All the kinkiness you've read about?"

She frowned at him and squared her shoulders, pulling away and fisting her hands at her sides. "I read a lot. I hear a lot. I'm curious, but I want to see what I'm getting into. People tried to scare me away from you. Because you're so wicked and dangerous. And I decided to see what you're all about for myself. Not because you fit what I've read in any book—you really don't." She grinned and ducked her head again in that cute way she did that made walking away impossible. "You're everything I'm told to avoid. I need to know why."

"Sometimes, when you're warned about something, you should listen."

"I know." She inhaled slowly, looking down at the hand he'd held. "Should I this time?"

"Yes." He took her hand again, needing to touch her. He should be warning her off himself. Give her the speech. Do whatever it took to scare her off. Instead, he drew her closer. "But let me give you a reason not to."

Chapter Eighteen

There was a reason for original sin. Justina imagined the first woman hadn't hesitated at all to take that bite.

Not if the devil had looked anything like Shawn Pischlar.

Good girls didn't fool around with men like him. They might like the attention, the flirting, but a good girl wanted a good, solid man. One that made promises. That would sweep them off their feet and have them thinking of a pretty picket fence future.

Maybe she wasn't the good girl everyone thought she was.

He sees more. And that's...pretty awesome.

No man had ever looked at her the way Shawn was now. Heat spread over her flesh as she took him in. All that hard muscle, not thick, but sleek and solid. His scent was a mix of leather with a hint of cinnamon. The silk of his black shirt was cool under her hands, but everything else about him was damned hot. The plug in his ear, not something she'd ever found sexy before, but on him? Totally bad-ass! His hair, shaved close to his scalp on the sides, but long enough to run her fingers through on top, gave his features a hard edge. But the dimple in his chin, his crooked smile, and his eyes...oh god, his eyes would haunt her dreams at night.

Beautiful, piercing, entrancing. Having his focus on her made any doubt that a man could want her fade away. He wanted her, but the lust in his steady gaze didn't scare her. It pulled her in, and her pulse raced as arousal stirred deep in her core.

She'd felt this way before. Over a sexy movie star, or a hot scene in a book, but never for a person within reach.

This could happen. Right now. All she had to do was say the word.

Yes. It's not hard. Say it!

Only...it was. She needed to know what she was getting into. She inhaled a slow, quiet breath to get her body to calm down a little. Her brain was all over the place, and *that* scared her.

"What exactly do you want from me, Shawn? One night? A scene?" She pressed her teeth into her bottom lip. "Doing something light would be okay, but...well, I can't have bruises or anything that will mess with my performance tomorrow."

"I'll respect any limits you have, Justina." He brushed a strand of hair from her cheek, the tender gesture making her wonder if more than her body would be sore tomorrow. "You're a virgin, aren't you?"

He just had to ask, didn't he? She considered lying. Her inexperience was already painfully obvious. He'd probably get bored with her if she kept this up, and that would be worse than the idea of him using her.

She didn't expect flowers and long walks in the park. Sweet words and romance.

The experience. Wild passion she'd never forget. That was what she needed.

But if she lied to him, he'd know. Guys had their ways of figuring that out, right? And while she didn't think he'd lose respect for her after one night of pleasure, no one appreciated dishonesty. What if he thought she'd tricked him to make him feel guilty?

Best to be straight with him from the start. She put some distance between them and folded her arms over her breasts. "Yes. But it's not a big deal."

Shawn shook his head, putting both hands on her shoulders. "It *is*. But I have a feeling you believe my opinion of you will change. A good man would probably leave you alone, but I've never been accused of being one."

That made her laugh. "Strangely enough, I was just thinking a good girl would stay far away from you."

"Ah, so you plan to be naughty?"

"A little? Maybe?" She looked around the club, surprised that no one had come to save her from herself. The club was full, with plenty of people whose good intentions would spoil all her fun. But between the loud music, the scenes, and the drama, everyone was distracted. Which left her free to make all the bad decisions she wanted to. "I'm not sure I know *how* to be naughty."

"I'm almost positive you don't." Shawn chuckled in a way that made goosebumps rise all over her skin, sliding his arm around her and brushing his fingers along her throat. "But you will."

As he led her away from the bar, she expected him to take her to one of the few empty scening areas. Instead, he took her to a small lounge area with three cushy leather sofas and a long table. He motioned for her to sit on the sofa then settled down on the edge of the table, facing her.

This was much more relaxed than she'd expected. She'd totally braced herself to be spanked within the first hour. What time was it? Maybe she still would be?

"Now that was an interesting thought. Your face hides nothing. I like that very much." Shawn smiled at her in a way that made her press her thighs together and pray wearing this short, black dress she'd borrowed from Sahara hadn't been a mistake. He glanced down and put a hand on her knee. "Tell me what you're thinking."

The room abruptly heated so much, the leather under her thighs became almost as damp as her panties. She was going to have to send this dress to the dry cleaners.

Thinking of dry cleaners was much easier than answering Shawn's question.

He didn't speak again. Simply gave her a level look, making it clear he was willing to wait as long as it took.

"Do I have to answer?"

"No. But if you don't, we'll be sitting here all night. Which is fine, if you're not comfortable discussing how fucking wet your pussy is. Or how much you'd love for me to bend you over my knees and smack that cute little ass." His lips quirked slightly when she wet her bottom lip with her tongue. "Would you rather discuss my stats? Your favorite cookies? My mother's recipe for *gaisburger marsch*?"

Oh hell. His accent was sexy, but when he spoke German? Her panties might need to be burned. "What is…that last one?"

"A kind of stew. Maybe I'll make it for you one day. My mother refused to let me leave her home until I proved I could feed myself." He winked at her. "I think she also hoped being a man who could cook would be an asset."

"She was right. But play nice. I know I can't keep you!" She grinned, but he didn't seem to find her words as funny as she'd hoped. His smile faded. She swallowed hard, reaching out to take his hand. "I won't say no if you want to cook for me one day. But…well, to answer your original question, I was fully prepared to be spanked."

His brow lifted. "When? As soon as you walked in the door?"

"Maybe?"

He laughed, shaking his head. "That's not a bad idea. I should suggest it to Richter. A spanking right after coat check might discourage those coming in here, expecting to fuck their favorite player because, well, naturally if you're kinky, you'll fuck anyone."

"They don't really think that?" Of course, she'd come here, hoping to get the attention of the hottest player on the team. She couldn't judge anyone. She wrinkled her nose. "I guess I'm not much better."

"Oh my sweet girl. If you came here intending to fuck *anyone*, I'd be shocked. Sex might have occurred to you, but not in any serious way. The spanking however? Yes, I believe you were prepared for that." He cocked his head. "Are you still? If I asked you to lay across my lap, would that frighten you?"

"No." But the fact that she didn't think twice freaked her out a little. She hardly knew him. Akira would be fuming if she could hear this conversation. But Sahara had spoken fondly of Shawn. He'd been there for her. He wasn't a bad guy. Just a player. And Justina was ready to play. "Do you want me to?"

"More than I can say. But not yet." He rose from the table, standing over her as she leaned back into the sofa, her pulse quickening as he placed one hand on the sofa beside her and the other on her cheek. "First, I need a taste."

A soft brush of lips and then…then her head was spinning. Saying she'd been kissed before might as well have been a lie. She'd never been kissed like *this*. He took everything from her with the press of his lips. Control, resistance, all ability to form words. His mouth was hot, and he teased her gently with the tip of his tongue, raking his fingers into her hair and easing her head back so he could take more.

All her senses narrowed to the feel of him tasting her. He tugged her bottom lip with his teeth, then licked it, making a soft sound of approval when her tongue touched his. He tasted like cinnamon, spicy and sweet, and she couldn't get enough. She moaned into his mouth as he lifted her off the sofa, pulling her into his lap as he sat.

Her dress rose up her thighs as she straddled him, but she didn't care. With his hands on her hips, his lips soft as she leaned into him, she couldn't think of anything beyond this moment. The way he sucked on her tongue made her ache in a way she never had. She could picture him sucking on her nipples. Almost feel his mouth between her thighs.

Only a kiss, but more dangerous than anything. Because she craved all he could give. Everything the smooth dip of his tongue, the pressure of his smooth lips, offered.

His hands cupped her ass, and she gasped, breathing hard as she lifted her head.

He leaned up to press a tender kiss to her parted lips. "Shall we see if being spanked is as hot as you've imagined?"

Yes! Her body was ready. Her mind…well, it had taken a vacation. Leaving her without the ability to answer in any way but a short nod.

"I'll accept that as a yes this time, pet. But next time, you will answer me properly. 'Yes, Sir'. Or even 'Yes, Shawn'." He helped her down over his lap, petting her back in a way that had her eyes drifting shut. She should be nervous, but instead, she was completely relaxed. Ready to take whatever he offered. "I need to know if you're overwhelmed."

"I'm not." She could sense his approval at her words. She wasn't sure how, but there was a shift in his demeanor. A lessening of the cautious tension she'd hardly noticed before. "Yes, Sir. I want to know if it's what I imagined. Or more."

"Good girl." He ran his hand over her ass, his tone low. Lulling her into a comfortable place, despite the awkward position. "The club safeword is red. Say it and I'll stop. Yellow if you want to continue, but are frightened or uncomfortable."

"I'm not."

"No, but that may change. Don't let pride get in the way. We're getting to know one another. I need to trust you to tell me what works. And what doesn't."

"That makes sense." Talking so much about embarrassing stuff was weird, but she could get used to it. Telling him the truth from the start had been a good idea. They wouldn't have come this far otherwise. And she was ready to go so much further. "I'll tell you whatever you want to know."

"Yes, you will." He massaged her ass cheeks, his thumb trailing down to her panties, lingering over the swatch of material that had grown damp with her arousal. She couldn't hide how turned on she was, but his touch chased away any need to. He pressed his thumb against her and she whimpered at the surge of pleasure. "Some women prefer bra and panties as a barrier the first time. Would you like the same?"

A barrier? She wiggled, wishing she could feel more of him. Going slowly would be smart, but she didn't want to be careful. She had him tonight. And aside from the limits she'd set, she'd go anywhere he wanted to take her.

"Use your words, Justina. I won't assume you driving me insane, pressing your sweet little pussy against me, means I can take what I please."

"But you can!" She dug her nails into his leather-clad thighs as he slid his thumb under her panties, panting as he stroked her, spreading the slickness over her clit. "Oh fuck, please just..."

"I will, sweet girl." He bent down and pressed a light kiss on the base of her spine. "Brace yourself."

His hand came down and her whole body jerked as the shocking sting of heat spread. The smack hadn't hurt, but it wasn't a playful little tap. He hadn't used his full strength either. Just enough for the dull ache to spread, lighting along her nerves, making her even more sensitive to his every touch.

Another came quickly, followed by a third.

She moaned as he slid a single finger into her. Her core tightened, and if she'd been wet before, now she was pure liquid. He withdrew his finger, slipping it back in as his hand came down on the side of her ass.

"So pretty, *Röschen*. Your ass is already as red as your cheeks. You won't have bruises, but one day..." His voice trailed off. He smacked her again, hitting both cheeks, easing another finger in as the swell of pleasure dragged her under. "You're close. Spread your thighs, and hold on tight."

Moving into position without any conscious effort, Justina braced her hands against his thigh, pressing her face between them as he dipped his fingers in deep, smacking her ass in a steady rhythm. She muffled a cry against his leg as all the sensations built up within, bursting out like a violent chemical reaction, without the destruction. Cesium in water. Liquid nitrogen. Gasoline and fire.

Her brain was trying very hard to make sense of all she felt, but her body had decided to soak it all in and ignore the random science analogies. Her bones weren't functioning, but Shawn didn't seem to notice as he pulled her into his arms and held her close.

"So beautifully responsive." Shawn kissed her cheek, smoothing her sweat-slicked hair away from her face. "Rest for a bit. I'm tempted to take you home with me, but I value my life, and I do believe, if I tried, at least one of your friends would kill me."

At first, his words were nothing but white noise. But as the delicious buzz faded, she couldn't help looking around to try to figure out what he meant.

About ten feet away, Akira stood, facing Mason, looking like she was ready to slug the big man. Cort stood at her side with a hand on her shoulder. Ford was at her other side, rubbing his chin and clearly trying very hard not to laugh.

I love that woman, but seriously? Justina sighed and tried to sit up.

Shawn shook his head and wrapped his arms around her. "Not yet, pet. You may reassure your friend after you speak to me. How do you feel?"

She smiled, resting her head on his shoulder. "*Amazing.* But don't tease me. I'd so go home with you if you asked. No one else gets to decide that for me."

His brow lifted slightly. Then he grinned. "I was only half joking, sweet girl. I rarely tease, but let your head clear before you consider anything else. Give it five minutes and going home with me will seem like a very bad idea."

Wrinkling her nose at him, she went back to watching Akira. She wished she could hear what she, or Mason, were saying. The man clearly wouldn't let Akira pass. He kept shaking his head and giving Cort an irritated look.

But Cort just shrugged, like he had no idea what he was supposed to do.

Finally, Mason motioned for Akira to wait, then approached Justina and Shawn. He met Justina's eyes, a concerned look on his face. "How are you doing, sweetie? I trust Pischlar, but you're new here, so it's natural that some will worry."

"I'm good." Justina didn't want to lift her head. Being held by Shawn was nice. Everything was nice. No reason to worry. "Shawn is awesome. Akira was so wrong about him."

One brow lifted, Mason glanced over her head at Shawn. "Was she now?"

Shawn's shoulder shifted as he rubbed her arm. "That depends on what she thinks I did to Justina. If my girl is comfortable with it, let Akira come talk to her."

"I'm comfortable." Justina giggled when Mason shook his head and gestured for Akira to join them. People were being way too serious. Why couldn't she enjoy herself without everyone freaking out?

Akira stepped right up and knelt in front of her. "I shouldn't have left you alone, honey. I'm so sorry."

"Why?"

"Because... Damn it, Justina. I don't know what he told you, but what happens tonight? That's all you'll get from him." Her eyes narrowed as Shawn sat up, still holding Justina close, but she could feel him tense. "She wouldn't have played with you if she'd known, Pisch. I'm sorry, but you don't get to use her to distract you from how fucked up things are with White."

Shawn went still. "Is that what you think I'm doing?"

"Yes."

He laughed. "Pet, go back to your men. I understand that you're protective, but you've gone too far."

Akira straightened, looking pretty tough in her leather studded bra and booty short getup. Her eyes narrowed. "I'm not the one who's gone too far. You need to leave her alone."

Okay, that's quite enough. Justina pushed off Shawn's lap and faced her friend. She loved that Akira was looking out for her, but she was tired of being so sheltered that she felt guilty about doing anything new. Unexpected. She was done letting other people decide what she could deal with.

"Akira, I love you. You're one of the best friends I've ever had, and I hope this doesn't change anything." Her eyes burned and her throat tightened. But she couldn't back down. "I'm capable of saying no. I know what I want. Shawn hasn't promised me anything, and I don't expect him to." Tears wet her lashes, and she blinked fast, hoping they wouldn't spill and embarrass her even more. "Maybe I'm stupid and innocent, but—"

"That's not what I'm saying!" Akira paled, reaching out, then letting her hands fall to her sides. "I don't want to see you hurt. You might think this is fun now, but tomorrow—"

"Tomorrow I'll still be me. I know what I want. I want to put on an amazing performance. To prove myself so one day, I can teach other girls to do what we do. That won't change because I met a hot guy." Her cheeks heated, and she was tempted to glance back at Shawn to make sure *he* didn't feel used. But she had to finish. "Maybe, one day, my plans will include a future with a man. But they don't now. There's so much I need to experience first. Is that wrong? Maybe. But it's what I want and I refuse to feel guilty about it."

"It's not wrong, Justina. But you deserve someone who will take you seriously. Who won't make you regret what you've given them in the morning." Akira sighed as Justina hugged her. "I'm sorry. I need to mind my own business."

"No you don't. I won't." Justina laughed as Akira rested her head on her shoulder. "Those two jerks giving you a hard time? Do I need to threaten them? I might not be scary on my own, but with Sahara and Jami, they might think twice."

Akira snorted. "I might take you up on that." She cleared her throat, raising her voice a little, obviously so her men would hear her. "The worst thing is they're fighting about hockey, and it's making them *both* unbearable."

Cort's jaw ticked, but he flashed Akira a tight smile. "You're absolutely right, Tiny. I shouldn't give Ford a hard time. Hell, maybe he should get on his knees and start sucking off all the players. They need all the help they can get."

"I wouldn't object to that." Shawn smirked when Akira glared at him. "I apologize. I'll behave."

Justina snickered, pretty sure she should be shocked, but not feeling it. She liked Shawn's relaxed attitude about sex. And even if he was only half joking, he'd effortlessly defused the situation.

Ford laughed and shook his head.

Rolling her eyes, Akira muttered under her breath. "Like I believe that."

"Do you feel better, Shorty?" Ford put an arm around Akira, pulling her to his side and laying a kiss on her hair. "Justina's got this. And I want to get home so we can finish our…" He made a face, as though he tasted something sour. "Discussion."

"Cort's still working for another hour."

"Well damn, completely forgot."

"You're so full of shit." Akira shrugged his arm off, turning to face both her men. "If you two don't work things out, I'm spending the night at Sahara's."

Mason, who stepped away to watch over a nearby flogging scene, glanced over, his lips slanted with amusement. "You will not. Sahara's packed up most of her apartment and put it in storage for when we get our new house. There's nowhere for you to sleep."

"Oh…"

"You may come to our place though. I hate that she's had to do so much of the packing on her own—she refuses to let me hire someone." Mason tilted his head, turning his attention to Justina. "You're more than welcome to come as well. Kimber enjoyed spending time with you."

The kid was a sweetie, and Justina loved hanging out with her, but not tonight. The girl would be sleeping by now. And Justina had plans. "Thank you, Mason. I'll stop by tomorrow sometime and help however I can."

"That would be much appreciated." Mason smiled, inclined his head to Shawn, then headed off to supervise the various scenes around the club.

Closer to the front, play seemed fairly tame. The odd snap of the whip made Justina jump—she hadn't really noticed it before, but the one Callahan was using for a demonstration was long and *loud*. The club members milling around gave him a wide berth.

A soft crackle came from an area sectioned off by a tall divider. She had no idea what was going on back there, but she suddenly wanted to see everything. The expected spanking had happened, which had been awesome. She was seriously considering going home with Shawn, which would be…

Damn, she wasn't sure, but she imagined it would be hot. If Akira hadn't gotten all over-protective, Justina might have dragged him out the door already.

Since they were still here, would it be wrong of her to explore? What was the protocol? Maybe people didn't like being watched?

Curving a hand around her hip, Shawn spoke close to her ear. "Just ask, *Röschen*."

She nibbled at the tip of her tongue. Looked over to see Akira squabbling with her men. She hoped they worked things out, but she really didn't know how to help them out anymore.

Maybe she could be a little selfish. Just this once.

"Do you know if anyone would mind me checking out some of the scenes? I don't want to seem like a voyeur, but—"

"Voyeurism is one of the many kinks you'll find here, sweetie. And many of the players are exhibitionists. They'll enjoy you watching." He took her hand, guiding her away from the lounge area. "What are you most curious about?"

The strange crackling sounded again, followed by a low, masculine moan. She stared at the partition. It was probably there for a reason.

"Words, Justina. Don't make me remind you again." Shawn wrapped her hair around his hand, tugging lightly as he brought his lips close to hers. "I wouldn't be much of a Dom if I didn't teach you the rules."

"Are there rules for one night, Sha—Sir?" Her nipples tightened at his dark look. Oh, she liked this. Which was odd. She had a feeling she'd get in trouble if she pushed. Part of her wanted him happy with her, but a mischievous side she hadn't even known she had wondered if he'd actually punish her for breaking these 'rules'.

Shawn's low chuckle had a dangerous edge that made her tingle all over. "Who said I'll be done with you after one night?"

"Everyone?"

"Yes, but everyone isn't making decisions for us, now are they?" He lifted his shoulders dismissively,, then jerked his chin toward the partition. "That's likely Bower doing electroplay. Say 'That sounds so fucking cool, Sir! Pretty please, may I see it?'"

She giggled, rising up on her tiptoes to kiss him. "Those exact words? Or just 'Pretty please, Sir?'"

He slid his hands down over her ass and grinned. "Ask like that and I'll give you anything."

"Anything?" She spun away from him, reaching back to grab his hand before he said more sweet things that would have her thinking beyond a casual experience. The speech had to be coming at any moment. She'd braced herself to hear it.

The idea of him cooking for her. Of him teaching her about the lifestyle. Of this being more than one night?

She knew better than to let herself hope.

Better to take things one step at a time.

He stopped her at the edge of the partition. Gave her hand a little squeeze. "Just about anything, Justina. I'm enjoying myself a lot more than I thought I would tonight."

Her throat tightened. She inhaled roughly. "So am I, but…but I don't want to start worrying about why that is. I want us to be friends. I want to try things I never have before, with no regrets. I don't want you to feel used, but I can't think about tomorrow. I'd rather end this now if there will be hard feelings."

His lips parted. He stared at her, the edges of his lips quirking up suddenly as he let out a soft laugh. "So I can't keep you?"

"Isn't that how this works, Shawn?"

He inclined his head. "Yes. That is exactly how this works." He shook his head then took her hand again. "Come. If nothing else, let's make this a memorable night."

Karma was a bitch. Shawn wasn't sure what he wanted to do more. Laugh his ass off or bang his head against the closest wall.

Justina was everything he usually avoided, but somehow, exactly what he needed. He loved how she reacted to every experience. How willing she was to try new things. She had spunk and an easygoing attitude. She came off as shy at first, but once she gained her bearings, she was fun and sweet, and her inquisitiveness was damn sexy. The things he could teach her...

He needed more than one night to do so. More than a few hours to get to know her, to explore that beautiful body, to taste every inch of her. To learn what make her smile. What would make her scream out in ecstasy.

By his own rules, her proposition was perfect. No strings. No expectations.

Fuck that. How about a few ropes? Where the hell is Carter?

Likely at home, since his sister was here. Some club members made a point of avoiding nights family members planned to play. Oriana, Silver, and Ford didn't seem to have an issue with it, but they rarely played in the same area. Cam tended to watch the door when Mason played.

Carter was sometimes uncomfortable with his friends watching his scenes with Ramos and Jami. His sister would be an issue.

Is an issue. Shawn had managed not to dwell on White, but he couldn't help look back at where he'd been scening with Chicklet and that girl.

Sam was the one on the cross now, while White stood off to the side with Zovko, drinking a bottle of water and nodding at whatever Zovko was saying. Maybe Zovko had found another way to get a piece of White.

Which didn't bother Shawn nearly as much as the idea that his man would be going home with Sam at the end of the night.

Refusing to let that fact ruin his time with Justina, Shawn eased into the wide space between the partition and the brick wall of the club. Bower didn't usually mind people observing his scenes, but best to ask, just in case.

Bower glanced up as he changed the attachment on the violet wand, his wide, muscular, bare chest glistening in the dim light. "Hey, Pisch."

"Hey…" Shawn wet his lips, trying not to stare at Richter and Silver, who were on a wide, padded table, completely oblivious to his presence. Then again, if he had a woman sucking his dick like that, the roof could probably cave in and he wouldn't notice either. He kept his attention on Bower. "Justina wanted to see you using the violet wand, but maybe it's a bad time."

Silver lifted her head, a naughty smile on her lips as she fisted her hand around the base of Richter's dick. "Not at all. Hey, cutie." She winked at Justina. "You're just in time to see us torture our man. He's been working too hard. He needs to be punished."

Justina inched closer to Shawn's side, which pleased him. Her cheeks were red, but she couldn't seem to tear her eyes away from Silver's tight hold on Richter's dick. The man was still wearing his white dress shirt and black tie, like he'd just stepped out of a business meeting. His pants were undone, but he hadn't even taken his shoes off.

His submissive, Silver, was dressed just as properly. The whole scene looked like some naughty secretary role-play. Add Bower as the pool boy and…*fuck*. Shawn's dick pressed painfully against the snug confined of his leathers.

Wide eyed, cheeks rosy, Justina tightened her grip on his hand and nibbled on her bottom lip. "You can punish your Dom?"

"No," Richter said, even as Shawn and Landon echoed the word. Richter took a firm hold of Silver's wrist. "Don't corrupt the child."

"Relax, Dean. She's here with Pisch. Pretty sure nothing we do will bother her." Silver leaned over Dean so he wasn't completely exposed, shooting Justina a curious look. "Interesting choice, chickie. He give you the speech?"

For fuck's sakes. Shawn pressed his lips together, frowning at Silver. "No. She gave it to me."

Bower's jaw nearly hit the floor. Richter's eyes widened.

And Silver burst out laughing. "You are officially my hero, Justina. I think that earns a few pointers. Let me and our pet Frenchman show you how to make a man beg."

Grabbing a fistful of Silver's hair, Bower leaned over Richter and growled in her ear. "Excuse me, *mignonne?*"

Shawn smirked as Silver sputtered. The mouthy sub had earned herself a punishment. He probably shouldn't be pleased that Justina would get to see this side of the lifestyle, but Silver was definitely an example of what *not* to do.

"He's mad." Justina tucked herself against him, hugging herself as she whispered. "She was just joking."

Slipping his arm around her shoulders as Richter tucked himself in his pants and rose so Silver could bend over the table, Shawn rubbed Justina's arm soothingly. "Not mad, pet. Disappointed. Silver knows better, but she's showing off for you. We don't have to stay if you're uncomfortable."

"I shouldn't want to stay." She bit hard at her bottom lip, her brow furrowed. "They'll tell us to leave if they don't want us here, right?"

"Yes, neither Bower or Richter are shy." Shawn inclined his head at Richter's questioning glance. If Shawn was introducing Justina to the lifestyle, observing a punishment would be a good learning experience. Otherwise, it was unnecessary.

He was playing dirty, but he hoped seeing the dynamics of a solid BDSM relationship would appeal to her. There were other couples who played light that he could introduce her to, but he'd always been a little envious of what these three had. A connection he'd considered exploring in the future.

Maybe that future didn't have to be quite so distant anymore.

Too soon to tell, but why not plant the seeds in Justina's mind and see if she'd reconsider putting him in the friend zone after tonight?

Thankfully, Bower used only his hand on Silver's bare ass to punish her. Justina winced when the first two smacks came down in quick succession. Her jaw clenched when Silver cried out after counting six and seven.

She let out a sigh of relief when Bower stopped at ten.

"If you'd like to be an example to a new sub, Silver, please do so in a way that doesn't reflect badly on Dean and myself." Bower dried Silver's tears, then pulled her into his arms. "And next time you call me your 'Pet Frenchman', I'm using the cane."

Silver sniffled. Then giggled. "I called you '*our* Pet Frenchman'."

"Silver." Richter's tone held a hard edge of warning. "That's enough."

"Oh, *fine*. I'm sorry, Master. Sir." Silver shot Justina a playful wink. Likely to let the younger woman know she was all right. "May we please show Justina something fun now? I promise, I'll be good."

"Apology accepted." Bower shrugged when Richter arched a brow at him. "We're not getting anything better. And I want to play."

Richter's gaze softened as he studied Bower. His lips curved. "Do you? In front of an audience?"

I fucking knew it! Shawn wouldn't admit it to anyone, but he'd jerked off a few times, picturing Bower and Richter together. There was an undeniable chemistry between them, but he'd assumed he'd made up most of that in his head.

Part of Silver's punishment had probably come from the implication that Bower was both her and Richter's 'pet'. In his fantasies, Bower wasn't the least bit submissive. He didn't seem like a switch, he always co-topped with Richter at the club.

Did he get on his knees for Richter?

Fuck, that would be hot to see.

Rubbing his palms on his leathers, Bower squared his shoulders. "It's Easy. Not like he'll tell anyone."

"Landon." Richter's tone was low. Soothing. One he might use with a nervous sub. "You don't have anything to prove."

"You turning down a blowjob, Bossman?"

"Do I ever, Goalie?"

Against his side, Justina shivered. Shawn smiled as she tipped her head up, pure lust in her eyes. The girl *was* a bit of a voyeur. Hell, could she be any more perfect?

"Lie down, Dean." Bower's sultry French accent thickened and his voice was rough. He stroked Silver's hair as she peered up at him. "Are you good with this?"

She rose up to kiss him. "Yes, as long as you are. We don't scene in front of people very often. I miss it."

Brow furrowed, Bower curved his hand around the back of her neck. "I'm sorry. I can't...Pisch is one thing. And you know Justina, right?"

"Yes, she's not a gossip." Silver gave Justina a fond look. "We can trust her."

"Okay, but...I don't know if I can do anything out there." Bower motioned at the partition. "Becky suspects, but the idea of her seeing..."

"We're taking this at your pace, Landon." Richter's hard gaze fixed on Shawn, telling him, in no uncertain terms, that if he broke their trust he'd likely be playing for a farm team in Alaska next year.

"Richter...*Dean*." Shawn held Richter's gaze, hoping he could find the right words to express how much he valued their opinion of him. That they'd let him witness what was clearly still very private for them meant more than he could say. "I know everyone sees me as a player. Not on the ice, but as a man who can't commit to anyone. Justina's already been warned." He smiled as she ducked her head. "But I'm also a man of my word. Whatever I hear, or see, stays between us."

"Thank you, Shawn." Dean's whole bearing relaxed. He turned to Justina. "Despite what people say, he's a good man. I would warn you away as well if I thought he'd hurt you." He paused. "But I don't believe he will."

Shawn was fairly certain he'd never been given such a positive endorsement in his life. He'd earned his reputation, so he wouldn't complain that it had come back to haunt him now, but it meant a lot that Richter wasn't telling Justina to find a better man. A safer one.

"I think you're right." Justina pulled at her bottom lip with her teeth. "Thank you for letting us stay."

"Thank us if you're not completely traumatized when we're done, pet." Richter chuckled, adjusting the table into a reclined position, so he was partially sitting up. He undid his shirt and tie, took both off and handed them to Silver, who folded them neatly and placed them on the bench where Bower had his violet wand kit set up.

Stepping back to give Bower room to work, Shawn wrapped his arms around Justina, loving the way she leaned back against him as she took in the scene.

Stripped out of her pale gray skirt suit, Silver crawled onto the table between Richter's thighs. She pulled out his dick and took him into her mouth without hesitation. Bower stepped up to the head of the table, holding the wand with a laser knife attachment in his hand.

Leaning down, Bower slid his lips over Richter's. Not as though they'd never kissed before, but as though doing so in front of an audience made him nervous. All the assurance that this would remain between them wouldn't mean a thing if Bower was afraid of judgment. Shawn had a feeling the man hadn't truly accepted he was bisexual. He reminded Shawn a bit of White. Granted, White had fooled around with Richards, so denial was a moot point, but Bower had never shown any interest in men before. If he had, Shawn might have...

No, he couldn't even consider toying with Bower. Not with the way the man looked at Richter. Bower had never come off as the type to fool around casually. He gave everything of himself to those he cared for.

He never would have fit into Shawn's lifestyle. But he fit perfectly with Silver and Richter. The bond between them was palpable.

Justina let out a happy sigh as Richter took over, raking his fingers through Bower's hair and drawing him down for a rough, passionate kiss. He groaned into Bower's mouth as Silver's lips slid over him faster and faster.

Letting out a gruff laugh, Bower lifted his head and turned on the wand. "You're not in charge tonight, Dean. Silver was right. Time to get you out of your head for a bit."

"I won't submit to you, Goalie." Richter held himself stiff, as though the very idea stole all the pleasure from the scene. "I've told you before; I'm not sure why I agreed to this."

"Because you know we don't expect you to give up control. Just loosen your grip a little bit." Bower lowered his lips to Richter's chest, flicking his tongue over an erect nipple. "Let us serve you."

"Shit." Richter ground his teeth as Bower brought the tip of the knife to his nipple. His whole body jerked as the white spark jumped off the blade. "This one is more concentrated."

"Yes." Bower's lips slanted as he grinned at Shawn and Justina. "A new toy. I usually use the TENS on Dean and the wand on Silver. She teased him that he was missing out."

Challenge accepted then. Shawn brought his hands down to Justina's hips. She was trying so hard to keep still, but he could tell she was aroused. Very fucking aroused. Not that he blamed her. He was so hard, he had half a mind to take her home now. But they likely wouldn't get this opportunity again.

Drawing the tip of the knife across Richter's chest, Bower kissed along the path, soothing the man's flesh with each bite of electricity. He traced the knife over Richter's pelvis, taking Silver's lips as she lifted her head. He continued stimulating his man as he kissed his woman. Then he handed Silver the wand.

"Like we practiced. Pay attention to his reactions. Don't hold it in one place for too long." When she nodded, Bower took hold of Richter's dick. Circled the swollen head with his tongue. Then slid his lips down as Silver ran the knife over Richter's thighs.

Hands fisted at his sides, Richter's spine bowed. He cursed under his breath and brought his hand to the back of Bower's head. Not holding him down. The men had an interesting balance, and Shawn was torn between envy and lust as he watched them. He would have attempted to take over. To guide Bower, ease him into taking more and more until he came down the man's throat.

But Richter held back. Enjoying his sub, and his man, without finding his release. He was waiting for more.

When Bower came up for air, Shawn could tell Richter was ready to take things to the next level. He made a sharp motion to Silver with his hand, then gestured for her to come to him. She crawled up the table, setting the knife on the ledge.

Bower retrieved it, shutting the unit off as he watched his lovers kiss. He let out a low groan as Richter lifted Silver's breasts to his mouth. Silver tossed her head, whimpering as Richter tugged a nipple with his teeth.

"You want to give them a show, dragonfly?" Richter stood, spreading Silver's thighs as she rested back across the table. He slid two fingers into her, thrusting them in deep before lifting his hand to Bower's lips to let him suck them clean. "Let him fuck you, while I fuck him. I have a feeling they should see how it's done."

Shawn tried not to react, even though he heard Justina's soft gasp. She liked the idea, but Richter was playing dirty. He must have seen White with *that* girl at some point tonight. Yes, Shawn would love to tempt his man away from her, but he didn't have the first idea of how to do so. And he wasn't on solid ground with Justina. Or any ground, really. The idea of sharing her only reminded him of how badly he'd fucked up with White. Sharing could be fun, but only if you didn't lose everything you'd started with.

You started with nothing. What did you expect?

Fine, he knew he'd mishandled the situation. But he wouldn't make that mistake again. He'd see where things stood with Justina. Show her he was worth more than one night. Give her a reason to stick around.

Then…well, he couldn't see that far ahead. This was new to him. He'd never had to convince someone to consider the morning after. Or beyond. The issue had always been making sure they didn't expect what he couldn't give.

"I think we've seen enough." Shawn frowned at Richter's amused look. "We haven't discussed limits yet. She may be curious, but—"

"I'm fine, Shawn. If they don't mind…" Justina's breath caught. She squirmed against him. "I'd like to stay."

Damn it. He wanted to stay, but he *knew* they should go. If she considered exploring more with him after witnessing how perfectly in sync a triad could be, he wasn't sure whatever he could offer would satisfy her. They could play with others, but would that be enough? Would *he* be enough?

You've never tried to be. This isn't about you, Easy. Give her what she wants. What she needs. The voice in his head was done with his shit. And for the first time, he didn't disregard it. *You always walk away when things get serious. Time for a change.*

"We can stay, *Röschen.*" He spread his fingers over her pelvis, loving the way she pressed against him. She might be turned on by what she saw, but she wasn't seeking release elsewhere. She craved his touch. Found solace in his arms. That was a start. "I won't lie. What they have is something many never achieve. But I want it. One day."

Justina pressed her eyes shut and took a deep breath. They were being ignored now. Both men were kissing Silver. One another. Speaking softly and teasing and tempting. Justina tipped her head back and met his eyes.

"So do I. But you're not supposed to say things like that. I thought I knew who you were. But you're so much more."

"Does that change your plans for us, pet?"

"Not yet. But keep it up and it might. Which scares me." She swallowed hard. "Would it be horrible for me to ask you to be the man I'd planned for? The one I knew exactly how to walk away from?"

"Will you come home with me, Justina?" The air came a little easier to his lung when she nodded. If she'd said no, he wasn't sure he'd get another chance. He wasn't the type a girl like her would consider when the morning light put everything in perspective. But give him another hour. Maybe two. By then he'd give her something she'd crave even when her mind told her she shouldn't. "Then don't make any plans. In the morning, tell me what you want. If it's friendship, I'll accept that."

"Will you?" Her sweet, lush lips pursed. "Shawn Pischlar, if you're playing me, I'll let Akira do whatever she wants to you. And help her. One thing I liked when people talked about you if that they all said you were straightforward. You didn't pretend to want more than sex."

"They were right."

"Then what changed?"

"I don't know." He wasn't enjoying this conversation. And by the way the two men and Silver had eased off their foreplay, they were paying attention to it, which made him feel completely exposed. But he expected Justina to be honest, so he could give her no less than the truth. "Maybe I'm tired of the games."

Richter frowned at him, as though the older man doubted his words.

Shawn sighed. "All right, I love the fucking games. But when you invest nothing, what's a win? That's the only way I can explain it, sweetheart. Give me a chance."

"I am giving you one, Shawn." Reaching back to hook her fingers to his belt, she nodded toward the others. "This is their time though. After…well, what happens, happens. I'm not sure the things I want to do to you are legal, but we shall see."

The girl was killing him. He'd be fine going home now. Being forced to wait went against every instinct, but maybe he needed to test his own control. So far, all his rules, all his selfish needs, weren't serving him very well. In the lifestyle, the submissive had more control than they even knew. And maybe that's what he needed. To finally acknowledge that he wasn't in charge. That he needed to follow another's lead.

And this sweet girl was leading him right to his favorite place. He forced his racing thoughts to quiet as Bower sank his long, thick cock into Silver's glistening pussy. Bower restrained Silver's wrists in one hand, using the other at the small of her back to lift her to every thrust.

Richter watched them fuck for a few moments, then took a condom and some lube out of the leather bag on the floor.

Justina shifted and Shawn slid his lips along her throat, loving how she trembled with anticipation and desire. He couldn't look away from the erotic scene playing out in front of him, but he needed to make sure Justina enjoyed it on every level.

But when he drew the hem of her black dress up for better access to her most sensitive bits, she caught his wrist.

"Shawn, I don't know if I can…" Her lips parted as Bower pounded hard into Silver and the other woman moaned in pleasure. "Damn, that's hot."

"Does watching them make you wet, *Röschen?*" He gently pried her fingers from his wrist, then restrained both her small hands in his big one against her stomach. "I didn't get enough of that sweet little pussy. I want to feel you tighten around my fingers. To see if watching them fuck does as much for you as being spanked did."

"Mmm." Justina didn't resist this time as he lifted the hem of her dress and slipped his fingers into her panties. He curved two into her and groaned as her soft, wet heat constricted around him. She pressed her eyes shut.

He bit the side of her neck, just hard enough to get her attention. "Keep watching, pet."

With a subtle nod, she focused on Silver and Bower while Shawn teased her with the tip of his fingers. He could tell she was trying very hard to hold still.

A shame he was about to make it more difficult.

"I'm going to let go of your hands, Justina. Reach behind you and latch your fingers to my belt." He made a soft sound of approval when she obeyed. "Good girl. Now don't let go."

Sliding his hand over her ribs, her breasts, he dipped his hand into the V neckline. She whimpered as he freed her breasts, but didn't protest.

Such a very good girl.

As he stimulated her tiny, pink nipples, she squirmed, her harsh breaths almost matching Silver's. When Richter settled his hand on Bower's hip to still him, both women went quiet.

Shawn bit the inside of his cheek as Richter carefully prepared Bower, murmuring tender words as he pressed his lube slicked fingers into the other man. Bower's jaw tensed, and he rested his forehead between Silver's breasts.

Silver petted his close cut, brown hair and whispered. "Relax, my love. You know he hates hurting you."

Bower released a strained laugh as Richter eased another finger in. "I can take it."

Probably not as often as you could if you learned how. Shawn kept that comment to himself though. He tended to top men like Richards—well, actually even *more* experienced than Richards. Men who didn't need tons of preparation. Not that he couldn't seduce an anal virgin, but virgins in general were dangerous.

The one in his arms was the perfect example.

Or just perfect.

He was going with perfect.

A loud *CRACK!* Startled Justina and Shawn pulled her back a step.

"*Calice! Mon tabarnak j'vais te décalisser la yeule!*" Bower growled, moving to rise, huffing out an angry breath when Richter pinned him against Silver. "What the fuck are you playing at, Dean?"

Leaning over Bower, Richter rubbed the red handprint he'd left on the man's thigh. "You want me to hurt you, Landon? I can do that. But if I'm going to fuck you, I need it to be good for both of us."

"*Merde!* Fine!" Bower pressed his eyes shut, calming slightly as Silver cupped his cheeks and kissed him. "I'll fucking relax."

Despite his words, Shawn noticed Bower tense as Richter's dick stretched him. Richter had enough experience to add more lube and move slowly until the other man truly released enough tension to let him in, but it was painful to watch.

Shawn remembered being taken roughly too many times. Bower would be sore for days, and Richter, unlike Shawn's first, would feel guilty after.

Maybe I should invite them to the party. Show them how it's done.

At least the triad seemed to have found a good rhythm once again. He bent down to graze Justina's throat with his teeth, noting that she never looked away. Her body shifted as though she was feeling every deep thrust. Her cheeks were rosy red, and she panted as Silver threw her head back and screamed.

"Oh God." Justina clenched her thighs against his hand. Holding back as her inner muscles gripped his fingers. "This is so wrong."

"What is wrong, *Röschen*?" He pressed his thumb over her erect clit, using the fingers of his other hand to pinch her nipple. The bite of pain had her moving restlessly against him, so close to losing control. "What they're doing, or how you feel watching them?"

"Me." She shook her head, likely at a loss for words. Tears wet her lashes as she let out a needy little whimper. "I should be ashamed of how I'm behaving, but I'm not."

"Good. Because I like you shameless. Let them hear you, pet." He caught her earlobe between his teeth. Licked the soft shallow beneath it. Nipped and sucked at her throat until he could tell she'd lost the last of her resistance. "Come for me."

Her cries were drowned out by Bower's deep groan and Richter's rough curse, but Shawn hardly noticed the men. Justina trembled in his arms, escaping into the throes of ecstasy. As she went still, he gently withdrew, covered her breasts and adjusted her panties so she wouldn't feel exposed as she came down from her euphoric high.

Before he had a chance to lift her up into his arms to hold her close, she turned and pressed her face into his chest. He could tell she was a little unsteady, but that she'd sought out his comfort on her own tugged at his heart.

He wrapped his arms around her, simply holding her until she stopped shaking. Until she lifted her head and gave him the sweetest smile.

"Thank you. Tell them...thank you." She hid her face again, muffling her voice. "Would it be horrible of me to want to leave with you now? I can't face Silver. Not yet."

"She won't think any less of you, precious." He kissed the top of her head, meeting Richter's eyes as the man grabbed two bottles of water from his bag, sparing him a brief nod before beginning aftercare for both his lovers. Silver likely didn't need much, but Bower was sitting on the edge of the table, fists pressed to his knees, refusing to look at anyone.

A 'thank you' wasn't needed. And likely wouldn't be appreciated at the moment. Shawn put his arm around Justina and led her into the main area of the club. At the bar, he lifted her up to a stool and turned to the bartender to order two bottles of water.

His jaw ticked as he met Chicklet's broad smile.

"What can I get for you, Easy?"

The bitterness of betrayal soured in Shawn's throat. He swallowed hard, acknowledging that the emotion was irrational. The woman had her reasons for wanting to mentor that girl. And if anyone could keep White safe while he played with that snake of a wanna-be Domme, it would be Chicklet.

Shawn schooled his features into what he hoped was a pleasant smile. "Water, please."

"Got it. What about you, White?"

Fuck me. Shawn took Justina's hand in his as she shot him a concerned look. He'd scowled without meaning to. He couldn't let himself react like this. She didn't need to be dragged into the mess he'd made.

"Can I have a beer, please?" White cleared his throat, and from the corner of his eye, Shawn saw his man help that girl onto a stool. "What are you having, cutie?"

"I'll have a beer too. Thank you." She leaned forward and grinned. "Hey, aren't you Shawn Pischlar?"

Still standing, Shawn glanced over to incline his head, then thanked Chicklet for the water bottles she set in front of Justina. He watched Justina take a few gulps then took one himself before he bothered answering Sam. "Yes. You're Carter's little sister, right?"

Sam's bright smile faded a little, but returned in a blink. "Yes. And Ian's girlfriend. He told you, didn't he? I'd hoped to speak to you. I don't want you to think I'll come between you."

"Oh?" Fuck, the girl didn't pull any punches, did she? Should he deny any concern? He hadn't had a chance to talk to Justina about his relationship with White. Not that he could even say they still had one. He took his time downing a good half of his water. "White and I are friends. Very good friends. I don't believe there's any risk of that changing."

White gave Shawn a hesitant smile. "I'm happy to hear that, man."

"If you were worried, all you had to do was ask."

"I know. I'm sorry, things have just been…" White bowed his head, then sighed. "I'm sorry."

Sam rubbed his shoulders, holding Shawn's level gaze. "Now I feel bad. I've been taking up so much of his time. But you'll have him all to yourself on the road. I told him I was fine with him having a boyfriend. I can't give him *everything* he needs."

"I'm not sure what you mean, Sam." Shawn sensed Justina watching him. What was she thinking? She'd made it clear she wasn't sure about anything beyond tonight, but *he* wanted more. Would she even give him a chance to explain after hearing this?

Turning her attention to Justina, Sam bit her bottom lip. "Maybe this discussion should be private. I don't know the protocol with a sub you're playing with for the night. Am I allowed to talk to her?"

No! Shawn almost crushed the bottle in his hand, but stopped himself just in time. Justina was so innocent, he knew he had to be careful with her. But Sam wouldn't be.

If Justina wasn't suspicious already, Sam would trample over all his attempts to ease her into his world. What choice did he have though? Tossing Justina over his shoulder and hauling her out of the club wouldn't earn her trust.

He would make sure she wasn't treated like a temporary plaything though. He gave Sam a tight smile. "I think respect is fairly universal. You can manage that, yes?"

Sam's eyes narrowed. She pulled away from White and stepped around Shawn, offering her hand to Justina. "Please don't think I'm being a bitch. I'm new to this and Shawn clearly doesn't like me. My name's Sam, and it's a pleasure to meet you."

Finishing her water, Justina swiveled in her stool to face Sam. She took the other girl's hand, her smile unreadable. She didn't look upset. That was good, right?

"Justina." Justina cocked her head and let out a soft laugh. "I'm new here too, but I don't get the impression Shawn doesn't like you. Maybe you're assuming that because you've been rude?"

Shawn almost choked on his water. Holy fuck, if Justina kept this up, he was gonna fall for her hard and fast. She never ceased to amaze him.

Jerking her hand back, Sam glared at Justina. "Excuse me?"

"No, I don't think I will. I'm glad I got to meet you though." Justina stood and held her hand out to Shawn. "Are you ready?"

He took her hand, all the weight of uncertainty lifting off his chest. No doubt, he'd have a few questions to answer once they got to his place, but she'd made it perfectly clear he'd get the chance to give them.

Leaving White with that girl wasn't easy. She was everything Shawn had been afraid of. Worse even.

But he couldn't save White from his decisions. All he could do was be there when White saw her for who she was. Which might take a while, but Shawn was willing to wait.

Maybe all they would have in the end was their friendship. Shawn wasn't sure at this point. With Justina by his side, he wasn't sure of much besides the opportunity to have more than he'd ever known he wanted.

Someone who made him want to be a better man. Who would accept him as he was, without question, for a time. Who forced him to consider all the ways he could make that time last.

Bianca Sommerland

Chapter Nineteen

That hadn't gone at all as planned. Sam bit her bottom lip as she watched Shawn and his new chick walk out of the club. The girl had seemed shy. Like a little mouse, one that would scurry away at the slightest threat.

Not that Sam had intended to come off as threatening, but the girl ruined all her plans. She hoped Shawn wasn't serious about her, because, damn it, Ian was serious about *him*.

She wasn't even sure Ian realized he was completely hung up on the man, but the fact that he brought Shawn up in almost every conversation told her two things. One, no matter what Ian said, he wasn't 'fine' with an open relationship. Or not one quite so open. Maybe if he and Shawn had been in a better place, Ian could handle the asshole doing every cute piece of ass he could find.

They'd been having fun, but when Ian saw Shawn with that chick, Justina, he'd gotten all serious. When Sam asked him what was wrong, White shook his head.

"None of my business. I just wish I knew what the fuck he was doing."

He hadn't elaborated, but Sam wasn't stupid. Justina wasn't the type a guy like Shawn should mess with. Ian probably wouldn't have liked seeing the man with *anyone* else, but he would have accepted someone who looked like a one-night-stand.

Hinting that Justina was just that had blown up in her face. Ian had gone quiet.

And Chicklet was glaring at her.

Which brought Sam to the second fact she'd learned. No matter what Shawn 'Easy' Pischlar did, people accepted him.

She wasn't so lucky.

Taking a sip of her beer, she finally met Chicklet's eyes. "Please don't be mad at me."

"What the fuck were you thinking, girl? You disrespected another Dom—a Master who has earned his place in this club—and spoke down to a young woman you don't even know." Chicklet fisted her hand around the rag she'd been using to wipe the bar, looking like it was Sam's neck she really wanted to get a hold of. "Are you trying to make everyone hate you?"

"Leave her alone, Chicklet." Ian's jaw tensed when Chicklet snapped her hard gaze at him. "She's new at this. I don't think she meant anything bad by—"

"He speaks! A fucking miracle!" Chicklet tossed the rag and slapped her hands on the bar. "That man is your best friend. If that's all he is to you now, fine. But you won't have even that if the two of you don't figure out what you want. And if you sit back and let this little troublemaker speak for you, you're not going to have very many friends at all."

"Fuck this. Come on, Sam. Let's go." White slammed his beer down on the bar and took her hand. He paused, glancing back at Chicklet. "I thought I knew what he wanted, but now I'm not sure. We'll figure it out, but I assumed you were training Sam because you understood her. If you don't, you need to back off."

Chicklet tipped her head back and groaned. "Damn it, White, I'm seriously considering tying you up and tucking you away somewhere where you won't get hurt. If I'm not training her, you two are *not* playing here."

"I'm good with that," Ian said, his tone cold.

I'm not! Sam pulled her hand free. Chicklet's approval meant a lot to her. She'd enjoyed Chicklet explaining the lifestyle. Talking to her about how to use a flogger safely. Sure, she hadn't missed that Chicklet hadn't let her do more than take a few light swings before telling her to practice on a pillow, but she made Sam feel like she was capable of doing something good. Chicklet said Sam reminded her of herself when she was young.

And damn, if Chicklet had been like her…maybe she could be like Chicklet when she grew up. Maybe it wasn't too late to make something of herself.

"I don't want anyone to hate me. I wasn't trying to—"

"Careful, little girl." Chicklet's eyes narrowed. "I've played the game for too long not to see right through someone who knows *exactly* what they're doing."

Ugh, this fucking sucks. Sam frowned and pulled herself back onto the stool, feeling Ian standing close behind her. "Justina doesn't know what she's getting into."

"Which is none of your business. She's been warned by people who know her *and* Pisch." Chicklet's lips slanted, like she could tell Sam was running out of excuses. "Try again."

"Damn it, why do we have to talk about this? Ian and I are enjoying ourselves. Ian wants Shawn. I don't see a problem with that." Her brow furrowed. Was it weird that she *didn't* have a problem with it? She didn't think so, but most people probably would. She tried to sort out her jumbled thoughts. "Justina isn't the type to play around. She's going to spoil all our fun."

Chicklet didn't say a word. She smirked, glancing over at White.

Who was frowning at Sam. "I don't understand. You have no problem with me and Pisch, but you've got an issue with him seeing another girl? Honey, don't get attached to Pisch. He's—"

"Not into commitment. He won't commit to you. He doesn't even like me." Okay, she kinda liked that Ian paid no attention to all the scheming, all the underhanded bullshit she couldn't help but get wrapped up in, but she wished he could see how close he was to losing the man he was in love with. "When you told me you were with him, it wasn't a big deal. Do you think she'll be cool sharing him with you?"

Ian lowered his gaze and shrugged. "I don't know. But I don't want you worrying about it. You can't fix this, Sam."

"I can try."

He gave her a half smile. "I don't think you trying is gonna help. I probably missed half of the shit that went down, because I'm not good with all this. But I know Pisch. Even if he's not serious about that girl, he's watching out for her. Be a good idea to leave her alone."

"One of the smartest things I've ever heard you say, White." Chicklet took their half finished beer bottles, emptying them in the sink. "Now get out of here. And don't keep him up too late, Sam. He's got a game tomorrow. And you don't wanna see how I handle things that get in between my boys and the game."

Fucking hockey. Sam almost rolled her eyes, but she wouldn't test Chicklet's patience again. Besides, she wanted to prove she fit in Ian's life, so getting him home and making sure he was well rested for the game would probably earn her brownie points.

Which she desperately needed.

She bit her bottom lip and looked at Chicklet. "Can I have a hug so I know you ain't still pissed?"

Chicklet chuckled and motioned her around the bar, meeting her halfway, and giving her a tight squeeze. "We're gonna have another chat, Trouble. Behave yourself until then, you hear me?"

"I will." Sam smiled at Chicklet, the older woman's forgiveness meaning more than she could say. Chicklet was right. She didn't have many friends, and she couldn't afford to lose any. She had to be more careful.

Justina was still a problem, but maybe not one she needed to deal with. Shawn had taken her home. Maybe he'd be up all night with her, then he'd play like shit and see she wasn't worth fucking up his career, and his relationship with Ian.

Until then, Sam had Ian. He spent time with her, called her all the time, and if he had to make a choice, she was sure he'd choose her.

So long as that remained true, she didn't have to fight to keep him.

He was already hers. The fight would happen when Shawn tried to change that.

Maybe Justina was the perfect distraction. If Shawn focused on her, maybe he wouldn't bother Sam and Ian. And by the time he turned his focus back to Ian?

It would be too late.

Ian helped Sam into the cab Chicklet had called for them, hesitating

on the sidewalk, because he needed a minute to think.

And another to convince himself not to pull out his phone and call Pisch.

He wasn't even sure what he would say, but damn it, he missed the man. He wanted to be with Pisch. He wanted to stay with Sam. And he didn't have to choose, which he'd thought worked out, considering all Pisch's rules.

The idea of an open relationship hadn't seemed like a good thing until he'd met Sam. Now, he wasn't alone. Wasn't obsessing over what—or *who*—Pisch was doing. When they hung out, they'd have a good time. When they didn't, he and Sam could explore their own relationship.

Maybe he'd been wrong about how all this was supposed to work. He might have hated seeing Pisch with Richards, but he'd been involved in the decision to play with the younger man in the first place. Kinda.

There had been some discussion. He could have said no.

Part of him wondered if he should have reached out to Pisch before taking Sam home with him. But Shawn hadn't seemed upset, so…was there a problem, or was Ian making more of this than he should?

He needed to know their friendship was intact. Which was why he'd asked.

Pisch saying he should have called was the first clue that he'd fucked up.

Guilt was the second.

Fuck, he was tired. He hoped Sam would be good with going back to his place and getting some sleep. If she wasn't, he'd do whatever he could to make her happy, but tonight had drained him.

Submitting to Pisch—to *Shawn*—felt natural. He did it without having to think about it. But when Sam had mentioned Chicklet training her, he'd felt like he was playing a part. He'd almost used his safeword when Pearce restrained him to the cross. He didn't like the man touching him, but he'd closed his eyes and heard Shawn's voice.

"Not everything is a fight, Bruiser." Shawn's face was pale as he watched Ian get yet another line of stitches. "I wish I knew why you always throw a punch then think about it afterward. Even on the ice, you need to take a minute. Consider the end results. Sometimes, it's not worth spilling blood."

That was why he hadn't hit Pearce. Why he'd done the scene. It had been weird, but not as bad as he'd expected. For some reason, he'd thought Chicklet would whip him hard. Or let Sam do it. He was tough, so people expected him to take whatever they threw at him.

He never worried with Shawn. The man got him. Looked out for him.

If he lost Shawn, who would care enough to make sure he didn't get himself fucked up because he was stupid? Not Sam. She needed Ian to look out for her. Better than he was doing, because she'd pushed Chicklet too far and almost lost the woman as a mentor.

Sam was cool with him and Shawn. Which was good. Exactly what he needed.

But she was right. Justina might not be as cool with sharing Shawn.

He'd felt like an asshole even noticing the other girl. With Sam by his side, he shouldn't be looking at another girl and thinking she was cute, or that she and Shawn were fucking hot together.

Shouldn't be wondering if this whole 'open relationship' had benefits he hadn't considered.

Being with Sam, he'd wondered if Shawn would want to play with them. Unfortunately, even he couldn't miss how much the two disliked one another. He wasn't sure why, but that had to change. Even if that didn't lead to the three of them naked together.

The cab driver rolled down his window. "You getting in?"

"Yeah." Ian sighed and slid into the backseat beside Sam. He put his arm around her as she leaned against him and closed her eyes. Looked like they *would* get some sleep tonight.

Which was good. He wasn't in the mood for sex. Or much of anything besides resting his head on his pillow and letting today end. Maybe tomorrow would be better.

If he got to talk to Shawn, it would be.

His brain was stuck on fucking repeat.

I miss him.

Chapter Twenty

What the hell have you gotten yourself into, Justina? As she followed Shawn from his car to his front door, she considered all the reasons she'd given him—and herself—for not asking him to drop her off at home.

Most importantly, because she wanted this. Wanted *him*.

Yes, learning about his relationship with White could make things more complicated, but only if she let it. Shawn had *almost* convinced her to look beyond tonight, to wonder what more they could have. But she had to sleep on it.

Why not do that sleeping with him?

But of all that had transpired, one little issue had absolutely no impact whatsoever on her decision come morning.

Sam.

Making snap judgments on people wasn't her style, but she knew Sam's type. The girl was a bully. Whatever else she had going on in her life—having a baby, being kicked out of her father's house, the rumors had it all—hadn't suddenly made her into the kind of person who'd step over those that got in her way.

Justina was in her way.

What the hell does she want though? She has *White.*

Maybe, but White wanted Shawn. And while Justina wasn't sure what exactly was going on between the men, Sam clearly figured she couldn't have White without Shawn. It wasn't hard to imagine Sam planned to seduce Shawn so she could have her cake and eat it too.

Let her! You don't need to get wrapped up in this mess.

True.

So why haven't you gone home yet?

Because this wasn't about Sam. This wasn't about White.

This was about Justina and Shawn. And tonight.

No drama. Nothing beyond taking what he'd offered. An experience she wouldn't pass up. She'd missed out before because she'd always done the right thing.

He might be all kinds of wrong, but she still wanted him.

And he wanted her.

It's that simple.

If things were gonna get complicated? Well…she'd had to fight for things she wanted before. She might not be tough. She had no idea how to play the games the people around her were so wrapped up in.

She was a pretty fast learner though.

Shawn held the door open for her, reaching in to flick on the lights. "You're thinking hard. I know you said Sam won't be an issue, but I'll tell you again. If she becomes one, let me deal with her."

"No." Justina spun around as she stepped over the threshold. She grinned and poked him in the center of the chest as he pushed the door shut behind him. "You want to give me a reason to consider anything beyond tonight? Here's a tip. Don't try to protect me from your world. If I decide it's worth taking on, I refuse to be some fragile little thing you need to watch over."

Damn it, the concern in his eyes, the way his muscles tensed like he was already imagining the battles he'd need to fight for her, was fucking sexy. Unnecessary, but sexy.

"What if I want to watch over you?" He closed the distance between them, wrapping one arm around her waist, delving his hand into her hair and tipping her head back. The green in his early forest mist eyes darkened as he studied her face. "I hate how she treated you."

"I know." She lifted her hand to his cheek, loving the scruff, which hadn't seemed to get much longer since the beginning of the playoffs. It didn't look patchy, like some guys who couldn't grow beards tended to end up with. She'd watched a few of his interviews, and he'd never been completely smooth. He always had the same shadow along his chin and jaw, with a bit above his lips.

A little rough around the edges, but so controlled.

He grinned as she traced her fingers along his jaw. "That's very distracting."

"Good. I don't want to talk about Sam. She's a bitch." She frowned, hating the surge of rage she couldn't tamp down. She'd probably called less than a handful of woman that insult in her life. And Sam hadn't done much to deserve it. "Fuck, I'm sorry."

"Why? You're adorable when you're all worked up." He brushed his lips over hers in that soft, teasing way he had that made her head spin. Not even a real kiss, but it promised so much more. "You don't swear often. It's kinda hot when you do."

"Hot is better than adorable." She wrinkled her nose at him. "You have tonight, Shawn. You sure you want to waste time talking about your boyfriend's new girl and how cute I am?"

He blinked at her. Then chuckled in a way that made goosebumps spread all over her skin. "Touché. I should focus on giving you a reason to want more of me."

"Do you have more to offer?"

"So much more, *Röschen*." He kissed her cheek, then whispered in her ear. "Should I show you?"

Oh god yes! She shivered as he lifted her hair over one shoulder, then eased down the zipper at the back of her dress.

"Cold?" He didn't pause as he pulled the straps of her dress off her shoulders, slipping it down and letting it drift to the floor. He smiled when she shook her head. "Good, because I want to see you. All of you." He moved behind her, kissing her shoulder as he undid her bra. "And I don't think you're cute."

She pressed her hands over her breasts, keeping her bra in place. "You don't?"

"No." He stepped in front of her again, gently lowering her hands and taking her bra, leaving her breasts completely bare. "You're beautiful, Justina. So fucking beautiful and pure. Not just because you've never been with a man. There's something about you that's so good, I know I shouldn't touch you. Shouldn't want you."

"But you do?" She struggled to keep her hands at her sides. Covering herself would make this so much easier. She couldn't help wonder if he'd see something he didn't like. Maybe she wasn't as sexy as he expected. She wasn't bold, wasn't sure what came next.

But he the way he looked at her, none of that mattered. He saw something she never did in her own reflection. In his eyes, she imagined a woman that could be desired.

Who was.

"I do. But I will take my time with you." He brushed his knuckles over her nipples, sending sparks of pleasure straight down to her core. "Since, as you continue to remind me, I might not have much once I let you leave."

Her brain wouldn't shut up. Everything he said made her want to throw herself at him. To enjoy the next few minutes, or hours, or…all right, she was losing her grip on the time limit already. But she did know there was one. Maybe not for them, but on what they had to spare. She had to perform tomorrow night. Or maybe it was tonight now? Midnight had definitely passed, which meant the fairytale would end.

But she'd never been the type of girl to dream of princes and pumpkins and happily ever after. She kept to the real world.

The one where there were responsibilities. And tomorrow meant taking another step toward fulfilling her dreams. He'd fulfilled his. He was part of a team.

And they needed him ready to play that role.

"You'll probably take a nap tomorrow, but you still need to get some sleep." Ugh, did she sound like a nag? That would *definitely* turn him on. "I mean—"

"Exactly what you said. And you're proving you're a perfect fit. You don't see the game as an obstacle. You know how important it is." He kissed her, stealing all the air from the room, making her heart skip in a way that couldn't be healthy. His lips were hot. The touch of his tongue made it impossible to voice any more objections. Then he laughed, and she pressed her eyes shut, not sure she could take a rejection now.

She gasped as he swept her up into his arms.

"I should go to bed now." His muscles surrounded her as he carried her down the hall. "I'm not tired, but I will be when I'm done with you."

Hiding her face against his neck, she nibbled at her bottom lip. "That's a good plan."

"I hope you mean tiring myself out, because if you think I'll be done with you any time soon, Justina…" He carried her to his bed and laid her down, leaning over her and speaking against her lips. "I've never had to convince someone to stick around. This is new, but I'm up to the challenge."

"Are you sure this is a good idea, Shawn?" She laced her fingers behind his neck, wondering if she'd end up being the one hurting him. She couldn't make any promises. Not yet. "I meant what I said. In the morning—"

"Don't give me the speech again, Justina." He pressed a finger over her lips before she could protest. "I get it. And if anyone told me what I'm about to tell you, I'd show them the door. Don't tell me I can't keep you. Let me prove that I can."

Shawn imagined he'd earned himself a special spot in hell for the

depravity he'd committed in his life, but this proved he was truly damned. And worse, he was being a selfish dick. A girl like Justina should go on dates. Be greeted at the door with flowers and chocolates. Experience all the romance, the sweet words, long before being seduced into a man's bed.

For some reason, she hadn't had all that.

And rather than wait any longer for the right man to give it to her, she'd let her curiosity get the better of her. Decided she wanted to meet *him*.

He couldn't blame her for guarding her heart. For seeing him as a temporary rush. As someone who could give her a taste of all she'd never had, but nothing more. He should stick to that. Give her all she'd asked for, then gently hand her off to a man who could be everything she didn't even know she wanted yet.

Instead, he was already wondering if he could be that man. Somehow.

To be honest, he wasn't sure. But if he couldn't be, he'd still take care of her. Once she'd had her fun with him, he'd make sure she had no regrets. She'd know what she needed in a relationship. Accept nothing less.

The idea of any other man filling that role already pissed him off.

You're doomed, Easy. Accept it.

He already had. And really, if she walked away, he deserved the heartache. He'd been the cause of so much pain. His speech wasn't a shield for anyone but himself. Hearing it from her proved that much. Knowing in advance that nothing you did would matter, that the results wouldn't change...

It fucking sucked.

And who knew how many had felt that way before he toyed with them. How many were thinking exactly what he was now.

Maybe it will be different.

Maybe I can be the one to change the rules.

At least Justina's rules hadn't been in place for long. She was already wavering from them.

All she needed was a little nudge in the right direction.

If you hurt her, you'll pay.

He wouldn't hurt her though. No matter what he did, he'd make sure of it.

Knowing that was the only thing that kept him moving. He yanked off his shirt, tossing it aside. Bracing his hands on the bed, at either side of her head, he leaned over her.

Her long, black lashes rested on her pale cheeks. Her lips were slightly parted, soft and red and swollen from his kisses. She had the fresh scent of spring, with the hint of ocean air and something all her. Deliciously alluring. He wondered if she'd forgotten perfume, because there was nothing artificial as he laid over her and breathed in.

She inhaled roughly as he ran his hand down her side. "Is there something I need to know? That I should say, or do? I want you enjoying this too."

"Oh, my sweet girl. I already am." He took her lips as he hooked his fingers to the edge of her panties, easing them down her hips as he lowered his lips to her throat. "All you need to do is tell me to stop if it's too much. No safeword now. Just a 'no'. Or a 'Shawn, I don't know if I can take much more!'."

He grinned at her giggle. Fuck, she was the sweetest, most precious person he'd ever had in his arms. Another came close, but Shawn couldn't think of him now. He hadn't believed in second chances, but he'd been given one.

And he wouldn't waste it.

Every inch his lips touched brought a reaction. She gasped. She squirmed. She shifted her legs so much he had to hold her thighs once he'd gotten her panties out of the way to avoid getting kneed in the face.

But once he had her spread open, his tongue slipping over her slick folds, tasting her sweet, hot pussy, she was lost to the pleasure.

Moving against his mouth and drinking in each and every sensation.

She was fucking delicious. He pressed his tongue into her, loving the way she whimpered and dug her heels into his shoulders. Maybe, in the morning, she'd come to her senses and walk away.

But if he had his way, she wouldn't get far before she turned around.

For once, he would be patient.

As always, he was *'Easy'*.

But now that meant something different.

He wouldn't be easy to take and leave. He would be easy to come back to. Easy to need more of.

Easy to become addicted to. Because he needed her to want another fix. One she wouldn't find anywhere else.

Justina fisted her hands in the dark blue comforter, bright white flashing behind her eyelids. Shawn had already given her so much pleasure, she'd expected more of the same, but this…this made all the rest nothing more than a small taste of what he could do.

His tongue was wicked. He dipped it into her, using his fingers to open her to him. There was nothing she could hide. She moaned as his tongue flicked over her clit and flames licked along her nerves, leaving them firing in every direction, like a dozen, maybe a hundred flares, burning endlessly within.

He filled her with two fingers and she cried out, the fullness almost too much. Yet not enough. As her body tightened around him, she needed more. She wanted to hold him. To feel him everywhere.

"Shawn!" She called his name, but she wasn't sure what she was asking for. What he was doing was incredible. She wanted to beg him to keep going. But…but she was so close to finding that release. And she didn't want it with his hands or his mouth. She needed it with him. "Please… I need you."

"And I need you, *Röschen*." Shawn rose over her, bending down to kiss her lips and let her taste herself. Wet and musky and so fucking hot. He guided her hand down between them to touch her own slick heat. "Feel how ready you are? Keep yourself that way."

She wasn't ashamed to admit that she'd touched herself before. Reading a hot book. Watching videos online. She'd been curious, so she knew what felt good. And she didn't hesitate to do as she'd been told. She circled her fingers over her clit, positive she'd never been this wet before, no matter how hot the words or what she watched.

Pulling a condom out of his wallet, Shawn groaned, watching her finger herself. "That's so fucking sexy, Justina. You've done this before."

She bit her bottom lip and pressed her eyes shut. "I said I was a virgin. I never said I had no interest in sex. I read some pretty kinky books. And...and I watch porn."

"Do you?" He slid between her thighs, holding her fingers over her clit as the thick head of his dick pressed against her. "What kind of porn?"

"All kinds."

"What's the last one you watched?"

"I...I watched one with two guys and a girl." She could feel him stretching her as he eased in, but she was so wet, so turned on, it didn't hurt. It did make speaking very difficult though. She hissed in a breath as he continued to use her own fingers on her clit. "But it was boring. They just...they fucked her and ignored each other."

"Why did that disappoint you? It's the ultimate fantasy."

"If there's more than one person, they should all be...you know...involved." Okay, that hurt a little. But not for long. The second she tensed, he eased off. He kissed her neck, finding a spot that made her tingle everywhere. And he focused on it as he slipped in and out, never going any deeper. "I looked into it because...girls talk. And talk about Ford and Cort..."

"Turned you on." Shawn cupped her breasts, one after the other, leaning down to suck on her nipples. "Had you fantasized about Akira before she kissed you?"

"No!" She whimpered as he tugged at her nipple with his teeth. "She's my friend."

"So? I've fucked several of my friends." His dick sank in deeper. He went still. "Focus on me, Justina. You're so wet, so relaxed, this shouldn't hurt much. But it won't hurt at all if I can get your mind on other things. With all that porn, did you wonder how your new friend's pussy tastes? Or did you just want to watch her and her men?"

Yes! Justina could see it, like she'd seen on the porn vids. Kissing Akira had been...different. But she couldn't picture doing more with her. She wanted to watch though. See Akira finally getting her men where she wanted them. It wasn't all about her. She loved them both. There was tension, but getting rid of that would be so easy.

"I don't think of Akira that way...I wanted to see..."

"You like to watch."

"Yes."

"And do you want to taste?" Shawn framed her jaw with his hand, rocking against her. "To feel?"

"Not with her then, but...I've seen other vids. One with a lot of people. It was...fucking sexy. Everyone was touching, tasting, feeling." A slight pain and Shawn filled her. She pressed her thighs against his hips and took a deep breath. "When everyone's lost in it. When they're all going with whatever feels right... That's what I like the most."

"I can give you that, Justina. And I can give you this." He held her gaze as he thrust into her. "I can give you everything."

She tried to make sense of what that meant. Right now, what he was doing to her *was* everything. All her fucked up fantasies didn't compare to feeling flesh on flesh. To the sensations. To the sound of his breath coming hard and fast.

Without warning, all her thoughts, all she felt, came together and evaporated in a burst of heat and steam and pleasure. She was sure she screamed, but she only felt the rawness in her throat. Everything within took over, imploding, leaving her helpless to the aftershocks that shook her, wave after wave, never-ending until she was completely drained.

At some point she simply gave in. To the sensations. To the overwhelming emotions, to the exhaustion. Completely spent, she let him hold her close, waking only once, her mind uncertain of all she'd revealed in the heat of the moment.

"I didn't mean any of it," she whispered when she saw him watching her. He should be sleeping. Maybe she'd woken him up? "I don't know what I want."

"You do, Justina. And it's perfect." He kissed her hair and hushed her when she protested. "No judgment. No expectations. Do you regret anything?"

"Only what I said." Her cheeks heated. Why had she told him about the stuff she'd seen? How was that okay? "I don't regret you."

"The rest can wait, pet." Shawn held her close as his eyes drifted shut. "So long as you don't regret me, so long as I still have a chance… The rest is something we can explore. Together."

"I shouldn't want that."

"You should. Why deny yourself, *Röschen*?" He held her down when she tried to sit up. "Would you deny me?"

"No." She couldn't help picture him. And White. And wonder where she could fit with them both. She'd never ask, but she considered his words.

He wouldn't deny her anything.

And she wouldn't deny him.

Which was…perfect. Even if she couldn't keep him, she could keep this.

Tonight. Tomorrow. Fantasy and reality. All the lines blurred.

An offer she couldn't resist.

Chapter Twenty One

Ian was restless as he warmed up with Hunt, using heavy ropes in a new training regime they'd both started at the gym recently. Whipping the long, doubled up rope against the ground between them, they each tried to knock the ropes out of one another's hands. Which was harder than it sounded.

He and Hunt weren't fond of one another. Not since Hunt had the fucked up idea that Ian had done something to Richards—who Hunt treated like a little brother.

Fine, Ian had done a *few* things to Richards, but not when Hunt started being all overprotective. And seriously, Richards was at least eighteen. Legal and all.

Not to mention, Richards had more experience than Ian did.

But…bringing that up probably wouldn't make Hunt his new BFF.

The baby goalie was a good workout partner though. They'd reached a truce. He even trusted the kid to spot him when he lifted weights. Not that he didn't wonder if the guy would some day drop them on his neck, but so long as Hunt didn't find out he'd fucked Richards, he was probably safe.

A violent tug and the ropes tore against Ian's hands. He dropped them with a curse.

Hunt frowned at him. "Dude, where's you head at?"

"Right here, man. I'm good."

"You sure?" Hunt's brow furrowed as Ian rubbed his hands against his snug black shorts. "Wanna work with the medicine ball for a bit? Don't wanna fuck with your grip."

"Sure." Ian ditched his sweat-soaked shirt as Hunt went to grab a ten-pound medicine ball from the trainers. They tossed it back and force for a bit, then moved to rolling it between planks. Not many of the men warmed up this much before games, but Hunt matched Ian's need to feel all his muscles burning a bit before he hit the ice.

Hunt was in an unusually chatty mood tonight though. He held himself in a steady plank position as Ian did a pushup with one hand on the ball. "You're dating Carter's sister now, right? What's she like?"

Ian inhaled slowly, making sure to keep his tone level. No fucking way was this kid gonna make him feel old with all his talking and not even breaking a sweat shit. "She's nice."

"Nice?" Hunt stared as Ian rolled him the ball. He spoke as he did his pushups with perfect form. "She boring?"

"Dude!" Ian shook his head, blinking as the sweat dripped into his eyes. "Why the fuck would you say that?"

"Because nice sounds boring. Maybe you should try fucking Carter instead."

A shadow fell across them, but Ian wasn't feeling 'nice' enough to warn the rookie before Ramos rested his foot on the center of the baby goalie's back. "Interesting conversation, *chico*. May I join you?"

Well, *now* Hunt was sweating. He swallowed hard. "Uh…sure, Ramos. But, like, I didn't mean anything. Just…hell, dude needs to get laid or something."

Ramos held out his hands and Ian tossed him the ball one-handed. With his foot still on Hunt's back, Ramos threw the ball back to Ian. "He seems less distracted than you do, Hunt."

"Because you're fucking stepping on me, man!"

"If you've the energy to run your mouth, you're not being challenged enough." Ramos bounced the ball right in front of Hunt and the goalie startled. "But let's continue discussing my man and what White should be doing with him."

Hunt's arms trembled. He shot Ian a pleading look. "Did I say Carter? I meant someone else. *Anyone* else."

"Yeah, I didn't hear Carter." Ian pushed to his feet, catching the ball one last time and grinning as Ramos inclined his head. "Sorry about the misunderstanding, Ramos."

"Apology accepted." Ramos held out his hand and helped Hunt to his feet, patting the young man's shoulder when he stood. "It's good to see you two getting along. You have much in common."

Like the fact that we're both meatheads? Ian shrugged as Hunt glanced over at him, confused. They both watched Ramos walk down the hall and back into the locker room.

"That was…weird." Hunt scratched his jaw, which had sprouted quite an impressive playoff beard. He almost looked like an adult with that thick black layer of scruff. But his expression was like a little kid caught with his hand in Ramos's cookie jar. "He knows I was joking, right?"

"About me fucking Carter? Probably." Ian chucked his sweaty shirt in Hunt's face as they headed for the locker room. "But he's probably caught you checking out his man's ass."

"Asshole!" Hunt slammed into his side as he opened the door.

The kid didn't know his own strength. Ian managed to avoid crashing into Callahan and braced his hands on the floor. Too late. When Hunt fell on top of him, his chin hit the carpet, skimming across it.

"Fuck!" Even with his own beard, the carpet had taken a layer of flesh. And his chin stung like a motherfucker. He jabbed his elbow back into Hunt's ribs. "Get your fat ass off me, man!"

Hunt scrambled to his feet, his face ashen. "Shit! I'm sorry, White. I didn't mean to… Fuck!"

He spun around and bolted out of the locker room before Ian could even stand.

When he did, he was face to face with Demyan, whose eyes were sharp with rage. "Nice going, Bruiser."

"How is this my fault?"

"His dad's always on him about keeping his body fat down. He hit ten percent, and apparently, it's the end of the fucking world. Becky makes him come over almost every day to make sure he fucking eats right. He'd finally chilled out a little." Demyan's jaw ticked. "But it was awesome of you to remind him what his dad thinks of him. Thanks for that."

Demyan took off after Hunt.

And Ian stood there, staring at the door, wondering why he was so damn stupid. He vaguely recalled one of the trainers having a heated argument with Hunt about his diet. Telling him he didn't need more protein. That he was in good shape.

The kid doesn't need you saying stupid shit to him. Everyone knows his dad is an asshole.

"White."

I didn't think…I never do.

"Ian!" Pischlar's voice cut through the noise in his head. He motioned for Ian to come sit beside him. "I know that look. You didn't know; don't beat yourself up over it."

Grinding his teeth, Ian stared at his scuffed sneakers. "I shouldn't have said that."

"Maybe not, but I believe you were reacting out of pain." Pisch's lips slanted as he took hold of Ian's jaw. "You're not supposed to get banged up *before* the game, *Bärchen*. Hold still."

Grabbing a clean towel from his stall and a bottle of water, Pisch wet it, then held the towel to Ian's chin.

Bearkin. I didn't think he'd ever call me that again. Ian pressed his eyes shut, knowing they couldn't talk here. But they needed to. Soon.

"Please tell me he didn't hit his head." Callahan came to stand beside Pisch, looking down at Ian. "You good?"

"Yeah, just feel like a jerk." Ian scowled. Which hurt. *Fucking hell.* "And I have rug burn on my face."

Callahan covered his mouth with his fist and coughed. "No comment. But don't worry about Hunt. He's a goalie. They're all a little touchy."

"Hey!" Bower shouted from across the room where he was taping his pads. "I heard that!"

"Good! You fucking ready, *Frenchman*?"

Bower's cheeks went red.

Pisch chuckled and chucked the water bottle at the assistant coach. "That's inappropriate, Coach. Please don't say it again."

"Sorry?" Callahan looked lost. He glanced back at Bower, who made a dismissive gesture. Then he went around the locker room to check on the other men.

And Bower grinned at Pisch, mouthing 'Thank you'.

What the actual fuck? Ian glared at Pisch when his man smiled at the goalie. He might not be super smart, but he could tell there was something going on between them. Something he'd missed.

Was Pisch fucking the goalie now? The man was married. Or almost married? He'd been with Silver forever, and they had a kid. They were both with Richter, and he didn't share. Did he?

Who fucking knew anymore? Not like he had a say in who Pisch fucked.

He's 'Easy'. He does whoever the fuck he wants.

"Ian—?"

"Don't fucking call me that, Pisch." Ian pushed Pisch's hand away from his face and stood. "I gotta get ready to play. Thanks for the chat."

Before he got far, Pisch was by his side, a firm grip on his shoulder as he redirected Ian past the locker room door and into the hall. He shoved him into the equipment storage room.

Ian's pulse raced as Pisch pushed him against the closed door. This was such a bad idea. A really fucking bad idea.

Why'd you let him drag you in here then?

He wasn't sure, except, he needed to hear what Pisch had to say.

Also, Pisch being all commanding had short-circuited his brain.

His dick was very interested in whatever came next. Which wasn't so great. Putting on a jock with a hard-on wasn't much fun.

You've got just enough time for a cold shower.

Yep. Good plan. He tried to sidle away from Pisch.

Pisch fisted his hands in Ian's hair. "Don't even fucking think about it, *Bärchen*. I've given you space while you explore whatever the hell you've got going on with *that* girl, but there will be no misunderstandings between us."

Misunderstandings? Ian rolled his eyes. There was nothing even a dumbass like he wouldn't understand. "Got it. You done?"

"Clearly not. What's upsetting you?"

"Nothing."

"Bullshit." Pisch lowered one hand between them, pressing it against the front of Ian's shorts, sharpening the ache pulsing through his rock hard dick. "Is there something you need, White? Something you haven't been getting?"

Yes! His jaw clenched as he fought the overpowering effect Pisch had on him. The man didn't have to touch him to steal every ounce of control Ian had, but when he did? Putting together words, in a way that made sense, was a struggle.

Damn it if he wouldn't try though. "It's Bower."

Eyes wide, lips parted, Pisch stared at him. Then he frowned and shook his head, tightening his grip on Ian's cock. "You want Bower?"

"No! Hell, can you stop that? I can't think." Ian inhaled roughly as Pisch gave him room to breath. "Are you fucking him?"

"What?"

"Pretty simple, Easy. Are you fucking Landon Bower? Our starting goaltender?" Had Pisch gone braindead? He still looked confused. Ian slammed his head back into the door. "The big Frenchman?"

"The big… *Himmel arsch und zwirn!* White, where did you get that idea? Because I noticed he was uncomfortable with the nickname?" Pisch's eyes narrowed at Ian's shrug. "I happen to be very observant. Do you think I fuck all my friends?"

Honestly? Ian dropped his gaze, not sure how to answer that. He believed Pisch. The man didn't lie about shit like this. But he *did* fool around with a lot of his friends.

"Talk to me, Ian." Pain filled Pisch's eyes as he brought his hand to Ian's cheek. "I can handle just about anything, but I hate that you don't talk to me anymore."

"I don't know what to say." Ian pressed his eyes shut. "I miss you, but I don't know how to do this. I'm with Sam. She needs me more than you do."

Pisch made a sharp, irritated sound in his throat. "Obviously. But are you still *with* me, Ian?"

"Yes." He wasn't sure how their relationship would work, but he wanted it to. He still needed Pisch, but he was losing him. "But how… I mean, Justina's not your type. She's a sweet girl, and I was kinda worried, seeing you with her. I know you don't like Sam yet, but you don't know her. She'll be fine with the speech. She won't try to keep you."

"I have no interest in Sam, White."

Ugh…there goes that idea. Ian scowled. "Fine. So I guess you gave Justina the speech, and she pretended—"

"She didn't need to pretend anything. She's very clear about what she wants from me." Pisch's smile was different. Tender, like just thinking about Justina made him happy. "And I didn't give it to her."

"Didn't give it to…" All right, he didn't have to ask what 'it' was. Even he wasn't that slow. He kinda wished he'd heard wrong though. The idea of Pisch not making it perfectly clear he couldn't be kept… His stomach sank. "She's special, isn't she?"

"I believe so."

The tightness in Ian's throat made it hard to breathe. "Where does that leave us?"

"She won't make me choose, Ian. And I won't make you. But I'm here when you want me." Pisch looked tired suddenly. He drew away and rubbed a hand over his face. "I've made a lot of mistakes, and I'm sorry. I've never felt for anyone what I do for you. You're the most important person in my life. I would have accepted being nothing more than your friend, but when you opened up the possibility for more…"

"You told me *I* couldn't keep you." The thought had all the frustration, all the anger that had built up within bursting free. He wanted to grab Pisch. Shake him and yell at him and...and he couldn't. Not after seeing the way Pisch's ex had treated him. He wasn't like that asshole. But his eyes burned as he focused on Pisch. "I love you. I *fucking* love you, Shawn! And you told me we'd just have fun. Keep things open. Why wasn't I important enough to change your fucking rules?"

"Do you want me to change them? If you ask me to, I will. I'll forget everyone else. We can go into the locker room and tell everyone that I'm yours."

Tell people? Ian's pulse pounded hard in his skull. He swallowed hard as a cold chill ran over his flesh. He wasn't ready for people to know… Maybe his teammates wouldn't judge him, but what about the media?

Or his grandmother?

Fine, she didn't always know who he was, but when she did, she asked about the girls he'd met. Bugged him about settling down. She'd never accept him being...being bisexual.

He still had a hard time accepting it sometimes.

"Breathe, Ian. I'm not going to force you to do anything. I'm trying to help you understand why I made the choices I did." Pisch let out a soft laugh and leaned in, brushing his lips over Ian's in a gentle kiss. "I love you, too. And I know you. One day, you're going to meet a nice girl and marry her. You're going to have beautiful kids together. They'll call me Uncle."

"And me and you—"

"Will still be best friends. And have some awesome fucking memories." Pisch kissed him again then backed away. "And no regrets. You can't keep me, Ian. Not because I don't want you to, but because I want to keep *you*. And this is the only way I know how."

This really sucks. Ian tugged his bottom lip between his teeth, wishing he could just stay in here with Pisch. Lock out the rest of the world and not have to face that Pisch was right.

Is he though? The life he pictures…is that what you want?

He'd never really looked that far ahead, but yeah, he'd probably always planned on something like that.

But later. *Much* later.

He reached out, wrapping his hand around the back of Pisch's—of *Shawn's* neck—and pulled him close. He needed to touch him. To know he wasn't losing the man any time soon.

Their lips met, and it was unlike any kiss they'd shared before. Rough and desperate. Saying all the things they had and so much more. He slanted his head, slipping his tongue in Shawn's mouth, tasting the other man, doing everything he could to tell Shawn how much he wanted him. *Needed* him.

Shawn groaned and tangled his hands in Ian's hair, pressing him against the door. Using his teeth, his tongue, his lips to give Ian the only answer he would accept right now.

He hadn't lost him. And he never would.

The man who would always have a piece of Ian's heart wouldn't be the one to walk away.

But if Ian needed to, if he found that girl, and wanted that life Shawn saw for him…

He'd be the one to walk away.

And Shawn would let him go.

A quiet knock pulled Shawn out of the passionate haze he'd lost himself in. He felt Ian stiffen—his whole body, not his dick, which was still as fucking hard as Shawn's—and eased away from him.

"Relax, Ian. Anyone who would think to come look for us here won't say a word." They'd damn well better not, anyway. He and Ian were in a better place. He didn't want the little time they had left cut short because Ian was afraid of being exposed. "Move away from the door. Let me see who it is."

Ian nodded and backed into the shadows of the small equipment room.

Shawn cracked the door open.

Callahan met his eyes and inclined his head as though he saw something in Shawn's eyes that told him he didn't need to know more. "Time to get suited up. Everything kosher?"

"Yes, but...discretion would be appreciated." He trusted Callahan, and Ian had known the man even longer, so hopefully he did as well. "I'd rather if no one questioned why White and I have been gone, together, for so long."

"It wasn't that long." Callahan's lips slanted. "Head on in. I'd like to speak to White anyway, so we'll be in the locker room in a bit."

Asking what he needed to talk to Ian about would probably be out of line, but Shawn was tempted. He hesitated, sighed, then stepped out into the hall. He and Ian were in a better place. Hopefully, that would be enough and Ian would tell him later. They used to discuss everything.

He'd missed that. Missed his best friend. And he still had him. Sam couldn't change that. Their fucked up relationship *hadn't* changed that.

Whatever happened from this point on didn't matter.

He could keep Ian. And he considered that a win.

The door closed and Ian stood in the equipment room, rubbing his sweaty palms on his shorts and holding his breath. He couldn't hear Shawn and Callahan anymore. Maybe Shawn had convinced Callahan they really didn't need to have a chat.

Even Easy can't get you out of trouble if you've done something to piss of the coach.

Assistant coach.

Yeah...could be worse. You piss off Shero and you're done for.

With everything else going on, Ian hadn't really thought much about his contract ending or his shaky position with the team. He trained hard, put his all into the game... But what if he seemed too distracted? He picked apart ever second of his every shift on the ice over the past few games.

Nothing to write home about. He was decent, but they had kids like Richards and Ladd in their prime. While he'd hit his already. He'd never make the big bucks of the top lines, but what scared him was ending up as a player traded from team to team for whatever was left of his career.

Not really valuable to anyone for anything but heavy hitting and dropping the gloves once in awhile.

And if he kept taking those big hits, the time he had left could be cut in half. Or worse. He had other skills, but no matter how hard he worked, both he, and every scout in the league, knew his limits.

He didn't want to start thinking about what came next.

Twenty-seven years old and he knew he should have a plan for when he retired. If he was lucky, he had another five years left. Which wasn't long at all.

First stressing about maybe getting married and having kids one day and now retirement? Damn, White, wanna get more depressed before the big game?

Sighing, he shook his head, looking up as Callahan opened the door and gestured for him to follow. "This won't take long."

"Okay…" Ian glanced over at the assistant coach and frowned. The man looked stressed. Or tired. Ian hoped it was tired. At least he didn't have to worry about getting traded during the playoffs. "Where are we going?"

Callahan held open the door at the end of the hall; the one leading to the underground parking. "Just here. I'd rather not be interrupted."

Smart place to chat. Only the players parked here, so there was no one hanging around. Maybe he and Shawn should have come here.

Folding his arms over his chest, Callahan leaned against the cement wall by the door. His brow furrowed. "I probably shouldn't be asking you this. Feel free to tell me to fuck off."

"Uh…okay?" Ian bit the inside of his cheek. No way would he tell Callahan to fuck off. The man was a demi-god when it came to his career. Shero and Richter were the actual gods, but they weren't studying him like there was an important decision to make.

Taking a deep breath, Callahan smiled suddenly. "I'm impressed with your performance lately. You look worried, so let's start with that. If you continue this way, your spot with the team is secure."

"Really? Shit, man, that's good to hear." Ian grinned, pretty sure he could take anything else the man threw at him. "And I'll keep working my ass off. I know I'm getting old, but—"

"For Christ's sakes, White. You're getting *old*? Mind not talking that crap to a man six years older than you?" Callahan looked down at his hand abruptly and scowled. There was a faint scar on the back of it from the surgery that had repaired the bones. And cut his own career short. The longer, deeper one on his cheek grew harsher as his face darkened. "If I hadn't fucked up my hand, I'd have played for another ten years. You're not getting old, and I hear you talk like that again and I'll break my other hand on your face."

Fuck, he would too. Ian bit into his inner cheek and nodded. "Got it, sir. Won't happen again."

"Good." Callahan's expression relaxed. "I just heard from Sam. She sounds like she's adjusting well, but I wanted to get your take. You're dating her now, right?"

Ian blinked. Nodded.

Am I allowed to?

Before he could ask, Callahan continued. "Does she seem happy? You seem to be good for her. She's doing well with her new job. Staying out of trouble."

"Yeah, she likes working at the bar." Ian wasn't sure what more he could say. He and Sam talked on the phone a lot—well, she mostly talked, and he listened, but that worked for him. She was still at his place, and they watched movies. She wasn't ready for much else and he refused to let her do stuff for him when he couldn't do anything for her.

The light play at the club was the most they'd done since their first time.

He was getting callouses on his palms.

None of which Callahan wanted to hear.

Callahan rubbed a hand over his lips, nodding slowly. "Does she talk about my…about her son?"

"No." Okay, now he got it. He vaguely recalled Sam mentioning signing more papers. How she couldn't wait for the adoption to be final so she didn't have to think about 'the kid' anymore. He'd changed the subject. He hated hearing her talk like that. "She…she doesn't like anyone bringing him up. *At all*. I took her to a coffee shop, and she overheard Jami talking about how cute Westy is and—"

"Westy? Like the dog?"

"The kid. Your son." *Umm…awkward much?* "That's what Carter calls him. I thought it was his name."

"Yeah…me and Uncle Luke are gonna have a chat." Callahan shook his head, then reached out to pat Ian's shoulder. "Thanks, Bruiser. Tomorrow, the last of the paperwork will be filed, and I needed to know…well, that she's still sure. I didn't want to ask when she comes to meet you after the game. I'm guessing she's in the pressbox?"

Ian laughed, stepping aside as Callahan opened the door. "Nope. She'll probably be sleeping when I get home. She's not really into the game."

"Oh." Callahan's brow furrowed. "Well, not all the guys' girlfriends are. That's not a deal breaker, is it?"

"No, but…" Ian's brow rose. "You telling me you approve of me dating her?"

"Why wouldn't I?"

"No one else seems to. Except maybe Chicklet."

"Chicklet's a smart woman. She knows Sam needs a good man in her life." Callahan squeezed Ian's shoulder. "You're a good man, White. Don't let anyone make you doubt that."

"Thanks, Coach. That means a lot coming from you." Ian ducked his head, deciding the night wasn't going so bad after all. He hummed to himself as they entered the locker room, realizing one of Vanek's favorite songs was playing.

Team tradition. The Cobra's 'angel' got all his favorites blasted before the game.

At least it wasn't Disney music anymore.

Across the locker room, Carter was singing *Son of a Preacher Man* at the top of his lungs. The kid was fucking tone deaf, but his energy was contagious. Catching Shawn's eye as he went to his stall to get suited up, Ian grinned and joined in, not singing quite so loud, because he didn't sound much better than Carter.

Shawn smiled and shook his head.

Ready to hit the ice, Ian considered how messed up things had started. And how quickly his life had changed. For the better.

Things were good with Sam. He wasn't sure she'd be 'that girl' Shawn assumed he'd spend the rest of his life with, but she was happy with how their relationship was now. Which included him being free to keep what he had with Shawn.

He hadn't been sure *what* they still had an hour ago. But he didn't have to worry anymore. Not unless he started looking into the far off future. And why the hell would he do that?

Callahan was right. He was still young. He had a career he loved. His team. A good girl at home. And his best friend hadn't ditched him.

There were a lot of uncertainties, but why dwell on them? He was fucking happy.

Add a win tonight?

His life would be as close to perfect as it had ever been.

Chapter Twenty Two

Nearing the end of the second period, the Cobras led the game 2-0. But they were taking a beating physically. Shawn cursed as he lifted his glove to his mouth and blood trailed over the white leather covering the palm. The stitches he'd gotten under his lip at the end of the first period had split with that last hit.

No call. *Of-fucking-course*.

Thankfully, Ian wasn't on the ice. He'd already taken two penalties for fighting. Another and he'd be tossed out of the game. He'd gotten an instigator penalty on the last one. The refs were fed up.

Heading to the bench to get patched up, again, Shawn tensed as the crowd let out a bloodthirsty howl. He sighed as he sat for the trainer and saw Mason grab the man who'd nailed Shawn. The guy was called 'Kennel' by pretty much everyone in the league.

Ugly fucker who played dirty. He deserved a beat down, but Mason had spent even more time in the box than Ian.

Which meant he was getting a game.

Kennel smirked as he and Mason latched on to one another's jerseys. Mason took a swing. Kennel dodged. Cut his fist upwards, connecting with Mason's jaw.

Blood spattered on the ice. Mason swayed. Righted himself.

Blocked the next punch and rammed his fist right into Kennel's nose.

Face a bloody mess, Kennel laughed, talking some shit Shawn couldn't hear. Mason's next punch missed.

Kennel's didn't. He hit Mason right in the throat.

Mason dropped to one knee, hand going to his neck. The crowd gasped as Kennel hit him again in the side of the head.

One ref pulled Kennel away as the other checked on Mason. Head bowed, Mason braced both hands on the ice.

Fuck! Shawn waved off the trainer and stood. A few feet away from him, Ladd tried to pull away from Callahan, who had a firm grip on his shoulder.

"You fucking cunt! Fucking bloody cocksucker, you! Yes, you, you fuckwit!" Ladd's face blotched crimson with rage as Kennel glanced over, slowly making his way to the penalty box. "You're a fucking pathetic piece of shit! Fucking cunt, wait until I get on the ice! You think that's funny, cunt? I'll fucking—"

"God damn it, Ladd! Shut up!" Callahan shook the rookie. "You're gonna get yourself thrown out of the game. Sit down!"

"Fuck that, I'm not fucking sitting! That fucking cu—"

Ian covered the rookie's mouth with his glove. Which probably stunned the kid long enough for him to listen. And whatever Ian said to Ladd got the kid to sit.

Still shaking, but somehow he seemed to have escaped the ref's notice. They hadn't called a bench penalty.

Yet.

Shawn settled on the bench to let the trainer finish with his lip. How fucked up was it that, while the rest of the team was gaping at Ladd like they'd never seen the kid before, he was thinking about how hot that damn Australian accent was with *all* the swear words?

Maybe he'd hit his head a little too hard. Might be safer if he had a concussion, because if Mason even suspected he'd looked twice at the kid, Shawn would be a dead man.

And you wonder why Ian thinks you're fucking the whole team?

He winced as his lip was prodded with a gloved hand, and he turned his focus back on the play. Fine, he might have considered most of the guys as prospects, but he hadn't acted on it. Ladd was too innocent. And too dangerous. He wouldn't touch the kid even if the boy begged.

Don't go there.

Strangely enough, picturing Ladd on his knees had him wondering how Justina would react to him sharing his perverted thoughts. He grinned—which fucking hurt and got the trainer grumbling at him.

Justina would get it. And wouldn't judge him.

He went over their lazy morning, in his bed, eating waffles and strawberries and trying to outdo one another with their most twisted fantasies.

"I have a confession to make." Justina rose up on her knees, giggling as he sucked on the plump, juicy strawberry she held to his lips. "I'm glad it's Silver I got to watch."

"Really?" He bit the strawberry, savoring the sharp, sweet flavor before pulling Justina down to taste her even sweeter lips. "Do tell."

She bit her bottom lip, her cheeks almost as red as the berries when he finally let her up. "Because she's in a lot of my hottest dreams. She's...she everything I wish I could be. Strong, smart, and sexy. Some of the Ice Girls talk about her and call her a slut. They say she fucked the whole team, like that makes her horrible. But even if it's true..."

"You think that's hot."

"Clearly. I know you've fucked most of the team."

"Not most. And I only admitted to sleeping with a few players. I never said who."

"Will you?"

"No. But you don't really want me to. You want to look at them and wonder. Picture me with all the different men. Nothing I could say would be as erotic as your fantasies."

"I doubt that, but you're right." She bit into a strawberry and rested her head on his shoulder. "But I'm tired of the fantasies. I like that at least one is finally real."

"Which one, pet?" He already knew, but he needed to hear it from her. To remind her why she hadn't slipped out the minute the sun peeked through the curtains, waking them both.

She bit his shoulder playfully, letting her eyes drift shut as he brushed her hair aside to kiss her neck. "You, Shawn. Just...stay real. For a little bit longer."

The trainer moved away, motioning to Coach Shero to let him know Shawn was good to go.

As Shawn hit the ice, his focus back on the game, he let the words he'd said to Justina play over again in his mind, hoping she believed them.

"This is real, Röschen. The game was just a fantasy for me once. Just a dream of all I wanted to have. Watch me play and you'll see a dream that's become reality. One that lasts."

Justina was watching him now, from somewhere up in the arena. And that had him moving a little faster. Hitting a little harder. He caught a sharp pass and drove for the net, one goal in mind.

This one's mine.

And so are you.

Standing in the pressbox, Justina picked Kimber right up off her feet and held the young girl close. One plus to not being small and skinny. And the teen weighed next to nothing.

The girl needed to be held.

A few feet away, Sahara tried to calm Bran as the little boy sobbed. She didn't look steady on her feet, but Dean stood to one side of her, while Silver stood at the other, both offering support.

Pacing along the huge glass window overlooking the ice, Ford raked his fingers through his hair, muttering to himself. "He's a strong man. He skated off the ice with only a bit of help. That's good, right?" He looked over at Dean, who didn't answer him. "That has to be good. But...what's up with the fucking refs? Are they watching the fucking game?"

"Ford, please..." Sahara hid her face against Silver's neck. "Please stop."

Justina focused on Kimber, keeping her close as she lowered the girl to her feet. She used her thumbs to dry the girl's tears. "Ford's right. Dominik is strong. Remember all the times you saw your brother get hurt? You were scared for him, but he was fine."

"Right." Kimber sniffed and wrapped her arms around Justina's waist. "But that man that hit Dominik is a bloody cunt. I hope someone cracks his fucking skull open."

"Kimber!" Sahara bit her bottom lip as Bran held his arms out for Ford. It seemed to bother her when the toddler didn't want to stay with her. But she handed him over and crouched down in front of Kimber. "Sweetie, you can't say those words. Dominik would be very upset if he heard you talking like that."

"Bloody hell, why the fuck does it matter what I say? Why are you still fucking here? You should be with him!" Kimber's eyes teared as she drew away from both Justina and Sahara. "He needs you!"

Sahara pressed her eyes shut, tears spilling down her cheeks. "*You* need me. You and Bran."

"No, we don't! We'll be fine!"

Bran started to cry again.

Silver stepped up to Kimber's side and put her hand on the girl's shoulder. "Let's try that again, sweetheart. How about 'Sahara, I love that you're worried about us, but I need to know Dominik isn't alone. Silver will take care of me. And will make sure I understand why I shouldn't say the 'C' word."

"You gonna give me a fucking lecture too, old lady?" Kimber jerked away from Silver and stormed to the other side of the glass.

And Silver stared after her, lips parted.

Dean leaned close, kissing her forehead. "I know how to handle temperamental teenagers. Let me talk to her."

"But…" Silver shook her head, speaking in a hushed voice. "She called me *old*."

Obviously holding back a smile, Dean shrugged. "Which makes me ancient. She's little more than a baby, Silver. Don't take it personally. She's hurting and lashing out. Jami used to say much worse." He hesitated and glanced over at Sahara. "Go meet him at the hospital." He put his hand to his ear, likely listening to something on the earpiece. "He's stable, but he's been taken to the general in an ambulance. The EMT managed to get him breathing again."

All the color left Sahara's face. She looked from Bran to Kimber, clearly torn.

Justina wasn't sure she could help, she'd only spent a bit of time with the kids, but they were comfortable with her. She pulled Sahara into her arms and hugged her tight. "I'll stay with them, Sahara. They still need you, no matter what Kimber said. But Dominik needs you more."

"Okay." Sahara straightened and took a deep breath. "I just...I want to be a good mom. And I know I'm not their mother, but—"

"But you're the closest thing they have to one. And shut up, you're rocking it!" Justina smiled at Sahara, nudging her toward the door. "Go. And call me with updates."

"I will."

Once Sahara was gone, Justina wasn't sure what to do with herself. Kimber was doing her best to piss Dean off, but he kept speaking to her calmly as the second intermission began.

At the other end of the pressbox, Cort was standing alone, his features tight, watching Ford as the other man walked with Bran around the room. Justina didn't know Cort well, but she hated feeling useless. Something was bothering him.

Silver followed her gaze then took her arm and led her toward him, speaking under her breath. "My brother is a little slow when it comes to the third in his relationship. As a good future sister-in-law, I think I need to do damage control. You're cute, and you're going to help me."

"Umm...how?" Justina might admire Silver, but she also knew the woman could be a little nuts. What in the world was she up to?

"Cort, have you met Justina?" Silver's tone was light and cheery. "It just occurred to me that you're both new to this open relationship thing. Maybe you should chat."

Cort eyes narrowed. "What are you talking about, Silver?"

"Well, I heard my brother was making out with Scott. Apparently, we have the same taste in men." Silver smiled sweetly. "And since Justina's with Pisch…well, she's getting a crash course in just about everything. You look upset, and she's not bothered by any of it. Maybe she can give you some tips."

Rather than roll his eyes, or laugh—which Justina half expected—Cort swung away from them and cracked his fist into the wall.

The room went quiet.

"Do you think this is a joke, Silver? My relationship is falling apart because of this fucking game. And after seeing one of my closest friends get…" Cort swallowed hard as he noticed both Kimber and Bran staring at him. He lowered his voice. "I'm in charge of security, and I had to clear the way for the ambulance. I know *exactly* the condition Dominik's in. So no, I don't give a fuck if your brother takes after you and fucks everyone on this goddamn team. Have at it. And whatever you're playing at, leave me out of it."

Folding her arms over her chest, Silver shook her head. "I'm sorry, I didn't think—"

"I'm not surprised. He doesn't either." Cort looked down at his hand, which was dripping blood onto the black tiled floor. He shot Justina a forced smile. "I'm sorry, honey. Pisch is a great guy, but some people play the game so long…" He glanced from Silver to Ford. "That it's all they care about. And I'm not talking about hockey. Please excuse me."

Whispering to Bran, Ford approached Justina and Silver, glaring at his sister. "What did you do?"

"I was just trying to help." Silver hugged herself tight. "I didn't know—"

"Here's a tip. I can fuck up my relationships all on my own. Don't help. *Ever.*" Ford kissed Bran's hair, gently unwrapped the boy's arms from around his neck, and handed him to Justina. "Remember what I said, buddy. Tell a girl she's pretty and she'll give you anything you want."

Bran giggled as he clung to Justina. He gave her the most heart-melting look, not even seeming to notice Ford had taken off. "Tina is so pretty."

Justina laughed and moved away from Silver, who was hissing something to herself and seemed to be close to punching something just like Cort had.

Sitting the little boy on a high stool near the refreshment table, Justina bent down and smiled at him. "What do you want, cutie?"

"Cake!" Bran looked over at the table with its impressive dessert spread. "All the cakes!"

That he spoke to her, when he rarely spoke to *anyone*, had Justina wanting to give him anything he asked for. But her little brother had a sweet tooth too, and she'd cleaned up puke too often to make the mistake of letting a child indulge again.

But she'd learned a neat trick with Chris that she hoped would work with Bran. "I'll make you a deal. You can have a little piece. Then a glass of milk. If you're still hungry after that, you can have more."

Pouting, Bran folded his arms and shook his head. "*All.*"

Stubborn little thing. Justina placed her hands on her hips. "Bran Ladd, we're negotiating. Do you know what that means?"

He shook his head again.

"It means I will let you have a treat, but only with the milk. You know what you get if you don't agree?"

He shrugged.

"Nothing. No cake for you." She picked up a paper plate and a plastic cup. "So…milk?"

"Yes. Bran likes milk." Bran flashed her a toothy smile. "And cake!"

"Perfect! So we've got a deal!" She laughed at Bran's enthusiastic nod. "Which one do you want to try first?"

After two slices of cake, and two small cups of milk, Bran was full. And tired. As the third period began, Justina held him in a big cushy chair Dean had brought close to the glass for her. While Bran fell asleep, Kimber curled up on the arm of the chair and rested her head on Justina's shoulder.

Justina watched the game, breathing easy for the first time that night. She loved her own family, but for some reason, being here was like having so much more. With all the drama, and the heartache, and every single mess that came with a group of people who cared for one another, the Cobras were quickly becoming her extended family.

And being part of this made her feel special. Wanted.

Not that she didn't at home...

Or, well, maybe sometimes she didn't. She hadn't seen her parents in days. And the last time she spoke to her mother, all she'd had to say was someone needed to pick her brother up after practice. And...and was Justina being careful with her diet, because her jeans looked a little too snug.

None of her friends had her looking in the mirror, trying to see what was wrong with her. Shawn called her beautiful as though it was a simple truth.

One she'd started to believe.

Ford found Cort in the parking lot. Beating the shit out of a cement pillar.

He winced as he saw the state of Cort's knuckles, but he knew better than to catch Cort off guard when he was like this. Thankfully, Cort didn't get in this headspace very often anymore. Akira would have a hard time seeing him lashing out. Losing control.

He held on so tight for her, Ford had almost forgotten Cort didn't say a word until he reached the breaking point. Would hold everything in until it had to come out. And he wouldn't let that pain come down on anyone but himself.

"Cort..." Ford approached his best friend, careful not to get too close in case Cort was still in a blind rage. "Cort, can we—"

Cort closed the distance between them, fisting his bloody hands in Ford's white shirt. "You can answer one question for me. What the fuck are you doing? We have something amazing, and you're going to fuck it all up."

"Damn it, Cort. We argue about the game. It's not going to fuck up our relationship." Ford winced as his back hit the wall hard. "What Silver said...don't listen to her."

"Why not? She's right. You've decided we have an open relationship, which is real cool. So glad you discussed it with me and Akira beforehand."

Ford sighed and shook his head. "Is this about me kissing Scott?"

"Yes!" Cort shook his head. "No! I don't fucking know, all right? I hated seeing it, but I shouldn't give a fuck. Just like I shouldn't want to call my dad and take a hit out on that Kennel guy. Dominik is *fine*."

"Is he?" Ford frowned when Cort let him go and turned away. "Are you?"

Growling, Cort fisted his hands at his sides, stretching the cuts on his knuckles. Blood spilled from his fists. "No one fucks with my friends."

"I know, but we don't live in that world anymore, Cort. You can't kill the guy. I'll push for an inquiry. Maybe he'll will get suspended and fined." Ford put his hand on Cort's arm. "I'll do what I can."

Head bowed, Cort nodded. "Yeah, I know. But what about us?"

"What about us? Jesus, your hands are a mess, man. Let me—"

"Don't touch me." Cort jerked away, gritting through his teeth. "Don't pretend you don't know what I'm talking about, Ford. Tell me what you want from me."

Ford swallowed. He wasn't sure how to answer that. Things had changed between them. He'd considered the man a brother for so long. Getting into the lifestyle hadn't changed that. Cort was fucking awesome with a flogger in his hand. Both Ford and Akira had loved all the time he'd spent practicing. But Akira didn't enjoy pain as much as Ford did. So when Cort started using the whip, it was on Ford alone.

Akira needed a Dominant man. She had two, and they worked well together to make her happy. That had been more than enough.

Until it wasn't. She'd noticed before either of them had. Ford wasn't sure when it started. A little more tension in the bedroom. Enough that they rarely took her together anymore. Their big house had plenty of room for them to avoid one another for days if they wanted.

They'd managed. And they'd blamed team rivalries. If the Cobras made it to the Eastern conference finals, they would be facing Detroit. No one would wonder why he and Cort were barely speaking then.

But Ford knew it wasn't about the game at all.

He was confused, and he didn't have a fucking clue what to do about it. Kissing Scott had cleared one thing up. He'd enjoyed it too much to claim to be perfectly straight.

But he didn't want Scott.

And he *couldn't* want Cort.

"Coward." Cort shoved him against the wall. "Do you think I got into this lifestyle, training with someone like Dominik no less, and I can't see right through a sub that doesn't know how to ask for what they need?"

Ford glared at Cort. "I'm not a fucking sub, Cort."

"Right. You're a big tough Dom. One who's learned how to kneel and hand me the whip before Dominik or Sloan helps me restrain you to the cross. One who talks all kinds of shit before admitting he needs a scene to get out of his own head for a bit." Cort braced a hand on his shoulder, holding him in place as he moved closer. "You might not submit to just anyone, Ford. But you've always done what I told you to. You might bitch, but things go a lot better when you give in."

Giving in sounded like a horrible idea. Cort was scary, looking at him like this. And it shouldn't be hot. He knew exactly how dangerous Cort could be.

He'd never been afraid of Cort, but he'd also been a stupid kid. He'd grown up, and while he might push Cort sometimes, he knew when he'd pushed him too far.

Somehow, he'd done just that, without even trying.

"Cort, I get it. I pissed you off, and I'm sorry. Let me take care of your hands. We'll get an update on Dominik. Go back and finish watching the game."

"Give me your shirt, Ford."

Ford's brow furrowed, but he pulled off his charcoal suit jacket, then his shirt. Handed it to Cort.

Cort tore the expensive shirt into long strips, using his teeth and his big, bloody hands. He wrapped his knuckles, then tossed what was left of the shirt aside, bringing his hands back to Ford's shoulders, curving one around Ford's throat.

"Fuck the game. Tell me…" Cort ran his thumb up and down the length of Ford's throat. "What did it feel like, kissing Scott? I remember you as a little punk, talking shit about guys you thought were 'gay'."

"I grew up." Ford shuddered as Cort put more pressure on his throat. "You said a lot of shit yourself."

"I did." Cort leaned closer, his breath hot against Ford's lips. "But you didn't answer my question. You kissed a man, Ford. How didn it feel?"

Fuck this. Ford reached out and grabbed the front of Cort's shirt. He smiled when Cort lost his cool detachment. "It felt wrong. He's good and all, but there's only so much he can give me."

"Yeah?" Cort rested his forehead against Ford's. "What can't he give you?"

"He wouldn't get off on hurting me." The words that came out hit Ford so hard, he wasn't sure he could say more. He'd been pissed off for so long. Frustrated. Messed up because what he wanted didn't make sense.

Fine, it made sense for other people. Oriana loved pain even more than he did. So much that it scared him. Scared Silver, and he'd spent a few late nights talking to his younger sister on the phone as she envisioned every worst-case scenario imaginable. Most which ended with their older sister dead in a ditch.

Always a ditch, because that was where bodies went, naturally.

He talked her down and reminded her that Sloan wasn't a serial killer.

He was training Cort, after all. And Ford was still in one piece. Which led to questions about how much pain Ford enjoyed. Which was fun to talk about with his paranoid little sister.

"Not much. Just enough to reach that edge."

The same lie every time.

But he couldn't lie to Cort. Because Cort was learning to read him way too well. To see when he'd had enough. And when he needed more.

"I get off on it, Ford. And that fucked with my head at first. Still does." Cort wrapped his hand around Ford's throat and squeezed, just enough to bring on that brilliant haze Ford craved. "And Akira loves it when I go to her after. Because I can't get enough of her sweet cunt."

The man loves pussy. That hasn't changed. And doesn't have to. Ford laughed. "Hey, man. That you're good with one cunt, with hers, works for me. I never thought you would be."

"We're not talking about Akira though. We're both happy with her. Neither of us has looked at another woman."

"She has. Maybe she wants—"

"Maybe she does. And we'll figure that out. But this, right here, right now, is about you and me." Cort's brow furrowed. "I love you, Ford."

Ford smiled. "I know."

Cort's grip on his throat increased. "Shut up. Not another fucking word, boy. Listen."

Yeah, I'd like to continue living, so I'm good with that.

Laughing, Cort flicked his tongue over Ford's bottom lip. "The things I want to do to you… Are you afraid of me?"

"Right now?" Ford had to fight to keep his eyes open. He felt high. Like Cort had just given him some damn good drugs. "A little?"

"Good. You should be." Cort held Ford against the wall with one hand on his throat and the other in his hair. He spoke with his lips close to Ford's. "You kissed another man. Don't fucking do it again."

"Are you gonna kiss me, Cort?" Ford wouldn't stop him, but the teasing was torture. Like he was standing on the brink and everything would change. But he had no control over the next step. "Do it. Do it and we'll see what happens."

"No." Cort released him, and he braced himself on the wall to keep from falling. "Not here. Not like this. I could hurt you, Ford. And you'd probably enjoy it. But I'm fucked up. I'm angry. And I won't make you pay for that."

As Cort turned away from him, all the messed up emotions burst out, impossible to contain. Ford slammed his fist into the back of Cort's shoulder. "That's it? You make me tell you everything, then walk away? Fuck you! Did you want something to use against me? I'll give you plenty. If I want a man, I'll find him. And I don't need fucking permission."

Cort caught his wrists and dragged him to the wall by the door. He wasn't smiling anymore. His eyes were dark as he whispered. "You do. You need mine. Don't push me, Ford. I'll let you have everything, but when we're both ready."

"Fuck you." Damn it, Ford hated the way his eyes burned. Cort made him feel stupid, and young, and completely out of control. "I won't wait."

"You will. Ford, I think Akira is pregnant. She's been worried about Jami, who we both know *is* pregnant. She missed a few days on her birth control and, tough as she is, I can tell she's not feeling good. She isn't eating." Cort sighed. "She hasn't even considered it, but if she is? She needs us to figure this out. The right way. She's so set on her plans; this will hurt her. And we're hurting her." Cort shook him. "Do you hear me, Ford? We're hurting her. We need to show her she doesn't have to sacrifice her dreams, even if she has our baby. Can you do that?"

"Yes!" Ford said the word, but he was terrified. And Cort would understand why. Ford had fucked up before. Gotten a girl pregnant. Been ready to support her.

To protect his family, Cort had been the one to drive them to the abortion clinic. To make sure every expense was paid. To check on the girl after. Make sure she was okay.

Three times. Three times, Ford could have been a father. He knew it hadn't happened after because he'd finally smartened up. Those three times were all before he turned eighteen. With girls a bit older. Sweet butt, chicks that hung around the biker clubs and slept around.

Ford braced his hands on his thighs. "I was an asshole when...fuck, a girl can do what she wants. But, with Akira...I love her. We both do. If she doesn't want the baby..."

"Ford, we'll discuss it. Those chicks...kid, you probably weren't the one to get them knocked up. But you were the only one who cared." Cort pulled Ford up into his arms, framing Ford's face with is hands. "I told you to set you straight, not to—"

"Straight? Cort, I'm not straight." Shit, he wasn't, was he? He'd have let Cort do whatever he wanted. Which was apparently nothing. He laughed. "Forget it. We're good. Good talk."

"Damn it, Ford!" Cort's fingers dug into his jaw. He slanted his mouth over Ford's, giving him a rough, bruising kiss that made Ford's mind go blank. He could do nothing but groan as Cort deepened the kiss, cutting Ford's lip on his teeth before he pulled away. Then Cort sighed and traced his thumb over Ford's bottom lip. "Asshole. I planned to make the first kiss good."

Ford grinned and licked his blood slicked bottom lip, touching Cort's thumb with his tongue. "That wasn't bad."

"That was pretty bad. Maybe you should practice with Scott some more. You suck at this." Cort's brow furrowed. "Or...don't. Because then I'll have to kill him. And your team needs all their top scorers. He's got the most points, right?"

"No, Vanek does."

"Ah, cool, then don't kiss *him* if you wanna win. Scott is expendable." Cort smirked. "This could work out for the rest of the playoffs. You hit on the Cobra's best players. I take 'em out. Detroit gets The Cup."

"Or I distract you and they all live."

"A good option. I'd go with that." Cort cupped the back of Ford's head, pulling him close to press his lips to Ford's brow. "We can't afford to play the game, Ford. I mean the game everyone else is playing. Not now. For us, it's all or nothing. You got it?"

"You gonna hurt me if I say no?" Ford ducked as Cort's big hand swung at his head. "I kid, I kid! And I get it. I kiss Akira, or you, no matter how much *you* suck at it."

"Boy, I am *very* good at it."

"Meh, I've had better."

That got *exactly* the reaction Ford wanted. One hand on his throat, the other under his jaw, Cort kissed him again. Holding him still, but taking it slowly. Teasing and torturing. Sucking on his bottom lip. Dipping his tongue into Ford's mouth and stealing his last breath. He caught Ford's tongue with his teeth and flicked his own over it, smiling as he released Ford abruptly and let him fall into the wall.

"Sure you have, kid. You wanna fuck a few guys before I take my turn, or we done talking?"

Shit! He'd never thought Cort would even go there, but now that he had?

Ford knew it would be good if it happened. And it would hurt. And with anyone else, it would feel so fucking wrong.

"Done talking." Ford was done *standing* too, but he grabbed the hand Cort held out. "You serious? You'd—"

"Ford, I've had your dick in my hand when we're playing with Akira. You've had your tongue touch my cock while I'm fucking her. Will I fuck you?" Cort chuckled. "Maybe. If you ask nicely. Now, go do your fucking job and stop acting like a needy slut."

"Cort…" Ford's cheek heated as the other man arched a brow. "Not cool."

"I'm not the one hitting on the team, Ford." Cort checked his busted knuckles and shrugged. "Stop and I'll find a new word for you. We'll see how this goes down."

"You were in prison too long."

Ford, you need to shut up.

Cort's eyes hardened. "Don't go there. I know you like pain, but you're pushing it. I didn't fuck anyone in prison. But you want me to make you my bitch? Or would you rather me treat you like the man I love?"

"Cort—"

"Stop talking, Ford." Cort rubbed a hand over his eyes. "You suck at that too."

I really do, don't I? He followed Cort back inside, wanting to say something even half as sweet as Cort just had. Something that didn't involve jail time or killing anyone.

Maybe he needed to keep it simple. Just tell the man how he felt. "I've told you I love you, haven't I, Cort?"

A crooked smile on his lips, Cort flung his arm over Ford's shoulders. "Not since the last time you told me to go fuck myself."

"Which was about ten minutes ago?"

"True."

"So no?"

"No, Ford. And you haven't bought me flowers ever. You're a shitty boyfriend." Cort smirked. "But I love you anyway."

"Yeah…" Ford's head hurt. He was gonna be a dad, and he hadn't even gotten used to being in a relationship. And…he was going to puke. He bolted away from Cort and rushed into the closest bathroom. Made it just in time.

"What the hell did you do to him, Cort?" Akira sounded like an angry wildcat. Cort was in trouble now.

It also occurred to Ford that they were in the bathroom connected to the Ice Girl's locker room.

"Hey, why wasn't Justina down here with you?" Ford wiped his mouth with the back of his hand and sat on the floor beside the toilet. "Who's taking her place?"

"And he remembers his job." Cort snorted, cutting the sound short when Akira glared at him.

Akira knelt in front of Ford. "She tweaked her ankle during the opening performance. Nothing serious, but the trainers and I decided to give her some time to walk it off. Now, what's going on with you?"

"I don't think I'm ready to be a dad. I haven't had the best example." He took a deep breath. "But I'll figure it out."

"Good to know." Akira brushed the sweaty strands of hair away from his face. "We'll *all* be ready before we decide to take that step. I loved seeing you take care of Bran though. I think you'll be an amazing daddy."

"He better be." Cort petted Akira's hair. "When were you planning to tell us, Tiny?"

"Tell you...?"

"That you're pregnant."

Akira covered her face with her hands and groaned. "Everyone else is saying I've lost weight, and you two think I'm pregnant? Seriously?"

"You're not?" Ford didn't want to sound relieved. He wanted Akira to have their baby. Just...not until she wanted it.

She patted his cheek and laughed. "No. Is that why you look like you're gonna pass out? I swear, when it happens, it won't be a complete shock."

Folding his arms over his chest, Cort frowned. "But you haven't been eating. Or taking your birth control."

"I'm on a different kind of birth control. It affected my appetite, but that's it." Akira stood. "Next time, ask, Mr. Nash." She grabbed Cort by the collar of his shirt and kissed him. "Mmm, you smell like Ford's aftershave."

Damn, seeing Cort go all red was worth the humiliation of having burst in here to puke his guts out. Ford went over to the sink to wash his face and rinse out his mouth, chuckling as Cort shot him a dirty look in the mirror.

Then, because he really was a bit of an asshole, he grabbed Cort's wrist and lifted his hand. "Gotta go take care of our man, Shorty. Miss you!"

"What the actual fuck, Cort! What did you do?" Akira stuck to Cort's side, paling as she checked Cort's other hand. She towed him out of the locker room like a fiery little tugboat. But, being the smart girl she was, it took her only seconds to turn that glare on Ford. "If he hit a wall instead of you because you were being a jerk, I'm going to smack you myself. What did you say?"

"Nothing!"

"Cort doesn't flip out over nothing."

"Cort used to flip out if a man looked at him the wrong way, Akira."

"Cort's not like that anymore!"

Pulling away from them both, Cort shook his head and sighed. "Cort is right here. And I can get someone to look at this on my own. You're both at work, you do realize that, right?"

"So are you." Ford frowned as he considered Cort's hands again. "You think Keane will fire you?"

"Oriana's in charge of personnel. I don't think she'll fire me unless she thinks I can't do my job properly. Let's not give her a reason." He lifted Akira up, ignoring her laughing protests, and brought his lips to hers, kissing her softly. "Now that's how it's done. I'll meet you both in about an hour." He gave Ford a heavy lidded look. "I look forward to getting you home."

Lust hit Ford like a heavy fist to the guts, and he couldn't say a word as Cort took off down the hall. He almost didn't notice Akira staring at him, arms folded, tapping her little ballet slippered foot.

"Ford Delgado, what happened?"

Heat rushed up the back of Ford's neck. He didn't have any issue telling Akira everything, but *here*? "Umm…we made up?" She wasn't buying it, and he didn't blame her. Since when had he started sounding this uncertain? He grinned. "Cort finally admitted Detroit sucks, and he's gonna start cheering for the Cobras."

"You're a fucking liar. I'd say a horrible one, but I know better." She sighed. "Fine, don't tell me. He will."

Hooking an arm around her waist before she could storm off, Ford cuddled his beautiful, very squirmy little fireball against his chest and spoke quietly, close to her ear. "I'd rather not discuss it here, pet. Let's just say, the dynamics in our household are about to change."

She went still and peered up at him with her brilliant green eyes wide. "You mean—"

"Whatever you're thinking, yes, that." Ford planted his most professional smile on his lips as several staff members passed. Not very effective, since he was shirtless, in the hall, holding his scantily clad girlfriend. At least his reputation couldn't get much worse. "I need to go grab my jacket and...fuck, pray one of the guys has a spare shirt?"

"Scott's image consultant makes him bring a spare to every game." Akira straightened her skirt as she slipped away from him. "Game's almost done. Go ask him."

"Cort might not appreciate me going home wearing Scott's clothes." *Look at me, thinking ahead and everything. I can be taught!* "I'll ask Max. He's my brother-in-law, so should be fine, right?"

"Max's shirt will float on you." Akira took his hand and pulled him toward the locker room. "Cort can't get mad at you if *I* ask."

"Shorty, I don't need you to—"

"Shut up, Ford."

"Yes, ma'am." Ford chuckled as he gave in. Fuck, he loved this woman. And their man.

Right now, the idea of everyone knowing what he still hadn't adjusted to didn't sit well, but that wouldn't last. And then, if Akira and Cort were comfortable with it...

He'd tell the fucking world.

Chapter Twenty Three

Going to the game hadn't sounded like much fun to Sam this morning. Or this afternoon.

Or, hell, an hour ago.

Jersey Shore was on Netflix. *Finally!* Ian wasn't into it, but she binge watched whenever he wasn't home. And she'd planned to do just that while he played. Only, she wasn't a complete idiot. She knew a supportive girlfriend would be at the damn game. Showing interest.

Even *pretending* to was better than nothing, right?

By the time she got dressed in something cute, hopped in a cab, and got there, the third period had started. Trying to convince security that she was Luke's sister, and obviously should be allowed into the building without a ticket, took another half hour. To no avail.

She was still standing outside.

So she tried calling Jami. Then Chicklet. And finally, Silver.

"Hey, sweetie. Is everything okay?" Silver's tone sounded strained.

Sam glared at the guard. "Yeah…just trying to get in to watch my brother play."

Bringing up Ian would be pointless. She imagined fans tried dropping player's names to get free tickets all the time. But she'd *been* here before. It wasn't her fault the guard was new.

"Oh! What's the problem?"

"This security guy doesn't believe that I'm who I say I am." Sam rolled her eyes at the man when he gave her a dirty look. "He's being very mean to me."

Silver went quiet. When she spoke again, her tone was ice cold. "Pass him the phone, honey. I'll meet you inside in a minute."

The man was a lot nicer by the time Silver was done with him. Face blotchy red, he held the door open for Sam, walking with her and letting the other guards know that she'd been given a pass from 'management'.

As promised, Silver met her in the open area beyond the entrance and quickly took her hand to lead her to the first opening at the lower level of the rink. "You missed the last goal, but we're leading three nothing. Luke has two assists and one goal."

"So we're winning?" Sam frowned, looking around as a concerned hum spread over the arena. "Doesn't sound like it."

"It doesn't…" Silver glanced across the ice, the color leaving her face. "Why is Hunt in net? Where the hell is Landon?"

Without warning, Silver took off running back into the concession area, damn fast for a woman wearing stilettos. Sam did her best to keep up, but even in kitten heels, she found herself struggling to even keep sight of the other woman.

Cursing under her breath, she slipped out of her heels, picked them up, and bolted down the hall leading to the locker rooms. She scuffed her bare feet on the carpet and tumbled into one of the guards standing in the hall.

He saved her from pitching face-first into the floor.

"Whoa, there, cutie. Someone chasing you?" Big man righted her then held her close as he stared down the hall. One dark hand settled on her shoulder. "If you're in some kind of trouble, I can't hide you here, but you can duck out through the parking lot."

Sam tipped her head up. *Way* up.

Damn, this man is… Her pulse sped up, and she swallowed. She'd never cared about whether a man wore a suit or not, but this guy filled his out just right. He was huge, and she could feel his muscles bulging under the clean-cut black jacket. His skin was a rich, dark brown, and he had the most beautiful golden brown eyes.

Down girl. You have a boyfriend.

Very true, but…

But he'll be fucking his boyfriend in a couple of nights. And he won't touch you.

Even more true.

She smiled up at her new hero. "I'm not in trouble, but it was sweet of you to offer. I was trying to keep up with Silver. And failed."

"Ah. Well, then, I imagine she went to the locker room to check on Bower." The man motioned her forward. "Come on, I'll make sure you get there in one piece." He flashed her a panty-melting smile as they continued down the hall. "My name's Cam, by the way."

"Pleasure to meet you. I'm Sam." For some reason, the man made her want to sound more grown up. She cleared her throat. "Actually, it's Samantha. Samantha Carter."

"Luke's little sister?"

"Yeah…" *Well, there goes any chance of a good first impression.* At least she'd had a bit of time with Ian before he knew she was *that* Sam. The one who stole from people, who'd gotten knocked up, and who couldn't keep a job to save her life. She shrugged and sighed. "I'm sure you've heard of me."

"Yep." He winked as he opened the locker room door. "Wait until you hear about me, sweet girl. Everything they say about me?" He leaned close as she moved to step over the threshold. "Is true. So I'm in no position to judge."

She bit her bottom lip and spun around, walking backward for a few steps. "Now you've got me curious, Cam."

"Good." He grinned, looking her over in a way that had her trembling all over. "I'll see you around, Sam."

Once the door closed behind him, she didn't have time to dwell on the exchange. She heard Silver crying and followed the sound.

"*Viens ici, mon amour.*" Bower held out his hand, careful not to move as the team doctor put another stitch in his jaw. "I'm fine."

"That remains to be seen." Dean Richter put his hand on Silver's shoulder, his whole bearing tense as he watched the doctor. "Damn it, Landon, don't fuck around. Did you hit your head?"

Landon sighed. "No. I got a few guys piled on me. It happens."

"Your helmet came off. And you got a skate in the face." Dean looked over at another man standing close. A trainer or something. The man quickly nodded. "You're not going back out there."

"Ever?" Landon smirked.

The doctor scowled at him.

"Sorry, Doc." Landon remained silent as the doctor finished the last stitch. Then he braced his hands on his thighs. "Shero and Callahan already made the call. Hunt's finishing the game. I *am* going back on the bench so the fans know I'm all right."

Dean gently tipped Landon's chin up with two fingers. "Are you?"

Feeling useless, Sam quietly approached Silver. The most she could offer was a hug, but Silver looked like she needed one.

Silver straightened and wrapped her arms around Sam. "I didn't mean to abandon you, honey. There's still a few minutes left if you want to watch?"

"Sure...but I can stay if you are?" Sam wasn't sure what would be better. She couldn't imagine how Silver must feel. If she saw Luke, or Ian, hurt like this, she wouldn't want to watch the game. She'd be coming up with good reasons for them to retire early.

"Oh, I'm going to watch. Make sure my man keeps his ass on the pine." Silver pursed her lips as Landon stood, with his helmet under one arm. Her eyes teared as she took in the long, stitched up gash along his jaw. "Damn it, Landon!"

"Come here, *mon coeur*." Landon drew Silver to him, pressing his lips to her hair as she leaned into him. "I'm fine. I swear."

"I'm afraid to watch the replay. What if the skate had cut you an inch lower?" Silver lifted her head and placed her hand to Landon's throat. "It's happened."

"Yes, but not often." Landon led the way back to the bench, Silver tucked to his side, Dean close to the other. "You both convinced me to continue playing. And I'm glad you did. I love the game. It's worth a few little nicks."

"Little nicks?" Silver's face was red as Landon kissed her. She leaned back against Dean as Landon made his way to the bench.

The crowd went absolutely insane. The Cobras had just gotten that thing where a guy got to sit in the box for doing some shit—*Sam's* guy, actually—but the fans didn't seem to care. They stood and applauded.

Sam snickered as she watched Ian stand, banging his stick on the glass and throwing his fist up in the air. Damn, hockey players were crazy.

Standing a little behind Dean and Silver, Sam tried to follow the game as the final minutes played out. She spotted Luke at one point and cheered when he got the puck.

Which made her feel stupid, because no one else was cheering, but Silver looked back at her and smiled. Which was nice.

As Luke rushed across the ice, the crowd started getting excited. For some reason, the other team didn't have a goalie. But they had more players. And all of them were hot on Luke's heels.

Ian got out of the box. Collided with the player closest to Luke. They both trailed after Luke, who took a shot just as a stick cracked into his side and snapped in two.

He went down. Sam held her breath.

The noise was deafening. There was a red light going off and a buzzer, and she was pretty sure the Cobras had just won the game, but Luke was still kneeling on the ice. And then he bent over and there were people rushing toward him.

Her vision went black.

"Sam. Sam, look at me, baby." Warm hands cupped her cold cheeks. Silver's face was close. Her voice was soft. "As soon as you're ready, I'll take you to see your brother. He's going to be okay, I promise."

Shivering, Sam nodded and let Silver help her back to her feet. She didn't remember hitting the ground. Didn't remember much of anything beyond seeing her brother go down. She couldn't get enough air. And she couldn't see past the tears.

She choked back a sob and managed to get out the words she wanted to scream, even though they came out as a whisper.

"I hate this fucking game!"

Chapter Twenty Four

"Ian, I think I'm falling in love with you, but I...I can't do this anymore!"

This couldn't be good. Ian loved how Sam ran into his arms the second she saw him in the hallway of the hospital. He'd held her for a bit, ready to tell her there was nothing to worry about. Carter was gonna be fine.

Then she dropped this bomb on him and he'd forgotten what words were. And how to use them.

Callahan was suddenly beside him, one hand on his shoulder, the other cupping Sam's cheek. "Sam, I know you're scared for your brother, but the doctor said he'll be fine. He has a couple of fractured ribs. With the proper support, he won't even miss a game."

Sam's eyes narrowed and an angry red blush spread over her cheeks. "Are you fucking kidding me? His ribs are *fractured,* and you're going to let him play?"

"The team will follow the doctor's advice. If there's any way that Luke *can* play, I doubt anyone will be able to stop him."

"We'll see about that." Sam inhaled roughly and took Ian's hand, peering up at him hopefully. "You didn't say anything."

"I'm not hurt." Ian squeezed her hand and smiled. "I get why you're worried about Cart—about Luke. He's fucking fragile, but Coach is right. If he can play, he'll play."

"I fucking hate you both right now." Sam yanked her hand from his and stormed into Luke's room.

Both Ramos and Jami were already in there. Ian decided he'd let them comfort Sam for a bit, because he was apparently doing a horrible job of it. One second she loved him. Now, she hated him.

You're fucking useless, White. Go home.

Callahan's hand was still on his shoulder. He tightened his grip when Ian tried to turn. "Bruiser, listen to me. I won't tell you how to handle this, but let me give you a bit of advice."

Ian nodded. "Please do? I'm starting to think I should've waited for her at my place."

The assistant coach laughed. "Then she'd be mad at you for not being *here*. She's young, White, but in this, age has nothing to do with it. A woman doesn't expect you to read her mind, despite what some may believe. She *does* expect you not to take the easy way out when she needs you though."

"That sounds complicated." Ian sucked his teeth, pretty sure he wasn't the right man for this job. Or any job that didn't involve a long piece of wood, big smelly gloves, and blades on ice. "How about she just tells me what she wants and I do that? The 'I hate you' probably means she doesn't want me here."

"Or that you pissed her off by calling her brother fragile while he's lying in a hospital bed."

"Dude, I've broken ribs before. Did you see my ass lying in a hospital bed?" Ian didn't get it. Like, *really* didn't get it. Mason, hell, he wanted to go check on him, because the man had stopped fucking breathing. Carter was being a wimp. "I get that it hurts, but—"

"White."

"Yeah?"

Callahan's tone took on a sharp edge. "Don't ever call me 'Dude'."

Ian swallowed. Nodded.

Scratching his jaw, which had a nice layer of black scruff, Callahan looked over at the door of Carter's room. "I think Jami and Ramos pushed for Carter to stay longer than he would have otherwise, but that doesn't explain why the doctor let him. I think there's more going on."

"Really?" Ian frowned, feeling like an asshole. What if Carter was badly hurt and Ian was out here, calling him a wimp? "Du—Coach, I don't really think he's a wimp. But I don't get why people are freaking out. Mason's in a lot worse shape. I'd be checking on him if Sam hadn't asked me to come here."

"That's not a bad idea, actually." Callahan checked his phone quickly. "He's in room 513. I think he just got out of surgery."

A chill slithered over Ian's skin. "Surgery?"

"Yes. The swelling in his throat blocked his airway to the point that he needed a cricothyroidotomy."

"Ah what?"

"A temporary procedure…he has a tube in his throat to help him breathe." Callahan's lips thinned. "Fucking dirty fighter. Crushed his windpipe with that hit. If the league doesn't review, it's going to get ugly."

"But he'll be okay?" Fuck, Ian *really* needed to see Mason now. All this medical talk was freaking him out.

"He will be. I don't think he'll be back during the playoffs though." Callahan patted his shoulder. "Go see him. Most of the guys have already. I'll put in a good word for you with Sam."

"Will that work? I mean, she kinda wants me here, but doesn't?" His head throbbed. This was much worse than a concussion. At least, when he hit his head, he could sit in a dark room. He didn't have to worry about fucking up the one relationship he'd been sure of. "Like…am I allowed to be more worried about Mason than her brother?"

Chuckling, Callahan led him to the elevator and pressed the call button. "You are. I say so. Go see Mason. Then come back and she'll be ready for you to take her home."

"Sounds good." Ian knew *he* was probably being a wimp, letting Callahan give him an out, but he needed it. The night had been going so well, but when he'd gotten to the locker room, Shawn was gone and everyone was in a bad mood. He was sure he should be doing something, but...what?

He took the elevator to the fifth floor, then headed for Mason's room. Shawn stood outside the door with Justina, Ladd, and Ladd's little brother and sister.

Shawn smiled as he lifted his head. He was holding the toddler, showing the kid something on his phone. "Hey! I was wondering where you took off to!"

"Sam's worried about Carter. And I wasn't very helpful." Ian shrugged when Shawn arched a brow, obviously expecting the full story. "I kinda called him fragile. I was trying to make her feel better."

Snorting, Shawn shook his head. "I agree. Not helpful."

Ian glanced over at the closed door, feeling like a big hand had wrapped around his throat, squeezing as he considered the condition of the other player who'd gone down tonight. "How's Mason doing?"

"He's resting." Shawn stroked the toddler's back as the kid lost interest in the phone and stuck his thumb in his mouth. "We're waiting for Sahara to come out and accept that Ladd, Justina, and I, can take care of the little ones for one night."

"I guess I can't go see Mason then?"

"I don't think she'd mind. We just finished taking turns. Cam was here a few minutes ago." Shawn handed the toddler over to Heath, then stepped up to Ian, curving his hand around the side of Ian's neck. "How are *you* doing?"

Besides pissed off? Ian lifted his hand to brush his thumb under the stitches beneath Shawn's bottom lip. "Wondering why I'm one of the few that made it out in one piece? Fuck, I should have... I should have done more. Kicked more ass so they got the fucking message."

"Which would have gotten you thrown out of the game. Maybe suspended." Shawn sucked in a sharp breath, chuckling as he caught Ian's wrist. "I don't think you want to be touching me like that in public."

"I don't care who fucking sees right now, Shawn. I fucking hate that you got hurt." A painful spear of anger and regret stabbed into his chest. "Mason won't be playing. And Carter might be out too if he's worse off than anyone knows. I need to do something. I feel damn useless."

Justina stepped up to Shawn's side, chewing at the edge of her bottom lip as she met Ian's eyes. "I know it's not my place, but maybe being there for Sam will help. I hate feeling useless too, but knowing I can take care of the kids, that Sahara will talk to me if she's ready to fall apart... It's something, you know?"

Why would Justina want to help him at all? Fine, they weren't exactly competing for Shawn's attention. She had Shawn now. Ian would have him on the road. But she clearly didn't like Sam and who knew what Shawn had told her about *him*.

The idea of Shawn discussing his problems with this new girl, sharing all the things he'd once shared with Ian, irked him. But he couldn't hold it against her. *If* she really was okay with Shawn's lifestyle, she was just the type of girl Shawn needed.

Could give him everything Ian couldn't.

Her and Sam getting along would probably make life a lot easier.

Which gave him an idea. "Maybe after I see Mason, you can come back to Carter's room with me."

"Your girl that scary, Ian?" Shawn winced, then frowned at Justina. "Did you just pinch me, pet?"

Hiking up her chin, Justina held Shawn's hard gaze with one of her own. "Yes. Don't be a jerk."

"*Justina*—"

The girl ignored Shawn's Dom voice and smiled at Ian. "*I* would love to come with you. I want to see how Luke's doing. And Jami. Besides, Sam and I got off on the wrong foot. Maybe we can call a truce."

'A truce', not be friends. Ian nodded, not sure why he'd hoped for more. Or *what* he'd hoped for at all. He tongued his bottom lip. "You're cool with me though, right? Like, you don't mind that me and Shawn will be fu—"

"Damn it, Bruiser!" Shawn shook his head as Justina giggled. "We're not having this conversation in the hospital hallway."

Twirling a long strand of glossy, soft brown hair around her finger, Justina flashed Shawn an impish grin. "Why not? No one's listening. We've talked about all my fantasies and a few of yours. But you haven't told me about the man I'll apparently be sharing you with."

Umm yeah… Shawn's right. So not the place to be having this conversation. Ian glanced over at Ladd, who seemed to be watching YouTube videos with his sister, his brother fast asleep in his arms. They couldn't hear anything, but still. Kinda awkward to be talking about sex with them right there.

He cleared his throat. "If you're cool with me, I'm cool with you. Fair?"

Inclining her head, Justina smiled. "Fair."

"Good."

Pretty simple. He smiled back at her, liking how straightforward she was. Probably one of the many things Shawn saw in her.

That and the fact she was fucking cute. He looked her over, not sure why he found her simple outfit of blue jeans and one of Shawn's 'stylish' black and white plaid shirts so sexy. Sure, Shawn's shirt fit snug against her breasts, since the man didn't wear anything baggy, but the last time he'd seen Shawn wear that shirt, he'd had the sleeves folded up and the hem tucked in. Looked all clean cut.

Still sexy as hell, but Justina was beautifully casual. She had a sweet, girl-next-door appeal.

Not Shawn's type on first glance, but after talking to her a few times, Ian could tell she was smart and maybe a little sassy. She accepted a lifestyle most girls her age couldn't. Shawn didn't intimidate or overwhelm her. She took everything in stride and somehow kept the playing field level with the much more experienced man.

Hell, maybe she could give me a few tips.

Shawn put his arm around Justina and gave Ian a crooked smile. "You're both incorrigible. Maybe I should keep you apart until I figure out how to manage you better."

"*Manage* us?" Justina's eyes widened. She pulled away from Shawn and turned to face him, hands on her hips. "You were doing so well, too. The idea of being managed isn't very appealing."

Lips sliding into one of those seductive smiles that went straight to Ian's balls, Shawn reached out to tuck a strand of hair behind Justina's ear. "Doesn't it? Are you sure? I think you'd enjoy being taught how to be a good girl for me, *Röschen*."

Cheeks pink, Justina moved her lips like she'd lost the ability to speak.

A feeling Ian knew too well. He decided she needed backup. "You don't sound sure you could manage both of us. Maybe we should compare notes."

"I like that idea," Justina whispered, managing to shake off a little of the affect Shawn had on her. Her tongue flicked out over her bottom lip, and her throat worked as she swallowed. "Got any tips for when he makes your mind go blank with a few words?"

A raised brow from Shawn, with that cocky smirk, had Ian tugging at his collar. Fuck, was it getting hot in here? He exchanged a look with Justina. "Nope. Still working on that."

"So tempting…" Shawn let out a soft laugh. "Sahara's out of the room, Ian. Go see Mason. Then we'll work on your girl."

Who? What? Ian had no idea what Shawn was talking about at first. But then he spotted Sahara and the grim reality he'd briefly escaped came back to him, cooling his blood.

His jaw hardened, and he approached Sahara, whose face was blotchy, eyes bloodshot. "Hey, sweetie. How is he?"

"Better." Sahara's smile was shaky, but he could tell she was fighting hard to hold herself together for the kids. "You can go in. The nurse is being really nice about letting all the guys stop by, but it has to be quick. I think you're the last one."

"Are you staying with him tonight?"

Sahara sighed and shook her head. "I don't know. Leaving the kids with Justina before was one thing, but all night?"

She had a point, but as he watched Ladd with his siblings, and considered Justina and Shawn looking out for them, the answer was pretty simple. "The kids have a lot of people. Who does Mason have?"

"Cam's coming back in a few minutes."

"Sure, but..." Ian wasn't good giving advice. Opening his stupid mouth tended to make things worse. But he had a feeling Sahara needed to hear this from as many people as possible to know she was making the right choice. He could tell she didn't want to leave. "Who do you think he'd rather wake up to see? You or his ugly little brother?"

Sahara's eyes teared a bit, even as she laughed. "Cam is *not* ugly. But you're right."

Ian winked at her. "Happens sometimes."

"More often than you know." Sahara leaned in for a hug, then whispered in his ear. "I pushed her toward Shawn. I think he's good for her, but...don't let him hurt her. Don't make him choose."

"I couldn't if I wanted to." Ian kissed Sahara's forehead, finding it strange that he'd been doing much more not that long ago. And yet, it wasn't weird that they were just friends now. She'd moved on with a good man, and he was happy for her.

Maybe that was how Shawn had managed to be with so many different people, giving them his speech, then walking away without looking back. He knew they'd find what they were looking for.

With someone else.

When does Shawn get what he's looking for though?

For the longest time, Ian had believed Shawn wasn't really 'looking for' anything.

But seeing him with Justina, he wasn't so sure anymore. Maybe he just hadn't found the right person until now.

And it wasn't me.

"Do you want to, Ian?" Sahara pressed her hand to his cheek, drawing his attention back to her. "He would choose you."

Ian watched Shawn pull Justina against his side as they joined Ladd and the kids. And he shook his head. "I don't think he would. And...I don't know how I feel about that."

Sahara hugged him again, not seeming sure what to say. She let him into Mason's room, standing back as he approached the bed.

Laid out on the bed, with a blue sheet pulled up to his chest, the toughest man on the team lay way too still. His dark brown skin had an ashen cast to it, and Ian's chest hurt as he stood by the man's side. He stared at Mason, at the machines helping him breathe. At the bandages on his throat and the tube in his neck. Even in the dim light, he could see the thick swelling from the punch that had crushed his windpipe.

One more game against the Leafs. Only one more if the Cobras weren't too fucking broken to finish them. If this series went to Game 7...

Not happening.

"I'm gonna make Kennel pay, Mason." Ian took Mason's cold hand in his, his jaw tense. "He doesn't get to do this to you and get away with it. I'll fucking destroy him."

Pressure on his palm had his heart skipping a beat. His eyes burned as Mason's opened. He forced a smile.

Mason's dark eyes narrowed. His lips moved, but no sound came out. He pressed his eyes shut. Then shook his head.

"Aww, come on, Mason. You'd fucking kill him if our positions were reversed." Ian sighed when Mason opened his eyes again and glared at him. "Fine. I won't do anything stupid. But you hurry up and get better, or I'll hunt him down off the ice."

The edge of Mason's lips quirked.

"Glad we agree. I'm gonna leave you with your girl. I'd ask to be the best man at your wedding, but Cam's probably taking the spot. Or Josh...fuck, he'd look awesome, standing beside you in his uniform." Ian ducked his head as Mason's brow rose. "Not that I think your brother looks hot in his uniform. Or...okay, he does, but I won't hit on him. I swear."

Mason rolled his eyes.

"I'm gonna go now. But I meant it. Get better." Ian fisted his hand around Mason's, then backed away as Sahara took his place. He put his hand on her shoulder. "I'll tell the kids you said goodnight. Shawn and Justina should get them out of here. This place fucking sucks."

Sahara put her finger to her lips and looked pointedly at Mason, who winced as he made a weird sound. Almost a laugh, but like a really painful, strangled one.

"Ah...yeah, unless you've gotta be here. Then it's awesome. They've got...nice sheets." Ian winced when Sahara smacked a hand into her forehead. "I'll...see you around."

"Wait." Sahara pulled a set of keys out of her pocket and tossed them to him. "Give these to Justina."

Nodding, he got out of the room before he said anything else stupid. Or anything at all, because Mason looked like he was trying not to laugh, and with his throat fucked up, laughing would probably make it worse.

Back in the hall, everyone looked at him expectantly. He forced a smile, even though he felt like shit. Seeing Mason laid out sucked. Seeing Sahara so upset was hard.

But she'd agreed to stay, so maybe him being here wasn't completely pointless?

He handed Justina the keys. "She's staying."

"Good." Justina pocketed the keys then hooked her arm to his. "Now, let's go do some damage control with your girl. Little tip? All else fails, just *listen*. Say you're sorry she's upset. That you understand."

"Okay. I can do that." But when they got back to the first floor and reached Carter's room, Ian's mind went blank. Justina had retreated to walk with Shawn and Ian was left alone to face Sam, who was sitting alone on a chair outside the room, her head in her hands.

Where the fuck had Callahan gone?

Great, she's alone and I feel like even more of an asshole. Ian chewed at the inside of his cheek. Crouched down in front of Sam and put his hands on her knees. "Hey."

She lifted her head, quickly drying her tears with her hands. "You came back?"

"Why wouldn't I?" That wasn't part of the script, but he hated that she thought he'd abandoned her. "I went to check on Mason. Give you time alone with your brother."

Sam brushed her fingers through his hair, then looked down at his hands on her knees. "How is he?"

"Messed up, but I think he'll be okay." He rubbed her knees. "How's Luke?"

"Getting X-rays or something. He's coughing up blood. And they think one of his wrists is broken." She let out an angry growl. "Sloan yelled at him when he found out Luke hadn't told the doctor everything. And Sebastian...*damn*. He went really quiet, but it was scarier than Sloan yelling. I think if Luke has so much as an ingrown toenail the doctor's gonna know about it now."

"Shit. I'm sorry." He really was too. It wasn't like Luke had a damn cold. "I was a jerk before. And Luke was a moron for not telling the doctor everything."

"Ian!" Justina shook her head. "No."

Sam laughed and stood, lacing her fingers with his and grinning at Justina. "He's right, Luke's a moron. But I can tell Ian's trying. And I have a feeling I have you to thank for that."

Justina's cheek reddened as she lifted her shoulders. "He would have tried either way. I just wanted to make it a little easier for him."

"Thank you." Sam cocked her head. "Not sure why you bothered since I was a bitch to you, but—"

"It's forgotten, Sam. Your brother's hurt. The rest is just...stupid drama." Justina looked down at her hand in Shawn's. "This is a weird situation. I'm pretty sure there's no instruction manual for how to handle it."

"True." Sam slipped her hand into the back pocket of Ian's jeans and leaned against his side. She let out a happy sigh when he rested his arm over her shoulders. "This isn't high school. We probably wouldn't have been friends there, but it's not about who's the cool kid anymore. Maybe we should hang out sometime."

"I'd like that."

"Cool. I'm busy tomorrow, but maybe when the guys head out, we can grab a drink somewhere."

"Sure! We can catch the game Tuesday night if you're not working."

Ian grinned at Shawn, liking how well the girls were getting along. Rather than smile back at him, Shawn focused on Sam.

Who simply shrugged. "Maybe. I think I've had enough of this fucking game though. Feels like it's gone on *forever*."

Shawn's brow furrowed.

Justina looked uncomfortable.

Hoping to ease the tension, Ian laughed and pressed his lips to Sam's hair. "That's just because it's been a rough night, sweetie. Give it a couple days and you'll enjoy it again. I promise."

"Right." Sam snorted. "'Again'."

Lips thin, Shawn looked from Sam to Ian. "This has been fun, but we need to get the kids home. Give me a shout when you can."

"Will do." The sound of Luke grumbling as he was rolled back to his room drew Ian's attention. Sam slipped into the room behind her brother. Ian moved to follow. Then paused and glanced over at Shawn, who'd started to walk away with Justina, Ladd, and the kids.

He wanted to say something to Shawn. Like, he was looking forward to having him all to himself. Which would be a dick thing to bring up in front of Justina.

So he caught Justina's eye instead and said the only other thing that was important right now. "Take care of him."

Justina shot him a concerned look he didn't understand. "I will, but Ian...?"

"Yeah?"

"Take care of *you*."

Long after they were gone, Ian stood in the hall, trying to figure out what she'd meant. With everything that had gone down tonight, he was the *last* person anyone should worry about.

An hour later, he took Sam back to his place. She was exhausted, but as they snuggled in his bed, she got in a weird mood. Started kissing him. Slipping her hand into his boxers to stroke his dick.

Which felt fucking awesome, but he knew she was still too…sore to enjoy sex. And she wouldn't let him return the favor, which made any pleasure she gave him bittersweet.

As she kissed her way down his stomach, he laughed and pulled her back up into his arms.

"Honey, you don't have to do that."

Making an irritated sound, she braced up on one arm and scowled at him. "What if I want to?"

"Do you?"

She licked her bottom lip and gave him a seductive smile. "Yes. I want you in a good mood."

"I'm not in a bad one."

"I know, but…I want to ask you something."

This girl confused the hell out of him sometimes. What did sucking his dick have to do with asking him anything? He rose up, flipping her onto her back and resting his hands on the bed at either side of her head.

"You have my full attention." He kissed the tip of her nose to make her smile. "Just ask."

Her smile faded. She pressed her eyes shut. "Don't hate me, but I was wondering…have you ever wanted to do anything else? You could…maybe be a model? A sports announcer? A truck driver?"

He sat back, even more confused. "Huh?"

"I just want you to think about it. You can't play the game forever, right?"

Not something he hadn't considered himself, but after the talk with Callahan, he'd stopped worrying about the day coming when he couldn't play. The thing was, the idea scared him because he wasn't good at anything else.

He'd sucked in school. He remembered coming home with shitty grades. His grandmother used to call him her 'special boy'.

"You mean stupid." Ian never talked back to his grandmother, but he'd had a horrible day. His English teacher had made him read a book report in front of the whole class. One he'd gotten a really bad grade on. The whole class had read The Outsiders.

The book was sad. He didn't get the point of reading a sad book. So he wrote his report on all the things Ponyboy should have done. How the book could have had a happy ending.

In front of everyone, the teacher asked him if he was stupid. Why couldn't he follow simple instructions?

"You're a good-looking boy, Ian." His grandmother patted his head and smiled. *"You don't need to be smart."*

Ian wanted to be smart, but everyone knew he wasn't. The only time he wasn't treated like he was an idiot was when he played hockey. He was good at that. The coaches like him. They told him what to do and patted his shoulder and said he was a skilled player. The way he read the plays was 'intelligent'.

High School was a bit easier. The teachers liked that he was an important part of the hockey team. He'd gotten frustrated once when making up a math test he'd missed for a road game.

"I'm so fucking stupid!"

The math teacher chuckled. Gave him a few of the right answers. "You've got other talents. Keep winning games and none of this will matter, kid."

There'd never been a time when he'd had more going for him than his ability to play hockey.

"Ian?"

Sam was waiting for his answer.

He wasn't sure he had the one she wanted to hear. But he liked her. He didn't want her to give up on him because he had nothing else to offer.

So he held her close and nodded. "You're right. There's got to be something else."

Nothing else he wanted to do. But to make her happy?

He couldn't drive a truck. But he could load boxes. He was strong.

That has to be good for something.

Chapter Twenty Five

Fifteen messages were waiting for Shawn when he turned his phone back on. Half were from his parents, who'd watched the game with all his aunts and uncles and cousins, calling to give him their reactions every time they enjoyed his play or the team scored. He listened to them all shouting in German, and laughed as he heard his youngest cousin, Otto, repeat an enthusiastic curse from his father.

His aunt scolded his father. The message cut short.

The next wasn't quite so pleasant.

"Shawn, I'm not sure how this man got my number, but let me know if you want to hear from him. Or if we need a restraining order." His manager's tone was strained, as though she was fed up. *"I'm leaning toward the latter, but he says he's an old friend."*

Each message from her got a bit worse.

"He seems very...nice, Shawn, but I'm considering blocking his number. He expected to see you tonight and isn't happy that he didn't. He's going to the game in Toronto. Did you see him at the last one? Why didn't you say anything?"

"This man is obsessed. He got his wife to call this time. I'm worried. I don't care what time it is, call me."

"Shit, I just realized you're probably at the hospital. I've blocked his number and strongly advise you to avoid him. Please call me. I'm worried about you."

Charlotte didn't worry over nothing. Whatever Steve had said upset her enough for her to call Shawn more than she normally would in a week unless they had a good endorsement deal on the table. Shawn had no doubt that it was Steve calling her. That man was the only one who didn't seem to understand when he'd crossed the line.

Stepping into the kitchen while Ladd and Justina settled the kids into bed, Shawn called Charlotte, hoping she wasn't asleep.

She answered on the first ring. "Thank you for calling. After speaking to that man, I was tempted to call the police."

For fuck's sakes, this has gone too far. Damn it, Steve, what's your problem?

Shawn kept his tone level. "What did he say?"

"He... Damn it, it's not even what he said. He was very polite. He said he's known you for a long time and that you were 'close'. He's traveled a long way to see you and apparently feels entitled your time." She sighed and the sound of a baby crying came through the line. "You're lucky you pay me well. Paula's drained and our son is colicky. I'd bitch at you for this keeping me up if you weren't my favorite client."

Nice to hear, but Shawn still felt horrible for disrupting Charlotte's down time with her wife and new baby. The couple had been looking forward to becoming parents for so long. The baby bug seemed to be going around.

He'd never expected Steve to go to such extremes to get in touch with him. Thankfully, fans didn't usually consider hunting down agents and managers to reach their favorite players. Charlotte had fended off over-enthusiastic fans before, but it happened so rarely, it wasn't considered an issue.

"We dated back in high school. I probably should have gotten in touch with him." The very idea made Shawn's stomach turn, but the alternative was Steve finding another way to get to him. Which was unacceptable. And he didn't want Charlotte concerned. "Give me his number. I'll call him tomorrow. And I'm sorry he bothered you."

"Shawn...look, I don't usually get involved in your personal life. I know you enjoy your freedom, and you've managed to publicly maintain a positive reputation, regardless of how 'easy' you are."

Charlotte sighed. "But I need to know. Is this man going to be a problem?"

"Not at all." Shawn considered carefully how to make Charlotte believe him. "He's important in his field and isn't accustomed to being ignored. You have clients like that. Remember the one freaking that he couldn't get a last minute reservation at that fancy restaurant in New York? You called me because I knew the owner. I dealt with that for you. And I will deal with this."

She let out a tired laugh. "You're right. And this isn't the worst thing I've ever had to handle, but it's not what I'm used to with you."

"It won't happen again."

"Promises, promises." She lowered her voice. "All right, I'm going to convince Paula to go back to bed. But if you need me to deal with him, just say the word. It's the playoffs, Shawn. No distractions, got it?"

"Yes, ma'am." Shawn held his smile after ending the call, trying to convince himself to buy the story he'd told Charlotte.

Steve won't be a problem.

He'd traveled a long way. Chosen to use his vacation time to watch Shawn play. Shawn refused to delve deeper into what that might mean.

But he couldn't forget their last exchange.

"You want me to meet your wife after the game? I can do that."

"You fucking know that's not what I want from you."

Maybe Shawn should give Steve *exactly* what he wanted. It was just sex. Maybe the man just needed to scratch that particular itch. Once he'd gotten what he wanted, he would go back to his life. And leave Shawn the fuck alone.

Imagining Steve touching him again made his blood run cold. But at least it would be over. Steve could go back to being a mistake he'd made. A part of his past.

"Shawn?" Justina slipped into the kitchen, holding a blue plastic cup with a Batman logo. "Are you okay?"

Shawn placed his phone on the table and went over to hug her. "Why wouldn't I be? Is Bran sleeping?"

"Yeah, he just fell back asleep with Heath. Kimber was out like a light as soon as I tucked her in. She wanted to take care of her brothers, but she relaxed when I told her I had them." Justina laced her fingers behind his neck. "Thank you for sticking around."

"You would have managed without me; you're great with the kids." Shawn combed his fingers through her hair, tipping her head back so he could gently taste her lips. "I'm glad I was able to be somewhat useful."

"Somewhat? Bran loves you already. Heath seems terrified of the kid half the time, and Bran notices. If I'd been alone with them at the hospital—"

"Or tonight?" With the kids sleeping, Shawn knew his presence probably wasn't needed, but he was reluctant to leave. They'd be heading to Toronto tomorrow night to make sure they were well rested for game six on Tuesday. He didn't have much time left with her.

You'll have the whole summer, dumbass.

Only if she didn't wake up one morning and come to her senses.

You sure you're not just avoiding being alone, Easy?

No, it wasn't that. He didn't have to be alone. Tonight or any other night. One phone call and he'd have all the company he could want. Warm bodies to fill his bed. To fuck and forget.

If he stayed here, with Justina, he'd probably be sleeping on the floor.

And with kids asleep in the other room, he didn't expect more than a few soft kisses and sweet words. Justina might be a passionate young woman, but if he was uncomfortable with the idea of having sex in Mason's house, she likely wouldn't even consider it.

"You don't have to stay if you don't want to, Shawn. We'll be okay." Justina rose up to kiss him before he could open his mouth. "But I'd like you to."

He grinned, picking her up and carrying her to the living room. "I was hoping you'd say that. I can't seem to get enough of you."

Justina nibbled her bottom lip as he lowered her to the sofa. Her eyes went to the dark hall. "Shawn, we can't—"

"Justina, before you finish that sentence, please understand I don't mean sex. Though I will enjoy playing out a few of your dirtier fantasies when I get you back to my home. Into my bed." He framed her chin with his hand and bent down to give her a long, slow kiss. "I like being close to you. Enough that I'll probably be very sore in the morning."

Her nose crinkled in confusion. "That's an odd line. Why would you be sore?"

"It's not a line." Shawn's lips curved as he glanced down at the hard wood floor. "I told you I'd give you a reason to want more of me. If my sleeping on the floor simply to stay with you doesn't prove I'm serious, nothing will."

Putting her hand over her mouth, Justina let out a muffled laugh. "How noble of you, Shawn. So I get the sofa bed all to myself?"

Heat rose up the back of his neck. The voice in his head was howling with laughter.

Real smooth, Easy.

"Ah…yes. That's exactly what I meant." Shawn was pretty sure even Ian would be amused at his lame assed attempts to be a gentleman. This whole putting in an actual effort to win the girl was a lot more difficult than he'd imagined. "You're used to sleeping alone, so—"

"Nice try, Mister." Justina stood and gave him a little nudge toward the hall. "The closet right by the bathroom has some sheets and blankets. Go get them while I open this up."

"Pushy little brat." Shawn hooked his arm around her waist, kissing her cheek before turning her away from the sofa. "I'll open this. You're making me feel very foolish."

"I know, but it's cute."

"Cute?" He arched a brow at her. No one had called him cute since he'd hit puberty. "I think the word you're looking for is sexy. Handsome. Maybe well endowed?"

"Cocky, arrogant, and egotistical might be fitting as well." Justina smirked at him. "But I prefer cute."

Put that way, 'cute' wasn't so bad. He inclined his head. "Yes, let's go with cute. Can you get the sheets, cheeky?"

"Absolutely." She hesitated as he began piling up the cushions beside the sofa. "Have I earned myself a spanking yet?"

Oh hell yes! Shawn shot her a sideways glance as all the blood pumped into his cock. "Several."

She blushed, like she was excited by the idea, but embarrassed that she'd been bold enough to let him know. Padding down the hall quietly in her socks, she quickly grabbed the sheets and a thick, gray blanket. Once he had the bed pulled out, he helped her make it. Then stripped out of his shirt and pants, leaving his boxers on and climbing under the blanket.

Justina curled up at his side, her head on his shoulder. He could get used to holding her as he fell asleep. One of the few things he had little experience with. He usually tried to distance himself from lovers, even if they spent the night, because cuddling was dangerously intimate. But he wanted intimate with this playful, sexy, lovable young woman.

And despite her original plan to make their time together short and sweet, she didn't have the experience to avoid tender moments like this.

"I should probably tell you… I've changed my mind." Justina rested her hand on his bare chest, her soft fingers curling against the light hair, her lips brushing against his neck as she whispered. "One night with you won't be enough. I want to play with you again."

"That's good to hear." He trailed his fingers up and down her arm. "I've just gotten comfortable."

"So have I." She sighed and her fingers stilled. "And I shouldn't. I know better."

He frowned, not sure what to say to that. She was right to worry. If he was any other man, she could get hurt. She'd given him something precious, and no matter what she intended, she couldn't be completely detached.

If he'd tried, he could have made this simple. Offered to train her. Given her friendship and nothing more. To avoid hurting her, he *should* have helped her guard her heart.

But for the first time, *he* hadn't been able to set those boundaries. For her. Or for himself.

"You're safe with me, Justina. I don't blame you if you don't believe any of the promises I make, but believe this: I will do everything in my power to keep you from getting hurt." He could tell by her steady breaths that she'd fallen asleep, but he needed to say the words as much as she needed to hear them. And he would say them again. "I've never asked for a chance. I've never deserved one. But thank you for giving me one." He rested his cheek on her hair and let his eyes drift shut. "You won't regret it."

Chapter Twenty Six

Cleaning up after breakfast the next morning took forever. Justina finally finished sopping up the egg and orange juice that Bran had managed to get everywhere. Using the back of her wrist to brush away the hair sticking to her forehead, she looked over to where Shawn was scrubbing every frying pan Mason owned.

Kimber had been sweet to make a surprise breakfast for everyone. She'd tried to be so quiet, but Justina and Shawn had been jolted awake by the scent of something burning. Seconds before the smoke alarm went off.

Aside from burning the pancakes and the hash browns, Kimber had done a pretty good job. Which Justina had tried to convince her when the teen broke down in tears.

Shawn and Heath were more believable, polishing off enough food between them to feed the whole team. Bran, however, had thrown a full-blown tantrum and refused to eat more than a few bites of toast.

Crazy start to the day, but while the kids quietly watched a movie in the living room with Heath, Justina got to admire one of the sexiest men she'd ever met, proving himself even more perfect. She wasn't used to watching a man clean, but for some reason, it was *hot*.

She might not have grown up imagining Prince Charming, but she'd always told herself she'd find a man who wouldn't sit back and make her do everything in the house. Much as she loved her father, she hated how he left all the chores to her mother when they both worked the same crazy hours.

Her mother had often warned her not to expect anything else.

"That's just how it is, baby. You'll grow up very lonely if you don't learn to let a man be a man."

Strangely enough, Justina had been perfectly fine with that idea. She'd been too busy training to bother with boys in school—not that any had shown interest. Maybe if she hadn't been so shy, so focused on her schoolwork and on taking care of her little brother, she would have cared more about being noticed.

Then again, looking back, would any of those boys have been able to give her what she'd experienced with Shawn?

Letting out a soft snort, she shook her head. *Not likely.*

"What's so funny?" Shawn glanced over his shoulder at her as he wiped down the sink. He frowned when she shook her head and squeezed the sponge over the mop bucket, using it to clean the orange juice under the chair. "I wish you'd have let me handle that."

She grinned as she inspected the underside of the table, finally satisfied that there was nothing sticky left anywhere. "I chose this because those pans were bad. You should have let them soak for a bit."

"I've handled worse. This is why I do the cooking and White…" His brow furrowed and he turned back to the sink. "Sorry."

"Why?" Standing, Justina dried her hands on her jeans and slipped up behind Shawn to wrap her arms around his waist. "I know you miss him. Things were different for you two before and a lot's changed. We haven't discussed much about your relationship, but I don't think we have to."

Letting out a low growl, Shawn turned, picked her up by the waist, and sat her on the counter. He braced his hands by her hips and gave her a hard look. "Of course we 'have to'. Why would you say that?"

"Because it's none of my business."

"None of your… Damn it, Justina. What if I say it is? What if I say I won't do anything without considering your feelings?" He lowered his head and lifted one hand up to rub over his eyes. "Fuck, I'm doing this all wrong. Forget I said that. I'm gonna scare you off."

"Shawn Pischlar, stop assuming I scare that easily. I'm trying to keep this from becoming too serious between us, but I like you. I accept *you*." She palmed his cheeks and smiled down at him. "Is it that hard to believe I don't want you to change?"

"Just a little." Shawn turned his head to kiss her palm. "I expect to have to make some difficult choices at some point."

His lips were so soft; focusing on his words, rather than how much she wanted to kiss him, was a challenge. But he'd be leaving in a few hours, and the last thing she wanted was for him to second-guess every move he made because of her.

She had an idea. A crazy one she'd never have dreamed up with anyone but Shawn.

One she hoped would appeal to his 'Easy' side.

"This is going to sound bad, but I meant to ask…" She pressed her teeth into her bottom lip. "Would it bother you if I tried to seduce Ian?"

Shawn blinked.

Somewhere behind him came the sound of something hitting the wall. *Hard.*

She peeked over Shawn's shoulder, relieved to see it was only Heath. The poor guy had grape juice all over his chin and splattered on his shirt. He stood there, lips parted. Then dropped his gaze to the floor.

"Bloody fucking mess. Sorry." Heath hurried over to the counter to grab the paper towels. "Be out of your way in a minute."

Shawn shot her a wicked smile, then cleared his throat. "Ladd, stop."

Heath dropped the paper towels and straightened.

"Come here. Let's get you cleaned up first." Shawn leaned his hip against the counter beside her as Heath approached. "We're going to have to wash that shirt. Take it off."

Bad, bad man. Justina punched his shoulder, sure she was earning herself another spanking. "Shawn, Mason will kill you. Behave."

"What? I'm just going to go throw his shirt in the wash." Shawn smirked at her as Heath handed over his shirt, a flush spreading over his tight, smooth, muscular chest. "I'm sure he can get cleaned up on his own, but feel free to help him if he needs it."

With that, Shawn walked out of the room.

Justina snickered as Heath crossed his arms over his chest, his cheeks going red. He wasn't that much younger than her, but she had a feeling he was much less experienced.

After the last few days she'd spent with Shawn, anyway.

"Don't worry, I'm not going to jump you, Heath." She hopped off the counter and pulled a rag from one of the drawers, tossing it to him to dry his face before moving the mop bucket to clean the spill. "Shawn's teasing you. Go take a shower, I've got this."

Heath shook his head. "Don't feel right, you cleaning up after all of us."

"Okay." She stepped back, letting him wipe up the mess, hating how stiff and uncomfortable he looked. Maybe Shawn had gone too far. "If he bothered you, just say so. He'll stop."

"He didn't." Heath hunched his shoulder, his hand fisted around the sponge. "My agent got me on this team for a reason, Justina. I just...I haven't been ready to talk about anything."

"Or talk much at all, from what I've heard." She considered the young man, wondering if she could help him. Shawn certainly could, but her warning about Dominik had been only half joking. "You don't have to tell me anything, Heath. But I hope you know you can talk to your teammates. Mason or Shawn. Or almost anyone else."

"Yeah...I might." He shrugged. "It's weird, how chill everyone is. In Russia, guys got real tense when stuff was brought up."

"Is that why you're so quiet?"

He shrugged again. "Always was."

"Ah..." She could tell he'd shared as much as he was comfortable with. Which was a start. Hopefully, being around Shawn and Dominik and the other guys would give him the confidence to come out of his shell. "Do you need anything before you guys head out? You probably want to spend time with Bran and Kimber, but I could go to the store for you."

"I'm good." Heath grinned, taking the bucket to the sink to empty it. "Hey, speaking of White..."

Were we? Her cheeks heated as she realized he meant the conversation he'd walked in on. "What about him?"

Rinsing out the bucket, then storing it under the sink, Heath remained silent until he turned to face her. His overgrown, dirty blond hair fell over his eyes as he ducked his head and tucked his thumbs in the pocket of his jeans.

"You won't have to try."

As he slipped out of the kitchen, she stared after him, shaking her head when Shawn strolled back in, a crooked smile on his lips.

He pulled her into his arms and pressed his lips to her forehead. "I think he was flirting with you. I'll have to keep an eye on him."

"Why? Jealous?" She tipped her head back, hoping he wasn't. He had no reason to be. She had her hands full with him.

And possibly Ian if Shawn liked her plan.

Shawn chuckled. "Nope. You're not the only one who likes to watch, pet."

Her cheeks were probably beet red. She hid her face against his chest.

He put his hands on her shoulders and eased her away from him. "Don't go all shy on me now. I want to hear more about you seducing Ian. You caught me off-guard, but I'm intrigued."

She lifted her shoulders, then realized she probably looked like Heath when he went all nonverbal. So she cleared her throat. "Well, it would probably be easier if we were close."

"That it would be, but he's with Sam. She might not mind sharing him with me, but you're actual competition." His lips curved into a sly smile. "Not that I have a problem with that."

"How I am competition if you're not?"

"You're a girl."

"So?"

"So, Sam rightly assumes—as I already know—that Ian will settle down with a woman one day. I'm a phase she can wait for him to get past." Shawn cocked his head, studying her with a thoughtful expression on his face. "You would give him another option. Which I shouldn't allow, considering I want you for myself."

Him saying that shouldn't make her stomach go all fluttery. Shouldn't have her thinking about how nice it would be to wake up next to him every morning. But she was having a very hard time containing him inside that 'temporary fun' box she'd planned to keep him in.

That box hadn't been sealed very tight after the first night. Now? She seemed to have lost the flimsy top.

But her chin jutted up as she considered his last words. "I didn't ask if you'd 'allow' it. I asked if it would bother you."

One brow raised, Shawn cocked his head. "Will it bother you that I'll spend every moment alone with him naked?"

Bothers me a bit that I won't be there to see you two. She took a deep breath. "No."

"Then no. But may I ask why?"

That was a little harder to explain, but she did her best. "I'm scared for him. He's trying to be there for Sam, and she's using that to make him into the man she wants him to be. I know what it's like to live for someone else."

"You hardly know him, Justina."

"True, but you love him." Loose strands of her hair slid over her cheeks as she lowered her gaze to the center of his gorgeously tattooed, sculpted chest. "I'm trying very hard not to care about you, but I'm failing miserably."

"It's only failing if you have regrets. You won't, *Röschen*." His lips covered hers before she could question him. He stole all her doubts along with her breath, holding her when her knees went weak. "Do you believe me?"

"I shouldn't." She wrinkled her nose at him when he frowned. "You *know* I shouldn't. But I'm still playing with you, so the game's not over yet."

He let out a soft laugh. "I'm starting to think I'm a bad influence on you. 'The game', Justina?"

"I know it's not a game. It's real. There are consequences to every choice I make." She wet her lips with her tongue, refusing to let the choices weigh on her now. She was enjoying her freedom. Enjoying every new experience. "I'm having fun. Taking chances. I'm aware of the risks, but I'm not letting them hold me back."

"Which is exciting and terrifying all at once."

"Yes."

He traced his thumb over her bottom lip before kissing her again. "I know exactly how you feel."

"I doubt that." Damn it, she wanted to feel him against her. To lose herself in his touch. Things had been so simple when it had been all about sex. Now she had to explore emotions she wasn't ready for. Emotions he couldn't possibly understand.

But the way he looked at her made her wonder. His eyes drifted shut as he shook his head. "I'm breaking all the rules. I have to leave soon, and I don't want you wondering if I mean what I've said. We'll discuss this when I can stay."

"Which gives us plenty of time. If you're winning the game, you can't stay long."

He kissed her one last time before letting her go. "That's debatable. A win means I'm not going anywhere."

"That's not the game I mean."

"I know, but it's the one I want you to keep in mind." He took her hand, lacing their fingers together. "I plan to win them both."

Chapter Twenty Seven

A soft cry and Sloan's son was lifted from his bassinet stroller. His boy would never learn to self-comfort if this kept up, but after such a stressful morning, he wasn't going to tell Max that their baby didn't need to be held.

Sliding his arm around Oriana's shoulders, he walked with her away from the courthouse as she pushed the empty stroller.

She put her head on his shoulder and let out a happy sigh. "It's over. We have our family."

Slight moisture seeped through his shirt under her cheek. He stopped, turning her to face him before she could wipe away her tears. "What's wrong, Oriana? Were you worried she'd change her mind?"

"They're happy tears, Sloan." She shook her head and glanced over at Max, who stood a few feet away, James cradled in his arms. "But yes, I was worried. I might not have let Samantha kiss me." Her lips quirked as Sloan shifted his gaze, scratching his jaw. Her eyes went to Max. "Or stopped doing my job. But I was just as afraid as you two this was all too good to be true."

"Why didn't you say anything?" Max joined them, a soft smile on his lips as Oriana held out her arms for their son. He carefully laid him in her arms. "You seemed so relaxed. I feel damn stupid for carryin' on the way I did, but we've wanted this for so long."

"You weren't 'carrying on', love. You're a new father. I know you, and I expected you to be over-protective and consider every single thing that could go wrong." She pressed her lips to James' forehead, then lifted her gaze to Sloan. "And you, as usual, tried to find a way to control a situation you had no power over. You were both a mess. A beautiful, loving mess. I decided, the day we brought James home, that I'd give you a few weeks to pull your shit together."

Max snorted, brushing his fingers over James' fluffy, blond hair. "Only a few weeks, pet?"

"Don't you 'pet' me, Mister." Oriana gave Max a hard look. "We're in the middle of the playoffs. You're lucky I gave you this long. And now that we're two players short, you need to step up your game."

Sloan's jaw hardened as he considered how they'd manage to win the game tomorrow night without Dominik *and* Carter. Fucking pissed him off that Carter had tried to downplay a serious injury. The kid was too young to fuck up his career for a couple of games.

You did it.

Fine, but he'd been older. And he'd hid a fucked up hand, not a pulmonary contusion.

"Sloan?" Max rested a hand on his shoulder. "We're good now, right? I'll work my ass off on the ice. And James…James isn't going anywhere."

Neither Max or Oriana had paid much attention to the lawyer's warning that with a private adoption, Sam could legally contest giving up her rights for a full month, but Sloan wouldn't bring that up. Sam hadn't hesitated to sign the paperwork finalizing the adoption. She was in a good place. Stable and comfortable that she'd made the right choice.

He'd been a little worried, seeing the way she hung onto White, but the man was an adult. If it worked out between them, great. If not…?

Well, hopefully she'd explore all the opportunities available in her future. He knew Chicklet was giving her some light training in the lifestyle. Not something he would have considered, but it gave her and Chicklet some common ground to bond over.

Chicklet would tell him if Sam started second-guessing her decision to give up James. And likely be Sam's biggest supporter if she believed Sam was doing it for the right reasons...

She won't change her mind, Callahan. You know she won't.

Right. And Oriana had a point. It was the playoffs. He still had a job to do. Even with his son at home and two players out of the lineup.

He didn't think *he'd* let all the uncertainty affect his work behind the bench though. He'd made one mistake that had shaken Max's performance on the ice, but they were past that.

Aren't we?

Dropping his gaze to Max's hand, he inhaled slowly. "Are we good, Max?"

"Yeah. I reckon we've done all the talkin' we need to about what happened." Max's cheeks reddened. "Oriana didn't see it as no big thing, so...neither do I."

Liar. Sloan inclined his head as they continued to the car. He waited until Oriana leaned into the car to strap James in his car seat.

Then he backed Max into the driver's side door, bracing his hands at either side of Max's broad shoulder, his lips slanted in a cold smile as Max's eyes went wide. "Whatever you do, Max, don't ever fucking lie to me."

"I'm not." Max swallowed hard, looking over at Oriana as she stood beside Sloan, her arms folded over her breasts. "You fixin' to lose your damn mind here on the street, man? Like I said, we talked. It's over."

"You were pissed that I let Sam kiss me."

Max's jaw hardened. "You're damn right I was."

"You were jealous."

"No." Max grabbed Sloan by the collar of his pale gray dress shirt, his voice low, his tone hard. "I don't want to lose you. Part of me is still raw from losing Dominik. You want the truth? I always wonder if you'll be next. If one day you'll feel you don't fit. If things will get so tense that a clean break will be better than us all hurting any more."

"How many times do I have to tell you I'm not going anywhere, Max? I love you both."

Nodding, Max lowered his gaze. "And I believe you, but what do you and I have besides friendship? What do we have to hold on to? All the pressure is on Oriana to keep this family together."

What? Damn, now Sloan was confused. He and Max had been close as brothers before even meeting Oriana. That hadn't changed. "Since when is our friendship not enough?"

"It is, I just…" Max shook his head. "Shouldn't there be more?"

Ah… Sloan had a sinking feeling he knew what Max was getting at. He took a deep breath. "Do you mean sex?"

He could almost laugh at the face Max made. The man didn't want to fuck him. Or be fucked *by* him. But he seemed to believe the lack of anything physical between them was an issue.

They weren't uncomfortable with one another in the bedroom when they shared Oriana. Sloan didn't panic when Max touched him. Didn't try to keep his distance. He was comfortable having Max close. *Needed* him close.

He couldn't picture their relationship without Max. It would be like losing a vital part of himself.

"Max, listen to me. I don't know what will happen years from now. I won't say we will never explore a different level of intimacy. But…" Sloan chose his words carefully. "If it's something you need, I'm willing to explore it now. I don't believe it is."

Max shrugged. "Yeah, I don't even fucking know anymore. Seems like everyone else has gone there. And if you're missing something, it's my fault. Oriana gives you everything."

"Do you want to give up control, man? I can take that from you." He actually liked the idea. Max liked watching everything, even the twisted mix of pain and lust Sloan and Oriana always pushed to the very edge. Sloan enjoyed Max watching them. Found satisfaction on how hard he got with every lash of the whip. With every head game.

"To be honest, I'd fucking *love* to give you a taste of what I give our beautiful woman."

Chuckling, Max curved his hand around the side of Sloan's neck. "That doesn't surprise me at all. I'll think about it."

Perfect. Sloan smiled and patted Max's cheek. "Glad we had this chat. We should negotiate more often."

Before he could back away, Max tugged at the collar of his shirt. "Wait."

Why? Sloan's lips thinned as Max stared at him. Apparently their 'chat' hadn't been enough. Max just had to fucking push the limits. He held still as the other man's lips brushed over his and felt…nothing.

He almost wished he'd been turned on. If he had, they'd have something to discuss. A different angle to their relationship. One Max apparently thought they needed. And he couldn't really blame the man. How many other relationships like theirs involved sharing in every way. Lust and passion exchanged, bringing every person involved closer.

What if Max needed that? Needed a partner he could experience everything with? Oriana made no secret of how often she fantasized about he and Max exploring more. What if Sloan was the one holding them both back?

Oriana giggled.

Sloan's brow furrowed as she and Max exchanged a look he couldn't read. "What?"

"You satisfied my curiosity. I reckon I'm good now." Max grinned then slipped into the backseat beside James's car seat.

The door closed.

And Sloan stood there, trying to figure out what the fuck had just happened.

"Would you like to drive, Sir?" Oriana shot him a playful smirk as she reached for the door. "You look a little stunned, maybe I should—"

"Explain."

Licking her bottom lip, Oriana took both his hands in hers. "I think that was more awkward than Silver hate flirting with Ford before she knew he was our brother. There was always this underlying...repulsion. Mostly from Ford. Thank God he already knew..."

This was true. Knowing both of Oriana's younger siblings, things could have gotten very *Star-Wars*-style-love-triangle if they'd both been ignorant of the facts. Not that he thought he and Max were *that* bad.

He scowled and shook his head. "I don't believe that's a good comparison. If I wanted to fucking kiss him, he'd damn well enjoy it. The man couldn't get enough of me."

"But you *don't* want to kiss him Sloan. If you did, this would be a very different conversation." She rose up on her tiptoes, brushing her lips over his, much the way Max had done, only this time, lust pumped through Sloan's veins. He cupped the back of her head, fingers delving into her hair, and tasted her lips in a long, hungry kiss.

From the open window of the car, Max cleared his throat. "As much as I enjoy watching you both, could we continue this at home?"

Sloan smiled against Oriana's lips. "Feeling left out?"

Max chuckled. "Just a bit."

All right, this was better. Sloan kissed Oriana again, swiped the car keys from the pocket of her sweater, and shooed her to the passenger side of the car. Their relationship would continue to evolve, but the tension of not knowing where they all stood was gone. Nothing had to change. They were comfortable. More than satisfied.

He did enjoy teasing though. A little uncertainty was a healthy part of any relationship involving a sadist.

Keeping his tone light, he pulled out onto the road. "You know, a good Dom always strives to meet the needs of those who belong to him. Even if he can't satisfy those needs himself."

He caught Oriana's frown from the corner of his eye. She shook her head. "We agreed to keep things between us."

"Yes, but if Max has other needs—"

"He doesn't."

"You don't speak for him, pet." At a red light, Sloan caught Max's eye in the rearview mirror. "You're awfully quiet, man."

Lips quirking into a lazy smile, Max shrugged. "Sorry, I got stuck on one part of what you said and ignored the rest."

The man knew Sloan too well for him to be much fun to toy with. Sloan brought his attention back to the road as the light turned green. "Which part?"

"I belong to you."

Not a question. Sloan's heart swelled, and he remained silent for a few moments to avoid saying anything sappy. The bond between him and Max was strong. Stronger than some who fucked like horny dogs. Fulfilling in its own way.

Together, they gave Oriana everything she could possibly want. They worked together, for her, for one another, and for their family. Which was all they would ever need.

"You're damn right you do."

Chapter Twenty Eight

It was over.
Done.
The end.

And the relief at signing the last of the adoption papers made Sam feel horrible. There had to be something wrong with her. Seriously wrong.

As soon as she walked into Ian's house, she kicked off her shoes and headed right to the living room, curling up on the sofa and pulling the thick blue blanket she'd left there last night around her. She kinda wished she'd gone straight to Chicklet's place. Staying with Ian for an hour before he took off seemed pointless.

"Hey…" Ian came over and crouched down in front of her, rubbing her blanket covered knees. "Are you sure you're okay? I know you said you were, and I should probably leave you alone, but—"

"I *am* okay. And it's freaking me out!" She slammed her fists down on the sofa. "And I don't want you to leave me alone."

Ian inclined his head. "Then I won't. Do you want a beer? Are you allowed to have one?"

For some reason, him being all sweet and careful pissed her off. She ground her teeth, fighting back the urge to take out her irrational irritation on him. "Yes. I can drink."

He rubbed his lips. "You're not on any meds?"

"No, and I'm not fucking breastfeeding either. Damn it, why did you offer if you were gonna make a big deal about it?"

Throat working, Ian straightened. The man looked fucking lost. "Sorry."

"Why are you sorry? You didn't fucking do anything!" Sam dropped her head back into the sofa, covering her face with the blanket as she let out a loud groan. "*I'm* sorry. I'm being a total bitch."

"You aren't. You've been through a lot. I understand—"

"*I* don't understand why you're being so nice." Sam let the blanket fall and hugged herself. "You didn't sign on for the insanity that is Samantha Carter."

Sitting at her side, Ian wrapped one arm around her and kissed her forehead. "Actually, I did. I like you a lot, Sam. I know I'm not around much, but that's gonna change soon. I'm not here for just the fun stuff."

"Or *any* of the fun stuff." She wrinkled her nose. "And you're here because it's your house."

His lips parted. His brow furrowed.

Then he grinned. "So about that beer."

Watching him bolt to the kitchen, Sam struggled not to laugh. He was trying so hard, and she appreciated everything he did, but she could drive herself nuts trying to figure out why he bothered with her.

And she had to. She had to know what he 'liked' about her so she could keep doing it. Once he headed out for the game in Toronto, he would belong to Shawn. And Shawn had every damn advantage. He was fun. Uncomplicated.

They call him 'Easy' for a reason.

He was all the things she wasn't. Her pathetic intro into BDSM wouldn't put her on his level anytime soon. What did she have to offer that Ian couldn't get from Shawn?

You mean Shawn and *Justina.*

She fisted her hands by her sides as she considered the other girl. So adorable and innocent. A good girl. The type of girl Ian would probably want if he wasn't stuck with Sam.

Got a wild pity party going on up in here!

"Shut up." Sam shoved the blanket off and stood. No way was she going to lose her man to Miss fucking purity. Of course, the chick wouldn't be so pure, now that Shawn had gotten his hands on her, but that was even worse. Shawn knew what Ian liked. He could mold Justina into the perfect woman for him.

Sam could sit back and feel sorry for herself, or she could stand up to the challenge.

She heard the distinct sound of a chip bag being ripped open in the kitchen.

Then Ian's phone vibrating. She glanced over at the sofa, bending down to fish it out from between the sofa cushions.

"Ian, your phone!"

"I'll be right there. Can you answer and tell them to give me a minute?"

"Sure!" She cleared her throat and accepted the call. "Hello?"

"Oh dear, I must have the wrong number." The woman sounded very upset. "My nurse called for me. I apologize."

Her nurse? Sam spoke quickly before the woman could hang up. "Are you calling for Ian? He'll be just a minute. I'm his…friend. Samantha."

"Yes, I am! I'm his grandmother." The woman let out a soft laugh. "Have we spoken before? I don't remember him having a young lady in his life, but I forget so much."

"No, we only started dating recently. But it's a pleasure to have gotten a chance to speak to you." Sam looked up as Ian came over, holding bowls of chips and dip, and two beers. "He's here, I'll pass him the—"

"No rush, sweetheart. I'd like to know more about you. Do you live in Dartmouth?"

"Yes. Actually, I'm living with your grandson." Maybe she shouldn't have said that. Her cheeks heated. "I mean…well, he was nice enough to give me somewhere to stay until I find my own place."

The old woman chuckled. "That's my boy. So giving. I've been hoping he'd find a sweet young thing and stop running around with all those loose women. Not to say there's anything wrong with a young man sowing his wild oats, but I think he's ready to settle down."

"I hope so." Sam bit her bottom lip and lifted her gaze to Ian, who was gulping down his beer, staring at her like the conversation was making him nervous. "I'm really enjoying our time together."

Ian visibly relaxed, his lips curving slightly at the edges.

"I'm very happy to hear that, my dear. Now let me talk to my grandson. If you're not too busy this summer, maybe you could come with him to visit?"

"I'd like that very much." Sam grinned, deciding she really like Ian's grandmother. The woman didn't know her, but it was cool to have someone treat her like she wasn't the biggest mistake any man could make. "Goodbye, Mrs. White."

"Please, call me Estelle. It's been a pleasure, Samantha."

After handing Ian the phone, Sam picked up her beer, idly flipping through the stations on TV as she enjoyed the light, malty flavor. She loved how calm Ian was, talking to his grandmother. There was something about the way he spoke that made it seem like he hadn't heard from her in a long time.

"Yes, I'm still playing for the Cobras, Grandma." He laughed. "No, I'm twenty-seven now. I eat just fine. No, she doesn't cook for me. Yes, she's cleaned…I know I'm messy, but I'm getting better." He went quiet. "Umm…yeah, I have my plane ticket for next month, but I can get her one. I'll ask her." He sighed. "No, Grandma, I'm not ashamed of you! None of those girls were important enough… No, I don't mean that I used them. Can we not talk about this?"

Sam hid her smile behind her beer when Ian shot her an exasperated look.

"I know I'm not a kid anymore. At this point, I'll beg her to come, all right?" He snorted. "That's not funny. Grandma! Bribing me with food isn't fair. You don't need to do anything special. Yes. I promise. I will. She loves you too." His voice hitched. "I love you too."

Placing his phone on the coffee table, Ian lowered to the sofa beside her, staring blindly ahead as he rubbed his thighs.

"Hey." Sam put her hand over one of his. "What's wrong?"

He lifted his shoulders and swallowed hard. "She was doing awesome until the end. Then she thought I was my father. And she told me to give my mother a kiss for her."

"Oh, Ian…I'm sorry." Sam set down her beer and pulled him into a tight hug. He hadn't shared anything about his family with her, but she had a feeling the reminder of his parents hadn't been pleasant. "They're…they're not around anymore?"

"No. I lost them both when I was little. She raised me." He rolled his shoulders. "It's tough, but she wouldn't want me getting all depressed. And she was herself when she asked me to take you to see her. You don't have to. She'll probably forget, but—"

"I'd love to." Sam grabbed both beers off the table, handing Ian his. "Look, I know we haven't known one another long, but you've been here for me. I'm not just here for when things are easy."

Taking a sip of his beer, Ian arched a brow. "Do you mean exactly that, or am I missing something?"

Okay, she had sorta, 'accidentally', thrown in Shawn's nickname, but she meant what she'd said. The good thing was, Ian would take her at her word. So she simply smiled. "You're not missing anything. I mean it. Actually, it'll be nice to do something for you for a change."

Ian's beer hit the table hard. He pulled her into his arms, lips claiming hers in a rough, passionate kiss that left her breathless. Then he tangled his hands in her hair. "Do you really believe you've done nothing for me, Sam? Just having you here, just coming home and holding you, and relaxing while watching a movie… Hell, just holding you at night. I love it. I love how comfortable I am with you. And people might think comfortable is boring, but it's not. I need this, Sam. I need you."

Those words…damn it, she never thought anyone would *ever* say them to her. Never say them and mean them anyway.

'I need you.'

In that moment, Ian had gone from being a great guy, to being the most amazing fucking man in the world. He knew how messed up she was, and he didn't care. He'd seen her at her worst, accepted when she couldn't give him what he could find anywhere else, and still wanted her.

She didn't deserve him. Wasn't sure she knew how to keep him. But she had more reasons—more now than ever—to try.

Shoving him back, then rising to push him onto the sofa, she latched onto the button of his jeans, snapping it open. "If you even try to stop me, I will hurt you."

As she fisted her hand around his dick, he let his head fall back and groaned. She grinned as she circled the head of his cock with her tongue. Already, the slick, salty taste of precum wet the tip. She wrapped her lips around his hot length as she knelt, palming his heavy balls and slipping her wet lips down slowly.

"Sam…oh fuck, that's good." He stroked his hand over her hair. "You don't have to—"

"Shut up, Ian." She grazed her teeth over him, letting out a soft laugh when he hissed in a sharp breathe. "Hands by your sides. Take what I'm giving you. Nothing more."

Sucking him in deep, pleasure filled her as he obeyed her commands, latching on the cushion by his hips and holding perfectly still. She licked up the length of his cock, enjoying the steady pulse under her tongue, taking her time tasting his hot flesh. Right now, in this moment, he was all hers. Completely powerless.

Which was a heady feeling. She'd never come from giving a guy a blowjob, but she was close. She undid her own jeans and slid her hand into her panties, matching the rapid stroke of her lips as she rubbed her clit.

The spark of pleasure intensified, and she lifted her head, letting Ian slip from her mouth as she cried out. Her core tightened on nothing, but the sizzle along her nerves burst out, pulling her into a flood of pure ecstasy.

Her first instinct was to languish in the pleasure. Her second was to make sure Ian found his release as well. Then the strangest thought occurred to her.

What would Chicklet do?

Not that they'd ever discussed this kinda thing in detail, but Chicklet could be mean. And she always had her reasons. She managed two men, one a fucking Dom, and the world seemed ready to bend to her will.

Sam was tired of playing Shawn's game on his terms. He always seemed so in control. He probably expected any efforts Sam made to be pathetic. To show Ian how much more he had to offer.

What if she changed the rules on him?

Resting on the floor, thighs pressed together, she sank into the sweet, dwindling sensations of bliss still lingering in her core. That Ian didn't move pleased her. She was able to enjoy the lazy euphoria soaking into her without distraction.

Feeling a little high on power and pleasure, she rose to her feet. Did up her jeans.

And smiled down at the man who'd clearly reached a level of need that was almost visibly painful. "You should get ready."

Uncertainty filled Ian's eyes. "What?"

"I don't want you to be late. But I enjoyed that very much." She leaned close to him, brushing a tender kiss over his lips. "Tell Shawn I said 'You're welcome.'"

Chapter Twenty Nine

Joining the crowd in the private lounge at the airport, all there to see the players off before their flight to Toronto, Justina couldn't help feeling out of place. With Bran in her arms, she'd at least had a purpose, but within minutes of stepping into the room, he was calling out for Ford.

"Little bloody traitor." Kimber held tight to Justina's hand as Ford swung Bran up in the air and the little boy giggled. "Don't he care that Heath is gonna be gone for days? He can see Ford any time."

"I don't think he understands that, cutie." Justina bumped against Kimber's side playfully as she made her way around the throng of wives and children, losing Heath somewhere along the way. A few of the families would be making the trip as well, but they'd be taking commercial flights later today.

Shawn had suggested Justina go. Take the kids to watch their brother play. Which was sweet, but the Ice Girls were involved in some local fan events, which she couldn't miss.

And Kimber had no interest in making the trip.

Acting all tough, fists clenched, bottom lip trembling, Kimber had glared at Shawn when he asked her if she wanted to go to Toronto.

"Really? Dominik's still in the hospital. Shit, what if something happens to him? What if Sahara needs me?" Her eyes flooded with tears. *"Bloody hell, she probably won't. I've been a fucking cu—"*

Placing one finger over her lips, Shawn inclined his head, his expression grave. "You have a point, little one. Sahara cares about you. I think you can be there for one another."

"She might not want me around anymore."

"Oh, Kimber." Shawn pulled the fragile teen into his arms, holding her as he met Justina's eyes. She could tell he wanted to comfort Kimber. To erase her insecurities. And being the man he was, not having all the answers bothered him. "You've had it rough. And I understand you not trusting people. But trust Sahara. Believe me, she not only wants you around. She needs you as much as you need her."

This man was going to steal his way into Justina's heart without even trying. He was with Callahan now, looking very serious as he listened to the assistant coach, nodding. He was taking Carter's left wing spot on the first line. And he was ready.

As soon as they'd reached the airport, he'd gained a focus she couldn't help but respect. Taken a few minutes to speak to all the rookies. To greet the players' wives and kids. She wasn't sure he knew how important he was to the team. How the very atmosphere changed the second he walked into a room.

There were other core members of the team who made up the heart and soul, but Shawn held his own unique spot. He was the vibrant pulse. The player whose steady rhythm didn't always fit with what was expected, but never stopped. Never slowed down. Despite all the challenges facing the team every day, they could count on him to find a way to get through the worst with a crooked grin and a never-say-die attitude.

Kimber was still giving her little brother dirty looks, so Justina led the girl over to Ford, who was gushing over his new nephew in the most adorable way as Bran tried to steal the baby's blue teddy bear.

Cort and Akira stood a few feet behind him, Cort grinning and Akira biting her bottom lip, her eyes full of longing. She'd called Justina this morning, confessing that she wished she *was* pregnant. And then went over all the reasons she wasn't ready.

Being a good friend, Justina had listened, not contradicting her, smiling as Akira talked herself into and out of having a baby. The call ended with Akira agreeing Justina could be in charge of the baby shower when she *did* make up her mind. Jami had too much going on and Sahara would make it a huge thing.

The three girls had such a close friendship, Justina had no words for how amazing it felt to have them include her.

Speaking of her friends, she spotted Jami with Ramos, eyes red like she'd been crying.

Justina glanced over at Akira.

Akira looked at Kimber.

And Kimber snickered. "Go do your girl thing. I wanna see the baby. And Ford needs to stop letting Bran be a brat."

Umm... Justina hesitated as Kimber joined the Delgado siblings and their partners, snatching the blue bear from her brother and laying it back in the stroller by the baby. Bran glared at her, clinging to Ford with one arm and sticking his thumb in his mouth.

Striding over, Akira hooked her arm to Justina's and led her toward Jami. "He's got this. And if he doesn't...well, Kimber hasn't met Cort yet, has she? He'll teach her some new words. Expand her vocabulary."

Justina stopped short. Sahara would not be happy if Kimber went home swearing more than she already did.

"Relax, I'm teasing." Akira chuckled. "My men are good with kids. If they weren't, my life would be much simpler. Ugh!"

"Aww, I feel sorry for you. I really do."

"You're starting to sound like Pisch. Not sure if that's a good thing." Akira let out a soft huff. "At least you won't have to worry about baby drama."

Ouch. Justina pulled away from Akira, frowning at her. "Why would you say that?"

Akira's brow furrowed. She tugged her bottom lip between her teeth then sighed. "I stopped worrying so much because you were clear that you were just having fun with him. I just meant... Damn it, I'm sorry."

Inhaling slowly, Justina shook her head. "No, it's okay. I'm not even sure why that bugged me. I'm turning twenty in a month. I don't *want* kids for a long time. And me and Shawn aren't…well, it's not something we would even…" Could she sound even more ridiculous? She rolled her eyes. "Even *if* it was serious, or going to be, we've known each other just a few days."

"Yeah…" Akira's gaze fixed on something across the lounge. "Pretty sure you've crossed the serious line, hon. I've never seen him look at a girl like he looks at you."

One look at Shawn and Justina's pulse sped up. He was still standing with the assistant coach, but Callahan had joined in on the teddy bear debate between Kimber and Bran. While Kimber blocked Bran's reach for the bear, she faced off against both Cort and Callahan, her stance all teen defiance. She'd probably said something they didn't like. Callahan seemed to be in lecture mode, and Cort was shaking his head.

With all the noise around him, Shawn was looking at her like they were alone. Like the distance between them could be crossed in a breath. Like he wanted to cross it and forget everything else.

He winked and turned his attention back to Callahan, stepping closer to Kimber and saying something that made the teen smile triumphantly.

Pressing her hands to her hot cheeks, Justina shifted her own focus back to Jami. She exchanged a look with Akira and joined their friend at the edge of the crowd.

"*Mi amor, estare contigo una eternidad. Nunca me iré de tu lado ni cuando respira por última vez. Eres la razón de mi existir. Sin ti no soy nada.*" Ramos tipped Jami's chin up with a finger, his Spanish accent thick as he whispered to her. "What you have…given us both, is not something to fear. Your father says you are not ready. *I* say we are."

Tears spilled down Jami's cheeks. "Are we? Luke…Luke is a mess."

"*No tengas miedo, mi vida. Juntos podemos con cualquier cosa.*" Ramos spoke slowly, and Jami seemed to understand most of what he said. She let out a soft, relieved laugh and hid her face against his chest. He kissed the top of her head.

"I'll give him shit while you're gone. But I won't tell him until you get back."

Ramos frowned. "Jami, he needs to know."

"He will. When I'm not mad at him." Jami jutted her chin up and scowled. "No one else needs to know yet."

Brow lifted, Ramos glanced over at Justina and Akira. "I think it would be good for you if your friends did."

Akira crossed the distance between her and Jami in a split second, laughing as she kissed Jami's cheeks. "Baby, I already knew. You turned down a cheeseburger with bacon and cheese and—"

"Akira," Ramos said, soft, but firm.

Justina approached Jami, laying her hand on her friend's shoulder. Jami had gone white. Food apparently wasn't her friend. "Deep breaths. No more talk of food. Your doctor will help you figure out how to eat what you need. My mom couldn't eat anything when she got pregnant with my brother, but the nausea passed after the first trimester."

Jami let out a soft sob as she hugged Akira, then Justina. "This is gonna sound lame, but I want my m…I want Silver. I didn't want to tell her, because she'll tell my dad, but she'll get how scared I am."

"Your mom." Akira rubbed Jami's back. "Silver is your mom. I think she's earned the title."

"Yeah." Jami sniffled and leaned back against Ramos. "I want to tell her first."

"Do you want me to get her?"

"Please?" Jami reached out and took Justina's hand. "Thanks for being here. I keep wondering why anyone would want to be my friend. I'm a train wreck and you…well, you've got it all figured out."

Justina laughed softly. "I play it well, don't I? I didn't think I was doing a good job, but now I do."

"I don't care if you do or not, Justina. I've claimed you as a friend. And if you aren't sick of me yet, anyone who fucks with you better watch out." Jami's lips thinned. "Even Sam. I'm trying to get where she's coming from, but…well, she needs to calm down."

As much as Justina appreciated having Jami in her corner, she felt bad for Sam. So she shrugged. "Everyone has their issues. I'm not worried about her."

"Good." Jami grinned. "Didn't I tell you Pisch was awesome? And he's still around, even after the speech."

'The speech' seemed to be a huge deal to everyone else. And hadn't been one for Justina at all. She wasn't sure how to respond. She didn't want to tell everyone that she hadn't heard it. That felt a bit too much like bragging.

She didn't end up having to explain anything.

Akira returned with Silver. Richter looked like he wanted to follow, but Bower put a hand on his shoulder. He cooed to his daughter, whispering something to Amia that had her letting out a high-pitched baby laugh and reaching for her other daddy. Richter grinned, taking his baby girl in her fluffy pink dress and leaning over to whisper in Bower's ear. Bower smirked at him.

Meanwhile, Silver reached for Jami, holding her close as Jami let out a muffled sob. "Talk to me, honey."

"I'm scared, Mom. Real scared." Jami sucked in a shaky breath. "I can't do this without you."

Rubbing Jami's back, Silver shot Ramos a fierce look, like a wolf sensing a threat to a cub in her pack. "What did you do to her? Is this about that damn boy you can't seem to control?"

Ramos's eyes narrowed, and Justina wondered if getting Silver involved had really been the best idea. She seemed to lash out before considering potential damage.

Before Ramos had to defend himself, or Carter, Jami drew away from Silver. "Please don't. I'm so tired of all this bullshit. We're supposed to be a family. Which includes Sebastian *and* Luke. How would you feel like if I started on Landon the way my dad—and apparently *you*—constantly attack Luke?"

Regret filled Silver's eyes. "I'm sorry, that's not what I'm trying to do, Jami. It's just…damn it, he does stupid shit, and it hurts you."

"I do stupid shit too!" Jami lifted her hand to her stomach, her expression softening. "Not this time though. It's not a mistake, it's just…" She shook her head when Silver's eyes widened. "I don't need a lecture. I need you to tell me everything's going to be okay."

"Oh honey…" Silver cupped Jami's cheek, lowering her voice. "Are you pregnant?"

Chewing on her bottom lip, Jami nodded.

By Justina's side, Akira tensed. Justina held her breath and took Akira's hand. If Silver reacted badly, Jami had them. And Ramos. They'd make sure she didn't feel completely alone.

A brilliant smile spread across Silver's lips. "That is amazing! Jami, you're going to be fine. I promise. I have a feeling I know what you're worried about, but I'll set you up an appointment with one of my doctors. She's the best. She'll do some tests to see if there's any risks."

"But there might be?" Jami closed her eyes and Ramos wrapped his arms around her, kissing the top of her head, showing support, even though he'd remained silent. "I wish I hadn't been so stupid."

"*Mi cielo*, you cannot change the past. You've come so far. You are a strong young woman." Ramos met Silver's eyes. "We haven't shared the good news with Luke yet, so I would appreciate you keep this to yourself."

Silver inclined her head. "Of course, but, Jami, don't wait too long to tell your father. I think, once he considers how happy both your men make you, how good they are with kids…" Her lips quirked. "Actually, I've seen Luke with Amia and Casey. He's great with Westy too. But I haven't seen you spend much time with the children, Sebastian. Are you sure *you're* ready for this?"

The big man blinked at Silver like she'd started speaking in tongues. "Why wouldn't I be? Jami has Amia in our home quite often."

Akira giggled. She apparently knew something Justina didn't.

"Yes, but have you ever changed a diaper?" Silver arched a brow when Ramos' brow furrowed. "Walked around for hours while she cries? Fixed a bottle?"

Ramos chuckled. "Ah, that will not be a problem. Jami will breastfeed."

Jami frowned and turned sideways to stare up at her partner. "I will?"

"I simply assumed..." Ramos cleared his throat. "It seems we have much to figure out before our daughter is born."

"Or son."

"*Gatita*..."

Jami rolled her eyes. "Don't '*gatita*' me. You can't command the sex of the baby."

"I am aware of that."

"And you don't get to decide if I breastfeed." She leaned close to Silver, kissed her cheek, whispering 'thank you' before towing Ramos away from the crowd. "And Silver's right; why don't you ever change diapers?"

Once they were out of hearing, Silver faced Akira and Justina, a satisfied smile on her lips. "I think they're going to be just fine, don't you?"

I can see why she meddles so much. Justina bit the inside of her cheek so she wouldn't laugh at Akira's stunned expression. *It can be strangely effective.*

"When I tell Cort and Ford that news, I'm going to make sure you're far, far away," Akira said dryly. "Preferable not in the country."

Eyes wide, Silver put her hand over her parted lips.

Oh no. Justina winced as Silver spun around.

"Ford Delgado, get your dumb ass over here!" Silver put her arm over Akira's shoulders. "You let me deal with him. I don't know why you're afraid to tell him. This is so exciting!"

Akira glanced back at Justina over her shoulder, mouthing, "*Help!*"

Ford and Cort rescued Akira before Justina had to figure out how. Hell, she couldn't help but love all these crazy people. No risk of things *ever* being boring.

Hands settled on her hips and she smiled, not even needing to look to know it was Shawn. She could sense his presence with the same ease as moving around a familiar place in the dark, knowing things were exactly where they should be.

His lips brushed her ear. "I was tempted to save you for a minute, but you clearly didn't need it."

Turning in his arms, she brought her hands up to cup his cheeks. "Good boy."

He chuckled, bending down to kiss the tip of her nose. "I should seriously nip this habit you've developed of disrespecting your Dom in the bud, but I like you cheeky."

She wrapped her arms around the back of his neck. "Damn, how am I gonna earn spankings then?"

"You don't have to earn them." He rubbed his scruffy cheek lightly against her smooth one, which reminded her of how good it felt when his face brushed over other places. He slid his hands down to her ass with a soft laugh. "I can be very generous."

His playful demeanor dropped abruptly, and he went still. She looked over her shoulder, not surprised to see Ian.

The poor guy slunk into the room, head down, shoulders hunched like the weight of the world rested on them. His hair was wet, pulled back away from his face in a tight, low ponytail, sharpening his features. His suit was wrinkled, his tie crooked, as though he'd been tugging at it.

Shawn moved to go to him. Then stopped.

Justina hated that he even second-guessed where he needed to be. That had to stop. She gently nudged him forward. "Go. I've had you all to myself for long enough."

Jaw hardening, Shawn opened his mouth. Then closed it, nodded, and crossed the distance between him and Ian.

Only superficially, because physically, he couldn't seem to get very close. Emotionally, she could see how shut down Ian was.

She didn't want to assume Sam was to blame. He could have gotten bad news. A family tragedy. A setback with his contract. Hell, maybe he hadn't slept well without Shawn. At least, for the next few days, that wouldn't be an issue.

That didn't bother her, but knowing Ian would have once reached out to Shawn for any of those things did. Sam had taken on that role in his life. And like her or not, Ian needed her to be there for him as much as he was there for her.

Too bad life wasn't fucking fair.

Ian was giving and giving, because he was that kind of man. Everyone had to see that he was drained. Tired. Needed to lean on someone else for a change.

A role Sam couldn't fulfill, even if she tried.

Shawn can be that someone. Justina went to join her friends and give the two men some privacy.

Hoping it wasn't too late for them to recover what they'd lost.

Chapter Thirty

The man standing in front of Shawn looked completely lost. Ian wouldn't meet Shawn's eyes until Shawn jutted his chin toward a quiet corner of the room. Then he simply followed, hands in his pockets, head down.

Shawn would have taken a walk with Ian, but the team would be heading out any minute. They could talk on the plane, but he needed to know what was going on with Ian. *Now*.

He brought his hand to the back of Ian's neck, studying his face, noting the chill of the skin under his hand. "What's wrong? Is it your grandma?"

Ian's lips twitched, but he shook his head. "No. I talked to her. She was... *her*. She remembered me until the end of the conversation. It was nice."

An issue, but not the big one. Shawn had seen Ian after a phone call from his grandmother when she didn't know him at all. Those precious moments where she was the woman who'd raised him would have been good, but losing that abruptly must have cut deep.

The man always clung to the positives though. So he would fight how much it hurt, because at least he'd gotten those moments. Shawn could dig deeper and force him to acknowledge the pain, but that wouldn't help. Not yet.

There was more going on, but Shawn had to get Ian to relax enough to discuss it.

He gave Ian a little smile, tugging lightly at his ponytail. "Why is your hair wet? It's a bit cold out today."

Ian shrugged, his jaw ticking. "I didn't notice. I just needed a shower. A fucking ice cold one."

"Do you want to talk about it?"

"No."

Shit. Shawn was usually better at this, but he'd let Ian back them into a corner. He'd have to knock down a wall to make any progress, but this wasn't the place for major emotional renovations.

"All right, guys!" Callahan shouted to be heard over the chatter. "Let's roll out!"

Looking up, Ian grinned suddenly, and Shawn decided he loved the assistant coach. While Shawn was racking his brain for a way to get through to his man, Callahan had managed it with a quote from one of Ian's favorite cartoons.

He caught Callahan's eyes. The assistant coach inclined his head, and Shawn mouthed "Thank you."

Setting a heavy hand on his shoulder, Ian took the lead, sights set on Justina. "Quit worrying about me. I'll be fine. It's stupid, but…maybe we can talk later. Give your girl a hug and kiss so she don't feel abandoned."

How the fuck do all these triads manage? Shawn struggled against the guilt cementing in his guts. Fine, he hadn't needed the reminder from Ian to give Justina a proper goodbye, but he'd hated walking away from her to be there for Ian. And he was torn about how much time he and Ian spent apart. *Cloning an option yet? Someone should fucking get on it.*

"Hey, Ian." Justina rocked in her sneakers, thumbs tucked into the back pocket of her jeans. "Ready to send the Leafs to the golf course?"

"Damn right we are." Ian squeezed Shawn's shoulder. "I'm gonna leave you with your man. Thanks for lending him to me."

"I only charge for late fees." Justina blushed, ducking her head like she felt silly. "You don't have to go though. I need the mental image."

Lust surged into Shawn's cock. Fuck, he loved the naughty side of his girl. He glanced over to see Ian's reaction.

Ian's brow furrowed. "What mental image?"

Justina's face reddened even more. "Never mind."

If this is her idea of flirting, we've got some work to do. Shawn bit back a smile as Ian's expression went from confused to surprised.

"Oh, shit. You mean...?" Crimson spread over Ian's cheeks. "Were you hoping to see...uh... We don't do that. Well, we *do*, but not in public."

Giggling, Justina shook her head. "I don't need to see it. In public."

"Okay, that works." Ian tugged at his collar, his gaze dropping down to Justina's breasts. He gave her a crooked smile. "You're a Dark Horse fan?"

"Yes! I know it's not as cool as DC or Marvel, but I love *ElfQuest*."

"*ElfQuest* used to be Marvel."

"Was it? I didn't know that." Justina nibbled on her bottom lip. "I'm not a very good geek. I've never been to a con, and I couldn't tell you all kinds of details, but I like reading all kinds of stuff. Including comics and manga. I've started watching Anime."

All right, Shawn had gotten a comic book 101 from Ian, but he was so not on the level of this conversation. He had absolutely nothing to contribute, but he enjoyed seeing his two favorite people finding common ground.

"With that shirt, you're doing a good job representing." Ian licked his bottom lip, running his hand over his bound hair. "Umm, forget I said that. I shouldn't be perving on my best friend's girl."

Shawn took a moment to admire the snug, black t-shirt with its horse logo. He couldn't blame Ian at all for admiring how her beautiful breasts were displayed.

"You shouldn't?" Justina's eyes widened. She looked over her shoulder as Akira called for her. Almost all the players had headed for the pre-approved TSA screening area, and most of the families had left. Justina hopped up to Shawn, giving him a soft kiss before shooting Ian a sly grin. "I guess I missed the memo. I assumed it was one of the perks of belonging to this man."

Ian's mouth hung open.

Shawn snorted, and turned all his focus to Justina. "I'll call you tonight, *Röschen*."

"If you're too busy, I completely understand." Justina patted his cheek, blew Ian a kiss, then scampered off to join her friends.

Placing one finger under Ian's chin to close his mouth, Shawn smirked. "She's incredible, isn't she?"

"She's…" Ian shook his head as they made their way to TSA. "She really doesn't have a problem with me, does she."

"No. She worries about you."

"Is that why she was flirting?"

"If you call that flirting?" Shawn's lip curved, a sweet warmth filling him every time he pictured Justina, cute and bold and shy all at once. "I'm surprised you noticed."

"I'm not stupid."

That word again. Fuck, he hated that word. He frowned at Ian. "Have I ever treated you like you are?"

"Yes." Ian's lips thinned. He sighed. "No, but you're like everyone else, thinking you know what I need. And it's fucking with my head, and I don't like it."

Okay, this was new. Shawn tried to think of anything he'd done differently that might have pissed Ian off, but he drew a blank. Dropping his overnight bag on the belt, he stepped up to the metal detector, which didn't usually give him any trouble.

He spotted the two healthy trouble triplets apart from the rest, getting patted down, and sighed. If they'd been stopped, no way was he getting through.

As predicted, he was motioned off to the side.

Thankfully, he hadn't gotten his dick pierced yet. He wanted to, but the idea of months without sex had him putting it off indefinitely. He did have two in each of his nipples and five in each ear. Those in his ears were small, except for his one plug, so he wasn't worried about them. But he'd assumed there wouldn't be any problem, so he'd worn his small, titanium circle loops with spikes in his nipples.

Spreading his arms as instructed, he remained still as the TSA agent went over his body with the wand. The man stopped at his chest and shook his head.

"I'm sorry, I'm going to have to pat you down."

The man was kinda hot in his uniform. Shawn gave him a crooked grin. "I'm good with that."

Standing in the area where everyone was stuffing their laptops back in their bags and their change back in their pockets, Ian gave him a dirty look.

Behave yourself, Easy.

He kept his mouth shut as the agent used the back of his hand to feel over his piercings.

"I apologize, sir, but I'm going to have to take you to a private room to—"

"Oh for fuck's sakes." Shawn rolled his eyes and pulled off his shirt. "Hold this for me, cutie."

The man's face lost all color. He took the shirt, shaking his head. "Sir, the procedure is—"

"Are these going to be an issue?" Shawn pointed to his piercings. He could hear Vanek snickering and Ramos telling him to be quiet. Ian was growling and Callahan, thankfully, was making sure he stayed put.

Clearing his throat, the agent eyed his loops. "I'm afraid the spikes could be considered a weapon."

"Got it." Shawn popped one loop open, then the other, palming both and holding them out. The agent waved off another uniformed man who approached as though making sure the guy didn't need backup.

"If you have someone who saw you off, you can leave the jewelry with them, then come back through."

Well, Ian had his bags, so that wasn't a bad idea. He nodded, then glanced over at Ian. "Can you grab my phone out of the pocket and call and see if Justina's still here?"

Ian scowled, but nodded.

Shawn winked at the agent. "I'll be right back."

Jogging back to the lobby, Shawn smiled as Justina ran up to him, gasping in air.

She was still on her phone. "Yes, I found him. I agree, he's completely insane. It's sexy as hell though." Her cheeks were rosy red as she stared at his chest then at a group of teenage girls that were making catcalls. "Where is your shirt?"

"Left it with the sexy agent." Shawn lifted Justina up in his arms, giving her a deep, hungry kiss. "I regret nothing."

"I can tell." She gave his bare chest a playful slap when he set her down. "What am I going to do with you?"

"Never let me go."

"Right now, I have to, goof." Justina held out her hand. "Give me."

He dropped the loops in her palm, dipping down to give her another kiss. "If I tell you I love you, will you smack me again?"

Her lips parted. She swallowed hard, shaking her head. "Don't play with me, Shawn. Don't say that before you have to take off. *Why would you say that?*"

"Because I..." Fuck, she was right. He sighed, the burst of energy that had flooded him fading away. He wasn't trying to play her. He wasn't saying meaningless words, but he couldn't prove they were true when he wasn't around. "I'm sorry, that was thoughtless of me. You're so perfect, and I couldn't help myself."

She shook her head again, cupping his cheek. "I like you. A lot. I can see myself falling for you, because you turn my brain to mush. Now go. The man I lo—like doesn't ditch his team."

"I heard that." The rush was back. He didn't need time or space to accept how he felt. Yes, there were details to iron out, but the exchange between she and Ian had him more than willing to explore all the possibilities. To find a way to take everything he wanted. "Tell Ian I love him too, and I'll be right there."

"Shawn!" Justina laughed, waving at him as he sprinted back to the TSA line.

The agent brought him his shirt and he passed through with no further issues. Ian was the only one waiting for him when he reached the terminal, and he was still on the phone with Justina.

"What makes you think I can get him to keep his clothes on?" Ian threw his shoulders back and laughed. "Yes, I guess I can do that."

"Do what?" Shawn arched a brow at Ian, curious about how he and Justina were conspiring against him.

Ian made a dismissive motion, quickening his pace to catch up to the rest of the team.

"That's pure evil, Justina. Yes, I'll do it anyway, but you're so bad."

Now I'm worried. His girl was crafty. He might pay for his little performance at TSA.

"Yep, he's listening. I think we're freaking him out." Ian smirked at Shawn. "Thanks. You too, sweetie."

After Ian hung up, they weren't left with any time for Shawn to interrogate the man. Or call Justina back. But as soon as they sat down, Shawn turned in his seat and gave Ian a hard look.

"Talk."

"Okay." Ian folded his arms behind him, more at ease before a flight than Shawn had ever seen him. He was nice and distracted. "You know those comics she was talking about? *ElfQuest*? Well, I think the elves are hot. I need to go to ComicCon one day and see the people that dress up, because—"

"You know very well that's not what I mean."

"Not sure what you *do* mean?" Ian's lips slanted. "You said talk. I'm talking."

Anyone who thought subs were all meek and obeyed every command needed their heads checked. Of course, Shawn would get bored with a sub who didn't challenge him a little. Being easy was his job.

He folded his arms over his chest, trying his best to look stern. "I mean what are you two planning?"

"Absolutely nothing. She wanted to tease you after you said 'Do what?', so I played along." Ian stiffened and lifted his hands to the armrests as the plane started moving. "Fuck."

"You forgot your pillow."

"I don't need it."

"Yes, you do." Shawn thought back, sure he'd seen the pillow with Ian's carryon stuff. He started to stand. "Did you put it in the overhead bin?"

Pressing his eyes shut, Ian nodded.

The flight attendant came over as Shawn tried to open the bin. "Excuse me, sir, but you need to take your seat and keep your seatbelt on."

"I will, I just have to get something." Damn it, the pillow was stuffed behind both his and Ian's bags. Where the hell was his head at? He usually checked everything for Ian before they left the runway.

"Sir, I'm going to need you to take your seat." The flight attendant's tone was stern. She pulled down the bin door, pausing just long enough for him to move his hand. "Any belongings can be retrieved once we've reached cruising altitude."

"But—"

"Shawn, I'm fine." Ian grabbed his wrist, pulling him back to his seat. "Thank you for trying, but I need to deal. Team therapist said so."

Snapping his seatbelt in place, Shawn turned to Ian. "You're seeing the team therapist?"

"It was that or a 'real' one. I've only gone a few times."

"And he told you to 'deal'?" Shawn was going to find the asshole and hurt him. What the actual fuck?

Ian's jaw moved, like he was grinding his teeth, as the plane sped down the runway. "No. He said I should try to fly without so many comfort items. The pillow. A movie. You."

"Me?"

"Not specifically you, but anyone who lets me avoid facing my fears." As the plane left the ground, Ian grabbed for his seatbelt. "I'm going to be sick."

The team therapist was going to get his ass handed to him. Who the hell did he think he was? Ian's issues with flying weren't something that he could be forced to 'face' so carelessly. That he got on a plane, or in a car, at all took a lot of strength. He couldn't do underground tunnels or subways either. Would the 'therapist' tell him to head on down and 'face' it without delving into the reasons for his fears?

Just wait, asshole. Shawn took Ian's hand, holding it tight as he fought to keep his features relaxed. *You're fucking done here.*

Stroking the back of Ian's hand with his thumb, Shawn spoke softly. "You can't get up now, Ian. Grab the puke bag if you're going to be sick, and listen to me."

"I'm listening."

"I know you. You want to be tough, but you already are. You've dealt with some hard blows, and they've left a few scars. And that's okay." Shawn inhaled roughly, not sure he'd ever get used to seeing Ian like this. He wanted to shield Ian from all his fears, and he couldn't. Since Tim's death, many of them had gotten worse. And he couldn't fix this for him. "I'm right here. Let me be your safe place. The place where you can hide from all your fears. All the memories that haunt you."

Ian groaned as the altitude continued changing and the plane jolted a little. "I don't even know why flying freaks me out. It's just…it's a small space. We're stuck in here if anything happens. There's no…there's no way to escape."

Just like a mineshaft. To Shawn, the comparisons were obvious, but cementing the image in Ian's head wouldn't help him now. He hadn't made the connection, but a good therapist would. Obviously *not* the one that worked for the team.

"You told me once that Madeline made flying a bit easier. She told you how she was scared to fly at first. Do you remember?" Shawn continued to run his thumb over the back of Ian's hand. Over his knuckles. "She learned how rarely planes go down, and exactly how to be prepared if they do. Being prepared helped her get over her fears."

Throat working as he swallowed, Ian nodded. "I miss her too."

"I know. And so do I. She was an amazing woman." Shawn

rubbed Ian's forearm, hoping he hadn't just made things worse. "But the tools she gave you are what's gotten you through hundreds of flights. Even though you can't quite shake how much you hate flying, she made it easier."

"She fixed my pillow."

"She did. And I'll get it for you as soon as I can." Shawn fought to keep his tone level. Something about Ian's behavior was like subdrop. Like he'd been pushed too far and had been left off balance. He'd been good after talking to Justina, but there was still a vulnerable edge that a good Dom would watch for. Only, Ian hadn't played recently, so it must be the phone call. Or maybe seeing Sam sign over her baby.

Either way, Ian was with Shawn, and Shawn would make him feel solid again. Secure.

Safe.

"Tell me something that I don't know." Shawn pressed his fingertips into Ian's palm to center him. "Anything."

Ian's lips curved. "Iron Man is a better hero than Captain America."

"Maybe, but Captain America is prettier."

Blinking, Ian turned his head to stare at Shawn. "Dude, he ain't pretty."

"He is. And so is Thor."

"You're so weird." Ian looked down at their clasped hands. "And I'm so fucked up."

"Because you're into me?" Shawn wouldn't take it personally. They'd already discussed this.

Shifting in his seat, Ian held Shawn's gaze, something in his eyes telling Shawn he was very wrong about what he'd assumed. Ian opened his mouth, looking angry at first. Then all the fire sparking in his eyes lost its heat.

He let out a heavy sigh. "No, but I get why you'd think that. I'm fucked up because I'm in over my head. I want to be there for Sam, but I'm making a mess of it. She was so frustrated today, she hated that I had to leave, and she's trying to adapt to this 'open' thing. I'm not sure it's working out so well."

A shallow pool of dread filled Shawn, but he schooled his expression, refusing to let it show. "Would it be easier if we went back to being just friends?"

"Maybe, but I don't want ea—" The edge of Ian's lips slanted up slightly. "Actually, in this case, I *do* want 'Easy'."

"Oh yeah?" Shawn's lips slid into a sly smile, all his uncertainties banished to the dark corners of his mind, where he could deal with them later. Ian was in a better place. Shawn didn't have to let him go yet. Anything else could wait. "Care to visit the mile high club again?"

"The mile…?" Ian pressed his tongue against his bottom lip, his cheeks growing red. "Oh. Umm… Damn it, that's tempting. But I need…I need more tonight, Shawn. I'm not even sure what, but all the light stuff? It's just not cutting it."

Those words brought more relief than disappointment. He'd refused to even consider that Sam might have tried out her feeble new 'Domme' skills on Ian without Chicklet there to supervise, but it had been a possibility. So far, it seemed to be more of an irritating tease than anything.

"Is there anything that you've done that you enjoy?" Shawn kept his tone casual, so Ian wouldn't feel pressured. "That you'd like to experience fully?"

Ian freed his hand gently and rubbed his thighs, dropping his gaze to the floor between them. "I need something real. Something that doesn't leave me feeling empty."

Real had never been something Shawn could offer before, but he'd come to terms with the fact that things between him and Ian would never be anything less. He didn't have to worry about hurting the man. He'd given him all the power in how long their relationship would last.

He nodded slowly. "I can do that for you, Ian."

Easing back into his chair, eyes closed, Ian let out a heavy sigh. "She said to tell you 'You're welcome'. And I've tried over and over to figure it out, but I can't."

A cold chill trailed down Shawn's spine. The flight attendant let them know it was safe to leave their seats, take out their laptops, or move about the cabin. He stood, pulled both his and Ian's bags out so he could grab the pillow. After storing their things, he nudged Ian, who smiled sleepily before propping the pillow against the window to rest his head.

Shawn inhaled deep, let it out slow, and waited until he knew his tone would be completely level before he spoke. "When did she say that, Bruiser?"

Without lifting his head, Ian snorted. "Before the cold shower."

"Were you expecting…?"

"Her to finish? I don't know. I guess…I shouldn't have? She doesn't owe me anything." Ian lifted his shoulders. "But when she said that, I guess…I wondered if it was some weird punishment. She didn't seem mad. And, like…well, when you're mentioned, she's fine with it. Unless I'm reading her wrong. Which I probably am."

Yeah, there was no way a straightforward, honest man like Ian could even begin to understand the game Sam was playing. Shawn wasn't sure *he* did. It sounded like she'd explored edging with Ian, but Chicklet wouldn't have suggested that. Not so early in their relationship. They were still getting to know one another. Learning to trust each other with their desires, with their needs.

If Sam had done that soon after Ian spoke to his grandmother?

Damn it, that girl…

"Why you growling, man?" Ian sat forward, his eyes open now. "Something wrong?"

"*No-pe.*" Shawn reached out, gently freeing Ian's hair from the tight binding. "Take a nap. You're gonna need plenty of energy for what I've got planned."

You want to leave him for me to take care of, sweetie? That's fine. Shawn idly smoothed Ian's hair as the man settled back down, his cheeks a little red at the implication, but a sleepy smile on his lips. *You might not get him back.*

Chapter Thirty One

Hours later, Ian was finally able to take his stupid jacket and tie off and relax in the hotel room. Shawn's hotel room. He had his own, but going to it hadn't even occurred to him. He plunked down on Shawn's bed, flicking on the TV.

"Turn it off, *Bärchen*." Shawn strode across the room, removing his own jacket and tie. He hung up the jacket, but kept the steel gray tie in his hand. He eyed Ian's jacket, which was lying on the floor. But he didn't speak until Ian turned the TV off. "Knowing you as well as I do, that's likely the only jacket you brought. Is that where it belongs?"

Shaking his head, Ian pushed off the bed and bent to retrieve his jacket. For some reason, the subtle change in the air between him and Shawn gave him a heady rush. He didn't really care about the jacket, but he wanted Shawn happy with him.

"Good." Shawn smiled as Ian hung his jacket carefully in the closet. "Now give me your tie and strip."

Ian's mouth went dry, but he didn't hesitate to hand over the length of dark blue linen. A tie Shawn had picked out for him.

Shawn held both ties in one hand then motioned Ian to continue.

Hands shaking as a surge of lust spilled through him, Ian undid the buttons of his white dress shirt. He was still near the closet, so he grabbed a hanger, hoping that taking care of his shit would please Shawn.

A smile curved Shawn's lips. "You learn fast, Ian."

Pride swelled in Ian's chest. Damn, maybe he wasn't that stupid after all. Shawn always did that for him. Even if, in his own head, he was calling himself an idiot, Shawn seemed to read his mind and say or do something to banish the self-hate. Which was fucking cool.

After folding his pants in half and clipping them awkwardly to another hanger, Ian hooked his thumbs into his black boxer briefs, goosebumps rising all over as he considered what would happen next. He wouldn't be thinking for long, he knew that. Shawn would take him out of his head. Send him to that zone where all he felt was pleasure.

Where he and the man he loved were the only two people on earth and nothing else mattered.

He slipped off his boxers and tossed them aside.

"Lie down, Ian."

Moving to the bed, Ian climbed onto it, laying on his back and relaxing into the cool, smooth comforter. Shawn took hold of both his wrists, bound them together, then used the other tie to restrain Ian to one of the thin wooden planks on the headboard.

"This wood isn't strong, so don't tug hard." Shawn's tone had taken on the lulling quality that always eased Ian into a peaceful place. "What's your safeword, Bruiser?"

Bruiser. Strangely enough, the nickname made Ian feel like Shawn was saying 'I know you're tough, but now's not the time to be.'

And he was fine with that. He didn't want to pretend anything. If something was off, he'd speak up. But he doubted he'd have to.

He inhaled slowly. "Ultron."

Shawn arched a brow. "Really? I thought you liked him."

"Oh, he's cool, but bad news, you know?" Ian's cheeks heated. Was that a silly safeword? Maybe he should have chosen a vegetable. "Is onion better?"

Chuckling, Shawn shook his head. "No. Ultron is totally you. And if you make it onion, and start shouting other vegetables in the heat of the moment, I might misinterpret."

All right, Ian wasn't sure what other message Shawn would get if he shouted out something like…cucumber? Either way, best not to chance it.

"Ultron then." Ian tugged at his bottom lip with his teeth, testing the binding on his wrists. "You think I'm gonna need to use it?"

"No. But you may come close." Shawn gave him one of those ball-tightening, evil smiles of his. "I'm going to cover your eyes. And you will be silent unless asked a question. Understand?"

His pulse stuttered, and a cold sweat covered his whole body. Shawn's gaze slid over him, from his face, to his chest, rising and falling, faster and faster with each breath, to his pulsing erection.

He needed everything Shawn would give him. No matter how fucked up. He wanted it all. So he nodded. "Yes."

"Perfect." Shawn folded his sleeves neatly high over his forearms then went to his small overnight bag, returning seconds later with a blindfold. He leaned over Ian and placed the blindfold over Ian's eyes.

"Wait." Ian sucked in a breath. "Kiss me first. I need to see you when you kiss me…at least one last time."

"That's ominous, man." Shawn dropped the blindfold by Ian's head and framed his jaw with on hand. "I hope the 'last time' won't be soon."

Shuddering as Shawn's hot breath skimmed his lips, Ian met the other man's eyes. "It won't be."

The bruising pressure of Shawn's lips, the way he claimed Ian's mouth with the deep stroke of his tongue, sent lust crashing deep into the pit of Ian's stomach. Ian groaned, tugging restlessly at his wrists as Shawn eased back a little. A firm hand settled on the tie between Ian's wrists, pinning him in place as Shawn took his time exploring his mouth.

With his tongue and teeth and lips, Shawn made Ian feel more from the kiss than he'd ever felt from a good, hard fuck. His dick jutted out, twitching as arousal throbbed with each beat of his heart. His nerves were on high alert, and the soft brush of Shawn's hand over his chest made him jerk with a surge of pleasure.

Pulling away again, Shawn chuckling, flicking his tongue over Ian's bottom lip. "You really do need this."

"Fuck, yes. Damn it, Shawn, just—"

"*Mein Herr.*"

"What?"

"High protocol, *Bärchen.*" Shawn patted his cheek then straightened. "Let's see how well it suits you."

It took a moment, but Ian remembered. The special names he and Shawn would use for one another during a scene. Instead of 'pet' and 'Sir'.

A soothing warmth filled him and he grinned, testing the words out, hoping he got them right. "*Mein Herr.*"

"Very nice." Shawn ran his hand down Ian's side. "Are you ready?"

"Yes, *Mein Herr.*" The words still felt a little strange to say, knowing what they meant, but an approving smile from Shawn made it worth getting used to. He held still as Shawn covered his eyes with the blindfold.

In the darkness, Ian heard Shawn moving around the room. He sensed the man close to his side. Shuddered as Shawn's fingers circled first one nipple then the other.

"There's something I will try that I believe you will enjoy very much. It may feel strange at first, but focus on the sensations." Shawn's fingers moved to the other nipple, tracing around and around, returning to the first, until both were tingling and erect. "I won't ask permission. I won't explain what I'm doing unless you pause the scene. Do so by speaking up, but otherwise, remain silent. Nod if you understand."

Ian nodded, not sure he could speak if he wanted to. He was so fucking turned on, just Shawn talking to him was pushing all the right buttons. He'd never come from words alone, but there was a first time for everything.

Shawn seemed to know what he was thinking, because he stopped touching Ian's nipples and laughed. "I can tell you're so fucking close, but hold back for me, *Bärchen*, just a little longer. This should help."

Silence and then the slickness of Shawn's tongue on his nipple. Ian hissed in a breath, fisting his hands as cold covered his pebbled flesh. Shawn had used something to make the cold last. Not unpleasant, but weird.

The other nipple got the same treatment, then there was a pinch on each. One that didn't go away. The cold had numbed Ian's nipples, but his nerves seemed to draw up tight under that combination of sensations.

"You've gone a little soft, *Bärchen*." Shawn clucked his tongue, pressing his warm hand over Ian's dick. "Are you in pain?"

Shaking his head, Ian swallowed as his pulse quickened. His cock didn't stay soft for long even with that casual touch. He shifted his hips.

A slap on his inner thigh was all the warning he needed. Shawn would give him pain and pleasure, but in his own time. Ian couldn't demand anything. He didn't have to.

All he had to do was let Shawn take whatever he wanted and reap the benefits.

I can do that.

"I can tell you understand. Very good. I'm pleased." Shawn rubbed down his inner thigh, over the slightly stinging flesh. His accent had thickened, adding a sexy, rough edge to his tone. "I will be in the bathroom for a moment. If you're uncomfortable, just call out."

Simple enough. Ian wasn't worried that he'd be abandoned like this, but Shawn taking care to warn him made it easier to hear him walk away and relax and wait.

He heard water running into a container.

Breathing evenly, Ian let his focus return to the chilled tightness of his nipples. Only Shawn had ever paid much attention to his nipples, and until him, Ian had never known how erotic them being touched and toyed with and sucked on could be.

When Shawn brought his little chemical toolbox into the mix? That attention became something Ian craved almost as much as having his dick jerked off. His nipples being played with could get him hard in seconds. And apparently, having them stimulated for a length of time kept him that way.

The unfamiliar bite of cold and pressure had thrown him off for a minute, but now his dick was rock hard again, straining upward. A cool breeze over the moist pre-cum made him shudder.

"Center yourself, just a little, Ian." Shawn was back, standing close to the side of the bed. "I want you to last."

With a firm nod, Ian forced himself to turn his attention away from how fucking aroused he was. The dull throb in his nipples proved to be the perfect distraction. The cold sensation had shifted, heating a little more the longer he focused on them.

"Better. Now lift your ass."

Ian went still. He swallowed hard, but didn't hesitate.

Shawn spread something beneath him, then tapped his hip. "Down."

Lowering his hips, Ian's brow furrowed as he felt the towel now covering the comforter. "Wha—?"

"Shh… You're doing so well. Trust me, *Bärchen*."

Not a problem. Until a warm cloth covered the base of his dick and his balls. He held his breath. A few seconds later, the cloth was removed and Shawn spread a thick lotion-like substance over Ian's balls.

"Hold very still."

The familiar feeling of a razor brushing over his skin banished any idea of disobeying. Actually, Ian was pretty sure he'd never stayed this still in his life. His lips parted as he heard Shawn rinse the razor.

"It's a good thing you keep the hair trimmed. This shouldn't take long." Shawn handled Ian's dick and balls carefully, removing all the short hair, his tone conversational. "It will make your skin very…reactive. Deep breaths and show me how much you can take."

Wasn't so bad. Ian inhaled. Maybe a little tender…like his balls were more sensitive to temperature…

No, it wasn't that. Ian's jaw tightened as a sharp, icy sensation spread over the flesh of his balls. Colder and colder, until it almost burned. Ian gasped, the muscles of his stomach and thighs tightening as he struggled not to pull away. It was like slapping aftershave on his freshly shaved face, only ten times worse. The burning spread, and he could feel it in his ass, all the way up to the slit of his dick.

His eyes watered as he sucked in air through his teeth. *Ok, this is bad. Fucking hell, I can't…*

Shawn finished, and the warm cloth returned.

The warmth intensified the sharp burn.

Shitshitshit! Ian choked back a shout, digging his feet into the mattress.

"Unpleasant at first, but together…" Shawn's lips wrapped around the head of his cock. Pleasure sank in deep, soaking through the burn until it thrummed into Ian's bones. "A chorus of sensations. Lose yourself to them, Ian. You don't need to fight them. Let them take you."

Shawn's mouth covered him again, and Ian was lost. Every inch of his skin lit up, like tiny sparks of ecstasy shot from every pore. He couldn't help but squirm as a long suck drew him in deeper, turning the sparks into a pure, white-hot pleasure. Shawn's tongue moved around the head of his cock, pressing to the underside.

Close, so fucking close. If he let go, he'd come in Shawn's mouth.

Not enough. He shook his head. His brain was not firing on all cylinders, but there was something he had to say.

"Not alone, Shawn. With you." Ian shuddered as the edge of release tugged at him, almost painful to resist. But he did, because he didn't want this alone. "Take me with you."

Fingers circling the base of Ian's cock, Shawn lifted his head. The dick in his hand was dark red, from the solid, well defined head, all the way to the root, thick with veins, hot to the touch. Without hair,

Ian looked even bigger, which was one of the reasons Shawn had shaved him clean. His balls were nice and heavy, his dick a bit longer than average, with an impressive girth.

Tightening his grip to help ease Ian away from the edge, Shawn considered his next step. He'd planned to suck Ian off until he came this time, letting the mint on his nipples from Shawn's favorite breath freshener, combined with the tea tree oil cut with conditioner on his newly shaved skin, heighten the experience. The oil could be almost painfully intense on parts of the genitals, both for men and women, but with some practice on himself he'd found the right combination to avoid it becoming pure torture.

Thankfully, Ian had used Shawn's shampoos and conditioners at home often enough that Shawn knew he wasn't allergic. The only question had been how he would react to the sensations.

He was so fucking close to coming. Shawn wanted to take him there, but he also loved how Ian had forced himself away from the edge, needing to share the pleasure. He didn't care for overly demanding subs, but when one asked so nicely…?

"I wasn't sure how much you were ready for, *Bärchen*, but you've done very well." Shawn rubbed his hands up Ian's thighs, the light hair and skin slick with sweat. "I have one more thing I brought in case you were willing to go further than before."

Ian wet his lips, and even with the blindfold, Shawn could tell he was thinking hard about exactly how far they would go.

"All I ask if for you to continue trusting me. I won't hurt you." Shawn grinned when Ian's lip pressed together, slanting slightly. "That wasn't actually painful, was it?"

Cocking his head, Ian shrugged.

"Fair enough." Shawn opened the small green bottle from his kit, squeezing the smooth lotion into it. The scent was pleasant, subtle tea tree oil, with peppermint and aloe, a pricey all natural conditioner he found safe for extracurricular activities.

Using the back of his wrists, he nudged Ian's thighs apart.

A notable shudder went through the man. He groaned, but didn't try to close his legs.

"Shh..." Shawn slicked a finger with the DIY warming lube and circled Ian's tight hole. "Relax and this will be quite...interesting."

"*Interesting?*" Ian panted as Shawn pressed the tip of his finger into him. "Oh fuck, I don't know if I can do this."

"Yellow or Ultron, Ian?" Shawn kept his fingertip within that snug ring of muscle, but didn't press deeper. "Do you need to discuss this, or stop?"

"Don't stop." Ian shifted restlessly, panting. The oil had begun to take effect. "It was burning, but now it's...damn, it's good. It's hot. Not a bad hot. I need..."

Shawn smiled. He knew exactly what Ian needed. One thing Shawn loved about chemical play was with the right combination, no impact at all was necessary for that perfect edge of pain and pleasure. Ian's endorphins were taking over, confusing the sensations until everything felt good.

Using a bit more lotion, he sank his finger into Ian, moving it in a slow rhythm as he spoke softly. "Bend your knees."

Ian obeyed, but the slight bend in his knees wasn't enough. Shawn used his free hand to press them up and apart, admiring how fucking sexy Ian was, his round ass bared, his most sensitive parts completely exposed.

"God, that's hot, *Bärchen.*" Shawn poured more lotion into his hand. He managed to get two fingers past the ring of muscle without much resistance. "How does it feel?"

Breathing in roughly, Ian subconsciously moved his hips in a way that let Shawn's penetrating fingers in even deeper. He opened his mouth, no sound coming out as Shawn curved his fingers and found his prostate.

Ian moved with Shawn's steady thrusts. He didn't need to answer; Shawn could tell by his face that he was relaxed. In a zone of pure ecstasy. All he would feel was more.

There were two remaining objects Shawn had retrieved from his bag, neither he'd really been sure he'd need. One was a condom. The other was a butt plug, only a little bigger than his two fingers, with the rounded end wide enough to provide a nice stretch for a novice.

Withdrawing his fingers, Shawn stripped quickly, then lubed up the plug. He knelt between Ian's parted thighs and pushed the plug into him gradually, his eyes on Ian's face. The plug settled into place and Ian trembled, like his body was trying to find a new way to absorb everything being done to it.

Opening the condom, Shawn climbed onto the bed, rolling the condom down Ian's length, grinning at Ian's confused frown. "Hold your breath. This might hurt a bit."

Time for the nipple clamps to come off.

A rough shout escaped Ian as the blood pulsed back into his nipples. He tried to buck against the pain, but Shawn pinned his hips, straddling him and gently brushing his hands over his tender flesh.

Ian hissed in a breath. "Shit, shit don't touch them. Fucking painful."

"Do you need to stop?" Shawn rose up, guiding the head of Ian's cock into his own body. He lowered, inch at a time, pleasure pumping into his dick and his balls, flaring at the base of his spine. "God, you feel so good, Ian. I want to fuck you."

Tugging abruptly at his restraints, Ian made a rough, low sound. "Then fuck me. I can take it, Shawn."

Once he held Ian deep in his body, Shawn leaned down, kissing Ian as he held his wrists firmly in place. "You *are* taking it, Ian. Everything I give you. You wanted this, didn't you?"

"I want it to be good for you too." Ian's fists opened and closed, as though he was fighting a battle in his mind. And losing. "Not like..."

Ah, I see the problem. "Not like last time?"

"Exactly."

"Does this feel." Shawn lifted his hips, driving down hard, before repeating the motion. "Anything." He licked Ian's bottom lip. "Like last time?"

Jutting his hips up, letting out steady, incoherent rasps of passion, Ian shook his head. His back bowed as Shawn increased his pace, and he growled out a sound of pleasure that must have grated his throat.

Palming his own dick, Shawn jerked himself off, coming seconds later, like the dam used to delay his release had splintered. He braced his hands by Ian's head, his arms shaky, as his cum hit Ian's stomach. His balls tightened as the last spine tingling burst of sweet fucking heat shot through him.

Kissing Ian's lips, Shawn lazily rested half his weight on the other man, enjoying the slight shift of thick muscles beneath his chest. He watched Ian's face, pleased to see how at ease he was.

Not demanding to be released, not regretting what he'd done, simply basking in the lingering sensations as though he had nowhere else he'd rather be. Shawn smiled, gently drawing off Ian while giving him a slow, open-mouthed kiss.

"Mmm…" Ian didn't budge, not even when Shawn removed the plug, though he winced as the thick part stretched his tender muscles. "Come cuddle."

Shawn arched a brow after he'd ducked into the bathroom to wet a facecloth. "You're into cuddling now?"

"Yeah, cuddling is nice." Ian's lips curved. He tugged at his hand, seeming confused that it was tied. "I think I'm stuck."

"I think you're over-tired and high on the feel-goods," Shawn teased, untying the makeshift restraints, then rubbing Ian's wrists. They weren't even that red. Ian hadn't tried very hard to fight them. "I'm going to clean you up, then lay down with you, okay?"

"'Kay." Ian closed his eyes, making a face as Shawn removed the condom and wiped him down. "I should be doing that."

Shaking his head, Shawn tossed the facecloth in the trash so housekeeping wouldn't have to deal with it. He washed up in the bathroom, leaving his clothes off to climb into bed with Ian for the night.

Ian plopped an arm over Shawn's chest, his eyes still covered with the blindfold, his lips in a crooked smile. "Do I gotta clear out in the morning?"

Shawn idly brushed his fingers back and forth over Ian's arm, trying to figure out what the man was talking about. *Yep, I got nothing.* "What do you mean?"

"The rules…" Ian smirked, sounding all sleepy and silly. "We're breaking 'em all."

Rolling his eyes, Shawn held Ian a little tighter, pressing his lips to Ian's hair. "Don't forget, I'm making them up as I go." He inhaled slowly, the fullness in his chest more than a little terrifying. "And I think you were meant to break every one."

Chapter Thirty Two

"You did *what?*"

Sam winced as Chicklet glared at her. Arms folded under her breasts, she shrugged, keeping her eyes on the sturdy linen sofas in the furniture store. Chicklet was replacing the one Thora had eaten. Apparently Raif's new dog had a thing for leather.

Trailing a few feet behind them with Thora leading him, Raif let out a soft laugh. "You may want to lower your voice, love."

"Why, so I don't embarrass her?" Chicklet scowled at Raif. "She's embarrassed *me!* A baby Domme playing at edging before she's even earned the trust of her sub? Damn it, I need a drink."

"Now *there's* a solution. Get drunk and none of this will matter." Raif shook his head. "White's with Pischlar, who *is* a responsible, experienced Dom. He'll be fine."

Chicklet ran her fingers through her short, spiky hair and sighed. "He better be. If his game is fucked up because of this—"

That again? Sam slammed her hand into her thigh, spinning around to face Chicklet. "Is that all that matters to everyone? The damn game? I don't fucking care—"

"Careful, girl." Chicklet's eyes narrowed. She glanced over her shoulder at Raif, who'd gone still. By his side, Thora whined and nudged his hand. Chicklet spoke softly, a sharp edge to her tone. "The 'damn game' means *everything* to some people. Including White."

Great, now Sam felt shitty. Raif wasn't smiling anymore. Chicklet was mad at her. And apparently, her one attempt at being a Domme on her own had been a mistake. She'd expected Chicklet to be impressed. Maybe laugh and help her plan out her next move.

Instead, she felt like a kid learning to ride a bike who'd taken off her training wheels too early and had the scrapes and bruises to show she wasn't ready.

She *had* to be ready. At this point, she was so far behind Shawn fucking 'Easy' Pischlar, she might as well be trying to win the Daytona 500 on a tricycle. Her best efforts were downright ridiculous.

There had to be a way to jump back in the race. She dropped her gaze as Chicklet watched her expectantly and swallowed. "I'm sorry. I didn't think it was… I didn't think. Please don't hate me?"

"I don't hate you, kid." Chicklet sighed as she put an arm over Sam's shoulders. "But next time you think 'What would Chicklet do', how about you call her and ask?"

"Deal." Sam bit her bottom lip, glancing up at the older woman. "So…what *would* you do? I mean, if you were me?"

Raif joined them, feeling the arm of a dark gray sofa Thora was sniffing. "Forfeit?"

"Unlikely." Chicklet reached out and took Raif's free hand, twining their fingers together. "Some people are worth fighting for, no matter the odds. If I wanted to prove I cared, to show I knew I fucked up, but I wasn't going anywhere, I'd look at what *I* had to offer, rather than worrying about the competition."

"But I don't have anything!" Sam looked down at herself, not sure she'd ever felt this plain in her life. She was young, fit, and cute. In her tight, black ripped jeans and her bright blue tank top, she'd gotten a few appreciative looks from men in the store, but those guys weren't Ian. Ian had Shawn *and* Justina.

Both were appealing in their own way. Shawn had *everything* going for him. And Justina was sneaky cute and sweet. More dangerous because she didn't even know how to play the games yet. She just had to stand there and be adorable for men to want her.

Sam couldn't do cute. She failed at sweet. And she'd fumbled trying to be sexy and in control.

"Honey, you're still living with the man. Maybe you should stop trying so hard." Chicklet plunked down on the sofa both Raif and Thora seemed to like, smiling as Thora sat at her feet and rested her muzzle on Chicklet's thigh. "Has he brought up you finding your own place?"

"No…"

"Well then, maybe you should mention it. See where he stands." Chicklet ran her hand over the arm of the sofa, cocking her head. She gave Thora a hard look. "You gonna eat this one too if we get it?"

Thora licked Chicklet's hand.

"Fine, but I'm trusting you." Chicklet smiled at the dog, then turned back to Sam. "He's asked you to go with him to see his grandmother this summer. That means he's not looking at you as temporary. So work with that. Show him where you fit."

That made a lot of sense. Sam slipped her hand into her back pocket where she'd stuck her phone, flashing Chicklet a hesitant smile. "Thank you. I know I fucked up, and you're not happy with me. But I'm so grateful you still want to help me."

"Good. Don't make me regret it again." Chicklet waved her away, brushing her hand over Raif's to get his attention. "Come sit. Tell me what you think of this one."

Wandering off, Sam took out her phone and pressed speed dial to call Ian. She found an armchair a little ways away from the sofa section and settled down, tucking her feet under her.

"Hey, Sam." Ian sounded out of breath, like he'd been running. It was still a few hours before the game, so he might have been warming up. "How you doin'?"

"Good. You?" Sam chewed on her bottom lip as he went quiet. Yeah, she'd definitely fucked up. "Look, let's not be all weird. I get it. I acted like a total head case, and I hope you aren't pissed."

"I'm not."

Great. She pressed her lips together. He sounded good, but careful. Like he had no idea how to talk to her anymore.

Time for some damage control.

"Okay, I'm happy to hear that, but I need you to understand something." She took a deep breath. "I really *am* cool with you and Shawn. With this whole open thing. I wanted to show you, but I think I messed up."

"You didn't. I'm fine."

Bullshit. You're fine with him. *Not me.* She rested her head on the backrest of the chair. "Cool. So when do you want me to pack my shit?"

"What?" He sounded like he was paying attention now. His tone changed, softening. "I don't want you to leave, Sam. I just… I don't get what's going on."

"What's going on is you're with me. And you're with him. And… Damn it, did you really listen to a word I said?"

"Yeah, but I'm worried you're just telling me what you think I wanna hear. Like you're giving me what you think I want."

"I'm not." She lifted her thumb to her lips, chewing on the edge of her nail. Something she hadn't done since she was a kid. "How can I convince you? There's no instruction manual for how to make a relationship like this work. I like living with you. I wanna meet your grandmother. I want…damn it, I want all of it. I love you."

She almost wished she could take the words back. His sharp inhale could be heard clearly. She held her breath, ready for him to end the call. Or to be the nice guy and tell her he cared about her, but…

That but would clear everything up real quick. She couldn't get past that.

Instead, he made a rough sound. Then cleared his throat. "You do?"

"Yes. You're a better man than I deserve. I know that." She chewed harder at her thumbnail. "But, like, I'm at a furniture store with Chicklet and Raif. And what they have? It's awesome. I wish I could have that. I wish I could be looking at furniture for your place. I think you'd like this chair."

Lame much?

Ian laughed softly. "What does it look like?"

"What Chicklet and Raif have? Hell, I can't describe it, it's like…special. Like they're so comfortable with one another. I thought it was weird at first. I tried to see who belonged to who, you know?" She'd figured Tyler was Raif's, and Laura was Chicklet's, and the four of them kinda fucked and then split off in pairs. But she'd been so wrong. There were no clear lines. The love wasn't limited. All four of them shared and had a bond she envied. "I guess I saw love like a pot of stew, you know? Like you could only give out so much."

"I saw it like that too." Ian sounded like he was smiling. Happy. "But I was wrong and it's good you see that too. I don't wanna have to choose. And I know that sounds selfish, but—"

"I don't think it does."

"Really?" He seemed hopeful. Like he'd been torn before, but she'd given him a reason to explore the possibilities. "So, just to be clear, you aren't mad, you're fine with Shawn, and you're not moving out?"

"I never really moved in." She knew she was pushing it, but better now than when she got comfortable. "But I'll go if you want me to."

"Nope." Ian paused, then laughed. "I was asking about the chair though. Before?"

"Oh!" She laughed. Damn, this man was awesome. He'd already gotten over the fucked up shit. She stroked the arm of the chair. "It's a soft brown leather chair." She reached over to pop up the footrest. "I could so sleep in this thing. And it's big enough to cuddle in."

"Buy it. Like, seriously. Take the phone to the sales person. I'll give them all the info."

"Do you mean it?" Sam hopped out of the chair, sure she must look silly, grinning so much over a chair. "You haven't even seen it."

"I don't need to." Ian's tone was all soft, as though he was smiling. "You like it, and I want you to feel at home in our apartment."

Her heart skipped a beat. She lifted her hand to her lips. "Don't fuck with me, Ian."

"I'm not! You like my place, don't you?"

"Yes, but...but I've been looking for my own, you know that. And we haven't known each other that long..." Not that she really cared. She was happy at his place. Happy with *him*. If he was serious, she'd stay.

"Sam..." Ian cleared his throat, sounding solemn now. "You're going with me to see my grandmother. I think we know one another pretty well."

"True."

"So I'm gonna get the chair. And if there's anything else you want—"

"Let's start with the chair." Sam inhaled quickly, bouncing in place. "It's so awesome. I'm taking custody if this doesn't work out between us."

"Deal." There was a muffled noise, then the sound of Ian stepping outside. "I gotta head to the rink for warm-up soon as we get your chair, but it was awesome talking to you, sweetie. Wish me luck?"

"For what?" She slapped her hand into her forehead, remembering why he was in freakin' Toronto. "Shit, forget I said that. Obviously, good luck for the game. Kick their asses. And be careful."

"Will do."

"I love you!" Sam chewed at her bottom lip, wondering if he'd say it back.

He laughed softly, his tone warm. "I love you too."

Yes! Sam did a little dance, grinning at the salesman who'd been on his way over. He hesitated, giving her a bemused smile.

"My boyfriend wants to talk to you about this chair." She handed him the phone. "Because I'm taking it home.

"You're going with me to see my grandmother."

Shawn rubbed his scruffy jaw, eyeing Ian as they headed to the rink. He wanted to ask the man what the fuck that was all about, but he was still on the phone, giving his credit card info to order a damn chair Sam had apparently fallen in love with.

Because, naturally, she needed furniture at his place.

She wasn't a guest anymore. She was living with him.

As soon as he finished buying the chair and giving directions for where to have it delivered, Ian hung up and stuffed his phone in his pocket. He grinned at Shawn.

And Shawn did his best to smile back.

Ian's brow creased. "What's wrong?"

"Nothing." Shawn hooked his thumbs to his pant pockets. "So…Sam's going to meet your grandmother?"

"Yep." Ian's eyes fairly glowed as his grin grew even broader. "Grandma loves her. I don't know if she'll remember talking to her, but fingers crossed."

Nodding slowly, Shawn wet his bottom lip with his tongue. "So I guess you don't want me to go anymore?"

The man stopped short, his eyes wide. "Shit, I didn't even think.. I mean, I figured you'd want to spend time with Justina."

"Of course I do."

"This works out better then. Right?" Ian scratched his thick beard, wrinkling his nose as though he still wasn't used to the thing. It made him look wild—not quite a caveman, but close. His eyes held a softness though, all warmth and caring, like he was worried Shawn would be hurt. "You didn't really want to go. I begged you because I didn't think I could manage alone, but I'll have Sam."

Keep smiling. Just fucking nod and smile. Shawn let out a tight laugh. "So long as you're not alone. Your grandmother should meet your girlfriend."

"Yeah…" Ian rolled his shoulders as they continued walking. "I'll miss you, man."

"You're not gone yet, buddy." Shawn put his arm over Ian's shoulders, squeezing his arm. He didn't want Ian getting all depressed before they hit the ice. "We win tonight and we're headed to Detroit. I'll get you to myself a few more times."

"Yeah…and, it's not like we won't hang out when I get back."

Maybe not, but things will change. A lot sooner than I thought. Shawn inhaled even breaths, forcing himself to look completely relaxed despite the sharp splintering pain in his chest and the tightness in his throat.

Might as well have been goodbye already.

Ian didn't need him anymore.

Chapter Thirty Three

Ian let his mind wander as he taped his stick, not really paying attention to the conversations going on around him. They needed to win this game. And then all the ones against Detroit. Maybe let it go to game seven in both rounds. Make the post-season last a little longer.

For some reason, he had a feeling everything would change once they hit the offseason. And he wasn't ready for those changes.

He might never be.

"White, check these out. These should be good, right?" Bower shoved something in Ian's face and Ian took it, not really seeing anything. "I think those should go well with her dress."

"Yep. They're perfect." Ian tried to focus on the magazine. When his eyes fell on a bunch of flowers that looked like they had little clits in them, he blinked, looking from Bower to the magazine and back again. "Dude, what the fuck is this?"

"Flowers?" Bower rubbed a hand over his face. "Look, Silver wants me more involved in all the planning shit for the wedding. Dean's an asshole, so he found the place and picked the chairs and the music. I'm stuck with flowers and tableware."

Ian held a thumb to the page and flipped the magazine closed. Seeing BRIDES GUIDE on the front made it hard to breathe. He dropped the magazine and slid away from it.

"Sorry, man, but I'm pretty sure that shit's contagious. Go with the pussy flowers, they're interesting."

"Pussy flowers?" Richter chuckled, ambling over, a big smile on his lips. He picked up the magazine and flipped to the page that had crumpled on impact. "Ah, cymbidium. Not a horrible choice, but I think Silver will agree with White on their resemblance to a woman's vagina." Richter flipped to another page and handed the magazine to Bower. "Whatever she says, her heart's already set on these."

Bower's whole bearing eased up, like a heavy load of pressure had just been lifted from his shoulders. "I fucking love you, man."

Richter smirked. "I know."

A few feet away, Vanek started humming the Star Wars theme. By his side, Demyan snorted and ruffled his hair before joining in.

Rolling his eyes, Richter looked over at Ian, speaking in a mock whisper. "At least it's not that Lion King song again."

"Dean!" Bower groaned as both Vanek and Demyan started crooning out *Can you feel the love tonight?* Which they apparently knew very well and sang very badly. While the rest of the team laughed, Bower thumped his forehead into his goalie mask, his cheeks blazing red. "You are aware they don't have an off button, right?"

"I am." Richter leaned close to Bower, as though speaking to him, but Ian caught him brushing his lips over Bower's ear.

He looked away, returning his focus back to his stick. He didn't have an issue with PDA, but damn, most of the guys kept it real private. Bower and Richter more than most. Ian hadn't even been sure they fucked until...well, *now*.

Usually, Richter didn't like the guys being too friendly in the locker room, but the way the GM eyed the stitches along the goalie's jaw, Ian had a feeling he was a little worried.

Not that Ian blamed him. That had been a close fucking call.

"Be safe out there." Richter moved away from Bower, straightening his dark gray suit as he looked over the entire team. "You guys have had a solid run. Not everyone can be here, with us, but..." The GM's tone wavered, but he quickly recovered, flashing a smile. "But in a way, they are. They're counting on you to finish this.

They believe in this team. They gave *everything* to see us all reach further than most of the league believed we'd be capable. So you fucking go out there and show the world the Cobras are a damn force to be reckoned with. We're taking home a win, boys!"

Standing and tapping his stick on the carpet, Ian joined the rest of the team in shouting out a loud cheer. Donning the rest of his uniform, he headed out to the ice with the men, ignoring the boos from the crowd. With long strides, he circled the Cobra's zone, bumping Vanek, then Richards, his heart racing as got himself ramped up for the game.

Positioned in front of the net, Shawn and Ladd shot pucks at Bower, not getting much by him, but doing what they could to get him in the right headspace. A few other guys picked up pucks and tested the goalie, but Ladd seemed more determined than most. His shots were precise, and when one went in Bower laughed and waved him over.

Ian could hear both Ladd and Shawn laughing at whatever the goalie said. Then Ladd nodded. He'd probably been warned not to show the other team Bower's weak spots.

Which was kinda funny. Bower didn't have many, and few matched Ladd's incredible aim and speed. He'd be an elite level player in a few years.

Fuck that, he's pretty much there now.

One hand curved around the back of Ladd's neck, Shawn pulled the rookie close and bumped helmets with him. Ian slowed his laps around the zone, wondering if he should worry about the attention Shawn was showing the kid. Not out of jealousy, though he couldn't completely avoid the slight sting. He was more worried how Mason would react if he thought Shawn was fucking with the kid.

Ten minutes later, Ian sat on the edge of the bench, watching Shawn take the faceoff. He held his breath as seconds later, Shawn took a solid check into the boards. His man still managed to snap a crisp pass to Demyan. Jetting across the ice, Demyan whipped the puck over to Vanek.

Vanek dodged the big, brutish Leaf's defense and skated almost completely past the net. He tucked the puck back to where Shawn had positioned himself on the edge of the blue paint. The Leaf's goalie stopped the first shot. Demyan cupped the rebound, lifting the puck over the goalie's pad.

Goal!

Throwing his fist up in the air, Ian leaned over the boards to congratulate the guys. He bumped his glove into Vanek's, then Demyan's, struggling to do the same to Shawn without pulling him close for a few extra seconds.

Shawn knew him too well. He laughed, leaning close and whispering, "*Later.*"

The game continued, fast paced, with brutal hits and a few close calls on both ends. In the last minute of the first period, the Leaf's crashed the net and tied things up. The goal went under review, but it was determined the Cobras own defenseman, Peter Kral, had knocked Bower over.

Good goal. Kral was still apologizing to Bower as the period ended and they headed for the locker room.

Bower gave Kral a one armed hug. "It happens, man. We're good. You'll make it up to me."

Second period and Kral more than made up for his sloppy play. He used his body to block a dangerous shot. Managed to send the puck rolling onto Ian's stick. Ian rushed across the ice, carrying the puck to the neutral zone. Absorbed a low hit, wincing as his knee buckled. He righted himself quickly, maintaining control of the puck just long enough to send it flying across the ice to Ramos.

Ramos passed to Manning. Manning sailed the puck over to Pearce. Pearce took the shot.

The red light went off.

2-1.

Well into the third period, the Cobras held on to the lead. The Leafs were always a step behind their goalie working some damn magic the only thing that kept the Cobras from burying them. Finishing up a long shift, Ian followed Ladd into the Leaf's zone, watching the kid zip around the players like he'd just gained the abilities of The Flash.

As Ladd reached the net, a stick hooked his legs, sending him crashing into the goalie.

And all hell broke loose.

Leafs piled on Ladd, grabbing at him and punching him before he could even stand. Ian hauled one of the bigger guys off the rookie, clocking him square in the jaw. The ref focused on the jumble of bodies as everyone but the goalies joined in the brawl. Equipment scattered across the ice.

Ian got his guy down with another solid punch, then turned to the fray, ready to grab the asshole who'd hooked Ladd, but Ramos had him. The huge defenseman was usually so fucking calm, but Ian knew he was downright scary when he lost his cool. Ramos' eyes flashed as he let one punch hit his jaw. Blood slicked his bottom lip as he gave the other man a tight smile.

Hand fisted in the Leaf's jersey, Ramos rained down punishing blows until the refs pried the two men apart.

The penalties racked up, most of the line from both teams crammed into the sin bin. Ian laughed as he found himself squished into the corner of the bin and the ref struggled to close the door.

Play continued, a little more even sided, as though the fight had given the Leaf's a much-needed burst of energy. Bower faced shot after shot, moving like he'd grown extra limbs. Perron took double shifts, guarding the zone and setting up some sweet plays. The man was on his fucking game.

But as he started losing steam, Callahan called him to the bench. And the Leafs took advantage of a sloppy line change, rushing the goal, only Kral between them and Bower. Kral went down to cut off the passing lane, but the puck sailed over him.

Bodies filled the net. Bower had stopped the puck, but it was still loose. The Leaf's jabbed at Bower's glove and pads, searching for the puck.

Kral managed to find the puck. He made a long pass, finding Ladd in the clear halfway across the rink. Ladd went on a breakaway, faking out the goalie with some fancy stick handling, the puck a blur as he spun around. He clipped the puck toward the net as he dove sideways to avoid slamming into the goalie.

The puck went in.

Minutes later, the game was won.

The Leafs were eliminated.

For most of the night, the team celebrated. Ian hung out with Shawn, Ladd, Hunt, and Ramos, tossing back a few beers and laughing as Hunt recapped the game from his point of view, just as excited as the rest of them even though he'd spent the entire game on the pine. Ladd seemed to have lost his ability to speak after Hunt congratulated him for the game winning goal.

Hunt didn't notice. He just bought Ladd another beer and slapped his shoulder, talking nonstop.

It was good to see the two getting along. Ian had been pretty sure they hated each other, but maybe they were just young and stupid sometimes. He'd had his moments with teammates before.

Speaking of teammates, Ian watched Shawn who'd been on the phone since they'd gotten to the hotel bar. His man was smiling and laughing, looking damn happy as he listened to whatever Justina was saying. Knowing her, she was probably doing the exact same thing Hunt was. From what Shawn had told Ian, she was passionate about the game.

Ian took out his phone, not all that surprised that he hadn't gotten a call. It was past midnight, so he didn't want to risk waking up Sam, but it bothered him a bit to know she probably hadn't watched the game at all.

She wasn't into hockey, which was fine, but it took up so much of his life, he wasn't sure how they'd manage with only their love of comic books in common.

Guess you'll find out this summer.

He took a long gulp of beer, all the elation from before fading. Maybe it was messed up, but he wasn't ready for the postseason to end. Seeing Shawn all dreamy eyed, his voice all soft as he talked to Justina, made him wonder how different things would be after a couple weeks apart. If Shawn wasn't already in love with the girl, he was headed in that direction. Maybe Ian wouldn't be the one to end things between him and Shawn after all.

How solid could a relationship that had been open from the start really be?

Doesn't matter. It's not over yet.

There had to be a way to keep it from being over at all.

Thankfully, Ian had plenty of time to figure that out.

Chapter Thirty Four

The conference finals against Detroit ended in a clean sweep. Fucking embarrassing, how easily the Cobras had been taken out, but Shawn suspected Bower had aggravated an old injury. Hunt had been thrown in for the last two games, and while he gave it his all, he didn't have the experience to hold the fort against a healthy team while his own was falling apart.

There was always next season. Shawn was proud of his team for going as far as they had. He managed to hold his positive front as he said goodbye to all the guys and cleaned out his locker. Somehow kept smiling long after Ian had taken off to catch his flight to Winnipeg.

But he stuck around the locker room for a long time, unable to shake the feeling that this was it. He'd abandoned his rules, hadn't been careful with his heart, and now he couldn't go back to being…well, *Easy*. At least Justina was off in Newfoundland to support her brother as his team finished off their own finals. No fucking way was he taking her down with him. He'd get past the hopelessness. Learn to live with Ian being his best friend and nothing more.

You knew this was gonna happen. Get over it.

Easier said than done.

Letting out a heavy sigh, Shawn grabbed his bags and headed out. After loading his trunk, his phone buzzed and he pulled it from the pocket of his black suit pants.

His stomach dropped as he read the text.

> **Steve: After talking to your agent, I realized I'd been acting crazy. I need to apologize. I know how important your team is to you, so I sold my tickets and *took* my wife down to PEI to enjoy the sights. I was sorry to hear that your team lost.**
>
> **I understand if you don't want to see me, but I would like to spend some time with you before I head home. Please let me know if this is agreeable.**

Shawn's first instinct was to reply 'Hell no', but damn it, it wasn't like he had anything else to do. Steve apologizing was kinda cool. And Shawn wasn't the scrawny, desperate kid he'd been back when Steve had fucked him up.

Some closure would be good. For both of them.

> **Shawn: Sure. You can come by my place if you want. We'll have a beer and catch up. Are you bringing your wife?**
>
> **Steve: No. She headed home yesterday. I told her I wanted to stay and meet up with you. That we're friends and I wasn't sure when I'd get this chance again.**

'Friends' wasn't what Shawn would call them, but whatever. He sent Steve his address, then made his way home, stopping at the store to grab some beer. Without Ian spending so much time at his place, he'd stopped bothering to keep any in his fridge.

There were a few things he'd stopped doing without Ian around. Cracking open a beer, Shawn took a sip, then set it aside to plug his iPod into the speaker in the living room. He scrolled until he found one of Ian's favorite songs. *Hell's Bells* by AC/DC.

Just as the bells sounded at the beginning of the song, he heard a knock at the door. Taking a few bracing gulps of beer, he crossed the room to let Steve in.

"Hey." Steve shuffled into the hall, standing off to the side as Shawn closed the door. "Thanks for letting me come over."

Shawn shrugged, holding up his beer. "You want a drink?"

"Sure, that would be great." Steve followed him to the kitchen, nodding his thanks when Shawn handed him a beer. He took a sip, making a face. "Not as good as Stiegl. Then again, I don't think anything here is as good as back home."

"I find this one pretty good. Ian usually gets Molson Canadian, but this is his favorite." Shawn's lips quirked at the edges at he looked at the bottle of Keith's, a beer brewed in Halifax. "I tried to get him to try some micro-brews, but he wasn't crazy about them."

Steve's eyes narrowed. "This...Ian. Is he your boyfriend?"

"He's my best friend." Shawn arched a brow, tilting the beer to his lips. He leaned against the kitchen counter. "You know, the guy you punched?"

"Ah." Steve gulped down half his beer then shook his head. "That was stupid of me. If he's around, maybe I can apologize to him as well."

Polishing off his beer, Shawn shook his head, going to the fridge to grab two more beers. "He went home to visit his grandmother with his girlfriend."

"So you are single?"

Fisting his hands around the beer bottles, Shawn frowned. "No. I'm seeing a girl, actually."

"And where is she?"

"Newfoundland." Shawn tried to shake the sinking unease filling him with Steve's questions. The man was asking about his life. Nothing unusual about that. He cleared his throat. "You said you brought your wife to Prince Edward Island. What did she think of it?"

"She thought it was beautiful." Moving closer, Steve brushed his fingers over the scruff on Shawn's cheek. "You should shave. I don't like you looking so unclean."

Stepping around him to set the bottles on the counter, Shawn snorted. "Not sure why you think I care, Steve. You keep yourself nice and neat though. That how your *wife* likes you?"

"Right now, I'm not thinking about what she likes. I'm remembering how you never cared how dirty I was." Steve stepped up to him, resting his hands on the counter at either side of Shawn's hips. "You would swallow my cock right after a game if we could find somewhere private. Fuck, I never met anyone who sucked dick as well as you do."

Yeah, so much for spending time together as 'friends'. Shawn reached back for his beer, pretty sure he was going to need it. "Is that what you want, Steve? You want me to suck your dick?"

"No." Steve pressed against him suddenly, laughing as Shawn clinked the mouth of the beer against his teeth. "I miss your fucking tight ass. I want *you*, Shawn."

"And your wife's okay with that?"

"My wife doesn't need to know." Steve's jaw hardened. "And you won't tell her."

Shawn pressed his hand against the center of Steve's chest, pushing him back so he could slip out of reach. "You're right. Because there'll be nothing *to* tell her."

Nodding slowly, Steve watched him. The predatory look in his eyes made Shawn's skin crawl.

Get him out. Now! Doing his best to sound calm, Shawn strode across the kitchen. "Time to go, Steve. It's been great and all, but—"

The weight of Steve's body slammed into him. He cracked his head on the edge of the hall table as he fell. He braced his hands on the floor as Steve fumbled with his belt. He shuddered as Steve sucked at the side of his neck.

"Please, Shawn. Please just let me…" Steve wrapped his hand around Shawn's dick, groaning as he roughly tugged, grinding against Shawn's ass. "Just once. Just once and I'll never bother you again."

The idea made Shawn nauseous, but it was just sex. If it would get Steve out of his fucking life for good? It would be worth the few…what, *seconds* it took to get the man off?

"Hurry up." Shawn lifted one hand to his face, swiping away the blood trailing down from his forehead. "Just fucking get it over with."

The man rose up and Shawn pressed his eyes shut as he heard the sound of his zipper coming down. At least he used a condom. And he was quick. Rough, but over fast. Now Shawn just had to get rid of the man so he could take a damn shower.

As he rolled over to pull up his pants, a sharp kick hit him in the ribs. Then another.

"You fucking disgusting piece of shit. Look what you fucking did..." Steve snarled as he straightened his clothes. He dropped the condom on the floor, staring at it, his face twisting with rage. He leaned down and grabbed Shawn by the throat. "I know what a big mouth you used to have, but I'm warning you, if you tell *anyone*—"

Tearing Steve's hand away from his throat, Shawn shoved to his feet, snapping his fist right between the fucker's eyes. He slammed another punch into Steve's gut. "You'll what, Steve? Kill me? I'm not a kid anymore. You don't fucking scare me. And you don't have your buddies here to help you beat the shit out of me."

"I don't need them."

A fist hammered into the side of Shawn's head. He struggled to stay on his feet, bracing for the next punch.

His vision blurred. He leaned against the wall. Footsteps sounded, further and further away. His front door opened and closed.

He was alone.

So very fucking alone.

Exactly how he'd wanted to be, for so long. Which had been perfect until he'd let himself see how it felt to have someone who cared. Someone who would be there for him. All he had to do was ask.

One phone call and Justina would be on her way. Ian would drop everything and come back, ready to destroy Steve. Hell, any of his teammates would be here in minutes.

Except, Shawn couldn't make that call. He didn't know how.

So he locked the door and helped himself to another beer. Kept drinking until he forgot the words he wanted to say.

I need you. I was so fucking wrong. He pressed his hand to his side, every breath pure hell. The pain reaching deep. He'd gotten everything he'd asked for.

Too bad he didn't want it anymore.

It was too late.

Justina lifted Chris up in her arms, equipment and all as he let out a victory yell. She handed him over to their father as he chattered excitedly about how he'd made the perfect pass, and he hoped everyone knew he was going to be better than Crosby one day.

Dad took Chris back to the locker room to get changed as Justina waited with her mother in the hall. Her mom smiled, giving Justina a one arms hug.

"I don't think I tell you this enough, but you're the reason he's so happy. All the practices you've gotten him to, all the extra time you've spent at the rink with him." Her mother grinned. "Your father and I can't keep up with him, but you've done an amazing job."

Smiling at her mother, before resting her head on her shoulder, Justina laughed. "I do my best. He's a pain in the butt, but I love him."

"Yes, but I'm glad you're doing more of your own thing. You don't talk to us much, but you seem…well, you're practically glowing lately." Her mother drew away and tipped Justina's chin up with a finger. "Have you met someone?"

"I have." Justina bit her bottom lip. "Actually, I was thinking of heading back early to see him. I have enough money saved up to pay to change the flight."

"He's that special, is he?" Her mother patted her cheek. "Go ahead, my love. But I expect to meet him soon. Not *so* soon that he feels weird about it, but a man who's made my little girl this happy must be pretty great."

"He is." She stepped aside as her father and Chris joined them. They made their way to the parking lot. "Umm...I've been putting this off, because I know you and dad are busy, but my friend, Sahara, is renting out her apartment and I was thinking of taking it."

Her mother frowned, shaking her head. "Justina, you're not making enough with the Ice Girls to manage an apartment on your own. I thought you liked the setup in the basement. You come and go as you please, no one bothers you—"

"I know, but I just feel it's time I look into being on my own." Justina sighed as her father grumbled. "What?"

Folding his arms over his chest, her father faced her as Mom opened the car. "If you're not living at home, who's going to watch your brother while we're at work?"

Guilt tightened Justina's throat. He was right. Her parents needed her, and she was being selfish.

Her mother shocked her by giving her father a playful shove. "Stop it, Harold. Justina's finally met a man! We can't expect to hog all her time. I'll talk to Mrs. Sampson—the nice old lady a few doors down? Chris mows her lawn for her, and she's been teaching him to bake when he stays with her while Justina's working."

Justina managed to hold her smile, but she hated that her mom was only on her side because she 'finally' had a boyfriend. But whatever made life easier on everyone, she'd go with it. Mrs. Sampson was a sweet old lady. Chris would have fun with her.

Less than an hour later, Justina managed to book a last minute flight and her parents dropped her off at the airport. She texted Shawn to let him know she was on her way, but didn't get a reply.

By the time she got home, it was almost 4 AM. Shawn must be sleeping. She decided to try him again in the morning.

When she woke up and still hadn't heard from him, she started to worry. Waiting until 10 AM in case he'd slept in, she drove to his apartment. His car was there, so she knew he was home.

But he didn't answer the door for what seemed a very long time.

Maybe she'd been wrong about him being home? She turned down the hall, wanting to text or call him again, but feeling silly. He might have gone for a walk. His phone might need charging or he was visiting a friend.

His front door opened. He called out softly. "Justina?"

Spinning around, she smiled at him. One look at his face and her stomach dropped. She crossed the hall in a few long strides, bringing her hand up to his face, afraid to touch him. There were cuts and bruises all over. He hadn't sounded hurt when she'd talked to him last night.

Freakin' men, acting all tough. She sighed, wrapping her arms around him, grinding her teeth when he winced. "Damn it, why didn't you tell me you'd gotten roughed up on the ice? I didn't see you get in a fight, but I only caught bits of the game while I was watching my brother play."

"It didn't happen on the ice."

"It didn't…" Justina shook her head, confused. "Don't you dare tell me you tripped." She looked him over. "Damn it, Shawn, there are bruises on your neck! Did you get mugged?"

"No." Shawn drew her into the apartment, shutting and locking the door behind her. "Do you want a beer? I should probably explain a bit so you'll understand."

A beer? Justina double then triple checked the time on her phone. It was only a little after ten. As far as she knew, Shawn wasn't a big drinker. What the fuck was going on?

"No, I don't want a beer." Justina took his hand, noting that his knuckles were swollen and bruised too. He *had* been in a fight. "Please come sit down. Tell me what happened."

They settled down on the sofa, facing one another. Shawn rubbed his scruffy jaw, staring at the floor. Then he swallowed hard. "I dated a football player in high school. It was a big secret—him being 'straight' and all. I was young and stupid, and he treated me like shit. But he was hot. Still is." He let out a pain filled laugh. "He came down while we were playing the Leafs. Said he wanted to hook up. I turned him down at first, but last night…well, I let him come over. Things went south."

Bile flooded her throat. She inhaled roughly. "Shawn, did he... I mean, I can see he hurt you, but what else—"

"He didn't rape me. I gave consent. I just wanted to get it over with." Shawn shrugged. "I figured he'd fuck me and go back to his life, but he was just as disgusted with himself as he used to be. My fault for being so irresistible."

Tears flooded her vision, but she blinked them away. "Shawn, you were there for Sahara when her ex came after her. This is—"

"Very different." Shawn's tone hardened. "It's over. He didn't abuse me like Sahara's boyfriend abused her."

Looking from the cut on Shawn's forehead, to his split lip and the bruises all over his face, Justina couldn't see how this was different at all. But Shawn needed support, not pressure.

"Do you want to go to the hospital?"

"No."

"All right." She wasn't giving up on getting him checked out, but for now, she'd focus on doing what she could. "Will you let me take care of you?"

Pressing his eyes shut and leaning his head back on the sofa, Shawn didn't say anything at first. Then he spoke so quietly, she could barely hear him. "I know we have an open relationship, Justina, but we've only ever discussed Ian. Why aren't you pissed that I fucked my ex?"

"I'm more pissed that you think that's an issue right now." Justina fisted her hands on her bent knees, not sure she was saying the right things, but absolutely positive there was no perfect way to handle a situation like this. "Do you want me here?"

"Yes." Shawn blinked fast, turning his head away from her. "Fuck, that's the one thing I'm sure of. I should tell you to go, but I...I need you close. I need to know you don't hate me."

Damn it, she wanted to hold him, but she was too afraid to hurt him. So she took his hand and lifted it to her lips. "I love you, Shawn. I started falling for you way before it was smart, but no regrets, right?"

He let out a shaky laugh. "Maybe a few. You deserve better."

"Better than what? Better than a man who makes me happier than I've ever been? Than a man who's shown me that the things I want aren't as fucked up as I once believed?" She cocked her head. "You're right. I should so totally go through dating a few assholes first."

"A lot of people will tell you I'm one of those assholes."

"And those people are wrong. You're a better man than you know." She ran her thumb carefully over the scabbed over flesh on his knuckles, silently hoping the fucker who'd hurt him looked a hell of a lot worst than he did. "People love you, Shawn. A lot of people. But they can get in line. You're mine."

He smiled, wincing as though it was painful. Then he pulled her against his side. "I never liked all that possessive shit, but it sounds damn good, coming from you."

"Good." She rested her hand on his thigh. "Because I'm not going anywhere."

They sat like that for a long time, just holding each other, Shawn seeming relaxed, just happy that she was there. Justina was happy to *be* there, but she hated how helpless she felt. She wanted to find the asshole who'd done this to Shawn and make sure he never even considered coming back. Or better yet, get the law involved and make sure it wasn't an option.

But even more, she wanted to talk to Ian. He would know far better than she what Shawn needed.

Mentioning Ian brought all the tension back to Shawn's body. He shook his head. "I'm not cutting his time with his grandmother short. I'm fine, sweetie. I promise."

He might believe that, but Justina didn't. He put on a pretty good show. He offered to make tea, chuckling when she gave him a dirty look and went to make them both tea herself. While she was in the kitchen, she decided he was right. Ian was with his grandmother, and making him worry wouldn't do anyone any good.

No reason she couldn't touch base though. Let him know he should call Shawn when he had a chance. They were kinda friends, so her texting him wouldn't be weird.

Justina: Hey! Thought I'd give you a shout! How's the weather out West?
Ian: Who the fuck is this?

Justina frowned. That didn't sound like Ian at all.

Justina: Your best friend's girlfriend? Sorry, I didn't mean to bother you.
Ian: Well, you are. Get a life. Ian's busy.

Ah, well that explained it. Sam had his phone. Wasn't she just the sweetest thing? Justina put the tea in the mugs after the water boiled, taking her time thinking out her reply.

Once both teas were ready, she typed it out then pressed send.

Justina: I hope you and Ian are doing well. Please tell Ian I messaged him. You know how guys are, they won't tell you when something's wrong, but I think Shawn misses him.
Ian: Right, because Shawn's shy and can't tell Ian himself.
Justina: I get that you've been through a lot, but do you have to be a complete bitch?

The second she sent the message, she wished she could take it back. She was just tired of Sam's attitude. The girl acted like she owned Ian. He wasn't a fucking prize, but he was a good man. One Sam could use. And had been using.

Ian: I'm a bitch? You know what, you're probably right. But at least I don't pretend to be all sweet and innocent. You want a piece of me, you stupid slut? I'll fuck you up.
Justina: And this conversation is over. Have a great day, Sam.

Tempted to throw her phone, Justina took a few long, steadying breaths. Thankfully, she *hadn't* tried to tell Ian what was going on. Sam didn't need to know something so personal about Shawn. The girl would probably find a way to use it against him.

The only problem was, Justina wasn't sure she could help him on her own. But who else could make a difference? Could actually convince him to go to a doctor without it being weird?

She took a deep breath and called Sahara.

"Hey, baby! How are you doing?" Sahara sounded breathless. "One second, Bran. I've got two hands. Kimber, use a freakin' oven mitt!"

In the background, Heath was yelling at his sister.

"You sound busy." Justina winced as Kimber called her brother every foul name she could think of, along with some she was sure the girl had made up. "Do you want me to call later?"

"No, not like there's a better time!" Sahara laughed. "Do you know Dominik is looking into adopting these kids? That man is insane. I love him so much."

Justina smiled. "He's a great guy. But I thought Heath was their guardian."

"He is, but child services isn't sure he can manage on his own. He's got so much going on. He's heading to Russia next week to do something with his old team. We've been talking to the kids' caseworker and if Dominik adopts them, getting citizenship will go faster." Sahara drew in a sharp breath. "We're thinking of getting married so we can raise them together. His mother is over the moon!"

"Oh my God, I'm so happy for you! Did he propose?"

"Kinda? He can't speak very well right now, but he wrote down the question. Like…as an 'if' he asked, would I be interested." Sahara giggled. "I'm mean. I told him when he asks, he'll get the answer. He's working with a speech therapist and told me he'll ask again when he sounds like himself."

"That's awesome. I'm glad he's doing better. I know you were scared for a bit." Justina decided she probably shouldn't dump her problems on Sahara. Not when the woman had finally gotten a break from her own. "I just wanted to see how you were doing."

"You are the worst liar I've ever met." Sahara chuckled. Her voice moved away from the phone. "Kimber, can you get him some juice?

And Heath, stop acting like you're five! I saw you pull her hair! Yes, I know you don't like her cooking. Unless you can do better, stay out of the way!"

Snickering, Justina stirred the tea. Much longer and it would get cold, but she missed talking to her friend. "Are you adopting Heath too?"

"Seems like it sometimes!" Sahara's tone shifted abruptly. "Nice try, Miss. How are things with you?"

"Good." Justina sighed when Sahara cleared her throat expectantly. "Fine. I'm worried about Shawn. He...he had a visitor. An ex. A really nasty one from the look of him. But...well, I tried to mention how he helped you, and he doesn't see it as the same thing. So I don't know what to do."

Sahara went quiet. And within seconds, Justina couldn't hear the kids around her anymore. Her friend spoke softly. "That doesn't surprise me. I think there's a reason why Shawn took such good care of me, but guys are always told they have to be tough. Not that it's good when it happens to anyone, but when a man is... Damn it, Justina What did the guy do?"

"I can't tell you everything, Sahara. I trust you, but he's very private."

"I know. Do you think he needs a doctor? Or a cop?"

"Maybe?" Justina pressed her hand to her eyes. "I don't think he'll file a report, but I need to know he'll be okay."

She could picture Sahara nodding. "Let me call Scott. He's dealt with his own shit and he can visit all random. He told me a bit about his past and how he felt he couldn't speak up because he's a guy. Maybe they can find some common ground."

"But I have to tell Shawn he's coming."

"Do you? Girl, you need to learn how to be a little sneaky when it's for their own good. Make him something to eat. Check emails, make a few calls. Look busy." Sahara's tone took on a sly edge. "You can't lie, but you can avoid the truth for a little bit."

"Okay. That I can do." Justina grinned as she heard the kids again. "Thank you."

"Hey, that's what friends are for. I've got you, babe."

After she hung up, Justina took Shawn his tea. Finished her own as she found a new movie On Demand. Then she decided to do some laundry. The stench of Shawn's equipment bag was driving her nuts.

"Leave it, Justina. I'll deal with it later."

The pain in his tone tore at her heart, but she kept her own voice light. "*Or* I can deal with it now. Don't argue with me, man of mine. Watch Superman destroy the city."

"I hate this asshole. Even though he's hot."

"He's not that hot. He's too pretty."

Shawn barked out a laugh. "Ian's said the exact same thing."

Smiling as she stuffed his uniform in the washing machine, Justina wondered how different things would be if Ian were here now. They could probably work together to get through to Shawn. Which was exactly what the man needed.

There was a knock at the door. Justina hurried over to answer.

Halfway off the sofa, bent over, clutching his ribs, Shawn rasped out. "Check who it is first."

She checked and grinned. "You have visitors."

Opening the door, she stepped aside to let in Demyan, Vanek, and Carter. Demyan held out his arms, hugging her tight.

"Thank you, Justina. I've got him." He kissed her cheek. "He's lucky to have you."

"He may not agree." Justina nibbled at her bottom lip as she watched Carter cross the room to sit beside Shawn.

Cast on one arm, holding a wiggling thing in the other, Carter leaned down and set it on the sofa. "I got you a puppy. Or...well, I found it. And Bear doesn't like it, so I figured it would be good with you."

"He's such a liar!" Vanek petted the little bundle of fluff. "This is the third stray you've taken home this week. Ramos has him working at the local shelter. He took a cat home, and it was licking its lips and eyeing Jami and Ramos' birds. Then he found a baby sparrow that was hurt. Which is with the vet. His man wouldn't let him in the house with this little thing. He said, with a new baby on the way, the last thing they needed was another pet."

"Asshole." Carter punched Vanek's shoulder. "Thanks for spoiling that for me. *I'm* the dad. I should be the one telling people."

Vanek smirked. "True. And I so wanna be there when you tell Richter he's gonna be a grandfather."

Demyan looked over his friends, shaking his head. "Do you really, Tyler? I'm pretty sure I wanna be far, far away."

Carter threw his head back, laughing, though he couldn't quite hide the underlying fear. "Not like he'll kill you two. This is all on me and Seb. Or…me *or* Seb? They'll be both our kids either way."

Shawn's eyes went wide. "*They'll* be?"

Justina knew that already, since Jami had called her, Sahara, and Akira right after the doctor's appointment, but Shawn's reaction was kinda funny.

"She's having twins. That's why she's been so sick." Carter plunked down on the sofa. "She on all these special meds and vitamins, and she's miserable. But happy. If that makes any sense."

"So, technically, you may each have a biological child with her." Shawn tilted his head to one side, his lips curving at the edges. "Which is perfect."

Staring at him, Carter shook his head. "Dude, this isn't sci-fi."

"No. It's biology." Shawn squeezed Carter's shoulder, his other hand on the small dog. "Congratulations. And thank you. I was thinking about getting a dog, but I didn't have time to visit the shelter. Does she have a name?"

"Not that I know of. We literally just found her and took her to a local vet to see if she had a chip. You may wanna put up posters to see if someone lost her." Carter focused on Shawn's face. "Enough of that. Who do we need to kill?"

Vanek held up a hand, clearing his throat. "Umm, dating a cop. Should not be hearing this."

"Fuck off, you know you're feeling homicidal, too." Carter glanced over at Demyan. "Right?"

Demyan met Shawn's eyes. Shook his head. Then motioned to Carter and Vanek. "Go take the dog for a walk."

"We don't have a leash."

Tossing Carter his keys, Demyan pointed at the door. "Go get one. And some food."

Lips parted, Vanek looked from Demyan to Carter.

Carter grabbed Vanek's arm, bent down to pick up the puppy, then walked out silently.

Sitting on the edge of the living room table, Demyan faced Shawn. He said nothing for several, long moments. Then he rubbed his freshly shaven jaw. "Look, I get it. Shit went down and you don't want to make a big deal about it. You're Shawn 'Easy' Pischlar. You have complete control over everything."

One brow raised, Shawn gave Demyan a slanted smile. "Not everything. The speech includes not kicking my ass if you're unhappy with my performance."

Justina hugged herself, not understanding how Shawn could joke about this.

But Demyan seemed to. "In the fine print? Did you add that before or after the first time this asshole hit you?"

Shawn's smile faded.

"I did some stupid shit when I thought I didn't deserve any better. I lost friends. I almost lost Becky and Zach." Demyan rubbed his thighs. "You need to get checked out. And you need to make sure the son of a bitch can't come back for round two. You have no idea who might get caught in the crossfire."

Shoulders hunched, Shawn shook his head. "He went home. To Austria. He won't come back."

Demyan's jaw tensed. "I didn't think my brother would come back. And he almost killed both Zach and Tyler."

"Shit." Shawn brought a hand up to the back of his neck, dropping his gaze. "I didn't know."

"Of course you didn't. And if I hadn't gone through lots of therapy, you still wouldn't know. I was a boy. Boys don't get sexually abused." Demyan shuddered, the color leaving his face. "At least, that's what I used to believe. I saw things differently when I looked at Zach's nephew. When I considered any of the shit that happened to me happening to…"

He swallowed hard, and Justina wanted to hug him. She knew exactly why Sahara had sent him now. This was difficult for him to open up about, but he was in the perfect position to get through to Shawn.

Taking hold of Demyan's hands, Shawn leaned forward. "What happened to you…damn it, Scott, it was wrong. You don't have to tell me more if you don't want to, but don't ever doubt that it was very wrong."

Demyan gave Shawn a tight smile. "Why am I sure I'm about to hear 'but'?"

"I'm an adult."

"Yes, you are." Demyan freed one hand, bringing it up to the cut on Shawn's head. To the dark bruise on his cheek. Then to the split in his lip. "What if someone did this to White? He's fucking tough. Hell, he should be able to fight anyone off, right? If he couldn't, maybe he got what was coming to him."

"Fuck you, Scott." Shawn growled, jerking away from Demyan and pushing to his feet.

Letting out a tired laugh, Demyan stood. "Not until you're in better shape, pal. Don't you have a party to plan?"

"Anyone ever tell you you're a pushy son of a bitch?"

"Not lately."

"I don't want to report this."

"Then don't. But this sweet thing is worried about you." Demyan brushed Justina's hair off one shoulder, shooting Shawn a sly smile as he leaned close and kissed her cheek. "Either you pull yourself back together and comfort her, or someone else will."

Shawn's eyes narrowed. "Did your man let you off your leash?"

"Hell no, I happen to love my leash." Demyan chuckled. "He's only lengthened it a little."

Moving closer to her, Shawn eyed Demyan as though he wasn't sure what to make of the other man. And Justina wasn't sure what to make of Shawn's possessive behavior. She didn't mind it, exactly, but it wasn't like him.

Wrapping and arm around his waist, she frowned at Demyan. "Be nice, or *I* won't let you play with my man."

"I don't think he needs to play with *anyone* right now, honey." The playfulness left Demyan's tone. "I think he needs you."

"He *has* me."

"*He* is grateful for that." Shawn pressed his lips to her hair. Then he shook his head. "And for you both forcing me to face how stupid I'm being. I just...damn it, I don't get to live like I do, and then bitch when things go bad."

"You're so fucking wrong about that, Easy." Demyan grabbed Shawn's shoulder and gave him a hard look. "You're a Dom. You know better. Those rules you use at the club to keep subs safe apply to you too."

Rubbing her arm, as though needing to feel her there, Shawn inclined his head. "Got it. Can you stay here?" He paused as Vanek and Carter stumbled through the front door, arms full of puppy and dog food and what looked like enough toys for a dog kennel. "Make sure the children don't wreck the place?"

"Dude, why do people keep calling us that?" Carter dumped the supplies in his arms on the living room table. "I'm responsible enough to be a dad. Which makes me an adult."

Vanek snorted. "Your dick gets hard, that's how you became a dad. The rest? We'll see."

Carter gave him the finger.

And Justina took the opportunity to tow Shawn out of the apartment as Demyan gestured for them to go.

In the car, on the way to the hospital, Shawn rested one hand on her knee as she drove, quiet at first. Then he laughed suddenly. "I don't think anyone's ever managed to handle me so well. You may not have noticed, but I'm a little stubborn."

"A little?" Justina rolled her eyes. "I was starting to think I'd need to use restraints."

"That's hot."

"You're impossible."

"Threaten me with a strap-on next. A great big one." Shawn wiggled his eyebrows at her, and she giggled. "Please?"

"Behave yourself and I'll think about it." The tightness in her chest loosened. He still looked roughed up, but not so broken. "Shawn, can I tell you something?"

"Anything, pet." Shawn looked over at the hospital as she pulled into the paid parking area. "Damn it, this is going to suck."

"I love you. I need you to know that."

"I love you too…is this where you say goodbye?" Shawn fisted his hands against his lap. "Because I get it. You should—"

"*You* should shut up. I love you. That's it. No fucking conditions. No chains, no limits." She got out of the driver's seat, slamming the door behind her, slowing her pace halfway across the lot when she realized he was having trouble keeping up. "Question me about that again and I'm going to find a Domme to teach me some tricks."

He didn't find that as funny as she'd hoped. "Unfortunately, that's *exactly* how Sam is trying to keep Ian."

Really? Well, we'll just see about that. Justina ground her teeth. "Looks like I'm gonna have my hands full between the two of you. Sounds like fun."

"Annnd now I'm going to see the doctor with a hard on." Shawn clucked his tongue and winked at her. "Still love me?"

Justina laughed, gently shoving him through the automatic doors before he could stall any longer. "Always."

Chapter Thirty Five

Tucking his grandmother into bed, Ian stood in her room for a bit, just watching her sleep, letting the day play over in his mind. He felt horrible, because Sam had seemed bored for the most part. He'd spent a lot of time talking to nurses and doctors. They hadn't even gotten to see his grandmother their first day here.

She was going through a new treatment and needed her rest. But at least she'd recognized him. She'd been so happy to meet Sam.

Which made *him* happy, but he couldn't help feel like something was up. Sam had been on his phone a few times with her brother. She didn't want to talk about what was going on, but he hoped it was just because they were still at the nursing home. Once they got back to the hotel, he'd get her to talk.

Only, he didn't have to wait that long.

In the cab, on the way there, she broke down in tears. "I'm a fucking horrible person. I'm so sorry!"

"Hey, I'm sure it can't be—"

"Shawn's in the hospital."

The weight of her words hit him like a hunk of lead dropping on his chest. He leaned forward and patted the driver's seat. "Change of plans. Take me to the airport."

"Ian, your grandmother—"

"How long have you known, Sam?" He wanted to hit something when she looked away from him. She'd forgotten to pay her own phone bill, so he hadn't minded letting her use his cell. He would have paid for hers, but she didn't want the money. No fucking wonder. He fought to keep his tone level. "How. Long?"

"Since yesterday. They kept him overnight because he showed signs of a concussion." She winced when he slammed his fist into the door. "I'm sorry. I just…you were waiting to see your grandmother and I didn't want you upset."

"So you lied to me?" Ian couldn't wrap his head around it. He covered his face with his hands. "Fuck, you talked to Luke. He told you, didn't he? You said he was worried about telling Richter about the baby."

"He *is*!" Sam hugged herself, tears trailing down her cheeks. "That was true."

"Why, Sam? You kept saying you were fine with everything. But you aren't."

"Yes, I am, but he's winning. He'll always win!" Her lips thinned. "For the first time, you chose me, and I liked it, okay?"

Damn it, he didn't know her at all, did he? "So this had nothing to do with my grandmother."

"What if it didn't? Are you going to break up with me because I was tired of coming in second?" She glared at him, like he was the one who'd fucked up. "I should have known you'd choose him."

Inhaling slowly, Ian shook his head. "He didn't make me choose, Sam. *You* did."

The cab pulled up in front of the airport. Ian handed the driver his credit card to pay for the ride then headed in, not even looking to see if Sam followed. Part of him felt guilty about being so cold to her, but he'd given her everything. Done his best to make her happy. And now his best friend was hurt, and she'd kept it from him because she saw this all as some kind of game she'd do anything to win.

Waiting as the airline agent searched for the next available flight, Ian sensed Sam beside him. He sighed, not finding it in him to just ditch her.

"They think they can find me a seat, but two will be tough. The hotel is covered for a few days. I'll get you the next available flight after mine." He pressed two fingers to the sore spot between his eyes. "I'm sorry things went to hell."

"But it's over, isn't it?"

"Yes." And fuck, he felt like shit about that too. But he couldn't stay with her. He couldn't trust her, and he wasn't sure he was helping her, no matter how much he tried. She needed more than he had to give. "I was stupid about this thing between us. You were trying to be the right girl for me, I was trying to be the right man for you, and none of it was real, was it?"

"I think you were, Ian." Sam wiped away the last of her tears. "I was hoping I could be good enough for you, because you're a great man. But this was going to happen eventually. You were going to see who I really am."

"You couldn't hide who you really were the whole time, Sam." He held out his arms, letting out a breath of relief as she let him hold her. "And I liked the girl I saw."

"But you were never in love with me?" Sam shook her head before he could answer, putting her finger over his lips. "It's okay. I don't think I was in love with you either. I was in love with the idea of having someone actually care about me."

"I still do."

The airline agent came over, handing him a ticket. "Since you have no luggage, I was able to get you on a flight leaving in less than an hour. But you'll have to hurry to the gate, they're about to start boarding."

"Won't be a problem, but can you get her on the next available flight? First class." He ruffled Sam's hair. "This girl deserves the best. And one day, she'll find it."

Once he'd secured Sam's ticket, he took off at a run, slowing only long enough to get through security before he was off again. He made it just in time to avoid dirty looks from the flight attendants.

Seven hours later, he grabbed a cab, his whole body stiff and sore from the two long flights, but feeling a bit better after talking to

Luke. Shawn was home now. With Justina. According to Luke, she was the only reason he'd gone to the hospital.

I could kiss that girl.

Yeah, he probably *could*, but that would be weird. He'd just broken up with Sam. And he hardly knew Justina.

What he did know made him like her a lot. While he'd been with Sam, completely clueless to how she actually felt about him and Shawn, Justina had been solid and steady for his man.

Or, well, *her* man. She'd never had to play games. She knew exactly where she stood.

She was flirting with you. Maybe Sam wasn't the only one playing games.

Handing the cabbie a twenty, Ian stepped onto the curb and took a deep breath. Damn it, could he really trust anyone?

Shawn. I trust Shawn. Nothing—no one—will ever change that.

He reached the front door. Used his key to open it.

His key slipped from his hand as he got a good look at Shawn. He looked like he'd been cracked in the face with a big fist. More than once. "Who did it? Tell me who and he's a dead man."

The detective sitting in a kitchen chair across from the sofa, who looked vaguely familiar, shot Ian an amused look. "I'll pretend I didn't hear that."

Shawn stood, moving toward him slowly. "What are you doing here?"

Ian crossed the distance, cupping Shawn's face in his hands. "Why didn't you call me?"

"You were with your grandmother."

"So? She totally understood me coming back. She knows you're my best friend. She raised me to take care of what's mine." Probably the wrong thing to say to Shawn, but Ian couldn't stop himself. "Sorry, Justina. I hope you don't mind sharing."

"Not at all." Justina grinned, as though seeing him and Shawn together made her happy. "I was going to call you, but he forbade it. I am very good at doing what I'm told."

Chuckling, Shawn glanced over his shoulder at her. "Yes. Which explains why the cop is here."

"Detective." The man muttered, not looking up from his notepad. "And you're both very lucky I don't hold a grudge. I've heard far more about you both than I ever wanted to know."

With a cocky smirk on his lips, Shawn leaned into Ian. "You hadn't claimed the boy yet. I make no apologies."

The boy? Ian's brow furrowed. What were they talking about?

"Clearly." The detective finished writing then stood. "Unfortunately, I can't promise much will come of this, but there may be enough evidence, combined with you being high profile, to issue a warrant. Which means if he tries to come back to Canada, he'll be arrested."

"That works for me." Shawn rolled his shoulders and sighed. "Thank you, Detective Hamilton."

"You're welcome, Pischlar." The detective held out his hand. "I'm sorry this happened to you, but you did the right thing. Take care of yourself." He touched his forehead and nodded at Justina. "Miss Davis."

"Oh shit!" It abruptly hit Ian where he remembered the cop from. "You're the dude that was a complete asshole about Richards' missing bike. Only…there was no bike."

"Figured that out all on your own, did you?" Detective Hamilton smirked. "Stay out of trouble now, you hear? Seems like you got your ankle monitor off early because of good behavior. I'd hate to be the 'asshole' forced to fit you with another one."

Yeah…calling a cop an asshole wasn't smart. Ian flashed the man his most innocent smile. "I'll be on my best behavior, sir. I've no intention of being arrested more than once this year."

Hamilton shook his head. "*This* year? Damn, sounds promising. Enjoy the rest of your day, folks."

Once the man was gone, they all got comfortable on the coach, Ian on one side of Shawn, Justina on the other. And then there was a fluffy thing, which hopped over Ian to curl up in Shawn's lap.

Ian stared at it. "What the hell is that?"

"She is my new dog." Shawn looked down at the white ball of fluff fondly, stroking her fur. "Her name is Edelweiss."

"Edelweiss?"

"It's a white flower." The edges of Shawn's lips twitched. "Fitting, I think."

Damn it, I was gone too long. The man's lost his mind. Ian rubbed his jaw, glad he'd shaved before going to his grandmother's. Shawn didn't need two hairy creatures in his life.

He cleared his throat. "So let me get this straight. You got a tiny little purse dog and named it after a flower? That's really—"

Shawn's brow rose. "Gay?"

"That's not what I was going to say. But why not a big dog? This one can't protect you from anything bigger than a mouse." Ian laughed as the dog stretched across Shawn's legs and licked Ian's hand. "She's cute though."

"She doesn't need to protect me."

"Someone needs to. You still haven't told me exactly what happened." Ian kept his attention on the dog. For some reason, seeing her all sweet and cuddling with Shawn made it easier to remain calm, despite how much he wanted to stand up and shout. Not *at* Shawn, but at the situation.

Sighing, Shawn picked up the puppy and placed her in Ian's lap. He stood and began to pace the room, hands laced behind his neck. "Remember that guy I told you about? My ex from when I was a teen…the one we ran into in Toronto?"

The fucker… Ian handed Justina the puppy and rose slowly. "He came after you?"

"I invited him over. Let him fuck me." Shawn stopped to stare out the window. "In return I got several bruises ribs, ten stitches, and a mild concussion. Sounds like a fair trade."

Fist clenched at his sides, Ian inhaled roughly as red flashed across his vision. His whole body shook with rage. "He's a dead man."

"He's alive and well and far, far away. You're here. I'd prefer to focus on that." Shawn's tone was strained, but Ian knew him well enough to get that he wanted the subject dropped.

Swallowing back the urge to describe all the things he wanted to do to the piece of shit who'd hurt his man, Ian moved up behind Shawn, carefully wrapping his arms around his waist.

He pressed his lips to Shawn's throat. "I'm here. And I'm not fucking leaving you again. Ever."

"Ian—"

"*Shawn.*" Ian used his teeth this time, grazing them over the hot flesh where his lips had touched. "What do I need to do? Name it. I'm not with Sam anymore. I dropped everything and came home. I'll get my agent to call a fucking press conference if you need me to tell the damn world."

"You decided all this right this minute, didn't you?" Shawn slanted his head to the side, shooting Ian an amused smile. "How about you consider all this when you're not feeling sorry for me?"

True, Ian hadn't thought over the press thing, or making any declarations, but all the thinking had been what kept them apart for so long. He didn't want to stop and consider what was simple, or easy, or how anyone would look at him if he admitted to being in love with Shawn. He was fucking tired of all the reasons why what they had couldn't last.

It was about time he started coming up with some that proved that they could.

"I didn't fall in love with you when I saw the bruises, Shawn. Or when I found out how fucking good it feels to fuck you. None of that changes what was already there." Ian rested his chin on Shawn's shoulder. "I started to fall for you the first time you explained a joke to me in the locker room without making me feel stupid for not getting it. You owned a piece of my heart the first time you took my hand on a flight when I was scared. The rest belonged to you the moment you talked me down from jumping in a fight on the ice."

A long time, but he'd been too blind to see it. He didn't blame Shawn for looking confused.

"I didn't understand the way I felt about you. You were my best friend within days of you joining the team. One of the most important people in my life." He took a deep breath, his cheeks heating as he considered the one time, early on, that he'd looked at Shawn differently. "You know I never got hard in the locker room. I never got turned on by the other guys, I considered myself straight. Totally straight. The idea of being anything else freaked me out. But you…"

Turning in his arms, back against the window, Shawn inclined his head. "Go on."

"Look, I don't have a problem with gay guys. I mean, maybe when I was a dumb kid, but I learned real quick that my grandmother was wrong, you know? So with the team, I saw everyone the same. If they checked out my ass, whatever. So long as they didn't touch me." Ian lifted his shoulders. He could still picture that day. He could feel someone watching him as he washed up after an intense practice.

After rinsing the soap off his face, he'd glanced over his shoulder to see Shawn, giving him an appreciative once over. Shawn didn't try to hide it either. He'd winked, then strode out of the showers like nothing had happened.

Fuck, Ian had turned the shower cold so fast, he was pretty sure his balls were gonna shrivel up and die. And his dick hadn't gotten the message for a long time. He'd stayed in the shower until it went soft, shivering as he returned to the locker room.

"You did things to me, and it freaked me out. I didn't know how I should feel, so I tried to keep things 'normal'. Our friendship had to be enough, because I wasn't like you. I couldn't be. I dated different chicks, had meaningless sex, and refused to even consider…" He bowed his head. "I stuck to what I thought I was supposed to feel. I'm good at that."

"Am I the first guy you ever got turned on by?" Shawn brushed his fingers through Ian's hair, tugging lightly until Ian looked up. His eyes held so much compassion. The same compassion he'd always shown Ian, no matter how messed up he was. "You say you're 'good at that', but I know you're attracted to women."

He was, but not all the chicks he'd been with had done anything for him. He shrugged. "I used to look at a lot of sports magazines.

My grandmother cried when I was little and I told her I thought Shawn Michaels was hot."

"The wrestler?"

"Yeah."

"You have good taste." Shawn closed the distance between them, brushing a soft kiss over Ian's lips. "You were conditioned to ignore part of who you are. It happens, but I'm glad you feel comfortable exploring it now."

Ian laughed, even though his throat tightened a bit. "I am, but it's going to be rough. My grandmother liked Sam. She once told her priest that she was worried about me, because I was slow and easily confused. A boy I knew was trans…he—*she* had a lot of trouble in school, and I stuck up for her. She was beautiful, and I wanted to date her, but grandma grounded me and started making me go to church every day. I swore to her I only like *real* girls. I didn't want her to hate me."

Shawn smiled. "Now that is interesting. You're likely pansexual, like your favorite superhero. Which is fucking hot."

"It is?"

"Mmmhmm. And now I have so many plans for you. You'll be mine, but we're going to have so much fun."

The hungry look in Shawn's eyes made Ian's dick harden in the confines of his jeans. Here he was, hoping honesty would prove he really was okay with a real relationship with the man, and Shawn was plotting out some kind of erotic game.

Not a bad thing, he knew how Shawn's mind worked, but he wanted the man to himself for a little while at least. Sharing with Justina was one thing. Knowing that Shawn had been beaten by the last person he'd let close had Ian wanting to put up some massive walls around the three of them.

"Is it…like, can the rest wait? I don't feel like I need more than what we have." Ian wished he could be clearer. Shawn was smart. He could make anything make sense, but Ian always felt like an idiot talking about this kinda stuff. "Like, Justina is fine, but anyone else..." Where was Justina? Ian looked over at the sofa, surprised that she wasn't still there.

"She slipped out when we started talking. My girl is very thoughtful." Shawn grinned, sniffing and letting out a sound of pleasure that went straight to Ian's balls. "I do believe she's making lunch."

"Oh..." Ian swallowed hard, half his mind in the gutter, considering all the things he could do to Shawn while they were alone, the other half still snarling about Shawn being hurt. It was too soon to even go *there*. "Maybe I should help her."

"Maybe you should stay here and help me forget." The slightest twitch of his lips was the only clue that Shawn was still raw over what he'd gone through. "Fuck me, Ian. Fuck me so I can feel you, instead of him."

The words cut deep, like a dull knife piercing his chest, over and over again. His throat tightened to the point breathing became difficult.

"Shawn, did he—"

"*No!* For fuck's sakes, I let him fuck me. It's just sex! Why the fuck do people keep assuming the worst?" Shawn jerked away from him, walking over to the living room table, pressing his hands against it. "I've let a lot of people fuck me. Does that change how you feel about me?"

Moving closer to Shawn, Ian put a hand on his tense shoulder, careful to keep his tone level. "No, it doesn't. But I've seen how you negotiate at the club. How you manage new Doms and subs as a Dungeon Monitor. You ask the hard questions. You don't accept a 'yes' that's forced."

"It wasn't."

"So you didn't let him fuck you so he would go away?"

A choked sound escaped Shawn. He swayed, lifting a hand up to cover his face. "I wanted him gone. I didn't...I didn't want to... Damn it, Ian, I swore I'd never let anyone hurt me like that again. But I did. I let him so it would be over with. "

"Shawn, I love you. I love you, and I hate what he did to you. But if you said yes because you were alone and…" Ian's vision blurred. Shawn had been alone because of *him*. "When you're ready, you need to talk about this. I won't force you to, but I think you need to."

Letting out a rough laugh, Shawn straightened. "So is that how it's going to be? You won't fuck me because of what he did?"

"I won't fuck you because I'm afraid he hurt you more than you're willing to admit. But I'll do anything else you ask of me. I'll do my best to help you forget for now."

"Okay." Shawn pushed off the table. "Then I need one thing."

"Name it."

"I…" Shawn shook his head and laughed again. "This is going to sound ridiculous, but he said I was dirty. I feel dirty. I've taken so many showers, I lost count. I think Justina was worried, but she's afraid to say anything. I wanted to shave, but my fucking hand was shaking…"

Ian took Shawn's hand in his and nodded. "Take a shower with me. I wanna see if you look at me the same way you did that first time."

"Keep talking like that and I'm going to fuck *you*, Bruiser."

Smirking, Ian pulled off his shirt and tossed it in Shawn's face. This he could do. He could see the strong, sexy, irrepressible man he'd fallen in love with hadn't gone far. He loved the vulnerable, wounded man just as much, but he suspected Shawn would fight to regain his strength as quickly as possible. And he was willing to help him in any way possible.

"That's the plan, Easy." Ian undid his jeans, pulling his belt free and letting it hit the floor before heading to the bathroom. "You coming?"

Bianca Sommerland

Chapter Thirty Six

By the time Shawn reached the bathroom, the shower had already filled it with steam. Standing naked by the bathroom counter, Ian held up a razor and pointed to the toilet, which he'd covered with a thick, dark blue towel.

"Sit."

Eyes on Ian's hard length, Shawn sat, licking his lips. Fuck, his man was hot. All those thick, tight muscles. The hair, unruly and wild, much like the man. The golden-brown hued curls on his chest and stomach formed a messy arrow pointing down to his thick, fully erect cock. Standing proud, with veins lining the hard length, pubes short on his heavy balls from the last time Shawn had shaved him.

There was no way Shawn could keep his hands to himself as Ian held a hot, damp cloth to his face. The reasons Ian was being so careful with him were easily forgotten as Shawn slid his hand over Ian's cock.

Ian groaned. "Damn it, man. You're going to make this hard, aren't you?"

"Not sure it can get much harder, but I'd like to find out." Shawn bent forward, flicking his tongue over the hot, dark red head of Ian's dick. "Fuck, I miss this dick."

Curving his hand under Shawn's jaw, Ian frowned down at him. "I'm up here, buddy. And you're not distracting me."

"Aren't I?"

"You're trying, but if you've taught me anything, it's the difference between 'need' and 'want'." Ian gave him a crooked smile as he filled his hand with shaving cream, then smeared it over Shawn's cheeks. "You *want* my dick in your mouth. And I *want* to feel your fucking hot lips around it. But we both *need* this scruff gone. My thighs were all raw the last time you rubbed your face between them. Kinda sucked."

They really needed to start sharing more details like that. Shawn's eyes narrowed as he held still while Ian ran the razor over his cheek. "Is there a reason you didn't tell me?"

"Yes. I was distracted by a girl who lied to me every chance she got." Ian went still, pressing his eyes shut. "I was stupid. Can we not talk about that?"

"If you can agree that I will find a fitting punishment for any time you call yourself stupid?" Shawn raised his hand to Ian's balls, squeezing just hard enough to get his point across. He lightened his grip at Ian's quick nod. "The conversation can wait."

"Okay." Ian inhaled roughly, continuing to carefully shave Shawn's face. "But…can I suck your dick this time? Not because I'm lost in the moment and tied up and following orders. Just because I want to make you feel good?"

Damn, I love this man. Shawn grinned, lifting his chin, not moving until Ian finished cleaning the hair from his throat. "I have absolutely no problem with you sucking my dick."

"Good." Ian smoothed his wet fingers over Shawn's cheeks, then nodded with a satisfied smile. "Now get in the shower."

"May I get undressed first? These pants are Tom Ford."

Ian glared at him. "Why the fuck are you wearing his pants?"

Shawn choked back a laugh. "It's a clothing brand, man of mine. And I'm wearing them because I'm a bitch with incredible fashion sense."

Blinking at him, Ian cocked his head. "You're fucking weird, you know that?"

"I'm aware." Shawn gave Ian a hooded look as he undid his belt, then his pants, letting both hit the floor. "It's one of the many things you love about me."

Stepping into the shower, Shawn tipped his head back under the spray, enjoying the way the hot water sluiced across his skin. He sensed Ian close to him. Then the man's lips sliding over his dick.

The pleasure was pure, sinful decadence. Even better without the games, without wondering if he'd manipulated Ian to get what he wanted from him. Ian was on his knees for him because he wanted to be there. And his mouth felt like heaven.

"Fuck, that feels amazing." Shawn stroked his hand over Ian's wet hair, moving his hips slowly, the slick pressure of Ian's lips wrapped around his dick bringing him to the edge of release after a few moments. He drew away, crooking his finger at Ian when the man tipped his head back, looking confused. "You tempted me with something I haven't had, *Bärchen*. Have you changed your mind?"

Tonguing his bottom lip, Ian rose slowly, shaking his head. "No, but..."

"You're contradicting yourself."

"Huh?"

Explaining the 'No butt' would spoil the mood. And make Ian feel stupid, which was the last thing Shawn wanted. He was trying to keep things light, so Ian wouldn't be nervous. And yet, this was new for the man. He rested his forearms on Ian's shoulders.

"I'm sorry, I'm teasing. I want you, Ian. I *need* to feel you around me." He smoothed Ian's hair away from his face. "I'm not sure this is the best place for your first time."

"It's not my... Ah, right. It is." Ian ducked his head, and his hair fell in wet strands over his face again. "I need it to be here. Or in the locker room, but I don't think they'll let us in to..."

"They might. I'm not that patient though." Shawn ran his hands down Ian's back, cupping his ass and pulling his hips forward so their solid lengths pressed together. "Tell me why you need it to be here."

Ian's lips parted. He lifted his lips to Shawn's, his kiss hot and wet, sweetened with desire and desperation. "Because if I'd just admitted how I felt about you then, I wouldn't have wasted so much time."

"The time wasn't wasted, Ian." Shawn flicked his tongue over Ian's bottom lip. "You used it to become the man who owns my heart."

"And Justina?"

"Will never be a man." Shawn chuckled when Ian sighed. "I'm sorry, I'll stop. Justina is the one who sidestepped all my walls, ignored all the warnings, and accepted me. She has my heart, my soul, and I've only loved one other person as much as I love her."

"Me?"

"Yes." Shawn lowered his lips to Ian's throat, moving against him as he bit and sucked, eager to show Ian, with more than words, how fucking vital he was to him. "You."

Ian's pulse pounded as he watched Shawn step out of the shower and reach into a drawer, taking out a condom and a bottle of lube that had the words 'Real Feel' written on it. He was starting to understand why Shawn had been joking around before. The teasing made it easier to enjoy each moment without worrying what came next.

Now, he couldn't avoid worrying. He wasn't afraid of the pain, but he was terrified of what this would mean for their relationship. Shawn had been in control before, and yet, he'd always bottomed. Which didn't make him seem any weaker, but he was...well, *Easy*.

He could make anything look strong and sexy. Even owning a little dog named after a flower.

Ian wasn't like him. Hell, he'd never been all that great at casual sex. He'd always felt shitty after. Like, if it meant nothing, what was the point? Because it felt good? Jerking off felt good too, and no one got hurt.

'Don't fall in love with me or anything, Bruiser. I'll break your heart.'

Things had changed. He didn't believe Shawn's speech applied to him anymore, but...damn it, what if this was the one last thing

Shawn wanted? What if, after he got it, he realized Ian wasn't worth more than great sex? What else did Ian actually have to offer?

"Bruiser, look at me." Shawn stepped back into the shower, setting the lube and the condom on the shelf, then curving his hand under Ian's jaw. "You don't have to do this."

Staring at the bruises on Shawn's face, Ian swallowed hard, regret clawing deep into his chest. The man needed something uncomplicated. Something to help him forget. Which Ian could give him. *Wanted* to give him.

"I know I don't have to. But I will."

Shawn arched a brow. "We'll see. How about you tell me what's bothering you first."

Inhaling the steamy air, Ian forced himself to meet Shawn's eyes. "You told me not to fall in love with you. And I did. I'm good with sharing you, to a point. I get that you need your freedom. But…" He shook his head, searching for the right words. "But I need this all to mean more. I don't want to be one of your conquests, and I don't really believe I am. I don't know why I'm even thinking it."

"Because my track record has given you every reason to."

"Yes, but you didn't tell any of the others that you loved them."

"True, but those are words, Ian. Shit has been rough between us, and that's not going to go away overnight." Shawn brushed his knuckles down Ian's chest. "If I was a good, patient man, I'd give you some space. Find another way to prove I'm in it for the long run. Instead, I'm going to take everything you can give me. And spend every fucking day making sure I deserve your trust."

They might be just words, but hearing Shawn say them shoved all Ian's fears aside. He was here. Now. Where he'd been headed before he'd gotten so damn lost.

"I trust you." Ian pressed his eyes shut as Shawn's hand wrapped around his dick. "Hell, I let you take a blade to my balls. I'm much fonder of them than my ass."

"Oh yeah?" Shawn chuckled, bringing his hand down to cup Ian's balls. "They're nice, but this ass?" His hand glided along Ian's hip. Curved over one ass cheek. Shawn groaned as he squeezed and Ian's breath caught in his throat. "Do you know how fucking hot your ass is?"

No, but I'm glad you think so. Ian's cheeks heated. "You gonna do more than talk about it?"

Shawn barked out a laugh. "Damn right I am. Turn around, Ian. Brace your hands on the wall."

Taking a deep breath, Ian faced the wall, planting his hands firmly against it. His whole body jerked as he felt Shawn's fingers slide between his ass cheeks. Then he felt Shawn's breath at the base of his spine. His hands holding him open.

"Oh *fuck*!" Ian pressed his forehead against the wall, panting as Shawn's tongue circled his tight hole. The sensation was strange, like nothing he'd ever felt, but he didn't want it to stop. A little pressure and Shawn's tongue penetrated him. "God, that's good. That's so fucking good."

Slicking him up with spit, Shawn thrust his tongue in, licking, then turning his head to bite Ian's ass. The sharp pain intensified everything, and Ian struggled not to pump his hips as Shawn used his tongue to tease him. And it was a tease. He needed more.

One finger eased into him as Shawn bit him again.

Still not enough.

"More. Please, Shawn. I want—"

"*Want?*" Shawn let out a soft laugh, pressing another finger into him. "If you only *want* more, you're not nearly desperate enough. Let's work on that, shall we?"

Standing behind him, Shawn withdrew his fingers, hushing Ian when he let out a needy sound he wasn't sure he'd ever made before. His brain was getting hazy. All his focus was on what his body craved. Which was Shawn. Shawn and whatever the hell the man wanted to do to him.

Two slick fingers filled him, curving and sending a surge of pleasure through him so intense, Ian's knees buckled.

Bringing a hand around the front of Ian's neck, Shawn spoke softly in his ear. "I want to hear you scream. I need Justina to know exactly what we're doing. When I'm done with you, you're going to thank me by making her come. I need to see my pets playing nice. You'll do that for me, won't you?"

Holy fuck! Ian nodded, pretty sure he'd agree to anything Shawn asked of him. He'd only spoken to Justina a few times, hadn't even kissed her yet, but if Shawn wanted to use him to give her pleasure? Yeah, they could get through the formalities some other time.

"Good boy." Shawn worked his fingers in deeper, moving them faster, his knuckles hitting Ian's ass with each rapid thrust. "Don't you dare come yet, but tell me how close you are. Tell me how much you need me to fuck this tight, sexy ass."

"I need you, Shawn. *Mien Herr! Sir!* Lord and fucking Master! God...oh god!" Ian bit into his cheek as the pleasure built up at the base of his spine. "Please...please, I can't..."

The emptiness came suddenly, and Ian muttered words. Or something like words. The water was cooling, but his flesh was burning hot. He fisted his hands against the wall.

"No, *Bärchen*. Keep your hands flat on the wall. Relax as much as you can." Shawn turned off the shower. He smiled as Ian glanced over his shoulder at him, ripping the condom wrapper with his teeth. "You didn't think I was done with you, did you?"

Ian shook his head, flattening his hands again, bracing himself as he felt Shawn's dick slide between his ass cheeks. Not pressing in, but moving against him. Shawn wrapped his arms around Ian, stroking his chest as he kissed his shoulder, then grazed his teeth up Ian's throat.

"You're so fucking hot, Ian. So hot." Shawn's flesh glided against his, still wet from the shower. "I need you to take me. Can you do that for me?"

One of Shawn's hands moved between them. The head of his cock pressed in gently, not going deep, simply testing him. A little deeper. The stretch burned and Ian hissed in a sharp breath.

"Can you, Ian?"

The pressure left him. Ian inhaled, trying to relax as Shawn's slicked up fingers filled him again.

"I'm trying." Ian gritted his teeth as Shawn's dick replaced his fingers again. "Fuck, when did you get so big, man?"

Shawn chuckled. "Flattery will get you everywhere. Press against me, Bruiser. The pain won't lessen if you fight it."

Pushing back, Ian cursed as the head of Shawn's cock penetrated him. It took everything he had not to jerk away. The liquid fire shit Shawn had used on him last time had hurt less.

"Shh... Hold still. It will pass." Shawn kissed his throat and brought his hand down to slide it loosely over Ian's dick. "Tell me when you're ready for more."

Pressure in the base of Ian's spine built up, flipping from pleasure to pain, back and forth as Shawn stroked his dick. The sensations melted into one, like molten metal, liquid in the heat. He moved his hips, tipping his head back as Shawn sank in deeper.

"Now." The friction wasn't enough. Ian's jaw clenched as he thrust back against Shawn. "I need more *now*."

Instead of giving him more, Shawn pulled out. When he pressed into Ian again, his dick was so slick, he glided in with little pain. His pelvis fit against Ian's ass. His hands latched on to Ian's hips. He laid an open-mouthed kiss on Ian's shoulder.

"Fuck, you have no idea how good you feel around me. Don't let me hurt you, Ian." Shawn moved slowly, drawing out slightly, then pushing in. "Swear to me you'll tell me if I hurt you."

"I swear." Ian shifted his hips, so turned on, he wasn't sure he could feel pain anymore. "That feels good. Keep doing that."

Working into him at a steady pace, Shawn bit his shoulder, sharpening the pleasure until Ian was shaking with the need to come. But he didn't. He wouldn't. Not yet...

Pulling out almost all the way, Shawn slammed in and Ian shouted as he lost all control. He couldn't hold back the violent wave of ecstasy. He shuddered as he came hard, his cum hitting the wall.

Hips slamming against Ian's ass, Shawn let out a low growl, his hand slapping the wall by Ian's head. He wrapped one arm around Ian, moaning as Ian's muscles tensed involuntarily.

"Holy fuck, don't do that." Shawn released a breathless laugh. "Shit. That hurts."

Ian frowned, but did his best to hold still. "What hurts?"

Easing out of him carefully, Shawn leaned against the wall, pressing a hand to his ribs. "I think the pain meds wore off."

Grinding his teeth, Ian stepped out of the shower, cursing as he realized they hadn't grabbed any towels. "Why didn't you say anything? This could have waited."

"No." Shawn's tone changed, gaining a rough edge that worried Ian. "It couldn't have."

A chill ran over Ian's damp flesh. He didn't doubt that Shawn had wanted *him*, but part of the timing was probably exactly what he'd said. He needed to forget. And the pain from his abused body made it difficult.

He needed to distract Shawn. Let him focus on what had just happened, rather than drift back to what had been done to him. He returned to the shower, turning it on, pleased to see the hot water was back.

After gently removing the condom from Shawn's dick, he reached out of the shower to toss it in the trash beneath the counter. Then he grabbed the body wash and rubbed his hands together.

Not sure anything else needed to be said, he rubbed the soap over Shawn's chest, kneeling to carefully wash his man's slackening cock. He loved Shawn's dick. He'd never really spent time to admire it before, there was usually a condom covering it by the time it was anywhere close to his face, but the snug foreskin fascinated him. He took his time running his curved hand over it, moving the skin over the thick head of Shawn's cock.

Shawn groaned as his dick began to harden a little in Ian's hand. "You need to stop that. I'm not as young as you are. I don't recover that fast."

Ian smirked as Shawn's dick proved him wrong. It wasn't fully hard, but hard enough to torture the man a bit. He let the water rinse off the rest of the soap, then licked away the droplets.

"Jesus, Ian!" Shawn thunked his head against the shower wall. Then brought a hand to his temple. "Oh shit...okay. Enough playtime. I need to sit down before I pass out."

You really are an idiot. Ian shot to his feet, quickly rinsing himself off, then helping Shawn out of the shower with an arm around his waist. He lead Shawn to the toilet, still covered with the only towel he'd brought in, then stepped out into the hall to grab some towels from the closet.

A tiny yelp made him drop the towels. He stared at Justina, who was standing there with a pile of folded clothes at her feet.

"Shit, sorry." Ian crossed the hall as she bent down, helping her pick up the clothes. "I...uh..."

"You're very naked." Justina blushed as they both straightened. "I knew things might... I mean, that we might..." She cleared her throat. "I didn't think I'd be seeing your dick before you sweet talked me out of my own clothes."

Eyes wide, Ian stared at her. Then he grinned. "Damn, girl. No wonder you handle Shawn so well. Hold that thought. I think I broke him."

Her eyes narrowed. She followed him to the bathroom, dropping the clothes on the counter and crouching down in front of Shawn. "What did he do?"

Lifting the back of his hand to his forehead dramatically, obviously feeling better already, Shawn sighed. "He's insatiable. Completely unsympathetic about my condition."

Justina didn't seem to realize Shawn was messing with her. She glared at Ian, then took Shawn's hand, helping him to his feet. "Maybe I need to repeat everything the doctor said, so he gets that you need to rest."

"Or..." Shawn stopped her in the hall, toying with the top button of her cute pink blouse. "You should strip, get in my bed, and make him suffer."

Lips parted, Justina looked from Shawn to Ian, stunned. She might be good at handling Shawn, but Ian had a feeling she still had a lot to learn.

No surprise there. After a few years, so did he.

Maybe, together, they could compare notes and gain the advantage.

Unlikely, but it would be fun to try.

Chapter Thirty Seven

Justina couldn't get past the doorway to Shawn's room. Despite Shawn's teasing, and how turned on she was after hearing the two men in the shower, she just couldn't bring herself to take that next step.

She liked Ian. She wanted to…to see how things would develop between them, but she couldn't dismiss how worried about Shawn she still was. She totally got Shawn needing Ian to help him forget the last man he'd let touch him, even if only for a little while, but how the hell would her and Ian fooling around help him?

Reclined on his bed, a white towel wrapped around his waist, Shawn folded his arms behind his head and glanced over at Ian expectantly. "You made me a promise, *Bärchen*."

"I know, but…" Ian shot her an apologetic look. "I don't think she's in the mood. And I don't blame her. She's right. You need to rest."

"I *will* rest. Come here, *Röschen*."

Approaching the bed, Justina glanced over at Ian. "*Bärchen?*"

"Little bear." Ian's cheeks went red. "It's a nickname."

Snickering, Justina let her eyes trail over him, thankfully he was covered with a towel now as well. It made keeping things light much easier. "What part of you is 'little' exactly?"

A crooked grin spread across his lips. "Nothing important."

She smiled at him slyly then crawled onto the bed, leaning over Shawn. "Is this a new game, Shawn? Can you teach me how to play?"

Trailing his fingers from her cheek, down to her throat, Shawn inclined his head. Little goosebumps rose all over her skin as he flipped open the buttons of her blouse, his eyes on her face as he slid it off her arms.

"This goes no further than you're comfortable with, Justina." He brushed his fingers along her collarbone, between her breasts, and over her stomach, his feather light touch making her shiver. "He is mine. He will be yours if you want him. I want you to enjoy him as much as I do."

All the talk of flirting and seducing the other man, and here she was, feeling like a virgin all over again. Whatever she'd said, she couldn't make the first move. She pressed her teeth into her bottom lip.

"Being shy isn't part of the game, pet." Shawn used his knuckles to lightly tip up her chin. "Would you prefer if I was in control?"

"But you're resting."

"And I shall continue to. Yes or no, Justina?"

She considered him, then looked at Ian, who hadn't moved any closer. This step had been expected, almost a natural progression of the relationship, strange as that sounded. But it wasn't one either she or Ian would have taken any time soon. From what she knew of her man's man, he was gentle, and used to giving what others needed from him. Which was exactly why Sam had been so dangerous.

From the sounds of it, Sam wasn't an issue anymore. Which made Justina more comfortable. As much as she disliked the other woman, fooling around with a guy in a relationship didn't feel right. Even if things were open, she needed to know everyone involved was on board. And Sam never would have been. Not when it came to Justina.

There was nothing stopping them now. And damn it, whether or not anything lasting developed between them, she couldn't resist the opportunity to take what Shawn offered.

He wouldn't share Ian with just anyone, anymore than he'd share her with someone he didn't trust.

The only question that remained… Was she ready to experience all that a relationship with 'Easy' consisted of?

Wetting her lips with her tongue, she nodded. "Yes."

"Good girl." Shawn stroked her arm, then leaned forward to whisper in her ear. "Kiss him."

Resting her forehead on his shoulder, Justina drew in a few bracing breaths. She could do this. Ian was a damn good-looking man. Strong and sweet and totally in love with the same man she loved. What more did she need?

"Justina."

She twisted around as Ian slid up behind her. The look in his eyes as he framed her face in his hands gave her exactly what she'd been missing. His clear blue eyes were filled with lust, but there was something else. He saw *her*.

Not just a woman Shawn was giving him to play with. Not another toy in their man's arsenal.

He gathered her hair in his hand, closing the distance between them, and her heart raced. His lips touched hers, and she gasped at the sharp spark of pleasure flowing through her. He must have felt it too, because he groaned, wrapping his arms around her to lift her against him.

She laced her fingers behind his neck, whimpering at the insatiable need building within. So hot. So powerful. Almost overwhelming, but the bruising pressure of his lips kept her from drowning in the desire. His rapid breaths, his strong hold, each smooth dip of his tongue, intensified the feeling of being carried away by a powerful current.

His hands slid down her back, unclipping her bra. His lips left hers only long enough to ease the white lace off her breasts. Then he kissed her again, lowering her to the bed, gliding his lips down her throat. He cupped her breast in his big, calloused hand. Her back bowed as he ran his thumb over her nipple.

"She's beautiful, isn't she, Ian?" Shawn latched on to her hands, anchoring her as Ian licked and sucked down to her tightening nipples. "Fuck, you two are hot together."

Ian circled her nipple with his tongue, then moved to the other, holding her breasts close together, making her squirm as he sucked harder. He let out a rough sound that sent a surge of longing deep into her core.

"Shawn, I need..." Ian hooked his fingers to the edge of her panties, working them down as she lifted her hips. "You sweet, gorgeous woman. Damn it, Justina, I want to taste you."

"Mmm." Justina threw her head back as his mouth covered her pussy, heightening the liquid heat building within. His tongue circled her clit in a rapid figure eight and she cried out as the climax hit her, bursting out so suddenly her whole body jerked with the overpowering sensation.

Kissing her hip, Ian brought his hand between her thighs, sliding two fingers into her. She clenched around him, her legs shaking as he quickly brought her up to the edge again with a few steady thrusts and his fingers curved just right.

And then he stopped.

"Ian!" Justina moaned as his fingers left her and the ache of emptiness took its place. She lifted her hips shamelessly.

Ian's body covered hers. His hips spread her thighs, and his dick pressed against her.

"Whoa there, my man." Shawn put his hand on Ian's shoulder. "You've already forgotten what you need, haven't you?"

Blinking at the other man, Ian swallowed hard. "I thought this was what you wanted. Should I have—?"

"Waited until you had one of these?" Shawn held a condom up between two fingers. "Yes, but you both got a little carried away. Let's be more careful next time, yes?"

"Ah...yeah. That would be smart." Ian let out a strained laugh, moving away her and reaching for the condom. His brow furrowed as Shawn pulled it out of reach. "What—?"

One hand up, Shawn motioned Ian to him. Opening the condom, he rolled it over Ian's dick, then latched on to the back of his neck, bringing their foreheads together. Justina chewed at her bottom lip, wondering if Shawn was mad. Or if he'd changed his mind about sharing.

But he simply laughed and gave Ian a rough kiss, letting out a low sound of pleasure as he sucked Ian's bottom lip. "Fucking delicious, isn't she?"

Justina sucked in a deep breath, arousal licking along her flesh. This was exactly what turned her on the most. She knew Shawn was in too much pain to do much, but she loved that he was still involved.

He whispered something to Ian. She let out a surprised yelp as Ian hooked an arm around her waist and slid her sideways on the bed. He knelt between her thighs, lifting her knees, raising her hips and pressing his dick into her slowly.

As his dick filled her, she moaned, trying to move with him, but the position made it impossible. The unhurried glide was pure torture.

Dropping her head back on the mattress, she whimpered. "Ian, please—"

"Don't blame him, pet." Shawn rested on his side by her hip, stroking his fingertips lightly over her mound. "This is the only way I can join in the fun."

He moved his mouth to where he'd touched her, licking over her clit. Over the base of Ian's dick, making his steady pace falter. His lips and tongue on her already sensitive clit, combined with the languid drag of Ian's dick, ignited a growing blaze that reached every inch of her. The heat spread, gathering inward until her core gripped him tight and she keened with the need to find her release.

Shawn lifted his head. Met Ian's eyes.

And nodded.

Gathering her in his arms, Ian lost all restraint, pistoning into her fast and hard as his lips found hers. She wrapped her legs around him, taking him in deeper. She combed her fingers into his hair, crying out into his mouth, her whole body shaking as the heat and pleasure and passion imploded.

Bracing his hands on the bed, Ian thrust in one last time, gritting out an incoherent curse as his dick pulsed inside her. Skin slick with sweat, he held her close, rolling to his side with what seemed to be the last of his strength.

She lay there with him, their bodies tangled together, for a long time. Shawn stroked her hair lazily, smiling when she peered up at him. His lips formed words she was too tired to hear, but she knew what they were. She could feel them, whenever he was near. Whenever she closed her eyes and pictured him, such an important part of her life.

Now and in the future.

The one night she'd given him had turned into forever.

Chapter Thirty Eight

Early July

The wind blew cool and crisp off the ocean, a balm from the heat of the sun glaring down in a clear blue sky. And with all the suits, the breeze was more than welcome. It was a perfect day, but Luke had a feeling Silver had made some kind of deal with the devil to make it so.

Hopefully the priest didn't find out before the wedding, since she'd been baptized...*Angelican?* He couldn't remember—just so she could get married here. It was a nice church, looked like a fancy white castle, but he was happy Jami wanted to get married on Halloween. Somewhere different.

Seb had vetoed a cemetery, but Luke had found an actual castle in West Virginia that their girl decided was perfect. He'd already reserved the spot and started the planning, without really telling anyone. He didn't want to distract from Landon's big day.

Might be unavoidable, but he'd done his best. He couldn't believe he hadn't been fired from the position of Best Man. At least Scott and Tyler would be close in case Richter decided he wanted Luke's head on a platter for his wedding gift.

Scott grabbed Luke's wrist, pulling it away from his tie. "Stop that, you're making it all crooked."

"You like me alive, right? Maybe I should go." Luke tugged at the sleeve of his suit, holding still as Scott straightened his tie. "You tell Bower I came down with...like, rabies or something."

Bouncing in place, close behind Scott, Tyler cocked his head. "You do look like you're foaming at the mouth a little bit."

Tyler is the man! Luke nodded, giving Scott his most charming smile. Scott had been put in charge of making sure the three of them were where they were supposed to be at all times. A job he was taking way too seriously.

Frowning at him, Scott shook his head. "Not happening, buddy."

"What if I fall in the ocean?"

"Then you'll be standing at Bower's side, soaking wet." Scott looked Luke over, then turned to inspect Tyler. "Damn it, Tyler. That's *not* the tie you're supposed to be wearing. It's too small and...shit, is it a clip-on?"

"Maybe?" Tyler ran his hand through his hair, making it stand up all puffy on one side. "I was in a hurry, *okay?* And Laura was busy with Chicklet and Raif couldn't..." Tyler's brow furrowed. "I didn't think anyone would notice."

Sympathy filled Scott's eyes. "Did you bring it?"

"Yeah." Tyler pulled the tie out of his pocket and handed it to Scott. "Thanks, Scott."

"No problem." Scott quickly tossed the clip-on tie, flipping Tyler's collar to fix the real one. All while using his super-dad power to keep an eye on Luke, which meant Luke's window of escape was slammed right in his face. "Try it and I'll tackle you, boy. And then I'll tell Ramos you tried to make a run for it."

Luke pressed his lips together and folded his arms over his chest. "Some friend you are."

"Some best man *you* are. Did you make sure Bower remembers his vows, that his shoes are polished, that he's not seeing how far out in the ocean *he* can swim?"

Snorting, Luke shook his head. "You think Richter hasn't got all that covered?"

"It's *your* job."

"And it's *my* neck on the line. He's going to know. One fucking look at Jami and…" Luke groaned and rubbed his hand over his face. "Why couldn't she tell him last week? Wait, don't answer that. She was sick. I get her not wanting to tell him while she's sick."

Tyler chewed at his bottom lip, glancing over at Luke as Scott finished with his tie. "She's better though, right?"

"Yeah, the doc has her on something new that seems to help her keep down food. He's awesome. I'm glad Silver made her see him." Luke laced his fingers behind his neck. "I don't know why *Silver* hasn't told him."

"Because it's not up to her to tell him. But she made sure the bridesmaid dresses were loose. Maybe he won't be able to tell." Scott didn't sound too convinced of his own words. Of course, Jami was almost five months pregnant, and she definitely showed.

"I'm a dead man."

"Demmy! Look, me and Amia have the prettiest flowers!" Casey ran up to them, stalling all talk of Luke's eminent death. She was carrying Amia, who had an armful of flowers. Becky was close behind the girls, not looking too comfortable with her daughter holding her cousin. At least both girls were in jeans and small Cobra jerseys, rather than dresses.

Casey knew exactly how to sweet talk her uncle, and Silver had decided, if Casey didn't want to wear a dress, all the kids should be comfortable. And match somewhat.

Which meant Casey was wearing a jersey with Scott's number and a Cobra cap with Pearce's. Amia's jersey had Bower's number. And the teeny tiny jersey Westy was wearing had Perron's.

Concern for the kids' comfort didn't apply to the adults though. Which meant tuxes and fancy dresses everywhere.

"La-La-La!" Amia strained away from Casey, dropping the flowers and holding her arms out for Luke.

Grinning at the little blonde cherub, Luke swept her up into his arms. "How's my Ami-bear?"

"Hey, I have an idea!" Tyler leaned close, offering Amia the end of his tie to play with, which got Scott muttering under his breath as he helped his daughter retrieve the flowers. Tyler ignored him. "If you walk down the aisle holding Amia, Richter definitely won't murder you."

Head shooting up, eyes wide, Casey stared at Tyler. "Uncle Dean won't kill Uncle Luke. They're family!"

"Of course he won't, *mon chou*." Becky glared at Tyler. "Uncle Tyler might want to be more careful about what he says."

"He will be." Tyler flashed Becky his most angelic smile. He crouched down in front of Casey. "You wanna go see Thora?"

Casey jumped up and down, clapping her hands. "Yes! Can I have a piggy back ride?"

"Sure! Hop on!"

"Tyler, your tux!" Scott sighed, his hands full of flowers, watching Tyler gallop across the churchyard with Casey on his back. "Silver is going to kill him if he gets dirty. When did he regress to twelve again?"

Becky wrapped her arms around Scott's waist, tipping her head back when he bent down to kiss her. "He didn't. *You* grew up, which makes him seem younger."

Scott grinned. "Probably. Hopefully having his own kids will get this one to grow up too."

Apparently Scott had missed Luke shaking his head and making a please-shut-your-mouth motion, which Amia copied. Very few people knew Jami was pregnant. Unfortunately, his best friends with big mouths were two of the people.

Pulling away from Scott, Becky spun around and stared at Luke. "Oh god, Dean *is* going to kill you. I thought Jami *wasn't* pregnant."

"Umm…well, seems like it didn't show on the tests the first few times. She was really sick and the doctor did an ultrasound and…" Luke cuddled Amia close and shrugged. "You couldn't tell looking at her, right?"

"Oh honey, I haven't seen her in almost a month. She wasn't showing then." Becky moved away from Scott and held out her arms, drawing both Luke and Amia into one of those motherly hugs she was so good at. "I think she's helping Silver get ready. Her father probably hasn't seen her yet. And I doubt he'll cause a scene during the ceremony."

"So that gives me another hour or two before I have to make a run for it."

"You're not making a run for it." Scott put a hand on his shoulder, squeezing supportively. "Though Tyler had a good point. If you hang on to the little one, Richter will have to be careful."

Becky shook her head and took Amia, blowing raspberries on her cheek and making her giggle. Then Becky gave both Scott and Luke a stern look. "We do not use babies as shields."

"Well, it sounds bad when you put it like *that*." Luke waved at Amia as Becky carried her away. There went his last hope.

Hooking an arm around his neck, Scott dragged him in the direction Tyler had gone. "Come on, it's not gonna be that bad. Let's fetch the angel before he gets grass stains on his suit. Silver will *definitely* kill him."

Over by the stone benches in the shade, Tyler was dodging Zovko's big dog, Thora, while Casey giggled and ran around in circles. Bran, Ladd's little brother, sat beside Zovko, sucking his thumb and staring up at the man as Zovko spoke to him. Chicklet sat on Zovko's other side, holding his hand and watching Tyler with a small smile on her lips.

Laura and Sahara had Kimber with them, and seemed to be trying to remove the very dark makeup she was wearing with wet wipes. Kimber sulked and said something that had Laura's mouth dropping open and Sahara's face pale. Mason watched them, rubbing his temples like he was getting a massive headache.

As Luke and Scott approached, Chicklet stood and gave Kimber a tight smile. She hesitated, looking over at Mason. "May I?"

"Please do." Mason's lips quirked as Kimber's eyes went wide. His voice still sounded gravelly, but much better than a few weeks ago. "And remember, Kimber, honey. We still love you."

"Yeah, right." Kimber bowed her head as Chicklet led her off to the parking lot.

Poor kid. Luke knew most people hated the teen's attitude, but she'd been through a lot. He had a feeling she expected Sahara and Mason to get sick of her and Bran, so she was pushing to make it happen now, rather than later.

She still didn't realize, neither was the type to give up on those they loved.

He met Mason's eyes. "Ladd should be back soon, right?"

"Yeah, he just had some things to take care of in Australia after his team in Russia was eliminated from the finals. Property he owns that his dad's family is trying to take." Mason's jaw hardened. "Most of them have criminal records, which is why they didn't get the kids. But they suddenly decided Heath was worth something. I'd be down there with him if my doctor had cleared me to travel."

"So he's there by himself?"

"No." Mason rolled his shoulders, relaxing slightly. "His agent is with him. The man might have no clue how to handle kids, but he's a bulldog when it comes to his clients. He has connections and a team of lawyers handling everything. Heath will be fine."

Luke nodded slowly. "But you're still worried."

"Naturally, but the best thing I can do is make sure Bran and Kimber are all right." Mason smiled, watching Bran hop off the bench, one hand in Zovko's, his thumb leaving his mouth so he could pet Thora, who'd raced back to her master, sitting nice and wagging her tail. "Bran's doing well. I found him a new therapist who suggested I socialize him as much as possible."

Moving away from Laura, Sahara looked at Mason, smiling, then stopping suddenly and changing directions. "Akira!"

Bran's head snapped up. A big smile spread across his lips. "Ford!"

As Bran went running, Ford bent down, throwing the little boy up in the air, then catching him. Sahara looked like she wanted to strangle the man, but Akira held her tight, laughing and shaking her head.

Cort joined Ford, putting an arm around him and giving Bran a fist bump.

Mason rubbed his temples again. "That child gets attached to the strangest people. Not that I mind, Cort's a great man and Ford..."

"Is Ford?" Luke supplied, trying to be helpful. "Hey, Bran loves you. And seems closer to strong guys. Jami says he isn't as comfortable with women though."

"Yeah..." Mason's expression darkened. "His therapist is concerned about that. Despite what Kimber's told us, he shows signs of neglect and abuse. Likely at the hands of a woman. He hides food and stops speaking for days if Sahara so much as raises her voice. She never yells at him, but Kimber tends to try one's patience... Anyway it's been rough, but he's doing better. He now has an obsession with motorcycles." Mason snorted when Cort pulled something out of the pocket of his leather jacket—a small toy motorcycle—and handed it to the little boy. "Not sure *why*."

Coming up to Luke's side, Scott held up his phone. "Almost time. You ready?"

"No-pe." Luke took a deep breath as Mason shot him an amused look. Where was Seb? He needed Seb. Seb wouldn't let Richter kill him. "Where the hell is my man?"

Looking around, Scott's attention went to the back of the church. He pointed. "Right there. And I think he might be just as worried about Richter killing you as the rest of us are. Proactive, isn't he?"

Oh fuck. Luke winced when he spotted Seb and Richter. Richter's face was red, and he was making really sharp hand gestures. And Seb...well, Seb looked real calm.

Scary calm.

Crossing the yard in long strides, Luke stepped up to Seb's side. He knew Richter didn't mind Jami and Seb being together. *He* was the issue. He wouldn't let Seb take shit for the mess he'd made.

Richter didn't seem to notice him at first. "Don't worry? You can't be serious, Ramos. The mother of my child had complications because of drug use. Do you really believe either you or *that boy* are ready to help Jami through this? Why hasn't she told me herself?"

"She was worried you wouldn't be happy for her." Seb's tone was dry. He folded his arms over his chest as he looked down at the GM. "Clearly, she was right."

"I'm worried! Damn it, Ramos, how can you not understand? I just lost my brother, I can't—I can't lose her!" Dean backed away from Seb, taking a deep breath. "You should have waited. Made sure her doctor said it was safe—"

"We did." Luke followed Seb's example and kept his voice level. "What don't you get, Richter? Our kids aren't a mistake."

Squaring his shoulders, Richter glared at him. "I didn't say they…" His brow furrowed. "*Kids?*"

"Uh…yeah. Seb didn't tell you that?"

Seb gave a subtle shake of his head.

"Ah… Well, now you know." Luke was a little worried about that vein pulsing in Richter's temple. That couldn't be healthy. "Congrats, Grandpa. We're having twins!"

Pain. So much pain, then stars. Grass on the back of his neck. There was yelling. Richter was growling, but someone was holding on to him.

Scott was suddenly kneeling beside Luke, helping him sit up. "What the fuck did you say?"

"Congrats?" Luke squinted. All right, there was Landon. Holding Richter. Looking down at Landon's shoes, Luke grinned. "See, I told you he'd be fine. His shoes are all nice and shiny."

"Get up, dumbass." Scott pulled him to his feet. Held up one hand. "How many fingers?"

"Eight. And two thumbs." The whole world spun, but there was a solid chest on his other side. A strong arm around him. Not Scott. Luke smiled, smelling Seb's cologne. "My man is here. You can go away now, Scott. But I love you, buddy. You're so fucking cool."

Minutes later he was sitting on a bench with an icepack over his eyes. Seb was still close, so life was good.

But when he moved the icepack, he saw Landon. Frowning at him.

Luke groaned. Stared at the grass. "I fucked up. I'm sorry."

Landon shook his head. "You didn't. Dean is fucking scared, and you paid for it. *I'm* sorry. Are you gonna be okay?"

"You're worried about me?"

"Damn it, Luke. Of course I am. You're my best friend. And my man just gave you two black eyes." Landon took hold of his jaw, cringing as he looked at Luke. "You have five minutes. Keep icing them. Maybe Silver won't lose her mind over you ruining the wedding pictures."

"Now I feel loved."

"You should. I sent Dean inside. Once he calmed down, he couldn't stop apologizing. I think he'll be nicer to you now. I warned him if he keeps this up, his daughter will never speak to him again." Landon rubbed his bent knees and sighed. "She loves you. She loves Ramos. She's lost so much, I think this baby is…hope. A future for you all. Truly believing life goes on."

"Did you tell him that?" Luke poked the swollen flesh by his eyes. Which hurt, but he did it again, just to be sure.

Seb grabbed his wrist and pushed it down to his side. "*Niño*, focus."

"I am."

Landon snorted. "I don't envy you, Ramos. And yes, Luke, I told him."

"Good." Luke leaned against Seb and closed his eyes. "Ugh, can you put off the wedding for a few days? You're right. Silver is going to be *pissed*."

"She'll be even more pissed if the wedding she's spent so long planning doesn't go perfectly." Landon brought the ice back over Luke's eyes. "Come on, Luke. It'll be fine. I need you by my side."

That was all Landon had to say. Luke pressed his lips together, took a deep breath, and brushed Landon's hand with the ice pack away. He stood and hooked his arm with Landon's.

"I've got you, man. Lead the way." His head spun and Seb steadied him with a hand under his elbow. "I think your second fiancé broke me."

"Can you walk in a straight line?"

"Yes. And I can recite the alphabet backwards. Z, T, L, Y—"

"Asshole." Landon let out a nervous laugh. "Shit, is everyone inside already? Are they waiting? I think you need more ice."

"I'm good." Luke focused on Landon's pale face. "Dude, are you scared?"

"No. Of course not!"

"You're full of shit." Luke laughed, his head feeling a bit better now. "Is it Silver or walking in front of all those people to condemn yourself for life?"

Seb let out a soft groan. "*Niño…*"

"Neither. Both. I don't know." Landon lowered his head to his hands. "I love her. I love him. This whole…*thing* is weird. Like it's all traditional, and we're not."

"I think I get it." Luke looked at the band on his left ring finger. Which Seb had gotten him after they decided he would 'officially' marry Jami. Their wedding wouldn't be traditional at all. Legally, it wouldn't be that different, but all three of them would recite vows. If he had to go through it without Seb being a vital part of everything?

He'd be just as freaked out.

Steady footsteps came toward them and they all looked up to see Callahan and Perron. If they'd just gotten here, Oriana had probably gone right in to see her sister.

Callahan held out his hand, shaking Landon's, then pulling him in for a quick hug. "How did I know I'd find you stalling?"

Landon frowned. "I'm not stalling."

"You are. And I heard part of what's bugging you. Come take a walk with me, Goalie." Callahan glanced over at Luke and shook his head. "And you. Not another word to anyone until the reception. I just got a dozen texts about you getting traded. Do I need to do damage control?"

"Not according to the groom."

"Huh. Well, try to behave. You look like hell."

It took a couple of minutes for Callahan to talk to Landon and get him looking more confident. Luke walked with Seb to the steps of the church. Seb went in to take his seat. Tyler and Scott joined Luke and Landon at the doors.

The music started. Nothing traditional, which was interesting, considering Richter had been in charge of the tunes. Landon paused, cocking his head as the song started. *Hallelujah* by Panic! At The Disco.

Rehearsal the other day had been really short. No music involved, so no one knew what to expect.

But Landon seemed to approve of Richter's choice. After Scott, then Tyler, then Luke walked down the aisle, he made his way toward them at a steady pace.

"Daddy!" Amia squirmed out of Becky's arms and ran to her father. Landon bent down and picked her up.

The music was powerful, but somehow, seeing Landon holding his daughter made the lyrics mean even more. He'd lost his firstborn, but his beautiful little girl looked at him like he was her hero...she'd helped him heal.

As much as Luke loved Landon, he knew the man wasn't perfect. He had a few scars to show for all he'd survived. But he was here today. Stronger than ever. An amazing father. And a soon to be husband who had proven he would stand by his woman—and his *man*—through the worst life could throw at them.

Marriage had always seemed like a trap until Luke had decided he wanted forever with Jami and Seb. Then it became something he wanted more than anything. But it was still scary.

Watching Landon carry Amia down the aisle to stand beside him and wait for his bride?

Not so scary anymore. Just all kinds of awesome.

Lips slanting, Luke caught Seb's eyes from where his man sat in the pews. And mouthed 'I love you'.

Seb grinned and pressed his fingers to his lips, before his lips moved to say, 'I love you too, *niño*."

Justina smoothed the skirt of her new dress, feeling all awkward as she rushed into the dressing room set up for Silver in the church. Sahara had sent her a '911, but no one is dead or hurt' message.

About ten minutes ago.

She'd been running late with Shawn and Ian. Shawn was ready almost three hours ago, and she'd been close behind, but Ian had locked himself in the bedroom and told them to go without him.

Naturally, they both refused. Shawn cajoled, then commanded, then knocked the door off its hinges.

Ian was sitting on Shawn's bed—which they all shared now—his face red as he met Shawn's eyes.

"Umm...the suit don't fit. I kinda ripped it trying to get it on." Ian dropped back on the bed, covering his face with his hands. "I suck, I know. Don't be mad."

Shawn placed his hands on his hips. "I told you to try it on last week."

"After a shower. And you and Justina were naked and...it didn't happen."

"Okay, I will totally take the blame for that." Shawn smirked. "You were both walking crooked for days."

Justina's cheeks heated. She sat next to Ian, taking his hand. "That doesn't fix the issue now."

"No, but give me five minutes." Shawn shot Ian a sly smile as he pulled out his phone. "You owe me. Missing the GM's wedding while your working on a contract is not an option."

"I'm aware." Ian flopped an arm over his eyes. "I will pay for the consequences. Go."

They didn't leave him. Shawn somehow found an expensive tux in Ian's size within an hour. They got to the church. Drama avoided.

But now there was a fresh end-of-the-world to deal with. One much worse than Ian ripping his tux.

Curled up on a loveseat in the dressing room, Jami sobbed. "He wasn't supposed to find out on your wedding day, Mom. I'm so sorry."

"Hush. He gave Luke two black eyes. Which is going to ruin all our pictures. The guilt will get me my own way for weeks." Silver kissed away Jami's tears. "Consider it a wedding present."

Jami choked on a laugh, shaking her head. "I got you a better one. You're gonna think it's stupid."

"I will not. Stop that, Jami Richter. You're tougher than this." Silver shoved the train of her elegant, mermaid style wedding dress out of her way and knelt in front of Jami. "Can I see it?"

Pulling a long, white box out of her gold clutch, Jami bit her bottom lip hard, then handed it to Silver. Reaching out, Jami squeezed Justina's hand as Silver opened the box.

On a long, delicate gold necklace was a heart pendant with two birthstones. An opal and a ruby.

"You and Amia." Silver's eyes teared. "Jami, this is beautiful. Thank you."

"You don't think it's weird?"

"Not unless you don't want to be my daughter. I get that I'm not old enough to be your mother, but…but I love it when you call me 'mom'." Silver blushed, lifting her carefully styled and curled hair over one shoulder. "Justina, can you help me?"

Justina nodded and silently took the necklace, clasping it behind Silver's slender neck. She stepped back and folded her hands in front of her, sure either Sahara or Akira should have done this.

Why was she here? Both of them knew Jami better than she did.

Silver spun around, cupping her cheeks and letting out a soft laugh. "Oh, my precious girl. You're so easy to read. Do you want to know why Sahara called you—and there's no point in denying it, darlin'." Silver smirked at Sahara when her lips parted. "I know you did."

Feeling like she should take the focus off Sahara, Justina cleared her throat. "Honestly? I'm not sure."

"Think about it. Sahara is so overwhelmed by her new brood, she's not sure she can help anyone. And Akira is with my brother, who has probably told her so much messed up shit about my family, she's afraid to say the wrong thing." Silver smiled fondly at both girls.

"Pisch has always been pretty neutral. You're the same. They likely hoped I wouldn't bring up how stubborn Dean is being, or how freaked out Landon is, in front of you. And if I did, you'd think of the right thing to say. Nothing that would piss off the bride. Or upset her expecting daughter."

All right, if Sahara and Akira expected all that of her, they didn't know her very well. She ducked her head. "I don't know what to say. It's your wedding. You should be happy. And Jami wants these babies. She should be happy too."

"Good." Silver inclined her head. "What about the fact that her fiancé, the best man, has two black eyes thanks to one of my men?"

"Luke?" Justina glanced over at Sahara, who nodded. "What did he do?"

"See, this is why you're awesome. She really is a perfect match for Pisch." Silver kissed her cheek. Then gently rubbed it with a finger. "He opened his mouth and inserted his foot. Now tell Jami things really are okay. I won't go out there without her and we've kept the guests waiting almost ten minutes already."

Justina grinned and took Jami's hands, pulling her to her feet. "What she said."

"My dad must be so mad at me." Jami sniffed as Sahara came over to touch up her makeup. "I don't want him to hate me."

"If he hit Luke, I'm sure he's feeling much better." Justina carefully wiped away a tear spilling down Jami's cheek. "Now he can focus on being a grandfather. And you can call Silver grandma."

Silver spun around, her lips parted. "What?"

Akira slid up to Justina's side. "This is true. And I'll be a great aunt. I think."

"This family is so fucked up. Does that make Ford Jami's uncle? Because...eww." Silver wrinkled her nose. "It's not too late to change my mind, is it?"

"Don't you dare!" Jami poked Silver's shoulder. "This is your perfect wedding. Everything is exactly how you wanted it."

"True. I did consider at least one of the groomsmen would have black eyes. Maybe if I'd put a wager on it with Landon and Dean,

Dean would have restrained himself." Silver snickered, then shrugged. "This is us. Bruises, scars, and all. Are you ready?"

Jami smoothed her hands over her flowy, golden dress, and nodded. "I'm ready if you are."

"I should head in." Justina spoke softly, feeling good about helping, but knowing she needed to step aside now. "It's only the maid of honor and the bridesmaids now."

"Honey, I don't think you read your invite very well. Even though you got the right dress." Silver curved her hand under Justina's chin. "You *are* one of the bridesmaids."

"I am? But…" Justina thought back on when she'd gotten the invite. She's looked at it quickly, then handed it to Shawn, knowing he was connected with people who could get her the right dress. And he had. Apparently the dress hadn't cost much because he was doing ads for the company. But he hadn't said anything about her being a bridesmaid.

Sahara bumped her shoulder. "It's okay. I didn't know either until I got here. The invite wasn't clear. Silver was busy planning all kinds of fan stuff for the playoffs. And swag and making sure her one year old gets into the right college."

"Pre-school." Silver stuck out her tongue at Sahara. "Speaking of which, who helped you make sure Bran goes to the same school?"

"I love you, Silver." Sahara gave the other woman a sweet smile.

"Right." Silver touched her hair, then her lips. "Do I look okay?"

"You're perfect." Justina helped Akira pull the veil over Silver's face. "Shawn said wars would be won if they paid as much attention to details as you did with your wedding."

Silver snorted, squaring her shoulders. "We'll see about that."

They headed out the back door of the church so they could enter from the front.

Sahara nudged Justina's shoulder. "I wondered why you weren't at the rehearsal."

"Please just don't let me look like a fool." Justina looked back at Silver and Jami, who waited at the bottom of the steps. "We go in now?"

"Yes. Just follow Akira."

The music began as Akira walked in, matching her steps to the beat. Justina matched her pace, smiling as she recognized the song. Sara Bareilles was awesome, but Justina never would have considered one of her songs to replace a wedding march. But if any could, *I Choose You*, definitely fit.

As she walked down the aisle, she searched out Shawn and Ian. Both were standing in the second row, eyes on her. Shawn winked at her. Ian stopped fussing with his collar to give her that soft smile that made her feel all warm inside. She was still getting used to having both men in her life, but it had become so natural, she didn't question whether it was right anymore.

She was still technically living at home. Luke had asked Sahara to rent Sam her place. And since Justina was spending most of her time at Shawn's, she didn't really need it.

Taking her place beside Akira, Justina watched Silver walk down the aisle, holding her brother's arm. She wasn't sure why Silver's father wasn't here, but Ford performed his duties effortlessly, escorting Silver to Landon, then stepping aside to stand between Luke and Dean.

The vows were exchanged, but Justina only caught a little. Enough to know they weren't meant for Silver and Landon alone.

In all the sweet words she'd spoken, Silver added one thing Justina knew included both Dean and Jami.

"When I give you my heart, I am trusting you with all that is precious to me. Love, life, and family. Two beautiful daughters. Both who belong to us, no matter how they joined our lives. The strength to take on the world for them comes from all three of us. Love can be shared. And committed eternally to those you love." Silver took a deep breath, glancing from Richter, to Landon. "I swear I will be yours. And his. For as long as I live. And longer, because a love like ours never ends."

About an hour later, the ceremony all done, everyone headed down to the beach where several huge, open tents were set up.

Torches were positioned around the seating area and a small stage had been erected for the band.

Once dinner was finished, the crowd circled the area in front of the stage as Landon and Silver came together for their first dance as a couple. Ford stepped up to the mic, grinning down at his sister as Cort pulled up a stool beside him and sat, holding his guitar.

Ford cleared his throat. "I totally planned to sing 'Bitch', but I value my life. *Ow!*" Ford winced, shooting Cort a dirty look as he rubbed the arm the man had playfully punched. "Why are you so violent? You know I chose a different song." Covering the mic, Ford nodded at something Cort growled at him. His face went red and he tugged at his tie, turning back to the mic. "Ah... I've been told to stop being an asshole. I love you, Silver. You've found two good men who will make you very happy. Or else me and Oriana will take 'em out."

Cort shook his head.

Off to the side of the dance floor, holding her son, Oriana laughed. "You're absolutely right, little brother. But I'm starting to understand why we weren't allowed to give speeches. Can we save the threats for after the honeymoon?"

"Aww, you're no fun." Ford grinned. "Anyway, like I said, I chose a song I hope is as special to you as it is to me."

Leaning against Shawn's side, Justina smiled as Ian moved closer to her other side and placed his hand on the small of her back. When their relationship had begun, they'd been more like friends with benefits than anything else, sharing their love for Shawn. But over time, things had changed. She wasn't sure exactly when it had happened, but the tender touches, the sweet kisses that didn't lead to getting naked, became more frequent.

Falling in love with Shawn had happened quickly, but with Ian, she started loving him without even realizing he'd claimed a piece of her heart. She missed him when he wasn't around. Just hearing his voice made her feel all warm and fuzzy. Weddings and romance had never been important to her, but what she'd found with Shawn and Ian?

Loving them, sharing her life with them, felt right. Something she hadn't known she needed, like heat and comfort surrounding her, when all she'd known was the cold. She was strong enough to stand on her own, but with them she felt like there were no limits. Nothing she couldn't reach.

The song was beautiful, and she found her eyes getting all teary as she listened to the lyrics. *Livin' Our Love Song* by Jason Michael Carroll. She'd seen how hard so many of those around her had struggled to be with the ones holding them, but she'd been damn lucky.

Ian put a hand on her shoulder, gently turning her to face him. "Hey, cutie. What's wrong? Why are you crying?"

Tears spilling as she giggled, Justina shook her head. "I'm not."

"You are."

"All right, I am." She lifted her hand to his jaw, her heart beating faster as she leaned up to kiss him. She'd never get tired of the effect he had on her. "They're happy tears. I think they're required at weddings."

Shawn curved his hand around the back of her neck, leaning close to brush his lips over her ear in a way that had her shivering with need. "Is this something you want, *Röschen*? Because you can have it all."

The haze of arousal made her slow to understand what he meant, but when she did, she joined Ian in staring at him. "Are you feeling okay?"

"Mmmhmm." Shawn's lips slanted into a devilish smile. "Why? Is it so far fetched that I'd consider marriage?"

"*Yes.*" She and Ian said in unison.

Shrugging, Shawn turned his attention back to watching the newlyweds dance. "Believe it or not, I've thought about it. Ian would make an amazing husband. I'll have him propose to you some other time though. Tonight would be tacky."

Ian's eyes went wide. "You're going to have me do what?"

"Hush, man of mine." Shawn closed his eyes, swaying a little to the music. "Ford's quite good, isn't he? Would you like me to ask him to perform at your wedding?"

Glancing around, Ian leaned close to Shawn and whispered. "You don't get to decide that, Easy."

"I agree." Justina reached for Ian's hand, taking a deep breath as he laced their fingers together. She didn't want him thinking she was in on Shawn's crazy plan. Even though she was well aware their man was teasing. "Besides, what if I want to propose to you? What would you say to that?"

"Yes."

She blinked at him. "Bullshit."

"Language, pet." Shawn's warning tone held the promise of things that would hurt so fucking good. He lowered his voice in a way made her want to either drag him out of there, or make a run for it. "Ask me again when we're alone. After I smack your ass until its nice and red and hot, while you've got Ian's dick deep in your throat. After I fuck you both so hard your screaming my name until it hurts to whisper."

Biting her bottom lip hard, Justina pressed her thighs together, not sure she could last until the end of the reception now. And by the way Ian was adjusting his pants, he wasn't in any better shape.

"Care to dance?" Shawn held out his hand, his smoky-green eyes glowing in the torchlight, sparkling with mischief.

"I love you, but you're driving me insane." Justina blew a strand of hair away from her face, grateful for the breeze that picked up over the water. Hopefully the air cooled her blood at little. At least enough for her to endure him toying with her. "What game are you playing, Shawn?"

"The best one of all. Where I figure out all the ways to make you happy. Where we all fulfill all our deepest fantasies. The one that never gets boring." He backed her into Ian, brushing his lips over hers in a soft kiss. "The one that never ends."

Closing her eyes, she smiled. "Mmm. That's my favorite game of all."

Epilogue

Late July

"This is a fucking awesome pool table, Cort." Shawn ran his hand along the dark wood as the big man racked up the balls. "Where'd you get it? I was thinking of getting a nice one for my new place once the renovations are finished in the basement."

"Came with the place." Cort positioned the pool cue. "But you should ask Ford where he gets his for the bar. They've got some nice ones."

Shawn inclined his head, resting his hip against the edge of the table. "Maybe I'll ask him after he's done sucking my dick."

The tip of the cue hit the table. The white ball rolled, touching the formation, but not a single one of the colored balls moved.

Pearce chuckled, stepping up to Shawn's side and patting his shoulder. "You've got to stop doing that, man. Cort's not gonna want to let us play with his toys anymore."

Grinning, Shawn glanced over at the 'toys'. Kneeling on the mats spread out along the other side of the game room were all the participating submissives. Each gagged, wearing a blindfold and soft, lined leather cuffs clipped behind their backs. The colors of the blindfolds indicated the limits the subs and their Doms had agreed on for the play party. Black for only oral and light impact play, red for sex and medium impact, and green for anything goes.

Both Ian and Justina *thought* they were wearing green. What could Shawn say, he liked keeping them guessing. He'd swapped for the black at the last minute, deciding to keep things light for their first real party.

Ford and Luke both had red blindfolds—interesting, since both their men had been incredibly possessive before. Scott and Becky had black. Akira was the only one without a blindfold, but she'd insisted she could try a few things. Cort hadn't seemed so sure, but he let her kneel with the others before taking all the Doms aside to warn them that she might not catch a trigger in time and no one was to take her out of his sight.

More than reasonable. They'd all be very careful with her.

With all of them.

Jami was here to simply watch. And she'd made them promise to have more parties when she wasn't as big as a house. Ramos decided it wouldn't happen until after their honeymoon, when they got married that fall, which made her happy.

Actually, both she and Luke seemed excited that their Master was letting them do group scenes again. Shawn wasn't sure why Ramos had stopped, but having him back in the mix made things more interesting.

Shawn was curious to see how Justina and Ian would react to the different styles of domination. Both Ramos and Pearce were stricter than he was. Cort was still pretty new, but he'd learned some fun tricks from Callahan. A few Shawn wouldn't mind learning as well.

Ford choosing to kneel with the subs rather than join the Doms had surprised Shawn. He'd trained as a Dom, and he'd been fun to co-Top with, but he'd admitted there were a few things he needed to experience.

Taunting Cort could be a useful way to learn what those things were. If done carefully. Shawn still wasn't sure how good the man was with sharing.

So he smiled and turned his attention to Pearce. "He chose pool for a reason. He's better than any of us, which means he'll be playing with *our* toys all night if we don't shift the advantage."

"Hmm... You have a point." Pearce rubbed his jaw thoughtfully. "I still don't believe Ford really likes dick. He probably gives horrible blowjobs."

"He won't by the end of the night if I have my way with him." Shawn cracked his knuckles then grabbed a pool cue from the rack on the wall, glancing over at Cort. "You have at least taught him not to use his teeth, haven't you?"

Over in the line of subs, Ford let out a low, angry sound.

Cort folded his arms over his broad chest, jerking his chin at Shawn. "If you want to find out, you might want to stop talking and start sinking balls."

"You didn't give me much to work with." Shawn shook his head as he realized he had absolutely *nothing* to work with. "I'm calling safety."

"Good choice."

The game continued, taking much longer than expected because, well, his cheating backfired. Cort might not have cleared the table as quickly as he would have without distraction, but Shawn wasn't the best pool player.

When Cort won, Shawn let out a sigh of relief. "Well played, man."

"That was a lot more fun than I expected." Cort chuckled, approaching the subs. Shawn assumed he'd choose Ian to make Shawn pay for all the comments about Ford, but instead, he stopped in front of Justina. He brushed his fingers down her cheek. "Come with me, pet."

Ducking her head, Justina gracefully rose to her feet. She let out a surprised yelp when Cort lifted her up and threw her over his shoulder.

Shawn wasn't fast enough to keep Ian from trying to get up and go after Cort, but thankfully Ramos had remained behind the line of subs, so he grabbed Ian by the shoulder, forcing him back to his knees.

"You know Cort can be trusted, *hermano*." Ramos fisted his hand in Ian's hair when he tried to pull away. He jerked his head back, bending down to kiss right over the cloth gag between his lips. "Careful, Ian. I am a fairly skilled player. You don't want me displeased with you when I win."

Fuck, that man is hot. Shawn adjusted his dick in his leathers, shaking his head when Pearce laughed at him. He turned his attention to where Cort had laid Justina on the pool table.

Cort moved away from her, then crooked his finger at Akira. "I missed out last time. It's Ford's fault."

Ford grunted.

"Ah, a shame you're blindfolded, isn't it, my boy?" Cort smirked, slipping behind Akira to remove her gag. He left her hands bound as he lifted her onto the pool table near Justina. "Pearce, could you get Justina's gag out of the way?"

As Pearce got Justina's gag off, Akira frowned at Cort. "Aren't *you* supposed to be getting off from the win?"

"Tiny, this totally does it for me. I'm a guy."

"Fine, but Justina's not into *me*." Akira's cheeks reddened. "And we're friends and I don't want it to be weird for her and—"

"Akira, will you just kiss me?" Justina smiled, her voice softening as she tried to shift closer to the other woman while still blindfolded and bound. "It wasn't weird last time. And didn't last long enough for me to be sure if I like it or not."

Akira inhaled roughly. Then nodded, a big smile curving her lips. "Should we make another trade?"

"Mmm, I like that idea." Justina wiggled as Akira's lips hovered over hers. "Who?"

Brow furrowing, Cort shook his head. "That's not how this works. You two are topping from the bottom." He looked at Pearce for confirmation and Pearce gave a firm nod. "Punishments will make this much less fun for you."

Batting her eyelashes, Akira gave him a pretty pout. "Please?"

"Brat." Cort's expression softened. "You don't see enough of guys making out?"

"Never! And you've only ever kissed Ford."

A crimson blush spread up the back of Cort's neck. "Yes, well... I guess you're going to make me do it?"

Releasing a heavy sigh, Ramos shook his head. "That is not at all how this works, hombre."

"You wanna show me how it works then, pal?"

Ramos smirked. "It would be my pleasure."

Swiftly untying Ian's gag, Ramos hauled him over to Luke then swept his feet out from under him. Grabbing Luke by the back of the neck, he pulled him over Ian.

One finger hooked Luke's gag, Ramos pried it free, letting it hang around Luke's neck. "Kiss him, *niño*."

Without hesitation, Luke claimed Ian's lips, only Ramos's grip on his neck keeping him from falling forward. There was something animalistic about the way the two men kissed, now that their control had been taken from them.

And it was fucking sexy to watch, but Shawn was getting a little tired of observing and not *doing*. He understood the point Ramos was trying to make, but the girls had given him the perfect opportunity to see if Cort tasted as good as he looked.

Before he could make his move, Cort pinned him against the edge of the pool table. He let out a soft laugh as he lifted his lips to Shawn's. "This is going to devolve quickly. Do you want to see how far the girls are willing to take this 'trade'?"

"That sounds like an excellent idea." Shawn teased Cort's bottom lip with his tongue. "And maybe I can give Ford a few tips."

The playful mood in the room changed quickly to one filled with pleasure and passion. Shawn had been to many erotic parties in his life, but somehow, this one was different. He'd been afraid relationships would cramp his style. That they would get in the way of him acting out his every desire.

Instead, he'd found someone to share those desires. *Two* someones. And neither saw his lack of inhibitions as a bad thing.

He still had his freedom. His games were actually a little bit naughtier than before. But no matter how much he enjoyed playing, he loved knowing he had something real to go home to. Two people who he trusted with his heart.

Who he could keep.

THE END

Visit the Dartmouth Cobras
www.TheDartmouthCobras.com

Game Misconduct
THE DARTMOUTH COBRAS #1

The game has always cast a shadow over Oriana Delgado's life. She should hate the game. But she doesn't. The passion and the energy of the sport are part of her. But so is the urge to drop the role of the Dartmouth Cobra owner's 'good daughter' and find a less . . .conventional one.

Playmaker Max Perron never expected a woman to accept him and his twisted desires. Oriana came close, but he wasn't surprised when she walked away. A girl like her needs normal. Which he can't give her. He's too much of a team player, and not just on the ice.

But then Oriana's father goes too far in trying to control her and she decides to use exposure as blackmail. Just the implication of her spending the night with the Cobras' finest should get her father to back off.

Turns out a team player is exactly what she needs.

"Ms Sommerland takes us on an extremely incredible journey as we watch Oriana's master her own sexuality. She comes to realize that there is more out there that she craves and desires, than she has ever realized." Rhayne —Guilty Pleasures

"With a delicious storyline and kinky characters outside of the norm, Game Misconduct pushes you outside of your comfort zone and rewards your submission with phenomenally erotic sex. If you're a fan of hardcore BDSM, then this book is going to top your list of must reads!" Silla Beaumont —Just Erotic Romance

Defensive Zone
THE DARTMOUTH COBRAS

Silver Delgado has gained control of the Dartmouth Cobras—and lost control of her life.

Hockey might be the family business, but it's never interested Silver. Until her father's health decline thrusts responsibility for the team he owns straight into her hands. Now she has to find a way to get the team more fans and establish herself as the new owner. Which means standing up to Dean Richter, the general manager and the advisor her father has forced on her. The fact that their "business relationship" started with her over his lap at his BDSM club shouldn't be too much of a problem. Their hot one-night stand meant nothing! But how can she earn his respect when he sees her as submissive? Can they separate work and the lifestyle she's curious to explore?

Balancing her new life away from Hollywood, living among people who see her as the selfish Delgado princess, has her feeling lost and alone until Landon Bower, the Cobras new goalie slips into her life and becomes her best—and only—friend. The time they spend together makes everything else bearable, but before long his eyes meet hers with more than friendship, reflecting what she feels. Which could ruin everything.

Two Dominant men who see past her pretty mask and the shallow image she portrayed to the flashing cameras. A gentle attack from both sides

that she can't hope to block unless she learns how to play.
    But she's getting the hang of the game.

Breakaway
THE DARTMOUTH COBRAS

Against some attacks, the only hope is to come out and meet the play.

Last year, Jami Richter had no plans, no goals, no future. But that's all changed. First step, make up for putting her father through hell by supporting the hockey team he manages and becoming an Ice Girl. But a photo shoot puts her right in the arms of Sebastian Ramos, a Dartmouth Cobra defenseman with a reputation for getting any woman—or, as the rumors imply, man—he desires. And the powerful dominant wants her...and Luke. Getting involved in Seb's lifestyle gives her a new understanding of the game and the bonds between players. But can she handle being caught between two men who want her, while struggling with their attraction to one another?

Luke Carter's life is about as messed up as his scarred face. His mother is sick. His girlfriend dumps him. When he goes to his favorite BDSM club to blow off some steam, his Dom status is turned upside down when a therapeutic beating puts him in a good place. He flatly denies being submissive—or, even worse, being attracted to another man. He wants Jami but can't have her without getting involved with Sebastian. Can he overcome his own prejudices long enough to admit he wants them both?

Caught between Luke and Jami, Sebastian Ramos does everything in his power to fulfill their needs. His two new submissives willingly share their bodies, but not their secrets. When his own past comes back to haunt him, the fragile foundation of their relationship is ripped apart. As he works to salvage the damage done by doubt and insecurity, he discovers that Jami is hiding something dangerous. But it may already be too late.

Offside
THE DARTMOUTH COBRAS

A pace ahead of the play can send you back to the start. And put everything you've worked for at risk.

Single mother and submissive Rebecca Bower abandoned her career as a sports reporter to become a media consultant with her brother's hockey team. A failed marriage to a selfish man makes her wary of getting involved with another. Unfortunately, chemistry is hard to deny, and all her hormones are dancing when she gets close to the Cobra's sniper, Scott Demyan.

Zachary Pearce 'came out' to the world last season to shift attention away from a teammate. And his one night with Scott Demyan had been unsettling. There could be more there, if only Scott was a different person. Instead, a night of sensual BDSM play with Becky leaves him wanting more, but she thinks he's gay and questions his interest. It's been a long time since a woman has attracted him both as a man and a Dom, and he'll do everything in his power to prove she's the only one he needs. Or wants. His one time with Scott was a mistake.

Scott might have forgotten what happened in his childhood, but the effects linger, and he specializes in drunken one-night stands...until he meets Zach and Becky and sees what he's missing. But neither one believes Scott can be faithful. Although he's trying hard to clean up his act to avoid getting kicked off the team, they want more from him. He's willing to make changes, but the most important one—putting their happiness before his own—means he'll probably end up alone.

Delayed Penalty
THE DARTMOUTH COBRAS

All choices have consequences, only sometimes they're . . . delayed.

Cortland Nash fled Dartmouth to avoid being arrested for murder, but his best friend, Ford Delgado, is in danger. Cort returns, prepared to keep his head down, and do whatever it takes to keep Ford breathing, but when he finds a beautiful young woman out in the snow, frozen in fear, his plans change. He needs to make sure she's safe—even if the greatest danger is him.

Akira Hayashi never thought she'd overcome her fear of men, but the care of an experienced Dom helped her achieve so much more. She's embraced her submissive side, and found her strength as the captain of the Dartmouth Cobras' Ice Girls. There's nothing she can't do—except function when she's mugged in a parking lot. The intimidating stranger who rescues her makes her feel things she never thought possible. The only problem is his connection with Ford, a man she'll hate forever because she refuses to feel anything else.

With the constant threats from the crime lord he once called "Dad," Ford Delgado has no room in his life for love. Unfortunately, Akira already has his heart—which is split in two when he discovers

Cort is dating her. The betrayal has him lashing out, trying to move on, to grow as a Dom, and free himself from Kingsley's criminal empire. He tries to forget what Akira means to him, but one look into her eyes shows him the last thing she needs is for him to let her go.

Iron Cross

Too many penalties may leave the goal vulnerable without the IRON CROSS.

After overcoming a potentially career-ending concussion, Tyler Vanek, Dartmouth Cobras first line forward, couldn't be happier with his life. Until his boyhood hero-worship for Raif Zovko, a newly acquired player, develops into more. His mistress, 'Chicklet' encourages him to explore his feelings, and with her enjoyment of toying with the powerful Dom, Tyler figures it might be fun.

Laura Tallent, a dedicated officer with the Halifax PD, and Chicklet's first sub, is tired of Tyler's fun disrupting the structure of her world. Devotion to her mistress kept her silent for two years, but a horrible case and more proof that Tyler is the worst sub in existence has her wondering how much better life would be if he was someone else's problem. Someone like Raif.

Raif won't deny the lust he feels for Tyler, but he refuses to play games with a young man who's questioning his sexuality--he won't be an experimental phase for an unruly submissive. But when Laura draws him into a plan to remove Tyler from her poly relationship with Chicklet, his protective instincts take over. He partners with Chicklet to protect Tyler and dig deeper into the reasons behind Laura's scheming. Chicklet clearly loves her boy, she won't let him go. And before long, Raif realizes neither can he.

Blindsided by the discord in her household, Chicklet struggles to fulfill her subs' needs as their careers throw challenges at them all. Control is slipping from her hands, but with Raif by her side, she prays her relationships can be saved. Salvaging the future means rebuilding with a new foundation. But the only way to make the base solid is for them all to work together. And with all the secrecy and lies, she has no idea where to start.

About the Author

Tell you about me? Hmm, well, there's not much to say. I love hockey and cars and my kids...not in that order of course! Lol! When I'm not writing—which isn't often—I'm usually watching a game or a car show while networking. Going out with my kids is my only downtime. I get to clear my head and forget everything.

As for when and why I first started writing, I guess I thought I'd get extra cookies if I was quiet for a while—that's how young I was. I used to bring my grandmother barely legible pages filled with tales of evil unicorns. She told me then that I would be a famous author.

I hope one day to prove her right.

For more of my work, please visit: www.Im-No-Angel.com

You can also find me on Facebook, and Twitter

Also by Bianca Sommerland

The Dartmouth Cobras

Blind Pass
Game Misconduct
Defensive Zone
Breakaway
Offside
Delayed Penalty
Iron Cross
Goal Line
Line Brawl

Also

Deadly Captive
Collateral Damage
The End – Coming Soon

Solid Education
Rosemary Entwined
Forbidden Steps
The Trip

Winter's Wrath Series
Backlash

Made in the USA
San Bernardino, CA
11 February 2018